Island J
By L.

MW01609954

PREF.

The following pages contain a theoretical account of the outcome of a modern day mystery.Based on the few known facts of Malaysia Flight 370, this fictional tale is one of secrets, deception, and the survival of many. Told from a narrator's standpoint, the plane's lead pilot along with two co-workers intentionally crash the plane on a deserted island. Months of planning and the gathering of life sustaining supplies precede the flight's disappearance. Throughout this book, you will learn how the crash survivors transform an uncharted Indian Ocean land mass into an island paradise. It will become evident how this multi-national group of survivors become a working community.

My special thanks go out to Google and Wikipedia for providing the facts of this flight, of which there are few. The websites where the information was obtained will be listed at the end of this preface.

It is of utmost importance to state that I know nothing of the crew members of the actual Malaysia Flight 370. It was by the combination of the Wikipedia reports and my own wild imagination that this yarn as spun.

Being optimistic by nature, I have trained myself to believe my deseased family members live in a distant town with no telephones. My heart feels they are happy there. My hope is this crazy story might bring this same comfort to any grieving family member who might read it.

Because I know nothing of any of the individuals aboard this flight, the names were changed to protect the strange. So sit back and enjoy as this narrator guides you through this amazing adventure.

Thank You,
L. A. Smith

Special thanks to:
William Smith
Leslie Tinsley
Arthur Nauman
Erlene Smith
Barbara Frazier

RESEARCH:
1) Wildlife - Thanks to Natural World Safaris.com and Animals in Indian Ocean
        All forms of reptiles, turtles, frogs, birds (Pelicans, Owls, Albatross),
        lizards, penguins, seals, sea lions.
2) Plane info thanks to Wikipedia
        Boeing 777-200ER: 209 ft, 1 in long, Wingspan 199 ft, 11 in.
        227 passengers and 12 crew members from 15 nations
3) Medical Advise thanks to Doctor Arthur Nauman and Wikipedia
        Pneumothorax, Burn treatments and child birth
4) Butterflies (Lepidoptera) of Christmas Island, Indian Ocean

Museum.net.au Australian Etomological Magazine. 14. (4,5):57-66
Citation: Moulds M. S. ; R. B. Lacian. 1987
Dark Blue Royal Pratapa
5) Foods grown Indian Ocean Islands
Thanks to Wikipedia and A Foodie's Journey into Indian Ocean Cuisine
Mango, pineapple, bananas, passion fruit, avocados, peaches

ISLAND JET 370
BY L. A. Smith

CHAPTER ONE

PRIOR TO THE FLIGHT

Five o'clock Saturday evening, the phone is ringing, and it's the airport again. Jack pauses a moment to curse under his breath before answering. "Hello, Captain Wellington, yes, I would be available to take the overnight flight to France. Yes I will report at 1900 hours."

He glances over at his wife, Janet, who has become instantly furious. "Damn it Jack, you know my parents are coming to dinner tonight. Not to mention Amy's piano recital is at 10:00 tomorrow and Johnny has a soccer game at 3:00. Once again everything is left for me to attend to. Honestly I am so sick of this that I don't know how much more I am going to put up with. If I divorce your ass, you can fly all the time and sign your paycheck over to me for alimony and child support."

Her constant clamering eventually seems a distant blur as he directs his attention to the traffic filled highway back home from unwanted dental checkups. Can't be happy about no cavities because Janet's mad. He soon surrenders to thoughts of a much happier time (his happy place of sorts) of his childhood. Being the son of a Migrant deep sea fisherman he remembers accompanying his father on two different vacations. They sailed deep into the Indian Ocean for two full days, picked an island, and camped for a week solid. Life seemed so calm on the island. He remembers feeling like they were all alone , free of the world's toxins whether they be human, animal, chemical, or any other source. The warm feeling of peace seemed to always engulf him when he surrendered himself to the memories of paradise.

Oops, gotta snap out of it. Pulling into the driveway. Five thirty-four, time to shower and put on my uniform. No time to exchange pleasentries with his in-laws other than hello and good-bye. Out the door by 6:02. Then two blocks down the road traffic is stopped dead. The car radio says small fender bender on freeway should be cleared in thirty minutes. Jack calls the airport to report that he will be late. The night supervisor informs him that he will be written up for his tardiness and says he will announce flight delay to waiting passengers. Then he tells Jack to consider himself warned that two more tardinesses would result in suspension or possibly termination. The call ends.

While waiting in traffic, his thoughts again return to the islands. He tries to google earth on Indian Ocean islands that would take at least two days to sail to from Malaysia. Once again, NOTHING. Regardless of the hundreds of other times he had tried it was worth one more chance. All the other times left him with a sense of loss, but not this time.

This time he decided to call Harold Renolds, his life long best friend, who worked as a baggage handler at Worldwide Malaysia International Airport. Jack and Harold had attended high school together. Jack went on to pilots school while Harold studied to become an engineer. Jack finished and landed a pilot's job. However Harold was not so fortunate . His father was an investment broker and was convicted of embezzlement when Harold was six months from graduation. His family was stripped of all assets including the money for Harold's tuition for the final semester before graduation. Jack helped him get a job at the airport to earn enough money to finish his education, but living expenses consumed his wages. It had been five years since then.

Harold answers, sounding out of sorts, "Hi Jack, what's up?"

"Got called in for the over-night to France. Are you still interested?" says Jack.

"Yeah man, more than ever," replied Harold. " Remember last month when I was out of work for a week with the flu?   I was running a week late on my rent and was served an eviction notice today on my way out the door to go to work. I can't deal with this bull anymore. The last shipment of supplies arrived yesterday. Let's do this. Janie has the pharmacuticals in three suitcases ready to hand off to you at the gate . It's the only thing we were lacking, and her father will recognize they are missing upon opening the store tomorrow. It is working out perfectly. Have you practiced enough night time landings to be confident enough?" asked Harold.

"Been practicing for months. I got my part down without a doubt. Paradise here we come." Jack answered.

Janie, Harold's fiance', was the flight attendant most often chosen to serve on flights with Jack and as usual was scheduled fatefully to accompany him tonight. She was the daughter of a wealthy local pharmacist who had denied the couple his blessing for marriage. His stated reason for his denial was Harold's family history. The two were inseparable with a deep and undeniable love. The were willing to risk everything for the opportunity of a peaceful life together.

Unbeknowance to anyone other than the three of them this was a one way flight like no other. They had with great care and planning devised a scheme to stock the cargo hold full of supplies rather than luggage and fly deep into the Indian Ocean in search of the perfect island paradise. They would then land on the island, and develope a Robinson Caruso type brave new world.

Jack had secretly had a separate bank account started one year ago when given a rather large raise upon being promoted to pilot. He had purchased 3 different life insurance policies naming his wife and two kids as beneficiaries, one per person to secure their futures. He had chosen to leave them all behind due to irreconcilable differences in personalities and diminished emotional bondings. The remaining funds in the separate bank account had been used to help fund the massive amount of supplies needed for such a daring adventure. He had also recently obtained as many as 5 credit cards which he very rapidly maxed out purchasing supplies. When he had reached his credit limit , Janie became of age to gain access to a rather large trust fund. Her father soon had it cut off because of her "unexplained, untraceable spending habits".

Harold had been named temporary supervisor of baggage and cargo for a 30-45 day period so the higher ups could take their annual manditory vacation. This offered a rare opportunity to receive shipments of the supplies as they arrived and store them in one area until the time was right to execute their plan.

The decision had been made long ago and finally, tonight the time was right. All the fates seemed to have been pushing them in this direction for years. Now with the darkness of recent events, no possible costs (even their lives) seemed too expensive to pay for a shot at a new life in paradise.

CHAPTER TWO

THE BACKGROUND

Jack's father, Jon Wellington, had been a hardworking individual, whose loyalties went beyond normal boundaries. His deep love for Jack's mother, Camilla, allowed him to turn a blind eye to the numerous red flags of her infidelities and selfish money hungry spending habits. His one and only goal in life was to make her happy. She, however, was a self absorbed woman who used the majority of his earnings to secretly pay for a modest but modern beach house used as a rendezvous location for her and her lover to carry on their adulterous affair. Jon Wellington worked so much that when he was not maping out the next fishing expedition, he was content to just be at home with his wife and only child. Jack remembered his father commenting a number of times during his childhood about Jack's seemingly endless growing. His clothing always appeared two sizes too small. His mother would blame it on them being sized wrong or the cost of children's clothes being too expensive. However, she always was dressed to the hilt.

From the time he was eight years old, Jack had been left alone all too often over night. He remembered eating three day old leftovers from the refrigerator or withered fruits and vegetables during her absences. She had sworn him to secrecy early on saying, "If Jon were to learn of this, he will leave us both forever,". That was the only threat she had to make knowing Jack's life would be unbearable without the only source of emotional support he had ever known. Sadly due to this fact her secrets were safe with him.

Jack's father had always encouraged him to stay on top of his studies. Jon dreamed of Jack being the first in their family to go to college or some type of technical training. He wanted Jack to break the chain of the family men having to do back breaking work, the first to make a living using their brain. Jack's main goal throughout his childhood was to make his beloved father's dream a reality. He threw himself into his studies. He was awarded a full scholarship to the college or trade school of his choice.

Jack's father's self driven work load left little time for spending with his son, so he prided himself with providing quality time with him. There was always a new adventure when his father was home. They spent a lot of time going on nature walks admiring the vegetation and wildlife. His father was especially fond of birds saying that they were sometimes the only animal other than fish one sees while at sea, his idea of a little merritime pun. Jack attributed his love for flight as being akin to his father's bird watching antics. Watching a hawk while he is soaring swoop down to successfully retrieve his prey never crashing. This had grabbed his imagination from a very early age. Between these wildlife hikes and the two wonderful sailing vacations to island paradises, his happiest memories of being a kid revolved around his wonderful father.

Jack and Harold became friends at the beginning of the 2004 school year. Soon their fathers met and decided to introduce a work ethic into their young stir-crazy sons before too much free time got them in trouble. Both boys got an after-school job at a beach side petting zoo riding with the little kids on live elephants. Surprisingly to them it was quite the enjoyable task. That is until late December of that same year when multiple nations on the Indian Ocean coasts were stricken simultaneously by a tsunami that swept hundreds of thousands of people out to sea. Somehow the animals seemed to possess a sixth sense and knew to run immediately for higher ground, taking Jack, Harold, their passengers and the other passengers and riders with them. All of them survived. Jack's parents did not however. His Mother and her lover were at their beach house. It was completely destroyed. His beloved father had been out on his boat on a commercial fishing trip and was thought to be lost at sea never to be seen or heard from again. Jack preferred to believe he had been shipwrecked on one of the paradise islands; it was bearable that way. Harold's parents took Jack in and he lived with them until he completed school.

Psychology tells us all too often it is human nature when selecting a mate our subconscious is drawn first toward an individual whose traits mimic a parent or family member due to the comfort of familiarity. Unfortunately for Jack this theory rang true. Unbeknowance to Jack until months after his wedding, Janet was very similar to his mother. She showed him very little emotion other than when she was angry. Her spending habits were out of control with determination that she and her parents would want for nothing. The children, however, got nothing unless it worked to further her statis in the social chain. Amy had been forced by her mother to spend four hours daily practicing piano. Nothing short of a reincarnated Beethoven was good enough for her. Johnny had been made to play soccer until he was beginning to show signs of Tendonitis. He had become nothing short of an embarrassment to Janet who had planned on him playing professionally. She had allowed Jack virtually no time with them and absolutely no say-so in their up bringing. Janet made sure to schedule as many practices as possible on Jack's days off. His children treated him only as an aquaintance, not a father.

Jack had tried to accommodate Janet's whims for years but 3 years ago he learned of an ongoing affair she was having with an early childhood olympic style soccer coach. This revelation was probably the last straw. He never again looked at her without remembering the years of watching as his mother deceived his father. Internally their relationship ended then. When at home he spent most of his time exploring virtual reality trying to find a peaceful alternate reality. He searched relentlessly for a place of serenity that existed only in his memories of those two trips to the uninhabited island paradises of his childhood. All of the wisdom of the world wide web seemed to have missed that part of the world. Google Earth didn't even offer it. Address unknown period.

So he wondered if he could fly a plane in the manner of the magnificent hawks he had loved watching; swooping down, skimming the ground never crashing. Somewhere along the way he studied plane crashes in various forrest areas. He marveled at just how the ground cover seemed to swallow up all traces of the aircraft in an incredibly swift amount of time. He began doing flight simulations, landing planes in small and difficult areas, then mountainous volcanic forrests. He became a "virtual" genius with the highest sucessful landing rates in all levels of difficulty. All this had even made him a better real life pilot improving his reaction time on yearly airline performance and endurance testing. His scores had risen so much he was promoted to head pilot and cleared for over night international flights. Still he practiced whenever he had time accumulating some 3000 hours doing simulated landings. These hours spent would prove very beneficial in the very near future as their plan played out.

From the day Jack and Harold had met they had an unexplained kinship, a brother from another mother of sorts. Harold's family seemed to be filled with love and laughter. His father, Montgomery Renolds aka Monty, was a very sucessful investment broker and was known for being extremely generous and well loved by the community. Monty seemed to thrive on providing for his family's every need and want while not going overboard. He still managed to instill morals, manners, caring and empathy into Harold making him the best friend possible. Harold's Mother, Ella, was a very kind hearted homemaker who was always ready to lend a helping hand to their household servants with their cleaning and cooking while praising them for their efforts and hard work. She always had a big hug and a smile for Harold and any friends he might bring home. She never seemed to see herself as better than anyone, truly a lovely lady. Harold's parents with no hesitation took Jack in after his loss of both parents providing everything he needed including the love and nurturing he had missed out on.

In 2009 Monty Renolds was arrested, tried, and sent to prison for being the master mind of what turned out to be the largest ponzi scheme in national history. He was convicted of defrauding all of his investors out of millions. As the trial went on it became all too clear that he was a modern day Robin Hood, stealing from the rich and giving to the poorest of the community, keeping very little for himself. It was even brought up in court that the homeless population had virtually deminished to nearly zero thanks to his individual efforts. The community actually rallied as a show of love and admiration for this "pillar of the community" during his court proceedings to no avail. A few of his largest victims refused to drop the charges (Janie's father, Amal Cordair, being one of them). The evidence was overwelming and he was sent to prison for what would probably turn out to be a life sentence at his age without the possibility of parole. His family was stripped of all their worldly assets short of one suitcase each including the money for the last semester tuition for Harold to finish engineering school. His dear mother was taken in by one of her beloved servants, one of which she had always treated with love and respect. Jack had been hired by the airline by then so he and Harold shared an efficiency appartment.

The largest sense of loss for Harold didn't come from the materialistic part but from the emotional loss of not only his father but also his lifelong mate had been stripped from his life as well. His parents being bound by tradition had long ago promised their only son to a pre-arranged marriage to the daughter of the largest pharamacist in the community. Throughout their childhoods Harold and Janie had twice monthly playdates to build on their relationship. They were always reminded that Harold would be responsible for providing for her and she in return was taught she would be expected to remain subserviant to him and provide him with sons. These two sets of parents had no idea just how strong the bond between their children would become with a love that surpassed all reason or logic.

Janie's father immediately following the conviction of Harold's father had totally forbidden Janie to ever see her beloved Harold again. Harold's family was no longer part of the class of people that his family was traditionally required to marry. Her father had promised to publically disown her as a daughter if she disobeyed his orders. Everyone knew what a hard cruel man Amal Cordair was. He was a money hungry individual who had probably never done any act of kindness for another human being. He would sell his pharmacuticals to anyone with a prescription and the money regardless of their drug history. Many family members begged him not to. Janie remembered on more than one occasion when people had come to the pharmacy asking for his help in reporting doctors who were overprescribing drugs for their already addicted loved ones. His only reaction was always loud outbursts of anger screaming that he was doing nothing illegal. He could care less about their "deadbeat drug addicted relative". As long as they kept paying he would keep filling their scripts. This almost always sent those customers running out the door in tears of dispair and embarrassment as he would do this in front of a store full of customers.

Janie's father had always been very cruel to her mother, Bonita, as well. Bonita had never been strong enough to stand up to this oppressive verbally and physically abusive tyrant. She reminded Janie of an empty turtle shell or a crumpled up old leaf. She would speak only when spoken to and even then never offering the slightest opinion of her own. Janie had found it very hard to feel anything other than sympathy for this shell of a woman. Her father had even forbidden her to be affectionate with her children. She feared her husband so much that she followed his rules to the letter even when he wasn't around. Clearly she had been broken years before.

Janie on the other hand had a very quiet mind of her own. She had fallen in love early on with Harold's robust laughter and kind demeaner. Ella Renolds had always been so loving to her, telling Harold to treat her as a fragile flower subject to lose it's beautiful petals if handled too roughly. It was one of the few times Janie remembered her own mother ever smiling and nodding in approval. After being taught and promised her whole life that she was to love Harold and serve him, and then to suddenly have him ripped from her life was unbearable for Janie. She was hopelessly in love and no one could keep her from him. The two forbidden lovers would sneak around for years. They would always find a way to be together. Somehow, some way true love will always prove victorious.

In Janie's family class it was expected of a young woman to find employment from age 18 till the time they receive their trust funds at age 25 or they marry, which ever comes first. Janie applied for and was hired as a flight attendant. Her father knew Jack was a pilot but was not aware that Harold worked there too. By this time Jack was already married so he posed no threat. This allowed for Janie and Harold to secretly spend time together.

During her teenage years Janie had worked at her father's pharmacy when she wasn't in school. She found it fascinating which medications were for which ailments. By the time she graduated, she could name what condition a customer suffered from just by reading the name of the prescription. Suprisingly this would prove beneficial later.

With Janie and Jack both racking up flight employee discounts as often as possible they used them to take Harold along on overnight flights. Six months ago Janie's father had become suspicious and threatened to rescind her trust fund. She knew she would never be able to break free of his barbaric treatment without it. She and Jack bought Harold a ticket to accompany them on a two day work flight with a stay over. During dinner after they had arrived Janie looked at them both and said," I wish we could take a flight to one of Jack's paradise islands and escape with our passengers to a fresh new world. This world would only consist of goodness, helpfullness, joy and love. My father would never be able to keep Harold and me apart ever again. There would be no social classes, only people pulling together to survive. It would be paradise, don't you think?"

CHAPTER THREE

THE PLAN

When Jack, Harold and Janie arrived back at their hotel, they spent half the night talking about Janie's idea. The next morning the three of them woke with a new resolve, a dream and a plan of how they might achieve it. They all agreed they would try to keep as many passengers healthy and alive as they could. This would require major planning and a great deal of luck and ingenuity.

Jack, being the son of a fisherman, would be responsible for all food, both immediate and long term. He would start with fishing gear: rods, reels, artificial bait, fishing line, cleaning and cooking instruments, nets and even a harpoon. He would include ropes and many kinds of string. They would need at least 5 guns of various calibers and multiple boxes of ammunition to aid in obtaining fresh game in the long term. He would add a few boxes of steel traps to further insure capture of game for consumption in the long term.

Jack bought books on regional island vegitation to learn which plants and tree fruits were edible and which were poisonous. He also got books on regional snakes and insects to learn which were venomous and which ones were beneficial. He even obtained books on growing crops. All these books he would put in the suitcase he always carried.

Jack and Harold devised a plan to fill both black boxes with items that had to survive. They would remove their contents during the flight and refill them with supplies. One would have seeds for future crops with everything from corn to tomatoes with high producing vegetables like beans and okra included. The other box would enclose all of their fire starters: lighters, matches and strikers. They would add 10 garden hoes and 10 shovels to the cargo.

Harold during his few weeks as baggage supervisor had been able to obtain a shipment of military MRE's(meals ready to eat)and store them in the unclaimed baggage section of the airport just days ago. These 3000 meals would be helpful in the beginning of their adventure. He had also allowed Jack to store the ten barrels of corn, rice and beans he had gathered. Jack also obtained 3000 life straws (an individual water purification system) to insure safe drinking water until natural pure water sources could be found. They would build rain troughs to gather fresh water during rain storms in the long term.

During their long discussions and planning they realized the corn they would grow could be used as food, cooking oils and biofuel. They obtained literature and tools to make this more than just a possibility.

They obtained many foods in dehydrated form: potatoes, eggs, milk, pre-sweetened drinks and powdered vitamin supplements. They would also include oats and cream of wheat with which to feed infants and toddlers along with a small amount of various kinds of baby formula.

Harold would be in charge of anything mechanical. He needed machinery: three generators, three push mowers, a plasma cutter, a small air compressor, and a welder. The generators would be run off some of the remaining airplane fuel and could be used to run the plasma cutter to cut up the remaining airplane wreckage to provide roofing materials for the shelters they would work together to construct. The welder would be used to weld the smaller pieces back together once they were in place atop the shelter structures. He would also provide hand tools like hammers,nails,screws, screw drivers and weed eaters. He would need multiple sets of hoses and gaskets for the gas operated tools as they will rapidly deteriorate being used with such high quality fuels like airplane fuel even though the machines will run well. The weed eaters and push mowers would be used to clear pathways, clear home sites, and keep weeds out of whatever crops they would grow in the long term. They would also run on the biofuel they would eventually make from corn. He would also need to bring 3 chain saws, a few hand saws and an axe to insure the ability to aquire fire wood.

Harold would be responsible for handling all baggage: inspecting and bringing one bag per person rather than the traditional 3 or 4 checked. All other bags would be placed in the unclaimed baggage area space cleaned out when he loaded the supplies he would store there. He would bring only clothing and medications. Everything else would be considered excess baggage. This would aid in covering up their planned escape to paradise while making room in the plane's cargo hole for the supplies to be brought aboard.

Janie had taken it upon herself to tend to personal health and welfare. She would use her knowledge of prescription drugs and the ailments they are used for to compile a mobile drug store for common ailments. She would take all the allergy and cough medications, all stomach medications, prescription meds for diabetes, heart disease, arthritis and kidney disorders, all otc fever and pain relevers. She would take blood pressure medications along with blood pressure cuff monitors and thermometers. She had to get bandages of all kinds, tape, and sauves. They would need calamine and anti-itch lotions accompanied by bug repellant spray. She ordered 5 cases of dish liquid actually a multi-purpose supply that can be used to bathe, wash hair, do laundry, wash dishes and kill bacteria while doing all of it. She ordered 1000 emergency style aluminum blankets offered by many emergency personel during multi casualty events. They would offer warmth and a way to stay dry. She ordered 1000 packs of baby wipes, 400 tooth brushes and 200 disposable razors. She even came up with the idea of making 400 individual care packages containing cough drops, baby wipes, tooth brush, razors, two aluminum blankets, a comb and two chocolate bars. She provided 50 pounds of hard chocolate candy and 50 pounds of cocoa to produce chocolate in the long run. She tried to tell herself that this was done to provide for the hypoglycemic, but she really loved chocolate and had struggled only with leaving it behind. She remembered to bring diapers, cloth not desposible, 500 in number for any infants aboard.

Janie had come up also with the idea that they could "slip a couple of mickeys" into the co-pilot's drink when she delivered it about an hour into the flight to knock him out for the flight. She was even able to get those at her father's pharmacy which she found peculiar. They were illegal unless obtained on the black market but for some reason her father had them shelved with the other medications. This only strengthened her resolve to fly away......

CHAPTER FOUR

LOADING AND BOARDING

Harold and Janie arrived at the airport 45 minutes before Jack made it through the traffic jam. As usual they split up before entering the airport. Harold went right to work loading their secret cargo onto the plane so he would have time to quickly go through the checked baggage keeping only clothing and medications. He had practiced this on three occasions recently, and he had even fixed an old bag x-ray machine to expedite the task. In 30 minutes flat he had reduced the amount of checked bags by 3/4 leaving ample space for their survival cargo.

Janie had met Jack at the gate to have him help with the 3 large suitcases of pharmacuticals she had gathered. Along with that they each had one carry on bag of clothing for themselves. They were able to avoid security due to the extreme delay to their flight's departure schedule. "Good thing the traffic held me up for so long. The fates must be smiling on our journey" Jack told Janie as they headed toward the flight boarding area. Neither of them seemed to have even one reservation about the actions they were about to take.

Jack took special interest in the boarding passes as he greeted each passenger individually. He wondered as he shook each hand how many of them would prove helpful in building their "new world". He noticed two gentlemen had listed their names with doctor in front of them. He wondered if they were medical doctors, dentists, psychologists, or college professors. He counted 24 children including infants. He uttered a silent prayer for both their safety and for his own children to have a good life. There were approximately 57 hands of the elderly he shook. This was pleasing to Jack. He had always had a keen awareness of the advanced wisdom of the advanced in age. He looked forward to picking their brains for survival techniques that he and his two accomplices may not have thought of yet. There were several younger able bodied men that would be able to help with the physical labor of building shelters and providing food in the long term. He wondered how many of them might have hunting and game cleaning experience. Both would be beneficial. There were also many women who would in the long term be responsible for preparing all food, tending to the children and the elderly, washing clothes and furthering the population of the island. Never once did it cross his mind that even one of these potential new neighbors could perish at the end of this flight. 227 passengers plus 12 crew members: 239 total would be the population of their island paradise. Luckily he had bought a solar powered language translator. To Jack's delight it worked perfectly during it's trial run. He had realized there would be people who had originated from many different nations. Understanding one another would be essential to the survival of one and all both short and long term.

Janie busied herself with making sure all of the passengers were comfortably secure. She was careful to put herself in position to be the flight attendant in charge of first class and caring for the pilot and co-pilot's needs in order to clear the way to drug the co-pilot when the time arrived to do so. Jack and she had decided that cappuccino would be the code word that Jack would request when he was ready. Janie had intentionally put the two "mickeys" into the left breast pocket of her uniform to symbolize that this trip was a product of the love she had for Harold and the ability to openly show that love forever once this flight landed on paradise. In her mind using them would set her heart free.

The flight would experience a 20 minute further delay while Harold finished loading the last of the cargo and baggage. He would need to attach a seat with seatbelt to the interior metal of the plane to secure himself in for the duration of the flight. He would hide in the cargo hold while his co-worker loaded the last of the bags and closed the hatch. Then Jack would know to begin the flight when he saw the co-worker drive the cart away. The two of them would have no contact during the flight until after landing. Since Harold would have no way of knowing when to expect impact, they had all agreed that he would remain seatbelted the whole time. But first of all he would need to re-route all unwanted cargo previously tagged to be on this flight. He was careful to cover all shipments by reversing the routing numbers and returning to sender both large and small lots of cargo. This would aid in covering their tracks.

Harold and Jack had previously devised a plan to use the plane's radar to aid them in locating and choosing their paradise island. By changing the beacon positioner of the radar system they would deny the air traffic controllers radar from knowing their position. This would work best if flying at the lowest possible altitude, basically flying under the radar. Jack likened this idea to the magnificant soar of his beloved hawk: ever skimming the surface never crashing. The radar plan would prove beneficial in choosing the perfect paradise. He would be able to see and judge the land mass in time to slow the air craft and begin the desent. Upon landing they would attach the radar beacon to a life raft and set it asail for parts unknown in the Indian ocean to further confuse any military radars as to the actual end result of the flight. They had no desire to ever be 'rescued' from paradise.

CHAPTER FIVE

THE FLIGHT

"Off We Go Into the Wild Blue Yonder" plays in Jack's mind as he and his co-pilot go through the plane's pre-take-off checklist. Jack even made sure to have the plane's fuel tank topped off "just in case we have to avert the course or do multiple circles around the airport destination prior to landing", or so he said. In his mind he knew they could use all the excess fuel they could get upon landing to build their island shelters. He starts the planes engines feeling more nerves and excitement than he had felt since his first experience flying. As he turns on the intercom to make his pre-flight announcements he decides to lay the groundwork for a few added safety precautions. He informs his passengers after the first hour of flight he was expecting to fly into weather systems that may produce extreme turbulance, and the passengers needed to be watching for the "fasten seatbelt" sign to come on. For their own comfort and safety, they would need to follow this instruction. He had come to realize while practicing flight simulations that flying under the radar can prove to be quite turbulant but felt himself to be experienced in this area. Upon finishing his announcement, he proceeded to taxi his plane onto the proper runway and begin his final assent into the "wild blue yonder". Rather than this realization being a bittersweet moment, it filled Jack with excitement and unknown expectations for their future.

The plan was that he would radio Janie approximately 45 minutes into the flight that he would like to have a cappuccino and the co-pilot would like a black coffee. Immediately realizing that the time had come, she hurried to the prep station and first poured the black coffee to allow herself time to adequately position herself so that her back was to any other flight attendant that might enter the room. Then she grabbed a cappuccino cup and put it in front of her. After one last glance over her shoulder, she quickly took the small piece of aluminum foil holding the "mickey's" from her left breast pocket and slipped them in the co-pilot's coffee. She then busied herself with making Jack's cappuccino. As she met a co-worker in the doorway of the prep-station, her friend said "Well, aren't you the cheerful one this evening. You must love France. I don't believe I have ever seen you look so happy."

Janie answered, "Yes I am happy tonight, but I can assure you it has nothing to do with going to France." Smiling she added, "I better get Captain Wellington his cappuccino before he strokes out." With that Janie made her way to the cockpit and was buzzed in. As she handed each gentleman his drink, she warned the co-pilot that the black coffee was extremely hot. It would need time to cool if he would like to stretch his legs. Unbeknowanced to the co-pilot even this was pre-planned to be sure the "mickey's" had dissolved totally. Also it would leave the co-pilot no reason to leave his post once the drug had taken affect. They couldn't chance their plans being discovered prior to leaving radar detection. The co-pilot left the cockpit. Jack asked Janie if all systems were still go. She simply asked him to please not let her down. He answered "okay, paradise it is."

Janie would then go back to her preassigned duties tending to the passengers. The co-pilot was soon to return to his post. Janie began to watch for the "buckle your seatbelt" light to come on. This was their signal that the co-pilot was fast asleep and their alternate route would begin as soon as Jack had done his final radio transmission to air traffic control before turning the plane toward the vast unknown Indian Ocean. In the mean time the plane had been put on auto pilot as usual after the route has been entered into the planes computer system.They were unsure how long it would take the drug to take affect. Twenty minutes after the co-pilot finished his coffee he was out.

Jack allowed his mind to wander for a few minutes while waiting for his coworker to reach unconsciousness. He inwardly laughed when he pictured Janet opening the 5 unexpected maxed out credit card bills. That would take a bite out of her part of his life insurance. It was nothing she didn't deserve after the inhumane way she had treated him for years. He reveled in the fact that he had named Harold's mother overseer to his children's life insurance policies. He considered this as insurance on his children's behalf. Janet had no desire to provide for anyone but herself. He was sure the happiness that had always seemed to evade him was to be found in his very near future.

Jack picked up the radio microphone after shaking the co-pilot to confirm that he would not awaken any time soon. The radio transfers had always been his least favorite part of flying so he smiled at the idea that this would be his final transmission. After all the call letters and coordinants were confirmed, Jack ended with "eye eye air control tower. Island Jet Flight 370 signing off. Good night gentlemen." And with that he turned off all radio contact. He could not be bothered with them trying over and over to contact them after the course had been changed. He then reached for the seatbelt light and turned it on. He turned toward the cockpit door to be sure all available locks were latched. Only then did he begin to turn the plane.

Once the new course had begun, Jack went right to work. He turned the radar beacon downward to be used to choose the perfect island. He unlocked both black boxes, emptied their contents, and placed the crop seeds in one and the fire starters and life straws for pure water in the other. He very carefully resealed each black box in the way he had found them to keep their contents safe. The boxes' interior was the only way to keep these precious essentials dry and fireproof during their landing.

Jack remembered he and his father had sailed for two full days to reach their island paradise destinations. He had studied ocean currents and how they change as the seasons change. Many times he had done the math. He was nearly sure one could fly at jet liner speeds for three hours and achieve roughly the same distance. This research was the only way that he could estimate the proximity of those islands. He would begin searching for "home" after two hours in flight. He realized he had approximately 9 hours worth of fuel available, but had the presence of mind to know that preservation was the key to easing many tasks as they set up their new shelters. The machinery they had brought along could be powered for possibly years on half of a tank of jet fuel. He had a set idea as to how far they needed to go and still be too close to never be found and how far was a waste of needed fuel for their future. He had no desire to ever be rescued from "paradise".

After studying ocean currents, Jack and Harold had realized that the beacons would be carried away very rapidly on the only life raft further confusing any military radars that might still have the plane in range. They would even convince the passengers this was being done to help the authorities to locate them. No one would ever be the wiser. As soon as all these things were in place, Jack lowered the flight altitude and began what would be a little more than two hours of rough turbulent flying.

Jack had kept a steady watch on the flipped radar beacon. He had marveled at the machine's ability to both watch for any upcoming land masses but also work as a depth finder. At some places the ocean's bottom registered at more than a mile below it's surface. The thought was chilling. Then suddenly a rather large land mass appeared on the screen. After flying internationals to Honalulu he recognized the island to be about the size of Auohu. He immediately checked the coordinates as the plane was flying at a high rate of speed and turning around in the darkness can be confusing. He then checked the time to see if his calculations were close. Three hours, fifteen minutes. Yes this could possibly be his father, Jon Wellington's, island. He swallowed hard as he calculated how far past the island would be best to go before turning around for the final approach. He knew he needed to make only one attempt so as not to be discovered. After he felt he had gone far enough, he slowly began to turn the plane back toward the island. When he had finally completed his reversal of directions, Jack began to slow the planes speed. Soon he lowered the landing gear and slowly began his dessent. The island seemed to have vast vegetation and some hilly regions. Great.

He would fly just above the oceans surface just as he had so often watched the magnificent hawks do. He would use the sandy beach to slow the plane as it progressed into the thick forest just beyond the inland edge of the beach. The rest would require both luck and skill. He hoped to stop the plane deep enough in the forest to be un-detectable to any search and rescue vessels that might be deployed.

Finally he could see the island on the radar screen. He slowed the plane to landing speed. "Here we go," he uttered, "in three...two.....

CHAPTER SIX

PLANE GROUNDED

The countdown never reached one. A one second miscalculation had ended in catastrophe. Everything went black. Jack was unsure how long he had been unconscious. He was awakened by screams and wailing from somewhere behind him in the darkness. He opened his eyes to see Janie seemingly wedged next to him shaking him vigorously screaming "Jack, Jack wake up. We have to find Harold." She was holding a flashlight in his face at first. But then everything became surreal as she turned the flashlight in the other direction.

Immediately beyond Janie, Jack had expected to see his co-pilot and the other side of the cabin. Instead there was solid rock. Suddenly the realization of Jack's actions hit him like a ton of bricks. Janie had been able to make her way to him only because the cabin door had been taken by the cliff as well as the entire right side of the cabin and 1/2 of first class. Jack began to sob uncontrollably thinking of the lives that had just been lost due to his actions. Janie slapped him hard across the face.

"We don't have time to worry about the dead; there are lots of people still alive to worry about. Don't you realize if they hear you blubbering on about this being your fault they will kill you! I had a feeling something like this would happen. I've been thinking about it this whole flight. Since the co-pilot perished along with two of the flight attendants strapped in across from me, we say this was all their idea and execution. I have kept a journal of our planning of this trip to paradise, and I just now put Penny's name on the cover. It's perfect Jack, just think about it. It will even explain why we know about the supplies. So compose yourself and help me find Harold. He should have survived because he was going to position his seat just under mine so if one died, we both would."

With that Jack seemed to recover instantly. His mind shifted back to the future of this brave new world. He must brace himself to speak to the remaining passengers, find Harold, launch the life boat with the radar beacon, and attend to the injured. He would need to do a head count of the survivors. His mind raced frantically as he reached what was left of the first class section. Even with the knowledge of the demise of half of the cabin and the partially destroyed first class, nothing could have prepared him for the extent of the disaster he was about to see.

"Everyone please remain seated at least until day break when we can see how to help one another. I shall return as soon as possible. I must go and assess the damage." Ahead of him beyond the beam of the flashlight, Jack could see what appeared to be three small fires. Then suddenly he reached the point where the cliff began. To his left there were 15 feet of debris from the entire destroyed section of the plane including the body parts of the occupants. That side of the plane seemed to have accordianed, folded many times during the crash.

The next thing he saw was the shocking sight of his co-pilot's lifeless eyes staring at him nearly eye level, his head being his only visible body part among the debris. First Jack screamed, followed once again by sobbing. But this time his words were different. He began loudly blubbering the words "Willard, you idiot. What did you do? Where are we? It was my shift to sleep. You said you could handle it."

Janie immediately stopped him by saying "Captain Wellington, please, we have to find the passengers who are still alive. Please, we need you." Understanding what she meant, Jack turned the flashlight toward the rear of the plane.

Janie's words when he had first awakened had etched their way so deeply into his mind that this lie was totally believable almost even to Jack. In this temporary state of shock and insanity, Jack noticed what appeared to be the left hand of a married woman sticking out of the end of the debris field. Her large diamond wedding ring set seemed to glisten and sparkle in the reflected flashlight beam. He felt her middle finger hand gesture to be quite appropriate considering her present state. Realizing how horribly bizarre his thoughts were, Jack shook his head vigorously for a moment. This seemed to bring him back to reality.

Approximately 20 feet away from the end of the debris field the plane had broken away. As he approached the end of the walkway he began calculating in his head. This Boeing 777-200ER was just under 210 feet in length. The spot he was standing in was roughly 75 feet from the nose of the aircraft. As he looked once again out into the darkness just in front of him now he saw again the three small fires. The light from the fires cast an erie glow but shed no light as to what they were coming from. He wondered in his current state of shock what happened to the other 130 feet of his plane.

Luckily there was an emergency exit door that was spared just 2 seats from where the plane had broken off. Janie called Jack's attention to the emergency ladder that might still deploy if they could get the door to open. At this point this might be the only safe way to get their feet on the ground. They were entirely too high up to try to jump to the ground without being injured and it was too dark out to attempt to climb down the cliff. So Jack asked for any men willing to help to attempt to open the door. Then Jack with the help of two rather large men were able to push the door open. Janie's hunch was correct. The emergency slide did deploy. However the ladder was a no go. Jack said to Janie "We must get the radar beacon and the life raft before we go outside. We will have to figure a way to get back in later." He pushed past Janie and headed back to the cabin to retrieve the items he had secured behind the seat. He was back in a moment. Then he and Janie exited the plane.

When they reached the ground the brush was quite thick. It was hard to walk and on this cloudy night it seemed much darker than usual. They could still see the fires in the distance. Just as they reached the bottom of the plane where it had broken off they could see a light coming out of it. They both started screaming Harold's name so loudly they couldn't hear him screaming for his love, his Janie. As the light got closer they realized it was strapped to Harold's head. He was struggling to climb through the supplies and the debris field. "Sorry guys, but I only thought of this head lamp at the last minute. It allows for hands free manuverability. I will be out in a sec," Harold yelled. As he reached them, Janie ran into his arms, and Jack joined their warm embrace.

Harold immediately told Jack they had no time to waste on getting the radar beacon launched into the sea. They would talk along the way to the beach. They would follow the path the plane had left behind enabling them to figure out where the rest of the plane had ended up.

As they made their way through the thick brush they soon came upon the next section of the plane. Yes the plane had actually broken into three pieces. The middle section was basically intact with the exception of the wing being buried into the sandy ground. Just yards beyond this section the beach began. Down the beach about the distance of a football field was the remaining section of the plane.

Before checking on anything, as soon as the three of them reached the beach they immediately launched their only life raft and the only way they could ever be found: the radar beacon. The ocean's waves grabbed the lifeboat instantly carrying it quickly out of the flashlight's rays and away into the night. If their studies and calculations were correct the beacon should take search teams thousands of miles deeper into the Indian Ocean. They would never think to begin their search anywhere near this point. YES NOW THIS WAS HOME!

Without delay they walked toward the tail section of the plane. Along the way there was cargo scattered all about. "We certainly have our work cut out for us for quite a while. Janie figured out a way for us to turn out the heroes in all this." Jack told Harold. Janie then explained about the journal and adding their co-workers name to it. They agreed to attempt to never speak of it again. Suddenly they could hear the survivors cries coming from up ahead in the tail section. Jack and Harold both whistled loudly on the count of three to gain the peoples attention. Jack identified himself as the pilot. He explained, "The co-pilot who was on shift to operate the air craft while I was on sleep shift crashed the plane." He told them he was unsure of their location but they had launched the radar beacon. (The survivors had no idea this was not to lure the rescue mission to them) He then asked that they stay put till daylight for further assessment and instruction.

They returned to the middle section where Jack repeated this speech. Then the three of them went back to sit on the beach to await daylight and maybe rest up for the great unknown.

CHAPTER SEVEN

THE BLOODY MORNING AFTER

Sometime afterwards, Jack awoke to the brightness of the sun coming over the horizon and the sound of the ocean waves splashing against the cliffs just down the beach. Knowing the enormous tasks that awaited them, just for a moment he chose to lay there. He wanted to take in the sounds of paradise, the salty taste in the air, the birds singing loudly, and most importantly the full sounds of untouched nature at it's finest. No autos, no industry, no phones, just God given nature. For only a second he allowed his mind to wonder if somewhere on this island he would find his beloved father. Then Janie awoke and woke Harold up so they could make themselves busy with the many tasks at hand.

They must first assess the number of people that would populate their island home. To do this they must find a way to safely get all the survivors to the ground. They would begin with the nose section of the wreckage since all of those survivors would be needed to aid in getting the other people to the ground. Jack and Harold would use the emergency slide to climb back into the remainder of that section to begin coaching those remaining passengers to go down the slide and make their way to the beach. Luckilly Jack's language interpreter was still buttoned in his uniform breast pocket making an otherwise impossible task do-able. Oddly enough to their benefit, the survivors in this section seemed virtually unscathed other than the minor cuts and bruises. Jack pointed them all in the direction of the beach to wait for further instructions. He made his way once again to the cockpit to retrieve a handfull of fire starters to hand out for people to build small bonfires to help them stay warm and help them recover from any shock they might be feeling. This should pacify them long enough for Harold, Janie, and himself to help the other passengers in the remaining two sections to the ground. Only then could they do a formal head count and start to delegate duties to their new neighbors. They would also need to bring them up to speed on the "awful deed their co-workers had committed" and tell them of the supplies available. They thought it best not to reveal which part of the world their trip had ended and just claim total ignorance in that area due to the fact Jack was supposed to be asleep at the time of the crash. After hearing instructions, one by one the survivors exited the plane. Janie stood on the ground below to help slow the landing of the passengers as they came down the slide.

As soon as Jack and Harold had exited the plane, Harold told Jack and Janie to wait there while he made his way back to his seat in the hull. He had left the battery operated impact drill connected to the bolts he had used to attach his seat to the plane. If it had survived he could use it to detach a built in ladder inside the hull. The ladder should be somewhere in the middle piece of the severed aircraft. He had made sure to use the size bolts used most in the structure of the body of the plane so if it survived it would prove very beneficial. Then he was off disappearing quickly into the darkness inside that hull. He returned approximately fifteen minutes later. As the light of his headlamp got closer they could see the drill in one hand and a large suitcase in the other. Janie recognized the suitcase immediately as being one of the ones she had filled with care packages for their passengers. She knew there were 50 packages per suitcase and thought one suitcase was a good start. They turned and made their way toward the beach. Harold spoke about the mess and disarray of the condition of the supplies remaining in the hull he had just exited. But even he had no idea how much that fact would ring true as to the scattered status of their life sustaining supplies.

As they approached the middle section of the plane, they marveled at the fact the plane appeared to have broken into nearly the same length sections, all 75 feet or so. The section in front of them was tilted to one side with the wing seeming buried deep beneath the sand. Harold stated the ladder was mounted just beneath where the wing attached. He hoped the ladder was next to the buried wing, but as they got closer he could see that this was not the case. With the way this section was sitting, the ladder hung high in the air. Most of this section's cargo was scattered all along the ground. There wasn't even enough cargo left in this section to stack up to reach the bolts that held the ladder. Jack suggested they use man power. The surviving men from the front section who were already on the ground were asked to go into the hull of this section and form a human pyramid of sorts to hoist Harold up to the ladder to remove the bolts. With this new life endevour they were embarking on there was no time like the present to introduce the teamwork ethic that would be necessary to insure their long term survival.

Jack went toward the beach to try to find help. As he reached the point where the thick brush and the beach's sands met, he saw that two barrels each of corn, beans and rice had been spilled seemingly everywhere. He made a mental note to self to have this addressed as soon as possible. They needed every morsel of food available to carry them until they were self sustaining. When he reached the place where the people had gathered, he used his translator again to communicate with the survivors. He short storied his explanation with a promise to provide more details later in 3 languages. All the men in the group followed him back to the middle section.

Using each other to pull and push, they soon had 15 men in the hull and 7 more on the ground. They found the location of the ladder and with some inner driven instinct the larger few of the men began hoisting each other onto their shoulders. They one by one climbed using knees, elbows and shoulders as stair runners until they were three levels high, sturdy and ready for Harold to ascend to the top to loosen the ladder. When the ladder released it nearly wiped everyone out. But it only knocked the wind out of two of the bottom row men as they got the brunt of the weight from the pyramid collapsed. They recovered rather quickly. Once the ladder was on the floor they soon realized at the angle this section was sitting the ladder would still be too short. They would have to open the hatch between the cargo hole and the passenger section of the plane. It should allow survivors to climb into the cargo hole and on to the ground from there. This too would require teamwork. Four people to hold the ladder on such an uneven surface and two people to climb up the sides of the ladder simultaniously as one person would surely not be strong enough to open the hatch alone. Screams and cheers rang out as hands from inside the passenger section helped open the hatch door. Jack climbed inside and once again using his translator to give instructions. He asked each one to climb down the ladder into the cargo hold and wait for help to reach the ground. He added that they would need to join the other survivors on the beach and that the flight attendant had built a campfire to warm themselves by. He would join them as soon as all survivors were safely on the ground. Once the last living passenger had climbed down to the hull, Jack checked the pulse of the ones remaining seated. Much to his dismay all 24 still seated had expired. Just as he was beginning to feel nauseous, Harold stuck his head in, "Jack, do you need any help? If you have done all you can up here, we need you."

"No, I'm on my way down now," he answered.

Once inside the hull they soon realized the ladder was about three rungs too short to reach the ground and unsafe for these survivors to try to climb down. Jack instructed the men on the ground to once again form a pyramid for the people to climb down. The men went down first to be able to aid the women, children and elderly safely to the ground. However unlikely this evacuation went off without a hitch. When only Jack and Harold were left to exit, Jack told him of the 24 passengers that had died in this section. They would need to deal with the dead soon out of respect but now they had to concentrate on keeping the living alive. They still had the tail section of passengers to evacuate. They exited down the human pyramid that awaited. As they reached the edge of the beach they could see a number of people now gathering on the beach. Suddenly from out of the crowd runs Janie. A little out of breath but smiling rather happily she immediately asked Harold if he thought he could locate another suitcase of her personal care packages. She was excited she had already given out 50 and was in need of more. "We have people", she exclaimed.

He answered, "There might be one or two more bags that survived." He then kissed her and went back to retrieve the supplies.

Jack and one of the passengers continued to carry the ladder to the severed tail section of the plane. Once they reached it they were relieved to see the ladder was a perfect height to enter the hull of this the final section of the plane. Soon he will know all the numbers: the survivors verses the casualties. Oh the horror of the knowledge that all this death was at his hand. The new secret he is now sworn to take to his grave. He inwardly hoped paradise would prove worth it. Luckily this section had rested nearly at it's original level. Jack was able to use the built in ladder that led to the rear kitchen/food prep area floor hatch. With one hard shove the hatch flew open. As Jack stuck his head through the floor he was greeted by the bloody face and dead glaring eyes of one of the other flight attendants. He instinctively let out a rather shrill scream of surprise startling the passengers. He then tried to calm the nerves of this group of already traumatized people that he had just scared the crap out of. Soon Harold arrived and helped him gain the attention of the group. They could now make their way down the built in ladder to the hull then down the other ladder to the beach. Once again he instructed them to go to the part of the beach where the others were gathered. Again Jack checked the pulse on each individual that did not go down the ladder. And once again everyone who didn't get up was dead, 26 this time. Dear God that made 50 he already knew were dead and he had seen a number of bodies up and down along the beach. Harold had to snap him out of shock by touching him on the sholder and saying "Hey man. It's like Janie said, we got people. We gotta go. We will deal with this later." They exited the section and began to walk down the beach toward where "their people" were gathered. Along the way they stared at all the supplies scattered everywhere possibly to locate any item that might be of immediate use. They would try to remember where they saw what. Jack asked Harold to help him check the people lying scattered on the beach for any additional survivors. They counted 21, all dead, some still strapped to their seats, some lying loose not connected to anything. This made at least 71 dead. The time had come to do the final head count of the survivors.

Jack used his translator to communicate that all the living must be counted. This time he only had to use it to communicate in four languages. Much to his surprise there were still 153 surviving members of their new community. Janie said she was still 3 short on care packages having enough for everybody. Next she reached behind her back and pulled out the journal which would clear them so they could acknowledge the supplies which must be located first. She suggested they try and locate the military MRE's. These people must be fed to maintain strength for the massive amount of work this first day would entail. Harold whispered soon after she would need to find the place in the journal that spoke of the plasma cutter and generator. Then he could begin preparing shelter for their scattered supplies to keep them safe from wildlife. Jack suggested that the male survivors form groups of five and begin combing the beach and the wreckage for these meals ready to eat. The women he instructed to walk along the edge of the vegetation to gather any sticks or logs small enough to drag out for fire wood. At night they would surely need multiple bonfires to keep this many people warm. The elderly were asked to not participate other than staying put, taking care of one another and watching after the children. All able bodied parents needed to busy themselves with the requested tasks. Once the food was found and everyone was fed there would be additional instructions as what they could do to help next. All of them instantly did what Jack had instructed; the amount of co-operation was everything that they could have hoped for. Jack and Harold soon joined the search for the food and Janie joined the fire wood retrievers as the women had chosen to call themselves. As they walked toward the nose section of the wreckage Jack began to count the dead verses living ratio again. "I counted 227 passengers and 12 crew members upon boarding, 239 total, with 71 dead accounted for and 153 still with us that leaves 15 still unaccounted for," Jack stated aloud.

"Sixteen, you forgot to count me. Remember I was not on the roster," Harold said under his breath in correction.

"Oh you're right, how thoughtless of me," answered Jack. They finished their walk in silent thought.

After about 20 minutes they heard shouting down the beach just beyond a mound of shipping crates. "Captain Wellington, old man, come and look. We may have found the meal bin just beyond this mound," a rather thin, tall, obviously british voice shouted from close proximity of the tail section of the plane. To Jack and Harold's surprise they were correct but this crate was buried underneath the 8 foot tall pile of debris that once was various supplies. The men yelled out for more help to expidite the task of digging the food out. To their delight, teamwork made the task go off once again without a hitch. Once unstacked they had a lot more supplies right here than they had expected including one plasma cutter and one pre-fueled generator not to mention 500 MRE's. It took eight men to carry the crate of food down the beach where the main group had set up a sort of camp. Janie greeted them with a new request. In the tail section of the plane in the food prep area, had it survived? If so, in the cabinet underneath the sink there should be a big box of 500 sets of good plastic ware to eat with. Would they please check, and if so bring the box back. She assured them it was not heavy. Harold set out immediately and was back in five minutes with the disposible flatware. They then proceeded to pass out meals to each person with the special request that they hold onto all used containers and each set of flatware for they would need to be used in the future.

For the first time since awakening that morning, Jack, Harold and Janie separated themselves from the herd and allowed themselves to sit down, rest, eat, and talk to one another in depth for a moment. They agreed to a moment of silent reflection and meditation both in honor of the dead passengers and to listen to the sounds of freedom and nature all around them; yes the sounds of paradise. Unplanned and almost simultaneously they each took a long, deep breath of the salty ocean air and let out a sigh of relief that they were really here. They all looked up at each other and laughed out loud. They began to plan which tasks must be attended to first. The fire wood retriever ladies had done a great job and gathered enough wood already to burn fires for two or three nights. Their next task would be to gather as many of the scattered supplies as possible and take them to the area between the middle part and the nose part of the plane. That is where they would quickly build a temporary shelter for their supplies the way Harold had it planned. The children would be asked to make a game out of picking up every grain of the rice, corn and beans that had been spilled in the sand just as the beach began. They would lay out 3 survival blankets, one for each (rice, corn and beans). The kids could go ahead and begin before the grain barrels were located. That should make the young ones happy and keep them busy for today.

The able bodied men would be split into three valuable groups:

Group #1 would form an expedition group to go inland scouting for anything helpful ie; fresh water sources, caves for shelter or possibly flat clear areas to possibly be used as building sites for future shelters.

Group #2 would be searching cargo both scattered and remaining in the front and tail sections of the plane. They were instructed to gather all pallet skids and take them to the supply holding area along with any string or rope. The skids and rope would be used to build the walls of the new structure which they would makeshift construct to house the supplies.

Group #3 would have the grusome task of bringing the dead to the waters edge and lining them up to be prayed over and left for the night's tides to take them out to their ocean resting place.

They would ask for volunteers for each group as only the passengers would know best which group they were best suited for. They still had 347 MRE's left in that crate. That would feed the people this evening and tomorrow morning before they would be required to search for another crate. The plan for the day had been made with Janie appearing to be gaining the information from the journal she had passed off as her co-workers just in case anyone was watching. They returned to the people to form the groups and begin the needed tasks.

Once again Jack used his translator to communicate the necessary instructions in four languages. This amazing group of people immediately separated themselves into their chosen task groups. Harold asked Janie in front of expedition group #1, "Didn't you say that journal had machetes listed in the supplies? They will help this group to maneuver through the thick vegetation and carve a path to follow back here."

Janie following his lead answered, "Yes, the journal lists them along with a host of other tools somewhere in a large wooden crate marked batteries of all things."

Harold then turned to Jack and asked, "Will you allow this group to take your service weapon for safety from wildlife?" refering to the pistol hanging on Jack's side.

"That would probably be a good idea" answered Jack as he turned to address this group. He asked for anyone who would be willing to carry the fire arm and take charge of shooting any threatening wildlife. Three men stepped up, two large and one medium. Jack handed the gun to the smaller gentleman along with an explanation that the two larger men might be more helpful clearing the path due to their obvious stronger stature.

Harold took half the group to search for the large wooden crate marked batteries. They returned shortly with the five machetes Harold had packed. After he and Jack discussed it they decided to send only ten men on the expedition. The rest of the 22 who stepped up for this task would be used to move any heavy supplies that the women could not move to the shelter area. They could also help Harold cut some metal from the tail section to make the roof for the supply shelter. Group 1 headed out past the mid section and nose section of the plane into the vast wilderness.

When they were out of sight Harold asked Jack about one of the men on the expedition being rather elderly to be accompanying this group. Jack explained while Harold had been gone to find the machetes, the man had approached him asking to be allowed to go along. He had said that being advanced in age didn't change the fact that he had been a scout leader for 30 years and had produced many Eagle Scouts. He knew his experience would be an asset on the trip into the jungle. He didn't seem to be lacking mobility skills so Jack had agreed to let him go. The old man had been very grateful he didn't have to help babysit the children today.

They proceeded to gather Group 2 whose task of locating and retrieving any skids to be used to build the walls of the structure. This group consisted of 18 men of three languages. Using common sense Janie suggested they separate the group into three mini groups: one would gather skids, one would locate rope or string, and one would need to cut thin trees into 8 foot sections to stab into the soft ground one foot deep to attach the skid walls to the ground for sturdying purposes. This would eliminate the language barrier while working. She then told Jack and Harold in front of the group that the journal listed 3 axes and some hand saws in the "batteries" crate. Harold once again took a couple of men and returned shortly with the axes and saws. Group 2 then were off to perform their mission.

Group 3 only needed a ladder to get started. Jack instructed them to begin by gathering the dead that were scattered on the beach and lay their bodies as close to the water's edge as possible. Then they could get the bodies first from the tail section. In the meantime he retrieved the one parachute that was available from the cockpit to be used somewhat like a hammock to lower the dead to the ground. He began to realize how difficult the task was going to be to retrieve the dead from the front section with such a large debris field. With those thoughts and the parachute he hurried back to the beach and Group 3. He would help this group with this very sad and gruesome task.

Janie would be in charge of getting the children started picking up spilled food, getting the elderly in position to take care of the children so no one wandered off, and searching for the storage barrels. She was responsible for making sure every grain of food was saved. Their lives depended on it.

Their next immediate concern was to locate a small air compressor also known as a pancake air compressor. It was needed to make the plasma cutter perform the duty of disassembling the plane to have to use to build shelters and various other things. After nearly an hour of searching it was found sticking out of the sand that had mounded up next to the buried wing of the middle section. This freed them up to begin the task of operation metal retrieval as they chose to call it.

Harold took advantage of the fact the plasma cutter and generator were so close to the tail section of the plane and the fact that section was the closest to the ground. Very soon the generator was started and he was dissecting the tail fins of the plane. They would be a lot of metal to construct a roof for the shed. He had his help to take each section to the beach next to the middle section and stack them up. His plan was to cut enough metal to put a roof on the shed approximately a 10x20 foot building. He would get the other guys to help him retrieve the cordless drill from the mid section when he disconnected the ladder. He would also need to go back into the cargo area of the nose section to locate his drill bits from the "batteries" crate. They needed them to drill holes in the metal panels to run the rope through to hold the roof to the walls.

Teamwork is a dynamic only surpassed by the assembly line. Once all the materials had been gathered, Harold found Jack so they could use the translator to give instructions as to how to tie the skids together and hold them up while other men sat on one another's shoulders to drive the posts they had cut into the ground through the openings on the bottom of the skids. They tied the walls together to further strengthen the structure. Then they built the roof one piece being tied on at a time. They intentionally made one side shorter so the roof would have pitch for the water to run off of during any rains that fell. They then entered the tail section passenger area to cut up any available carpet to cover any holes in the structure. Within hours they had built a fairly sturdy structure to house the supplies. They would leave the supplies in the nose section cargo hold alone for now. They would need to try to gather the supplies from the tail section and either put them in the shelter or try to get them in the remaining nose section cargo hold. Soon the shelter was being lined wall to wall with the once scattered supplies. Janie had been lucky enough to find the grain barrels washed up down the beach beyond the tail section but she could not locate the lids. The children had gathered around half a barrel of each of the three so far. She later discovered the lids had been found and put to use to stack the used food containers on by some of the older women who had cleaned and stacked them. She was relieved. Janie said the dishes could be restacked on top of the barrels after they were full and placed in the supply shelter.

Feeling as though this mission had been accomplished, this group decided to head back to the beach. Their lightheartedness was soon replaced with sadness as they reached the clearing of the beach. There they saw lying just at the water's edge was 45 dead bodies positioned side by side. Jack's crew were lowering the final 2 bodies out of the tail section. Even after retrieving so many, they realized they were barely past half done. They would need the help of Group 2 to retrieve the middle section's 24 bodies. They realized the nose section's 16 dead could take days to dig out of the destroyed debris pile. They allowed themselves to call it a day after the middle section had been cleared of the dead. They would pray over only this 71 tonight and tomorrow they would begin trying to free the remaining bodies to be taken by the sea.

After resting for a brief period, people began the building of five bonfires as night time was soon approaching. There was a quiet solitude among the 143 survivors other than the chatter of the kids still picking up the pieces of corn, beans, and rice. Suddenly off in the distance from somewhere in the dense island vegetation they heard the faint sound of multiple screams, followed by a single gun shot, followed by more screaming and then an erie silence. Being some 2 hours until dark, Jack and Harold decided to wait until morning to send a search party if Group 1 had not returned to the beach. They had been gone for 4 hours and they knew they might not be able to find them by dark. However, they didn't have to do this because the remaining 8 men from Group 1 reached the beach just as night fell with tales of both horror and triumph. Missing from the group was one of the large men who had stepped up to volunteer to carry the gun and the elderly scout leader who had wanted so badly to go. A very distraught elderly lady immediately charged up to the group screaming inquiries as to her husband's whereabouts. The shaken and weary group answered he had a heart attack and died while standing next to a man who had been surrounded by a 25 to 30 foot tropical snake, possibly a boa constrictor. The snake had fallen from a tree that they were pulling a vine from to try to save two men who had walked into a quick sand pit. The armed man shot and killed the snake but even death had not released the snakes sufficating grip. At this point there were 6 men available to deal with utter chaos. While 2 men worked to unwrap the snake from one man, another performed CPR on the scout leader in an effort to revive him, the remaining 3 were trying to pull 2 sinking men from the quick sand pit. By the time the man closest to the edge was pulled out of the pit, it was too late for the other man. He could not get one arm to pull out of the sand far enough to reach the vine and could not hold on with only one arm. They had watched in horror as his head went under the sandy surface and that last hand lost grip of the vine and followed it into the ground. The man pulled from the pit had a badly dislocated shoulder and the snake's victim obviously had broken ribs at the very least and could barely breath or walk by this time. The tearful wife of the scout leader seemed to retreat into her own world after uttering the words, "He was deathly afraid of even little snakes. How awful that must have been for my dear love." She sat down facing the sea and never spoke again.

At this time another of the passengers came forward stating he was a medical doctor and he would like to take a look at the two injured men. Finally a ray of hope Jack thought after a very somber day of retrieving so many dead bodies and then hearing the Group #1's news. Janie approached Jack and Harold opening the journal and reading about three suitcases of pharmaceuticals that were brought on board the plane "by her co-worker". She informed them those must have been the bags that Penny (another flight attendant) placed behind Janie's seat. The bags might have survived. They were said to contain many medications, insect repellant, and sunburn cream. Jack asked the people if anyone still had battery on their cell phones as they could use their flashlights to find the said suitcases. Five citizens offered up their phones and off went Jack, Harold and the five men. Janie yelled to ask if there were any more suitcases of those care packages left she could use 2 more of those as well. They shouted back confirming they would check on it. After about 20 minutes the 7 men returned with two bags of care packages and one suitcase of medications. The elderly women in the group were asked to apply sunburn cream to the whimpering children who had been in the sun all day picking up the rice, beans and corn. This would ease their pain and calm the nerves of everyone listening to them crying. The doctor being pleasantly surprised by the amount of pharmaceuticals he had to work with. He treated the two wounded men with anti-inflammatories as this batch of meds contained no antibiotics.

The two suitcases of care packages offered enough bottled water for everyone to have at least one bottle. Jack began handing the evening MRE's out. During this meal Jack, Harold and Janie asked the remaining Group #1 members to join them for further discussion of their discoveries of the day. As the discussion began, Jack thanked the men for their bravery. He asked them what happened to the scout leader's body. They answered they had left it behind next to the quick sand. They thought it best to ask any family members of the deceased if they preferred burial at sea or on land by slipping the body into the quick sand pit. Jack decided to discuss the burial the next morning with the man's widow. She had sat quiet and motionless staring at the sea since learning of her mate's death. The MRE and water she had been given sat untouched on the sand next to her so maybe tomorrow she would feel better.

The men told of seeing multiple forms of wildlife: turtles, frogs, lizards, squirrels and a number of bird species. They told of reaching the bottom of a cliff where two men had climbed atop to gain a better perspective of what the island might hold. From this additional altitude they believed they had seen a substantial size inland body of water, possibly fresh water at a point to the east of the cliff. Across from the body of water they saw a large cave opening in a cliff that ran along side of the water that might provide shelter if they could reach it. They could see different parts of the beach but the island appeared to be quite vast from atop the cliff. One part of the beach they could see had what appeared to be an old debris field, possibly washed up years ago during the tsunami. At some point they would have to make their way to that point to see if there could be anything beneficial in the rubble. Then the men told of climbing back down the cliff and turning their path toward the direction of the water source. About an hour later they had finally chopped a path to what had appeared to be a clearing in the jungle. Excitedly two men had rushed into the clearing which had turned out to be the quick sand pit. The remaining story had already been told.

After their meal was finished they all returned to the main group. It was not hard for Jack to gain the attention of this solemn group of people. He used his translator to communicate with the people that now was the time to say the prayers over all the bodies that had been placed by the waters edge. He asked anyone who desired could walk up the beach at the heads of the victims and offer up prayers for whomever they wished. That being said he led the possession followed immediately by Harold and Janie. Very few did not make that walk. Once finished Jack conveyed wishes for everyone to get a good night's rest. They found spots and retired for the evening. Harold and Janie made their way to the remaining tail section of the plane to sleep. Down deep they couldn't have been happier to realize they had the rest of their lives together.

CHAPTER EIGHT

DAY TWO, THE SMELL OF DEATH

Day two, Jack awakened to an unfamiliar, unbearable aroma in the air. He sat up in the sand to see first thing the bodies were still with them. They all seemed to be water logged and swolen now. He soon realized this was the smell of death. These bodies had started their rapid decay. He got to his feet and began to count the bodies. At the end of the line he had counted 68. Only 3 had been taken by the ocean. After breakfast they would need to begin burying the dead. He proceeded on down the beach to the tail section of the plane. He shouted good morning greetings inside to Harold and Janie and waited a moment to enter. This offered them an opportunity to discuss in private today's work activities. They discussed once again how to deal with the dead. Harold had brought along shovels thought originally to be beneficial to plant crops but they could use them to dig graves, or had he thought about cremating the remains. Then Janie came up with a workable idea. They would use the parachute that lowered the bodies from the plane to drag the bodies to the quick sand pit and put them in it. At least part of the bodies could be dealt with that way and it shouldn't take as long to reach the pit since the path was already cut out. Dragging the bodies would further beat down the path. Home spots could possibly be placed along the beaten path.

Harold would begin his day by working on an alternative fresh water source. The planes water tank had busted, but there was still an eighty gallon hot water heater of non-potable water in it. Although this water was not originally intended for human consumption it could be purified by the life straws. This would be enough drinking water for one or two days. Then Harold would continue disassembling the tail section to be used as building materials.

Jack would get help to cut the parachute into as many 4 foot wide strips as it would make. Each strip would hold three bodies lined up head to toe. When cut there were only 4 strips. That meant only a dozen dead could be dragged to the pit each trip which might be good considering they had no idea how many could be placed in the pit before it was full. He would use a different group of men to do the dragging each trip. He along with one man from the expedition team would accompany the first body moving team. After loading the first 12 bodies for transport, Jack would locate the scout leaders wife and explain to her how her husband would be buried with the other bodies. Jack realized now he had failed to ask the scout leader's and his wife's names. He would make it a point to learn the names of all the people in the next few days.

Janie would need to see to it the children had picked up every possible grain of corn, beans, and rice before all the birds found it. They had taken care of retrieving about 3/4 of the grain but they would need it all. The barrels had already been moved into the make shift shelter built so they would again utilize three of the aluminum warming blankets to separate and move the grain to the proper barrels. They would need every piece they could get their hands on in the long run. She would need to locate another crate of MRE'S for the next three meals. She would need to get some of the women to start weaving the wide tough grass blades together to possibly be used as building materials for the shelters. These women could begin by helping clear the home sites or they could gather their own grass to weave.

They would ask yesterday's Group #2 to continue to cut small trees to build homes but to leave any standing that were located in a 12 foot outer square that might be used to sturdy up the structures. They too would need to help clear the homesites. They would be responsible as well for moving any metal Harold retrieved to the new building spot. Being pleased with yesterday's performance, Harold would ask the same people to help him in his efforts to sever the air craft's metal exterior to be used for roofs or possibly even walls for their homes. As he went he would attempt to save even the seats along with the interior of the plane to eventually use to furnish the small homes with atleast a table and chairs. He planned to use the carry on baggage areas to build each home a table. But first thing first, they needed roofs over their heads.

Once all these plans had been made, the three of them rejoined their new neighbors on the beach. The smell of death was strongly evident but stopped just short of inducing nausea. They were just beginning to pass out the morning MRE's when they were approached by the doctor from the night before. "Captain Wellington sir," the doctor began, "I fear Mr. Patel may be coming down with pneumonia."

"I am sorry Doctor, I failed to get your name last night. Which injured gentleman is Mr. Patel?" Jack answered.

"I am Doctor Arthur Goodson from Dallas, Texas, and the man I speak of is the one who was attacked by the snake. It is my belief that his lung may have punctured over night while he tossed and turned. He is coughing up large amounts of blood and mucus. I am unsure as to my ability to save him in our current situation. I just wanted you to be aware of his medical status. Also I believe your scout leader's wife may have chosen to join her husband in death as next to her still uneaten dinner and unopened drinking water and the imprint of where she was sitting last night was one set of footprints leading out into the sea but after checking the beach, no footprints could be found coming out of the water."

Saddened by this revelation, all Jack said, "Three people died in the first 24 hours here and I didn't even know their names." He then pushed past Doctor Goodson and began helping pass out breakfast. He handed Janie a permanent magic marker that he had stuck in his uniform pocket along side his ink pen and asked that she would write each person's name on their shirts to help them all become acquainted. She promised to give it her best shot.

After breakfast was over Jack, using his translator, informed the survivors of the day's planned tasks. He asked in each of the four languages if anyone had seen what happened to the scout leader's wife and if anyone had learned her or her husband's names. Upon learning the people had no knowledge of the lady, he ended the morning's announcements and asked for volunteers for the first trip transporting the dead to the quick sand pit. Once again he asked for two members of Group #1 to accompany him along with seven other volunteers, ten men per trip to the pit. It was expected to take around two hours each way per trip. He asked Harold to find the shovels if they still existed and ask a few of the men to bury as many as they could. They would need to be buried at least 4 feet deep if placed in the beach's sandy soil to keep them from being washed back up by the ocean's waves. Even if they could only bury eight bodies it would allow the transport team to only have to make five trips instead of six. Harold remembered seeing the shovels in the "battery crate. It would not be a problem to retrieve them. He helped Jack and the other men to load the first twelve bodies onto the parachute strips and then went to get the shovels. Jack handed his gun back to his "trigger man" from the day before and asked him to lead the way. Jack noticed he already had his name written in magic marker; HABIB the shirt read. Jack shook the man's hand, called him by name, and reminded him the gun now only had five bullets left. Jack then praised the man for only using one bullet yesterday to kill the snake. Two men would pull each set of bodies. Jack would follow at the rear of the convoy.

Upon his return, Harold wasted no time getting busy. He went directly to the tail section of the plane along with the help of three men to move the plasma cutter, pancake air compressor and generator into the wreckage. They quickly located the 80 gallon water heater and began to remove the top with the plasma cutter. Sweet success: the tank remained full of water, but they would need to use the life straws water purifiers. He grabbed a large trash bag and two large pots from the food preparation area and asked his helpers to follow him. Once he had located Janie, he handed her the trash bag and asked that all of the empty water bottles be placed into it. They would refill the bottles with the unsanitized water from the hot water heater tank. Afterwards he asked Janie, "Didn't you say the journal listed a hand drill and some corking materials. I am going to drain the fuel tanks in small amounts to run the generator with?"

Janie answered, "Yes, indeed I told you that". She pulled the journal from the back of her waist band and began to look for the requested information for the continuation of their deception. Again the journal spoke of the non-electrical hand drill and corks being in a large crate marked "batteries". Feeling they had covered their tracks, they each went to work.

Harold began his fuel recovery mission standing on the ground beneath the middle section of the wreckage just where the buried wing came out of the ground. He and three helpers took turns with the hand drill, and after about twenty minutes the fuel began pouring out of the newly drilled hole. Harold grabbed one of the two large pots and placed it under the stream of air plane fuel. He instructed the men: as the pot fills up, two men would need to grab the filled pot while someone else placed the empty one in it's spot. As soon as it was nearly full he would need to cork the hole. As time went on they would need every drop of fuel and didn't need to waste any if at all possible. The cork worked but there was a small drip about every ten seconds. This would have to do. Harold would have one of his helpers bring one of the pots back after they filled the generator's fuel tank and place it under the drip as the wing was slanted into the ground. At this point, conservation was the key to survival.

Janie met Harold and his crew at the edge of the beach with the trash bag of empty water bottles. She suggested the men place the refilled bottles back into the bag to prevent them from being confused with what was left of the plane's rapidly deminishing bottled water supply. She had not been able to locate but one crate of the MRE"s and was concerned as to the status of the others. The journal stated there were 3000 MRE's aboard. One crate would only allot three meals. She asked Harold to work on locating more for the following morning? He agreed and took the trash bag of water bottles from her.

Harold and his men returned to the tail section and began cutting strips of metal from the passenger section roof at just the spot where it had severed away from the rest of the plane upon impact. They disassembled the interior knowing these materials could be used as furnishings in their shelters. Their last trip to the "battery" crate had rewarded them with a home maintenance tool kit equipped with hammers, screw drivers, a socket driver set and various kinds of wire pliers, all very helpful in this endeavor. The entire upper level would have to be disassembled before they would be able to start on the bottom which was ground level. It was yet to be seen how many structures could be constructed daily. Harold wondered how the tree and grass weaving crews were doing. As he looked out the gaping hole he was standing next to, everyone living was busy with one task or another. They all seemed to be trying to keep their minds off the ever growing stench of death. The aroma strengthened drastically with the heat of mid-day sunshine. He noticed there were 6 men burying three bodies, there were people gathering firewood and weaving grasses. Some of the children were helping the ladies with the weaving.

Janie and three other ladies were busy connecting a ten foot section of woven grass wall to three trees in an area they had cleared of grass. They had decided a women's privacy area was their priority. They would use available standing trees to sturdy the walls. They would leave the roof open to avoid any bad scent left after using the restroom multiple times. They would fill the used dinner plates they had already accumulated with sand and stack them in their new ladies room to cover the waste with. They would ask Harold to modify 4 passenger seats to have a hole like a toilet would but was open to the ground under the seat hole. She knew they had a limited number of trash bags but they were the strong kind. They would line their four new toilets with trash bags and empty them into the ocean when half full of sandbox waste. The ladies and children were weaving like a bunch of factory workers making sure the finished product was always at least three blades thick at all times. They had constantly staggered the beginnings and endings of each blade to avoid any holes in the finished product. Their efforts were deliberate and precise and their speed was impressive. At this rate they should be able to provide wall material for three or four 12 foot square shelters by the later part of the day when they would be needed for construction. Janie was pleased with the progress of these ladies.

Meanwhile Jack and the body movers were on their way back from the first trip to the quick sand pit. Delivering the first dozen bodies to their final resting place had been a grueling task, both physically and emotionally. Although they had not run across any dangerous animals on this trip, their arrival at the pit had induced fear and bewilderment as both the body of the snake and the scout leader had been partially eaten over night by some unknown source. With their hair and nerves standing on end they had placed these two bodies into the quick sand first. Jack marveled as those bodies along with the 12 additional bodies disappeared into the sand and the surface seemed to return instantly to it's original smooth surface. His mind wondered just what kind of creatures had met their demise previously in this sandy pit of death. He hoped they might fill the pit to compacity by the time all the bodies were placed inside. On the way back to the beach to load the second dozen bodies, Habib who was leading the way stopped to show Jack where they had climbed the cliff to look out over the terrain. They both climbed atop it to see what the two men from the day before had been talking about. They too saw an inland body of water, possibly fresh water, and the rather large cave opening in the cliff just beyond the water's edge on the pond's opposite side. Jack was pleased to see they seemed to be on a somewhat vast land mass. As he turned to scout out the complete 360 degree turn he saw the part of the beach where the debris field of Group #1's report was located. He too was under the assumption that this pile of rubble must be a result of the major tsunami that took his parent's lives years before. His heart wondered could his father's fishing vessel be among the debris. He knew it could take months for the residents of their new island home to reach the debris pile and examine it's contents. Realizing they had the rest of their lives he was content to climb back down their lookout cliff. Besides from high upon this perch the wind was blowing inland and the smell of the dead back on the beach was overwhelming.

While climbing back down the cliff, Jack noticed a small amount of water trickling down the side. Once on the level ground he watched as the water after was dripping to the ground from the cliff's jagged edge. He cupped his hands together beneath the drip and counted. Approximately two seconds separated the drips. He held his hands under the drip long enough to catch enough water to sip it. Much to his delight it tasted like cold, fresh spring water. He shouted a prayer of thanks to God as the other 9 men joined in his delight. As soon as each one had been able to taste the water, they continued on their journey back to the beach. The round trip only took three hours, a remarkable difference when not having to chop out a path which was good considering they were down to two machetes. The first man that had entered the quicksand pit yesterday had a machete that went into the pit when he did. The second man had dropped his on the ground before running into the quicksand clearing. They had only brought one with them on this trip and had left the other one at the shelter site with the clearing crew. The pathway had become clearer after just one trip making it much more visible and easier to follow. However they had left a pair of boots at the edge of the quicksand pit just to try and prevent any more accidents upon the next arrival with the second load of bodies. As they neared the beach, Jack noticed the roar of the generator and plasma cutters getting louder. He was glad that was the only modern equipment noise interupting the sounds of nature. As they reached the area just as the path begins into the jungle from the nose section, they came upon a work crew cutting out home sites. Two were nearly prepared already. He pulled his translator from his shirt pocket and thanked the people for their efforts as well as praising their finished product. As he entered the edge of the beach just beyond the middle section, Jack noticed the children were through picking up the grain. Impressed, he looked hard at the area where the corn, rice, and beans had been spilled but didn't see even one missed piece. While heading to the edge of the water to load a dozen more bodies, he yelled greetings to Janie and company. She said, "Building a ladies room. It won't take away from any metal needed for shelter. No roof, just walls." Jack told her of the good news about the fresh water drip and said he would take a pot from the kitchen area and a cup to leave under the drip. This would help on the many trips to transfer the bodies to the pit. A few swallows of water on a trip like that would go a long way. Once gathered they were off again.

Just prior to re-entering the forest, Jack was stopped by Doctor Goodson. "Please Captain Wellington, sir. I need to speak to you about Mr. Patel. His condition has continued to worsen. There's no way to really check my diagnosis but I am basically convinced that he is suffering from a pneumothorax."

Jack answered, "Forgive me doctor, but I am not trained in medical terminology."

"I believe him to have a collapsed lung on his right side. If so his only path to survival is to cut a small incision just between his ribs just over the lung, insert some sort of tube and drain the air and blood that is surrounding the outside of the lung so that the lung has the proper amount of space to re-inflate. Otherwise I believe this man will be dead before nightfall," stated Doctor Goodson.

"Well wait just a moment and I will recruit a couple of extra men to accompany these gentlemen back to the quicksand pit. I will meet you back at Mr. Patel's side to help you. Meanwhile, you get Janie to go through the ledger and see if there are any supplies that might be helpful with this procedure. I will be with you in five minutes or so." Jack finished his statement while motioning for his group to stay put for a moment. He headed toward the men who were digging graves. He asked for two men to join the body removal team for this trip so he could aid the doctor in caring for Mr. Patel. Two of the original expedition team immediately stepped up. He accompanied them back to his team, instructed them to place the pan under the water drip at lookout cliff on the way to the pit and keep track of the time it took to get back to it. Then they would know roughly how long it would take to fill the pan and how much fresh water could be obtained from this source. After wishing them a safe and speedy trip, he was off to meet with the doctor.

Upon arriving at the doctor's location, Janie and Doctor Goodson were looking through the suitcase of pharmaceuticals that had been found the night before. Doctor Goodson had already acquired gause, alcohol, peroxide and three tubes of extra strength mouth numbing gel. Puzzled, Jack asked about the mouth numbing gel. The doctor answered that it would have to act as a topical numbing agent on the area of the incision. He asked Jack to find him a bamboo limb approximately 8 to 12 inches in length and as big around as a pencil. Jack asked if a drinking straw would do. The doctor told him that the straw would collapse and bamboo would not. With that Jack ran as hard as he could to the home site clearing crew to inquire about a bamboo shoot that would meet the doctor's requirements. Alot of what they were clearing was bamboo, and after approximately 10 minutes of searching they believed they had found a suitable piece. Jack rushed back to the doctor's side. Janie had been sent to the tail section of the plane to retrieve a sharp knife from the basically intact kitchen area of the plane. By the time she returned the bamboo limb had been sterlized with alcohol. He asked Janie to rub the numbing gel all over the outside of the bamboo at least three quarters of the way up to provide additional numbing of the incision upon insertion. Having covered the area of the planned incision with mouth gel five minutes earlier, Doctor Goodson was ready to begin. He asked Jack and Janie to stay and hand him any tools needed and help him hold the tube while he tried to tape it into place with a roll of medical tape he had found in the suitcase. Then the doctor cleaned the knife with alcohol and uttered the words, "Let us begin."

After slicing through the initial skin layers the doctor stopped and wiped the knife once again with alcohol and then rubbed numbing gel onto the blade. Mr. Patel screamed out in agony as the doctor cut deeper into his chest cavity but became quiet again once the bamboo straw was shoved into it's opening. As he stopped screaming, they could hear air exiting the bamboo tube and that side of his chest began once again to rise and fall a little more with each breath. They taped the tube into place and wrapped the area in gause. The doctor asked for help with rolling the patient onto his side and prop him there so the blood that had also accumulated in the chest might partially exit the bamboo as well. Doctor Goodson seemed confident his diagnosis was confirmed and the patient might possibly survive barring any complications from infection. Janie returned to her ladies room construction. Jack told the doctor he would check with Harold on how long until a shelter could be erected for the doctor and patient to move into. He felt Mr. Patel would be better off out of the direct sunlight to prevent dehydration. He promised to return shortly.

Jack went then directly to the tail section of the plane to ask Harold about the shelter status for the doctor and his patient. He could already see there was one section of metal approximately 6'x 12' already severed from the wreckage and lying on the sand. He entered the lower level of the tail section and climbed the ladder into the upper level kitchen and passenger area. For a moment his mind flashed back to the first time he opened the hatch to this room of horrific death--being greeted by the cold dead eyes of the blood covered flight attendant. He remembered the shrillness of his own startled scream. Jack shook his head hard to clear his mind of the freshly burned memories. He looked around and to his surprise Harold's crew was making lots of progress disassembling the interior of the passenger section removing seats, carry on compartments and interior wall covering (a thinner layer of metal connected by bolts). Harold soon stopped cutting the outside of the plane about half-way through the next 6'x 12' piece. Jack asked him about the ETA on the next shelter having enough material to roof. He explained about Mr. Patel's condition. With his three helpers looking on, Harold answered, "Honestly, it could be as much as two more hours before I get this section cut out. The idiots that brought us here thought of almost everything...everything that is except that a compact pancake air compressor produces only enough air pressure to sustain a plasma cutter for about a six inch stretch. Then it quits again until the air pressure has time to build up again. Unless that journal Janie found has some passage about some miracle larger air compressor, this is going to take awhile. Unfortunately we cannot just rush out to the local hardware store and grab a bigger one. As soon as I am done with this section I have to cut the bottoms of four passenger seats out for Janie's ladies room. I don't expect for that to take long so two and a half maybe three hours we could possibly roof the doctor a mini-hospital shelter. By then we should be able to provide carpet to put on the ground for a floor, along with a couple of seats and four or five overhead compartments to stack up to use as medicine cabinets. Janie read in the journal there are two or three more suitcases somewhere full of pharmaceuticals. Once found he will need somewhere to store them where wildlife cannot find them. Really, man, that is about all I can offer you right now. Will you please get the site-clearing crew to have one 12' square site ready by then and please see that there walls woven and ready to close it in?"

"I will. Thanks man for all your help." Jack replied and was off.

Jack noticed Janie was now starting along with her three lady helpers to connect the third woven wall to the other two walls of their ladies room. He looked to the part of the beach where approximately 20 women and children sat weaving into walls the piles of grass blades that others were keeping stocked next to them. He noticed they had one approximately 8'x 8' piece set aside, but they were all weaving a 8' wide piece that was now around 20' long already. He marveled at the way the wicker began in the middle and was weaved outwardly making such a great width possible. Jack asked the women why such a long section. They answered they were intending to make it long enough to wrap all the way around the outside of the shelter making it sturdier. Jack smiled with appreciation of their intellect. He went on to the home site-clearing crew and requested they prepare the site for the doctor especially well so the salvaged carpet would work without an actual floor underneath it. They pledged their best efforts. Jack returned to the beach.

Jack decided to join the grave diggers. They told him he would need to find a digging partner due to the heat of the mid-day and the nauseating smell of the dead. One person could only dig for a few minutes at a time. Each two men had to take turns because there were too many bodies for the shoveling to stop period. Jack abided and soon returned from the site-clearing area with Nigel French, the tall slender British gentleman who had located the first crate of MRE's yesterday morning. An hour later the six of them had four feet deep graves for three more dead. Jack stopped for a moment to count once again the remaining bodies. Thirty-eight dead still remained: 71 to start with-3 washed away-24 in the quicksand pit-6 now buried. There was much still to be done. They took a short break to have a bottle of water each and went right back to digging.

While placing the three bodies into their graves, Jack had noticed many of the bodies still to be dealt with were small in size. He discussed with the other grave diggers whether it would be disrespectful to bury more than one body in each grave. Nigel French's response sealed the deal: "Considering we are using the quicksand pit as a mass grave, I don't see what difference it would make at this point." They made the decision to dig the graves a foot wider and place two bodies in each grave. They would bury the larger bodies and try to send four extra bodies on the next group to be sent to the pit. Jack believed each parachute strip could haul four bodies each since the bodies were smaller in size. This theory would be confirmed an hour later when the body movers came back from trip number two. These men wasted no time going right to the bodies and stretching the strips of parachute out to reload.

Habib reported to Jack the events of their trip while Jack requested that they choose the smallest corpses to increase the progress being made in that task. Habib was pleased to report there was obviously more room in the pit as it had once again returned to it's ever smooth previous state as soon as the last body of that trip sunk beneath the surface. Also there was good news about the water drip at lookout cliff; the pan was almost half full when they reached it on the return trip of ice cold refreshing water! The group had been so thrilled they had each drank one cup without remembering to use their life-straw water purifiers. One hour later, at this time, no adverse signs of stomach issues. This water source would help but would not be enough to sustain all 150 living members of this new community. But it was a step in the right direction, the direction of survival. They had seen two turtles along the way but no dangerous wildlife today as of yet. The path had become more beaten and easier to navigate with each trip. All good news. Soon the group had the 16 bodies loaded and were on their way. Now there were 22 bodies left.

Around an hour into the next grave digging session, Jack heard the loud sound of metal hitting metal. He turned to the tail section of the wreckage to see Harold had completed the removal of the second piece of roofing. He looked in the other direction to see that Janie had completed the fourth wall of her ladies room structure. He told Nigel that as soon as Harold prepared four of the passenger seats to become make shift toilets they would probably be needed to help construct the doctor's quarters. The two began digging harder to finish this grave for two more dead in the time left. It felt like only minutes before another hour had passed. Harold along with his three helpers had just walked out of the tail section each carrying a seat with one trash bag hanging from their back pockets. They told Jack they did not need any help when asked as they made their way to Janie's structure. After placing the seats inside, Harold stopped for a moment to help Janie hang one of the heating aluminum blankets across the entrance to serve as a door. By this time the grave had reached the proper width and depth to bury two more bodies. Jack was pleased that this day of dealing with the dead was nearly done. As these two bodies were moved they noticed the bodily fluids had begun to escape. The stinch of death was nearly unbearable. Only 20 left now and the other men were nearing completion of the two graves they were preparing. Soon they would be down to only 16 bodies left on the beach. They would all be glad when this morbid effort was finished.

Harold approached Jack and asked if he would get the site-clearing crew to help them transfer the building materials to the site of the doctor's soon-to-be office. They had cabinets, flooring, seats, and roofing to move. Not to mention the now approximately 45 or so feet of woven grass wall that would all have to be moved to the site. Jack asked Nigel if he could finish covering the two bodies they were burying and so he could go help. In a matter of 15 minutes, all the materials were transfered. Harold was pleased to see the site as it had 4 standing trees approximately the size of 4x4 posts located almost perfectly in the corner positions. There were plenty of posts already cut and ready to drive into the ground to support the middle of the walls. Everyone instinctively began doing the work they had done the day prior: drilling holes in the metal roofing to run ropes through to attatch it, men sitting on each other's shoulders to drive the wall posts into place, etc. Soon the framework and roof were attached. They wrapped the grass woven wall covering around the outer perimeter of the structure, cutting holes to run the rope through to secure it to the framework. Much to their delight the woven material proved to be strong and would serve nicely to keep the elements at bay. After the walls were added, they laid the carpeting. It laid smoothly needing no extra work thanks to excellent site preparation. They then stacked the carry-on cabinets making a nice 4 foot tall cabinet and brought in three seats. They had used some of the seat cushions to make a bed for Mr. Patel and added a warming blanket to serve as a door. Once the cracks were filled with excess carpet scraps the structure was complete and they all helped Doctor Goodson and his patient get moved and settled in. Another large task accomplished.

By the time this task was complete, the body transfer team had returned to load another set of corpses to be taken to the seemingly bottomless quicksand pit. Habib reported to Jack the pit had once again returned to it's smooth inviting surface after swallowing those sixteen bodies. He asked for any empty water bottles to be bagged so they could be filled at the now overflowing pan at lookout cliff. They would bring them back on the final return trip. He also requested they be allowed to take only 12 bodies on this final trip as the extra weight from the trip just finished nearly proved to be too much. Jack agreed knowing this would only leave 4 bodies behind... two more graves to prepare. Feeling a sense of urgency Jack had Janie quickly gather a trash bag of water bottles while he helped load the last of the dead onto the parachute strips. The people still working on the beach were relieved when the transfer team entered the jungle knowing the stinch of death would soon diminish. This day of odor induced nausea should improve greatly in the coming hours. Meanwhile the grave diggers were already starting the final two graves that would hold the last four bodies. Tomorrow they would begin to deal with the 16 dead still encased in the nose section wreckage but for now the dead had been dealt with.

"Now back to the land of the living," Jack told Harold as they walked toward Janie's ladies room. She was eager to show them the finished product. The two men couldn't help but smile as they passed through the curtained door opening to be greeted with 3 water bottles of fresh wild flowers cut by Janie's ladies. Each corner of the 10x10 enclosure had a toilet, a 3 foot stack of trays filled with sand, a place to stack the emptied trays, a roll of tissue and a large package of baby wipes and a trash can made of fresh woven grass. Janie informed them as the tissue would run out quickly the ladies had decided to use the clothing that would not be claimed by the living to cut into usable sections for clean up purposes after using the restroom. She had seen in the journal there were multiple gallons of bleach and dish liquid aboard the plane. If they had survived, the used cloths could be put into a container of bleach water to be reused at a later date. She and her crew believed that would just about cover the immediate restroom facility situation. Jack and Harold happily agreed. Knowing they had a little more than 3 more hours of daylight left, Jack, Harold and the three men who had been Harold's helpers returned to the tail section to resume dismantling the passenger section for the next shelter to be built. Harold told Jack they would probably be able to get one more section of roofing cut by the time they would have to quit for the day.

Approximately thirty minutes before dark, the body transfer team made their way back to the beach to the sound of praise for the massive task they had accomlished that day. The campfires were built and the evening MRE's were being handed out. All of the people seemed serene and exhausted at this point and were looking forward to a good night's rest. Finally they could all take in the peace and quiet of this beautiful new existence before tomorrow landed them a whole new set of tasks to conquer.

CHAPTER NINE

RED SKIES IN THE MORNING

Jack awoke as the sun was beginning to rise the next morning. There was a warm breeze blowing in off the ocean. As he sat up and looked across the horizon, he immediately rubbed his eyes and took another look. It almost appeared as though the sky was on fire. The multiple shades of reds, orange and yellows were almost hypnotic. Then out of the blue Jack's mind drifted back to his childhood and the very specific warning his father had given him about not ignoring the validity of the old saying "Red skies in the morning are a sailor's warning, and red skies at night are a sailor's delight." He had told Jack following that simple rule of thumb had saved his life on many occasions. To Jack this meant they needed to make some kind of preparations before night fall. He would speak with Harold. They would try to come up with an idea to tell the people about as soon as everyone started stirring. But just for a few moments he would just sit here and enjoy the magnificant spectrum of colors this sunrise was offering up for anyone who would take the time to notice it. Jack was thankful for the opportunity to watch it and excited to think he would have a lifetime of this same opportunity ahead of him. Inside he truly was happy to be here.

Seemingly all too soon, the sun's rays burned through the beautiful colors and became too bright for Jack to keep staring at. The sound of laughter of children caught his attention as he turned his back to the ocean. To his delight there were hundreds of beautiful blue butterflies flying just one or two feet above the beach's sandy surface. The children were dancing and bouncing around chasing them. Almost as soon as a big smile came over Jack's face he felt a tug at his heart. He silently prayed that his two children, Amy and Johnny, would somehow find a way to experience the kind of joy that these children were right in front of him just chasing butterflies. Deep down he knew his wife would have no part of it as Janet felt fun was a waste of time better spent practicing for recitals and soccer games. Jack decided to put this painful thought into a box in his psyche that now housed so much guilt and so many secrets to be opened and dealt with at a later date. He allowed his mind to return to his present surroundings and began to make his way to the tail section to have his morning meeting with Harold and Janie. They needed to discuss the best tasks to undertake for today.

After shouting "Good morning", Jack made his way to the passenger section. There he reminded Harold of the times he had told him of his father's ominous warning about the red skies. Harold said he remembered and then Jack told him about the firey red skies this morning. They needed to figure out how they could keep everyone safe in a storm. After thinking for a moment, Harold suggested they cut one more piece of metal that they would need to erect another shelter. They could use the thinner metal his crew had been able to unbolt from the interior to make the walls. Then they could use that shelter to store the supplies from the cargo department of the wrecked nose section. Once emptied this area could serve as a storm shelter. There might even be enough materials to make some kind of door for the opening. They would fill both the new shelter and the first one from floor to ceiling wall to wall with as many of the supplies as possible and the rest would have to remain in the cargo hole. They would arrange things to the best of their abilities. The three agreed this sounded like their best choice. They passed out breakfast and would talk this over with the people.

As they were walking toward the people waiting for breakfast and instructions on today's activities, Jack was approached by one of the men who had been helping Harold for the last two days. Jack greeted him by name, Sanjay his shirt read, and asked how he was doing. With his eyebrows nearly touching in an obviously concerned scowl, Sanjay answered Jack, "Captain Wellington, I fear your estimation as to our whereabouts may have been confirmed this morning by the appearance of the multitude of the Lepidoptera."

"Excuse me?" answered Jack looking puzzled.

"Forgive me, the butterflies," Sanjay began. "I just recently visited Christmas Island in the Indian Ocean. This particular butterfly breed is native to the Indian Ocean Islands. It is painful to inform you, sir, but depending on how far out into the ocean the co-pilot flew us before crashing the plane on this island will determine the likelihood of us ever being rescued."

"Why would the distance affect the possibility of us being found?" quizzed Jack, secretly already knowing the answer.

"Because," Sanjay continued "due to it's vastness most of the Indian Ocean and it's islands are uncharted and have yet to be added to the Google Earth network. We could be stranded here for years or possibly forever."

"According to the extensive writings in the journal, I fear you may be correct. I regret the fact that only two of my co-workers survived, but we will work as hard as possible to keep everyone safe and healthy to make adjusting to what may turn out to be our new home as easy as humanly possible." The two men shook hands in quiet sad resolve and proceeded on toward the crate of MRE's being handed out.

Jack took two MRE's and two bottles of water and headed toward the doctor's quarters to deliver their morning meal. Upon arrival Jack first saw the doctor had propped the aluminum blanket being used as a door open with a long stick. Jack said, "Good morning, Doctor Goodson. How are you and our patient doing this morning?"

"Mr. Patel seems to be resting comfortably on his bed you all made him and is showing signs of improvement. What would be the chance I could get someone to cut two flaps in the wall covering that I could tie back when the weather is permitting to let some air and sun light in and then tie back shut when it is raining or at night? As of now that is the only complaint I have about my new home/office. Also it may be wise to try to locate the suitcases of pharmacuticals listed in the journal to ward off any infection from setting up in Mr. Patel's wound and also to address any other ailments which might arise among the other survivors. Other than that I am finding my quarters to be surprisingly quite cozy and efficient." Jack promised to address the doctor's concerns after breakfast. He headed back to the beach to join Harold and Janie to eat before talking to the people about the plans for today.

As they sat there eating, Jack watched as people entered and exited Janie's restroom while the children quickly finished eating and went back to playing with the butterflies. Jack couldn't help but notice one woman who played with a small group of children in the sand laughingly teaching them to Ring Around the Rosy. Not only did her laughter catch his attention, but her tanned face, her flowing long black hair, her eyes were encircled with the most perfectly curled black lashes that he had ever seen. She looked like an Egyptian Goddess, as surely a beauty this pure would even surpass that of Cleopatra. Jack, finding it hard not to stare, turned to Harold and Janie to ask how they thought the day's tasks should proceed.

Harold suggested the women and children continue to weave the grass walls as they would need as much as they could make in the long run. He would ask Sanjay and his other two helpers to resume what they were doing yesterday along with cutting more roofing. He and Jack would lead a crew to begin building the new supply storage shed. They would use this same crew when clearing out the cargo hole for a storm shelter. First Harold would retrieve enough air plane fuel to refill the tank on the generator and he would be good to go. The rest of the daily tasks would have to be decided by Jack and Janie.

Jack asked for volunteers for a new expedition group; once again he asked for ten men including Habib. He asked if they would try to find the way to the water and cave he had seen from lookout cliff. He reminded them they would need to use extreme caution when finding a path around the large quicksand pit. He suggested they stop by the stack of brush from the site clearing crews and choose a couple of long walking sticks to test the ground ahead when in doubt. He filled a trash bag with empty water bottles and asked that they refill them at lookout cliff and leave them there until their return trip except what they took along their expedition. After giving them the only two machetes they had left, the group began their journey. Jack asked the site clearing crew to try to get one more site cleared and they would keep the grass weavers stocked at all times so that maybe two shelters might be finished today. After submitting his requests in four different languages thanks to his translator that thankfully was solar powered and still worked on this the third morning, the people went on to their chosen tasks. Janie asked Jack about the remaining dead in the nose section passenger department wreckage. Jack said their first priority was to keep everyone safe and alive in the event of a bad storm tonight. Once that was secured they would address the issue of the dead still awaiting burial.

As soon as Harold finished refueling the generator, he and Jack went to the site clearing area and asked the men who had helped in building the first two shelters to help them to build another storage facility for supplies. They told the men of their fears of an oncoming storm and the need to clear out the cargo hold for storm shelter usage. The threat of bad weather made the men all expedite their efforts. First they all went to the tail section wreckage to retrieve the one piece of roofing and the 6 pieces of thinner metal which once was the interior walls of the passenger area. They were pleased to see that Sanjay was already working on cutting the next piece of roofing material. Harold was glad to see the thickness of the interior metal was a little better than he had originally thought and should work fine for the exterior walls of the storage shed. There were only three available standing trees that were positioned right to be two corners and one center post on the opposite wall. This would require setting more posts than the other shelters had required but luckily there were already more than enough cut. As long as they secured it well to the horizontal brace posts it would prove plenty sturdy. Soon the framework was complete.

As soon as they began to attatch the first piece of roofing to the frame they began to hear shouting from the beach. The shouts continued to get more frequent and more frantic as the moments passed. Janie appeared so quickly it seemed out of nowhere. Scared and out of breath, she managed to pant "Quick Harold, Jack. Come quick--a child has wondered off...maybe chasing butterflies. Please help...can't find anywhere." Without another word Janie turned and ran back to the beach followed by Jack, Harold and all who heard her frantic plea.

Knowing time was of the essence, Jack quickly asked for 25 volunteers to walk side by side through the brush but to stay within arm's reach of one another to insure a maximum search sweep. He recommended that only the parents of the missing child shout the name and everyone else needed to be listening for the child to shout back. They also needed to try to listen for crying as may be the case when the child realizes he is lost. He asked Janie who the child's parents were. She answered the father was lost in the crash and took him to the mother who was standing away from the group facing the brush crying and repeating "Arianna, Arianna where are you?" Her voice already sounded hoarse and raspy from shouting for her lost child. When Janie touched her arm and she turned to face them, it was the lady Jack had been watching earlier. He explained their plan and asked if she had any idea which direction they should head. She pointed in the direction she had been staring and said she had caught her playing in the area twice today, and she had made her come out on the beach. Her daughter had been playing over near the grass weavers. She decided to go to the restroom. When she came out a few moments later her daughter was gone. After learning Arianna was 3 years old, Jack gathered the troops and the search began. He reminded the people to be aware of their surroundings and to choose their steps wisely as they did not know if more quick sand existed or not. He gave the girl's mother a bottle of water to keep her throat wet to help with shouting for the child.

Approximately 20 minutes into the search one of the rescuers heard the faint sound of child laughter. With every few steps the group would stop and listen again to be sure they were getting closer to the laughs. Suddenly from the other end of the 25 person line someone yelled, "Here she is Captain Wellington, right here playing in this stream." Everyone ran to see that the child, Arianna, was alright.

As her mother grabbed her up out of the 2' wide 6" deep stream she hugged her tight all the while swatting her twice on the bottom with promises of more if she ever ran off again. Then suddenly she said "Wait a minute, you found running water." She sat the child back in the stream, cupped her hands and tasted the water. "And it's fresh and cold. We have fresh water!" She stood, picked up her little girl again and thanked all her new family members for saving her baby. Then she asked Janie if she thought they would all ever find the beach again. The two joined the group once again in side by side formation and make their way back to the beach. In half an hour they were successful.

Once there Jack, Harold and their helpers went right back to work. They were discussing what had just occurred when Harold looked at Jack and said, "Marah."

"What?" Jack asked.

Harold continued "Marah is Arianna's mother's name. I saw how you were looking at her. Just thought you might like to know her name so I read her shirt." Jack just smiled and remained silent.

It only took about an hour to install the wall metal and the one piece of roofing they had already moved to the site. Surprisingly, just as they were securing the last piece of the third wall, Sanjay and his two helpers appeared carrying the last piece of roofing and two more pieces of the thinner metal to finish the walls. After sitting their load on the ground, Sanjay informed Harold they had reached a point in dismantling the tail section where a door might be salvaged. He needed to know what to do with it. Using a stick that the men had predetermined to be about 5' long the two men measured the remaining opening to the cargo hold hoping to be able to close out the storm's wind and rain. Once the measurements were obtained Sanjay and his men returned to the tail section to resume their disassembly. Half an hour later the supply storage shed was completed except for a door. It was already built and laying in wait to be added after they filled the shed with the supplies.

The men wasted no time beginning to fill the shed with supplies. Jack and Harold had made plans to check all cargo to see if there was anything that would be of immediate aid in everyday life. They planned to keep all luggage in the cargo hold to stack around the walls to use for seating and a place for the elderly and children to lay down should the storms last all night. They would also leave one crate of MRE's inside in case they had to eat dinner and breakfast prior to the completion of the storm. They soon found a crate that was filled with flashlights, candles and solar lights normally used in flower beds. They stratigically placed a few flashlights inside the cargo hold to light the way for their work and laid aside a number of candles before moving that crate to the shed. Very soon they realized both storage sheds were sure to reach capacity before enough cargo was removed to provide adequate space to hold 150 people. Facing this realization, Jack made a decision. They would have to prepare a spot for Mr. Patel and Doctor Goodson to relocate to inside the cargo hold and temporarily use his shelter to store the remaining supplies until they could build another shed possibly the following day if the weather was permitting. After discussing it, even Doctor Goodson was pleased not to have to ride out their maiden storm inside his hut. If the sheds came through the storm undamaged, they would all feel alot safer being inside them during the next storm. Their next task was to provide the door to close off the opening.

With the clouds rapidly thickening and the winds picking up, Jack and Harold were beginning to feel the pressure to finish the project. After going to the tail section to check on the progress of the door removal, they realized the door was not going to be ready in time. They decided to use the thinner metal from the interior walls that had already been removed. They would use the poles that were left over to frame out the door and attach the metal to them. They would attach enough roping to the to be able to tie the door over the opening. It would be completed just prior to the first raindrops beginning to fall.

Meanwhile unbeknownst to anyone else, the expedition group had finally reached the inland lake. Joyously realizing the water was fresh and clear enough to see the lake's floor, the men were able to witness multiple schools of various fish swimming freely through the lake. From this vantage point the cave Jack had seen was accessable by walking around one fourth of the lake's perimeter. The men would use the walking sticks they had brought to test the ground prior to every step along the lake's sandy narrow beach to avoid any surprise quick sand encounters. They had no more than reached the cave's entrance as the first bolt of lightening struck very close to them. It was followed immediately by a clap of thunder so loud it was nearly deafening. Fearing what kind of wildlife might lie in wait inside the cave, a very brief discussion as to the marksmanship of Habib ensued. Having had extensive training in target practice and skeet shooting, Habib could nearly guarantee a clean kill with no ricochet possibility. With the weather rapidly deteriorating the men had no choice but to take cover inside the cave. They quickly gathered enough firewood from the woods surrounding them and entered the dark cave. At first they only went as far inside as the light from the entrance had illuminated. It was there where daylight ended that they chose to build their campfire. Once the fire was lit, the men marveled at the vastness of this cavern just inside the surface of this jagged cliff. It appeared as though they had entered another world: a beautiful 35 to 40 foot wide room, possibly 30 feet deep. There was a cathedral ceiling looming above that had apparent veins of gold and silver shining back at them in the most beautiful shapes and swirls they could have imagined. The cave's floor was surprisingly flat and easy to navigate. In one corner was a place where a single drip of water every 2 seconds or so had etched out a basin in the stone from possibly hundreds of years of landing in the same spot. The water was clean, cold and fresh. The group would stay until the storm passed since no threatening wildlife appeared to live in this cave.

Back at the camp, the cargo hold had been prepared to the best of their abilities with flashlights and candles having been stratigically placed throughout to adequately light it's interior. Women, children and the elderly had to be protected first. Luckily there seemed to be more than enough space for all 140 of the people. Not knowing the whereabouts of the expedition team, and with the weather conditions worsening, Jack and Harold entered the shelter and tied the makeshift doors closed. Jack would remain close to the doors with his ears open in case the group returned during the storm. He offered up a silent prayer in their honor asking for their safety during this the first storm to hit paradise since their arrival. Soon the winds howled forcefully through any available opening in the badly damaged wreckage. Soon the heavy rains began to find their way down the massive cliff that the nose section was wedged against washing the blood and the smell of death down into the cargo hold and right out the doors. Doctor Goodson advised the group to quickly put their shoes on top of the luggage stacked along the walls where people sat to keep them as dry as possible to be worn in the coming days. He stressed the importance of taking care of one's feet.

The storm raged all through the night and at one point there had been a loud boom. Jack and Harold had thought it might have been a tree falling but couldn't be sure until the morning's light. Finally about an hour before day break the storm ended. Everyone had found a place to sit after the rain had subsided and stopped leaking down the cliff at the front of the section. Most were sleeping so Jack sat down and leaned on the door and dozed off himself. He woke up some time later to the sound of the people beginning to wake up and stir. "Drats," Jack said to himself, "I missed the sunrise. Now I don't know how to predict what the weather will be today. I guess we will have to play it by ear." By then Harold came to help get the door opened to let anyone who wanted out leave so he and Jack could access the damage left behind by the storm. As soon as they were able to open the doors they were face to face with the surreal reality of just how severe the storms had been. The middle section of the airplane was no longer wedged into the ground but now it sat flat on the ground with the wings still intact. It was at least 30 feet closer to the nose section. It had been put so firmly there by the wind and rain that the landing gear was what was now buried into the ground allowing the section to sit flat on the ground. After the "wow" factor wore off they were extremely pleased as now there would be more usable space with a roof on it. Also upon further examination, a tree had fallen at the other end of the middle section making the passenger level easily accessible. Both of the sheds and Doctor Goodson's office appeared untouched. After reaching the beach it was quickly evident that the tail section was forty or so feet closer than the day before and yet Janie's ladies room had only lost it's alumunum warming blanket door. Over all a good outcome everyone seemed to agree.

CHAPTER TEN

A NEW RAY OF HOPE

After everyone had made their way back to the beach, the morning MRE's were passed out. Luckily they seemed untouched by the storm and surprisingly dry thanks to their expert packaging. It was later in the day than usual when the morning meal had been passed out. It wasn't until everyone had finished eating--nearly mid-day when out of the path into the forest came the ten man expedition team from yesterday. They were excited to be bringing not only a trashbag full of full water bottles but good tidings about their findings while exploring this magical land. The third day on this mysterious island might have ended in terrible storms, but this new morning they told stories of a beautiful clear freshwater lake and cavernous caves with gold and silver swirls on their cathedral ceilings. As soon as Habib had delivered the news to Jack and an ever growing audience, the clouds parted and a ray of sunshine shone down on their group...a bright new ray of hope to all who believe in supernatural signs. Many were eager to go and see this wonderful place only so few had witnessed.

Jack requested they break the expedition into three groups of fifty people or so. Unfortunately there was still work needing to be done. He asked for volunteers to attempt to extract the dead from the passenger section of the nose section so that they could be taken to the quicksand pit for burial. Sadly he reminded them that their were still sixteen corpses inside the accordioned wreckage. Luckily the rains had washed away most of the bodily fluids overnight and the smell had somewhat diminished. He then asked for a separate group of volunteers to help in further dismantling the tail section. Today's materials retrieval would be used to close in both ends of the newly relocated middle section to use for housing purposes. This would offer a roof over many of the 150 island residents heads until further accomodations could be made. Upon the return of the first fifty people from the lake, they can trade places with fifty of those who stayed to work. Then the second group can go and view the lake. Almost like he was watching a bunch of well trained obedient children this amazing group of people went, one by one, to their chosen tasks. Jack was aware this sense of community was sure to be a rarity. He and Harold would work with the body retrieval team while they directed Sanjay and Nigel French to lead the tail section dismantling team. Habib would lead the fifty person group to explore the lake. Soon everyone had gone about their tasks.

Jack and Harold with some 20 or more people climbed the ladder that lead to this temporary graveyard of what was left of the casualties of the crash. They began to unpile the 15 foot debris field that immediately preceded the beginning of the cliff. Oddly enough each piece seemed to be just sitting there waiting to be removed to reveal the secrets lurking behind them, no longer really attached to anything and broken into strangly managable pieces. Jack noticed early on Janie and Marah were among the volunteers helping on this project. Jack approached the ladies and suggested due to the grusomeness of the possible conditions of the corpses, they might be better off helping on one of the other projects. Marah answered that her husband was among the sixteen dead still aboard this plane and with or without permission, she would have to help in the effort to give him a proper burial. It was for her own piece of mind and out of respect to Arianna. "Do you know which row you were sitting in?" Jack asked.

"I don't know. The third or forth, maybe the fifth. I wasn't paying attention. I just sat down across the aisle from him like he told me to. Then Arianna and I both fell asleep and woke up here in the dark next to a cliff. So I truly don't know which aisle we were seated in." answered Marah.

Janie said, "We're staying Jack." The two ladies had become good friends rather quickly. Jack agreed and they all went back to work. Within three to four hours the task was completed. The sixteen bodies had been placed on the parachute strips to be transported to the quicksand pit for burial. This body retrieval had been quite possibly nightmare inducing as some of the bodies had been missing limbs that had to be found and laid to rest with the proper torso. Jack and all who had been involved in the job would be glad when the last body was placed in their final grave.

Just as the group was about to head toward the pit, Habib and the second group of 50 people to visit the cave and the lake returned. Habib suggested that he follow the burial crew after about fifteen minutes allowing enough time for the completion of the procedure. He would be accompanied by the remainder of the people who had not seen the cave yet. Then they could all finish the trip as the beautiful things seen there would be sure to lift their spirits after the day they must have had. Jack and the group agreed Habib was right and they were on their way. Almost immediately after the last body had disappeared into the sand, the groups were reunited. Once this group got to view the lake/cave area, only the children and the elderly ladies who had stayed behind to babysit would have not yet made the trip. Doctor Goodson and Mr. Patel also chose to wait. A special message had been sent to Marah not to worry about Arianna as they would all keep close watch on her until she returned.

Habib had been right. The valley which housed the lake and cave held breath taking beauty even before reaching that point. The lake was surrounded by trees and appeared to be quite deep. Upon entering the cave, Habib stirred the campfire they had left burning all day and added firewood to it. In a few moments the blaze grew and began to show the gold and silver swirls he had spoken about. As the flames grew larger, the magnificence of this place became evident to all who had entered. Habib told Jack there had been talk among the first two groups here that the cave would make a great mess hall style cafeteria. The food storage would be somewhat refrigerated. Jack and Harold agreed and began making plans to disassemble the kitchen area of the tail section and move it to the cave. They could even use the over head luggage departments to provide cabinetry for storage. They would build tables from the floor between the passenger section and the cargo area of the tail section. They would have the site clearers and the grass weavers to work together to build benches to sit at the tables. Their excitement grew with each new segment of this plan. They talked about it all the way back to the camp at the beach.

Upon their arrival at the new spot that the middle section now occupied, they were met with a pleasant surprise. Sanjay, Nigel French and a group of men were finishing up attaching metal and a door to the cargo hold of the wreckage. The other end they had closed up using a massive piece of woven grass wall that the women and children had built today. The bottom level would be available for sleeping quarters starting tonight. Tomorrow they would try to close off the upper level, formerally the passenger area. Janie and Marah instantly jumped in and located candles to light the area during the night. Everyone agreed that the sick and elderly should be housed first with any extra space being given to women with children.

They proceeded to the beach and began getting ready to pass out their evening meals. Much progress had been made in many areas today, and there was much to be discussed with the people. Finally all of the dead had been laid to rest, and they could all begin to get on with living. The idea of a working cafeteria right next to a crystal clear fresh water lake full of fish was becoming more exciting by the moment. Possibly in the next few days they could all have a fresh cooked meal of fish, rice and beans. Luckily they had located the fishing equipment the day before while cleaning out the cargo hold of the nose section for the storm shelter. Fresh food retrieval would be a great reward they could offer the dead body team for a job well done. After everyone was finished eating, Jack would call a meeting of all the people to discuss a plan for the cave. They would all work together for a common goal and all ideas mattered. He would use his translator to give everyone a chance to offer their ideas on how to make anything easier. Janie and Marah ate together discussing asking for volunteers to help gather the bags from the overhead compartments in the rapidly disappearing tail section. They could be used to provide some comfort to the soon to be middle section residents. Tomorrow they would attempt to retrieve all the overhead luggage and get it to the rightful owners. They would also try to clean up the storm shelter (nose section) so it could also be used as sleeping quarters until more could be built. The two ladies seemed to have bonded into close allies with many common goals. Quite the forceful team they would prove to be.

After all had finished eating, Jack gained the attention of the people by first asking how many were yet to see the cave and lake. He was surprised that he had overlooked the fact Sanjay, Nigel French and their six helpers were among the 32 people who had not been there. Jack spoke of the idea many had shared about using the cave as a cafeteria. He told them about the plan to move the kitchen area of the plane and many overhead compartments to use for cabinets. He explained about them building the tables and chairs. Harold spoke up about an idea of using the recently cut open water heater tank to somehow mount above the basin that had been etched into the ledge on one side of the cave. The tank could be positioned to catch the water drip at all times and then filled to capacity with the clean water from the lake. Anytime the drip could not keep up with usage, they would just refill the tank. The bottom of the tank has a shut off valve so it would serve as having running water in the kitchen adding to it's usability.

Harold also said they would need to cut strips of metal 6'x10' to tie ropes to so they could be used as sleds to move the kitchen materials to the cave. The added ease of mobility would be a welcomed help with such a long move and so many materials to haul.

Jack then made a special request that a thick pile of brush be put at the entrance to the quicksand pit along the path. By the time all the kitchen materials were moved to the cave the path would surely be beaten down nicely. He was concerned with children running into the clearing if they saw it right in front of them and a large brush pile should hide it sufficiently.

Following the construction of the kitchen there would be large amounts of supplies that would also need to be transported to the cave. All food, dishes saved from the daily MRE's, used water bottles and three large sets of pots and pans listed in the journal would have to be moved. The fishing and hunting equipment located yesterday while cleaning out the storm shelter would be kept there also.

Upon using his translator he learned that a chinese restaurant owner named Chun Li was among the residents. He and his wife Su were more than qualified to cook for the amount of people here. Two elderly ladies spoke about having been retired school cafeteria workers. They volunteered to help with food preparation promising wonderful coconut cream pies out of only items found here. The two sisters, Jenny and Ophilia Parker even said that any fruits left over from fruit salads they made would be turned into dinner wines for the following months dinners. Everyone seemed to be on board and eager to do what ever was necessary to help.

With the evening meeting ending Jack asked for volunteers to help Janie and Marah in their efforts to move the overhead baggage from the tail section to the middle section living quarters. A few moments later there were four people throwing the bags out of the opened end of that section to the crowd gathered on the ground below them. With unexplained rhythm they each grabbed one or two bags and turned toward the assigned area. At this point it didn't seem to matter who the bags belonged to. They would sort all that out tomorrow. Right now they only had to make ready the new shelter for this night's sleeping arrangements. Soon the task was complete, the sick and elderly were shown to their new quarters and they all settled in for the evening. Jack, Harold and Janie all felt this had been a day well spent with the promise of a brighter tomorrow.

CHAPTER ELEVEN

TWO DAYS UNTIL DINNER

Day number five began as usual with blue skies and breakfast. Harold and Janie joined Jack almost immediately after he awoke bubbling with excitement over the prospect of building a working kitchen. Harold asked Jack to help him to retrieve the needed fuel to run the generator for the day. This task had increased in difficulty after the storm had moved the middle section to it's current position. They would need to use the ladder to get to the wing that once was dug deep into the sandy ground. Upon arriving at the middle section, both men were pleased to see the cork used to seal the hole already drilled in the wing was now facing down and was accessible. It had been drilled close to the body of the wreckage and could be reached from the ladder leaning against the plane. However it took 30 minutes to locate the large pan that was being used to hold the fuel. It had been blown into the vegetation close to the original resting spot of the severed tail section by the storm. With the tail section having been moved some forty feet or so by the storm, finding this pan had proven to be quite the task. There was never a mention of using a different pan as everyone knew their resourses were limited. All additional pans would be needed in the new kitchen. After the hole was re-corked, Harold and Jack returned to the beach to have breakfast.

Jack had done the math and realized the first four days had knocked quite a dent in their supply of MRE's. Twelve hundred of the available three thousand ready made meals had already been devoured by the 150 residents of the island. If it took two days to construct the kitchen area, this would use up an additional six hundred meals. He knew they would need to keep as many MRE's as possible for stormy days when food retrieval was more difficult. With any luck at all considering all the available manpower, a fresh meal was possible in two days. When they were through eating, Jack would hold a discussion as to the kitchen dismantle, transfer, and reassembly. He would inform the people of the importance of expediting this large job due to the rapidly deminishing prepared food availability.

Sanjay and Nigel French spoke up about the progress that had been made the previous day of the disassembly of the tail section. They were sure the two sections of metal they needed to transport the heavier of the kitchen materials could be made of the already removed lighter weight interior metal. There were several overhead compartments that had been removed and were ready for transport. They were confident the water heater could be removed and ready for transport in the amount of time it would take to drill the holes in the metal to attach the pulling ropes to. In a very short time the first load could be ready to move. They would need help to get the overhead cabinets to the ground level. They could not be thrown down like the metal and the carry on bags from the night before. Each cabinet would have to be handed down the ladder individually to remain intact and usable.

Habib mentioned they needed to gather large amounts of firewood to place close to the entrance of the cave. A fire would need to remain lit in the cave at all times for lighting and would require a lot of wood to maintain. Marah reminded them of the many solar lights they had located while preparing the storm shelter and suggested that they take a portion of them to the cave to aid in the lighting. She and Janie had charged the lights yesterday and used some in the sleeping areas of the middle section and storm shelter overnight to much success. Impressed with both ideas, Jack agreed.

Speaking in broken english, Chun Li asked permission to begin construction of the actual cooking fire pit himself. He needed the help of any chinese speaking people to avoid the burden of language barriers. Jack inquired what would be needed. Using the pocket translator he learned of Li's plan to search for the perfect stones to build an open furnace. He requested that at some point today a piece of metal 3'x 5' could be cut from the thicker exterior metal. Li asked that the plasma cutter be used to transform the solid piece into a large grate to cook on. Over night Li had been told by one of the elderly men in the group a morter mix could be made of the volcanic rock dirt, sand and grass. It would be much like stucco and hold the rock fire pit structure together. Su Li then asked permission for herself along with Jenny and Ophilia Parker to have the say as to how the kitchen would be set up. She reminded them the cave came equipped with a natural waist high ledge down one side which could serve well as a working space counter top. The ledges needed to remain empty. Chun Li agreed that it would be good for the three lady cooks to design their own kitchen.

Janie then asked all the ladies that weren't babysitting to help her transport as many supplies as possible to the cave while they were assembling the kitchen. It would be necessary to calculate the number of cabinets needed to store supplies. First they would bring all the used MRE plates, plastic ware and any empty water bottles. Then they could start on any supplies small enough to carry for long distances. If they all made the trip twice they would more easily be able to calculate how many more cabinets would be needed. "There are lots more shelters to build and it would be nice if each one had two of those cabinets so we have none to waste," Janie said. "Afterwards we can all come back, sit down and weave grass for the chairs to go in the dining room. If we can weave enough after we have the seats covered we can start another restroom close to the cave," she added.

Harold said, "I could use some people to help me build a stand for the water heater. Then I plan to start on tables and chair frames. Janie, when we were cleaning out the storm shelter, I saw a box with bags of nails and screws. If you ladies run across it please let me know."

Jack said, "I will stay behind and begin to cut metal. I can help with the disassembly of the kitchen while I am waiting for the air compressor to catch up every time. The people who stayed inside last night were pleased with their accommodations. I would like to get that upper level fixed for shelter purposes. I will go to the cave during today's last load's transport."

Then Doctor Goodson asked Jack, "Captain Wellington, Mr. Patel is showing signs of developing an infection. I realize you have alot to attend to. But please, I really need you to try to find out if the pharmacuticals spoken of in the journal survived the crash. Hopefully there will be an antibiotic available if they were not destroyed."

Jack lept into action immediately realizing he had forgotten that the doctor had made this very same request the day before. "Oh Doctor, please forgive me. I completely forgot. I will do it now before anything else can distract me." He then disappeared toward the nose section of the wreckage to see if the other two suitcases of medications were still behind his seat in the cockpit. Luckily the ladder was nearby leaning on the middle section. Jack leaned the ladder onto the nose section. He could barely reach high enough to climb into the cabin without help but he finally made it. When he got the suitcases from behind the seat they didn't so much as have a scratch on them. But both broke open and spilled upon impact when dropped to the ground. Jack spent the next half hour picking up bottles and boxes of every kind of medications imaginable trying to fit them all back in the suitcases. He took them then to the doctor. "Doctor Goodson, I found two suitcases of medications and such. Hopefully you will find something of use for Mr. Patel. We will try to have your quarters available again by tomorrow. There should be enough supplies moved to the kitchen by then to move anything else into the first storage shed. Can you take care of all of these meds until then?" Jack inquired.

"I don't see any reason why not. Thank you Captain Wellington." answered the doctor. Jack turned and headed to the tail section to get busy.

There was one sled of overhead cabinets loaded and ready by the time he got there. Holes were being drilled in the other sheet of metal to put the pulling ropes through. The water heater and the remaining spool of rope were waiting to be loaded when that sled was ready. The excitement was everywhere with so many eager to help. As Jack entered the wreckage, the kitchen sink was being handed down the built-in ladder followed by two more cabinets. That should do it for this load. Most of the people followed. Anyone who was empty handed stopped to take supplies that Janie and Marah were removing from the two storage sheds and the doctor's quarters.

On one of his trips to the cave, Habib had counted his steps. There were 880 steps with an estimated three foot gait. It equaled half a mile each direction. He had made sure to make everyone involved aware of this fact during the planning discussion this morning. It would be quite the hike and one should only carry what they could manage over a long distance.

Within ten minutes there was a convoy of people and supplies on their way to the cave to transform it into a working kitchen capable of producing 300 meals a day. No one made the trip empty handed. Upon arrival, Su Li asked Jenny and Ophilia Parker to help her decide where was best to put the cabinets from the first load. Once decided the three of them began placing the supplies both inside the cabinets and onto the natural countertop. Many left their arm fulls of supplies and headed back for another load. The sleds were soon unloaded and sent back for more kitchen materials. Some stayed to help Chun Li locate just the right rocks to build his furnace/oven/grill. Nigel French, being bilingual, understood when Chun Li asked if someone could let the metal cutters know he would need two of the requested grates, one 4 inches wider than the other. His design of the grill had evolved during the walk here. Now he believed that a two tier grill was needed, the bottom being the oven. French agreed to deliver the message while retrieving the next load.

Harold and a few men were attempting to design a stand for the water tank. They would use young tree trunks approximately 3 inches thick cut and tied to craddle the tank upright. This would allow the water faucet to work right. Luckily the box of nails and screws had been located early on. Sanjay had brought along one bag of each. This would make their job much easier. On the second load from the tail section they would grab the hammer and the screw driver from the upper level. They would position the tank under the water drip and mount the sink below it atop of the natural basin. Harold planned the following day to salvage enough tubing or piping from the wreckage to connect a drain pipe for the grey water to exit the sink and the cave. They would need to build a step ladder of sorts to ease the filling of the water tank and leave it there at all times. Harold had remembered to bring the hand drill. Their work was slow and enjoyable.

Upon arriving back at the camp, Janie gathered up 10 more water bottles. As she filled them with sand from the beach Marah asked, "What are you doing that for?"

Janie answered, "I want to use these bottles to put 10 of the solar lights in and set them around the cave for extra lighting. It seemed awfully dim in there so I thought this would help. You can't stick them into the ground inside a solid rock cave."

Marah chuckled, "Well I guess you're right. I really hadn't thought about it that way." They stopped at the shed that would soon return to being the doctor's quarters. They needed two boxes of supplies that had enough empty space inside to hold the sand filled bottles and the 10 already charged solar lights along with their original contents. Much to their delight they were successful. One box was nearly full of bottles of dish soap and the other contained multiple jars of pre-sweetened teas and instant coffee.

"Oh what a treat to have something besides just water to drink. The sodas ran out the first day here. I can hardly wait," Janie bubbled.

"I am going to find something to put enough water in to wash my hair. This dish soap will work fine for shampoo," Marah answered. With arms full they headed back to the cave for their second and final time today.

While walking the half mile path Janie asked, "How are you dealing so well with the loss of your husband? I don't know if I could take it if anything were to happen to Harold. I think you are alot stronger than I would be, and I admire your strength."

Marah, who was always visibly aware of her surroundings, looked around to be sure no one would hear. Then she answered, "Unfortunately I am finding it very hard to grieve my husband's death. He was very abusive to Arianna and me. I am not sure that he wasn't involved in organized international crime of some sort. We would travel to lots of countries, check into a hotel and that's where Arianna and I would stay. A number of occasions strange men would visit our hotel rooms. Arianna and I would be told to go to the bedroom and not come out. Once when Arianna was two years old she escaped from the bedroom causing me to chase after her. It looked like they were snorting drugs. He screamed for me to get both of us back into the bedroom. When the visitors left I was beaten so badly that I never let her escape again. After that I would sit on the floor with my back against the bedroom door until it was safe. Twice before I mistakenly believed that Ragish had been killed. First was one and a half years ago. We were leaving our hotel in Columbia South America when he was attacked by four men. They all had metal pipes and when they were through he was left lying on the sidewalk, beaten beyond recognition. I couldn't find a pulse and a witness called an ambulance. He lived through it just to be shot through the neck six months later right in front of Arianna and me. Since he had only waited two months after the beating in Columbia to break all my fingers on my left hand individually, I prayed for his death from the gun shot wound. He lived. Even on the day we boarded this flight he slapped me and kicked me in my stomach. It feels like Arianna and I fell asleep on a plane leaving my husband's evil grip and landed in paradise. Part of me thinks that maybe he didn't die this time either. Maybe me and Arianna died and this is actually Heaven. But anyway that is the true story about my so called strength."

"Oh my, that's awful," Janie gasped in horror. "What possessed him to break only your fingers on your left hand?" she asked.

"I was in the process of mixing a meatloaf and had taken off my wedding ring. It was too big and I didn't want to lose it in the meat. Arianna fell and skinned her knee so I went to her immediately. I forgot about my ring when I went back to finish mixing the meat. Ragish found it on the counter while dinner was cooking. He was enraged and that's what happened." Marah answered.

"I am so sorry that your life was so hard and painful. I'm with you on this place having the potential to be much better than the hustle and bustle of modern society at least until we eventually get rescued. But if not, there are way worse places to be in this world. Yeah, this place will work." Janie replied. "I mean have you noticed the fruit trees along this path. I saw both bananas and pineapples. Personally I'm looking forward to the food here after the kitchen is complete." she added. They finished the walk talking about fruit salads and sweet tea.

Everyone working on the kitchen was pleased with Janie and Marah for bringing the solar lights and the sand filled bottles to stand them in. Within ten minutes of their arrival, Ophilia Parker was stirring up a large pot of sweet tea. Su Li and Jenny Parker made a funnel from part of the cardboard box the dish soap came in. Then the three ladies filled as many water bottles as possible. Thirty minutes later they had three large pots of tea bottled and ready for drinking. They handed it out to all the people working on the kitchen. The refreshing sweet tea sent a wave of delight over the whole group.

Janie and Marah borrowed another big pot to get water to wash their hair. They had decided not to wash in the lake, but away from it. This water was pure and free from human contaminates and they wanted it to always be so. They would do one at a time and help each other rinse the soap out.

Nigel French and Sanjay then arrived with two more sleds of kitchen materials. They brought the hammer, screw driver, and the first of Chun Li's requested grill grates. There were nearly two sleds of over head cabinets and one 3' x 6' piece of flooring for building the first table. They were followed again by the large caravan of people with more and more supplies. Chun Li was satisfied with the grate and took advantage of being able to communicate with Nigel French. He had remembered the mortar would hold better if hair and grass could be in the mixture. Li asked French to request that Janie and all of the ladies that had access to a comb to save the hair from combings to be used this way. The mortar would be mixed the next day so they would need all they could get by then. Janie and Marah agreed to spread the word.

Most everyone headed back to the beach to either get more supplies or to help the grass weavers. Janie and Marah brought back as many tea bottles as they could carry to give the babysitters and the tail section disassemblers. Jack was working on Chun Li's second grill grate. He asked, "So what kind of progress are they making on the kitchen?"

Janie smiled and gave him a bottle of tea answering, "Amazing progress! That tea is an example. I understand Mr. Li has nearly all the stones needed to build the grill. He was stacking them in place while we were there this trip. Harold said he has to build it so he knows if he has all the right sized rocks and then rebuild it tomorrow with the mortar. Harold and his help have the water tank stand ready to screw together. They have a rope tied to a bucket that held supplies of some sort ready to fill it with water when installed. The sink is already installed. They used rocks to sturdy it. Many cabinets are installed and full with supplies already. Oh and there are already two large stacks of firewood gathered outside the cave entrance. You should go see on the next sled delivery."

"I will. That sounds great." answered Jack.

Janie joined the grass weavers, and Marah took her armload of tea to the babysitters and the elderly to share. Soon Nigel French and Sanjay led the pack of material transfer men to the tail section to aquire another load. Jack asked the two men to help him before the last load of the day was taken to the cave. "I feel confident that the doctor's quarters can be cleaned the rest of the way out. With all the supplies that have already been moved, the rest can be added to the two sheds. That way we can get Mr. Patel settled in and hopefully begin to battle his infection better," explained Jack. French and Sanjay agreed. Jack's theory proved to be the case. Doctor Goodson's quarters were nearly empty of supplies. There was more than enough room in the other sheds to house them. Fifteen minutes later they were able to help the doctor and Mr. Patel relocate to their original quarters. They also moved the suitcases of medications so he could store them in his cabinets. They loaded the sleds and headed to the cave.

Along the way Jack was glad to see the entrance to the quicksand pit had been blocked totally by a large pile of tree limbs. He saw no way for a child to be interested in the area. This load contained the actual cabinets from the plane's kitchenette and all supplies they contained. The Li's would be pleased with the cooking utensils they would have for use. Jack was especially pleased to provide the drawers they were kept in. He had also salvaged the microwave and the refrigerator which possibly could work with the generator once the shelters were complete. Otherwise they could be for storage as well.

Upon arrival Jack was amazed at the progress that had been made. The water tank was perfectly installed above the sink. Habib was sitting on top of Harold's sholders pouring water into it from the bucket that Janie had described. Jack laughed. Harold looked around and said, "We still have to build a ladder to fill the tank, but we couldn't wait to try it out."

Jack replied, "This place is really starting to look like a kitchen. I love how there is a natural counter top. It is crazy just how flat their surface is. How did you get those cabinets mounted above them?" About then the water started to spill over the top of the water tank and onto Harold's head. Jack really laughed then. Harold's hair was wet. Habib slid down off Harold's sholders quickly but it still looked like he had wet his pants. All three men seeing the comedy in the situation enjoyed a laugh together. Harold answered finally, "See the stands at each end. We cut small tree trunks to fit and screwed them together to hold the over head cabinets firmly. Then after screwing the cabinets to the frames, we sat them up on the natural counter tops. They seem to lean to the right but under the circumstances, I will give it a 'good enough' and move on."

Nigel French approached. Chun Li had asked him to get Jack so he could show him the grill. Li was very pleased with both grates and wanted to show him why one had been requested larger. This would be a two layer grill with the bottom grate at times serving as an oven. Li had very wide rocks on the bottom layer approximately 2 feet off the floor. Then he had placed the first more narrow of the grates. Next he stacked a layer of thin rock about 4 inches thick all around the grate leaving an inch or so in all directions. He followed with one foot deep rock that covered the edges of the grate by 2 or 3 inches but never touched the grate. After he placed the other grate on top of the three sided structure. Last he laid rocks one feet deep across the open side. Li asked Jack and French to hold down on the stones of the grill and showed them that the bottom grate was easily removable per his design. It slid right out the front. Using Nigel French to translate, Chun Li requested one 3 1/2' x 5 1/2' piece and one 40" x 6' piece of solid metal. One would cover the top grate when the oven was in use. The larger piece would be a removable door for the front of the grill. This would prevent sparks from catching clothing on fire and allow for coals to be added from the campfire to prevent wood ash from getting in the food. The row of stones placed at the front of the grill opening was to keep the coals from rolling out on one's feet. Tomorrow he would do the final build with mortar.

When the sleds were unloaded, everyone pitched in to attempt to make one corner of the kitchen a reconstruction of the actual kitchenette from the plane. The same people who disassembeled it worked flawlessly to rebuild it in only minutes. At one end of the natural counter top the cave wall curved quite similarly to the curve of the plane wall. This made reassembling the kitchen remarkably easy. Any supplies that were left over after filling all available cabinets were placed on top of the counter to await their new home. Being weary from a hard day's work they all decided to call it a day and head back to the beach for rest and dinner.

The beach was busy with grass weavers making tremendous progress on a wall sized piece of fabric. Three women were brushing children's hair and emptying the excess into a grass woven pouch about 2 square feet in size. Marah was showing a group of children how to build sand castles. Janie and two ladies who had been babysitters today were gathering MRE's and bottled water for the evening meal. Along the walk from the cave, twenty people had each grabbed an arm load of firewood for the night. Harold said to Jack and anyone else in earshot, "One more day of hard work and that kitchen should be usable, don't you think?" A five man chorus of affirmative answers rang out in aggreement. Although thankful for the nourishment, everyone on this island was ready for some fresh cooked food.

The tone of dinner seemed to be one of happy conversation. Jack said, "I realize that everyone is tired from the events of the day. I just wanted to say we were able to cut enough extra metal to close one end of the upper middle section of the wreckage. The grassweaving crew has provided a piece of fabric large enough to close the other end. First thing tomorrow I could use some help with that. We will also need to salvage some of the overhead cabinets from the nose section to finish the storage space for the kitchen. We have already stripped all of them from the tail section."

Harold said to Janie, "Yeah and you need to be picking out where we will be sleeping after the next two nights. By the time we get the materials for the tables and chairs or benches, the second level will be nearing nonexistence in the tail section. I trust your judgement and will agree to whatever you decide."

"Until more shelters can be built, maybe you could build a ladder of some sort and we can make a sleeping area in the nose section passenger area. We can weave a grass wall big enough to cover the wreckage area and clean it up a bit. That's the easiest thing I can come up with," answered Janie.

"Your wish is my command my love," Harold said with a smile.

That night's sleep seemed to last only moments as people began to stir early. All were eager to finish both the kitchen and gathering area with tables and benches. There was chatter of this being the last morning without hot coffee for the forseeable future. Jenny and Ophilia Parker had estimated just from the supplies stored yesterday that there was coffee available for 3 to 4 years at two cups each of instant coffee. Then there was probably 2 or 3 years worth of unground coffee beans. This information had excited each adult that had heard it and induced a new sense of urgency into the residents. This would be the sixth day of hard work to reach some level of normalcy. The completed cafeteria would be a nice step in that direction.

Before breakfast, Jack, Harold, Sanjay and Habib closed in the upper middle section passenger area. While they were there, Harold drained another pan of airplane fuel from the wing to run the generator. Sanjay volunteered to stay behind and salvage more metal from the tail section for the top of Chun Li's grill. He could also help cut the floor sections for tables. By the time this was done everyone else had finished eating and gone on about their business. The four men sat down on the beach and ate. Then they were off.

Harold and Habib went to the tail section to work on salvaging enough pipes or hoses to drain the water from the newly installed kitchen sink. Jack and Sanjay grabbed a few tools and headed to the nose section to start removing overhead cabinets for the cave. Nigel French had headed to the cave carrying two arm loads of supplies. He had asked Janie to let Harold know that he would get some help and start building tables. French had said Chun Li had taken the woven pouch of hair along with his shirt full of sand and left to gather mortar materials. Janie reported that all who had went to the cave so far had again carried supplies. Janie and Marah then left with a plan of starting another restroom near the cave.

Two hours later both sleds were once again filled with materials and on their way to the cave. They carried the two remaining pieces of thick metal to finish the grill, three more 3' x 6' pieces of flooring to be tables, and as many cabinets as the sleds could hold. Harold had grabbed the morning's grass weavings thinking the fabric would serve well as seat material for benches. He hoped to put two benches at each table alone with a chair at each end. He had calculated that 20 tables would be more than sufficient. If they ran out of flooring materials they would build some of the table tops with multiple layers of grass weavings.

The cave was very busy by the time they arrived. Chun Li was finishing the first later of the grill. The mortar appeared to be very sticky and dark in color. Su Li immediately started directing where to put the new batch of cabinets. Chun Li asked Nigel French to thank Jack and Harold for the storage cabinets as the cave had this morning's batch of supplies scattered everywhere. In his words Su was OCD and a clean individual. All the unstored supplies had been driving her crazy and she had been driving him crazy because of it. She had even covered Nigel French's newly built table with supplies right after it was completed.

Having already discussed the seating arrangement with Harold, French and his team of four other men had two bench frames and one chair frame designed and ready to be topped. Ten minutes later there were two benches and one chair completed. The first of this batch of cabinets were filled with the supplies off the table. Ophilia Parker then handed each man a fresh bottle of sweet tea and asked that they be the first to sit at the table and rest a few moments before resuming their work. Being fixed from the water stored over night in the tank inside the cave, the tea was cool and refreshing. As soon as they had finished their tea, Su Li rushed them back to work. Speaking in broken English she said, "Go now, need more cabinets now." Flopping her arms around she ran them off like a bunch of annoying flies. No one seemed to mind as all left giggling under their breath.

Janie, Marah, and the other two women who had helped to build the first restroom were working close to the cave entrance clearing a space to construct the next restroom. Janie asked Harold to please prepare 4 seats from the plane with holes in the center to be the toilets and bring them with this load or the final load this afternoon. He promised to attend to it. The ladies had once again chosen a spot that had four trees positioned almost perfectly as the four corner posts. The space was nearly cleared at this time. There was a large stack of grass to begin weaving for the walls. Janie had already asked that the ladies who would be weaving grass back at the beach to bring the first 10' piece they completed to them and they would try to provide the rest themselves. With any luck the restroom would be complete by nightfall.

Three hours passed before the next load arrived at the cave. Cutting the bottom of the seats out was time consuming. The kitchen was nearing completion. Chun Li was spreading a layer of mortar on the outside of his amazing new grill. Three more tables had been built. There were frames for benches that were awaiting tops. The restroom had two walls already. Nigel French was happy to see that there were three more table tops on this load. Chun Li requested that French to ask the moving group to wait to see if any more cabinets would be needed. He also inquired about the plan for the remaining MRE's and the barrels filled with corn, beans and rice. Would they be moved to the cave as well or would they be brought in small amounts as needed. Finally Li requested a wood box of some sort. Su Li had been upset about the dirt from the firewood in her kitchen and a storage container for it would keep her from "driving him crazy". French couldn't help but giggle when translating the last part.

A short while later Ophilia Parker approached Jack and company and reported that all the supplies that had been transported to the cave were now stored in the kitchen with two cabinets left. She said the ladies would like to have four additional cabinets brought to the cave to store fresh fruit inside.

Harold stayed at the cave while Jack, Sanjay and Habib headed back to get the final load of cabinets. Jack would handle the removal of the requested cabinets alone while the other two attempted to cut enough floor material for three more table tops. Sanjay felt that seven was a lucky number and they needed three more tables to make seven.

As Jack was about to climb the ladder to the nose section upper level, he was stopped by Doctor Goodson. The doctor was carrying the three tags from the suitcases of pharmacuticals. With a deep look of concern he asked, "Captain Wellington, I believe these belong to you."

Jack, being puzzled, asked, "Okay, but why bring me just the tags?"

"I did it to try to calm Mr. Patel's nerves. He is running a high fever from the infection and has been ranting for two hours about your name being on the pharmaceuticals. He keeps asking if your crew only learned of the medications from the journal then why is it your name on the tags. He got so worked up that I had to give him a sedative. He is sleeping now," answered Doctor Goodson.

Jack answered quickly, "I have no idea. I didn't bring those suitcases aboard. Oh God, were they going to try to frame me?"

Doctor Goodson replied, "Look Jack, if I may?" Jack nodded. "To tell you the truth, I couldn't be happier to be here on this island paradise. I came on this vacation because my life just went to Hell in a hat bag. My wife, who I love dearly just divorced me. She was determined that I was having an affair with the nurse who worked in my office. I was not. The nurse was one of my best friends. We were both happily married to our spouses, but we confided in one another trying to figure out how to best please our mates. We thought it helped to hear an opinion from the opposite sex. Instead this friendship cost me my marriage."

"I"m sorry for your divorce, but what does that have to do with Mr. Patel?" asked Jack.

Doctor Goodson answered, "In plain Texas talk, I am just saying that I will never know whether your co-pilot brought us here or if you did. I don't know but I like this place. I love the sense of community that seems to exist here. Patel's concerns can be blamed on fever and delerium but only if you destroy these tags. His fever was plenty high enough to induce hallucinations. I will try to convince him of this. Regardless of the answers, help me to avoid introducing chaos to paradise. We all need each other for long term survival. Please dispose of the tags permanently."

"Okay, I will take care of it. Thank you. If you will excuse me, I have four cabinets that need removing to finish our kitchen," said Jack as he turned and started up the ladder. Unnerved, he began to remove the overhead storage compartments. Annoyed by the fact he had overlooked something as simple as tags on the suitcases, he prayed for forgiveness and his own safety. He could quite possibly be killed if his roll in the crash was discovered. He rarely recalled anything his Mother had ever said, but at this moment he remembered hearing her on speaker phone with a friend. Her friend asked her what she would do if caught being unfaithful. Her answer was one word, repeated three times, "deny, deny, deny." It sickened him to think of where this advice had come from, but he would do just that: deny his involvement until his dying breath.

As Jack was disconnecting the last cabinet of the four, Habib and Sanjay arrived at the nose section with the three table tops. They climbed inside and helped to lower the cabinets to the ground with ropes tied to them. Soon they were headed back to the cave for today's final delivery. Prior to this trip he had not noticed, but some of the people were whispering and pointing in his direction. Unsure whether it was paranoia or reality, Jack decided to try to get out in front of the chaos that might be building. Tonight at dinner he would speak again about Willard, his co-pilot being the one in control of the plane when it crashed.

After reaching the cave and unloading the two skids, Janie and Marah approached Jack asking for him to look at the new restroom they had built. Seeing a very concerned look on Janie's face, Harold followed them. When they entered the restroom it looked fine. Janie's look never changed. Jack and Harold asked in unison, "Janie are you okay?"

"No, not really. Marah, will you tell them what you told me?" Janie replied.

"Yes, of course I will. I was told by one of the other ladies that when she and two others were getting supplies to bring to the cave, Mr. Patel was yelling inside the doctor's quarters. He was saying that you brought us here because your name was on the bags of medications. People are talking and many are angry." said Marah.

"Doctor Goodson made me aware of this when I was there just now. It appears our colleague was planning to frame me," Jack said as he pulled the tags from his pocket. "I swear to you all I had nothing to do with this. I will address the situation at dinner tonight."

Harold said, "Willard always seemed sneaky. I guess now we know why. I believe I can speak for Janie in saying we will both vouch for you."

"Yes absolutely," Janie added.

Looking sad, Jack exited the structure. The three of them followed him back to the beach. Harold and Jack decided to cut as many more table tops from the tail section as they could before dinner. Janie asked Marah to help her to prepare a sleeping area in the upper part of the nose section. Harold had again reminded her of the ever shrinking sleeping space in the tail section and that the time had come to prepare another one.

First the ladies went to the storage sheds to find five of the care packages to rob them of the aluminum sleeping blankets. They would try to use them to curtain off the blood stained debris from the crash. Also they planned to give both levels a good scrubbing. After dinner they would recruit some help to remove a few of the seats to place in the cargo section to make both levels more homey. Just when they had finished, they heard the remaining residents returning from the cave. Janie and Marah decided it was time to quit and pass out the dinner meal.

When everyone was served, Jack said, "May I have your attention please. It has come to my attention there is some concern among some of you that I may be responsible for crashing our plane. It seems that my co-pilot along with some of my other colleagues planned to frame me for this horrendous act. Apparently they put my name on the suitcases of medications and God knows what else. Mr. Patel noticed the tags and brought it to Doctor Goodson's attention. He in turn brought the tags to me and asked about them. I swear to all of you, I learned of the bags just like the rest of you, from the journal written by one of the deceased flight attendants. I have no way of knowing what other actions they took to make me appear the guilty party. Harold, Janie and I, being the only crew members to have survived, do feel a sense of responsibility to keep us all safe. The passengers who enter an aircraft are the responsibility of the crew on every flight that leaves the ground whether the flight is successful or not. We have attempted to use the journal and the supplies listed to insure our survival, not to dictate your actions. You have all done a wonderful job for the past six days. The spirit of community and pulling together is like none I have ever seen. I beg of you, please don't let my co-pilot and his co-conspirators win. I did not do this to us all. As we all begin to spend more and more time at the cave, I ask that at all times the fires on the beach remain lit. They are our signal fires in case a ship or plane comes near. At this point they may be our only hope of being rescued."

Doctor Goodson looked shocked at Jack's announcement about the tags. It had been unexpected after their discussion but had somehow solidified his belief in Jack's innocence. Mr. Patel, still having his doubts, uttered one word, "Oh."

Sanjay, visibly shaken by the tone of the announcement, said, "On the day we were visited by the multitude of butterflies, it was I who told the captain of the probability of our current location. It was obvious that he was taken by surprise even though he had feared the worst. Captain Wellington has been leading us all on the only possible path to survival. I believe he is telling the truth." Sanjay's statement was followed by a number of people vocalizing agreement that Jack was more than likely not responsible for the crash. But there were also whispers of doubt among the people.

Feeling the need to change the tone of the conversation, Harold said, "We found lots of fishing gear while moving supplies. There's more than enough bamboo on this island to tie fishing twine to for anyone who wants to fish tomorrow to do so. Many of us could use a day to rest after the week we have had. Nigel, please ask Chun Li if fish will be on the menu for tomorrow night's dinner if provided?" After asking, Nigel French answered that would be possible. Harold added, "I also saw a large fishing net that I believe we can attach to bamboo near the cave entrance end of the lake. It could provide a live well if too many fish are caught to eat in one meal."

Habib said to Mr. Patel and Doctor Goodson, "Tomorrow morning the two of you should attend the first prepared breakfast. Mr. Patel, I realize you shouldn't try to walk the half mile to the cave. Some of us will give you a ride on one of the sleds. It has already been my experience that the breath-taking beauty of the lake and cave has a calming effect to the soul. Once you see the new cafeteria and what can be accomplished when a community pulls together, I believe you will both feel better."

Marah then chimed in, "I too believe you will feel better afterward. The first time I saw the magical lake and cave was just after helping to recover my husband's body and watching as he was buried at the quicksand pit. There is a peace that engulfed me the moment I laid eyes on the sparkling fresh water, and the cave is magnificent. I have faith that place will have a similar effect on you." After Marah's plea, Mr. Patel agreed to the trip.

Harold said, "Hopefully in the next couple of days, we will finish building the tables and chairs for the dining area of the cave. Tomorrow I will cut and remove more of the metal from the tail section for housing purposes. That will allow for more flooring material to be removed for table tops. I was wondering if any of you are small engine mechanics? While moving supplies from the nose section a few days ago, among the debris was discovered 2 more generators, a welder, and what I believe were 3 push mowers. They were all badly damaged, but the right mechanic might be able to build a generator from all of them to use at the cave."

Being nudged by his wife, a gentleman with a strong French accent spoke up. He said, "I own a small mower repair shop in the south of France." His dark eyes were lit with interest. The name written on his shirt read Guillaume Rotge. "I don't know to what extent it will help, but I will be glad to take a look at them the day after tomorrow. I really liked the idea of fishing tomorrow if you don't mind."

"The day after tomorrow it is," answered Harold.

"If some of you will gather me a bunch of fruit tomorrow, I will make a large fruit salad to go with dinner. If it is all eaten, wonderful. If not, the remaining salad will be the beginning of next month's dinner wine. We all need to remember, when you have little, you waste nothing," stated Ophilia Parker.

Many voiced their agreement with her statement, and the conversations began to break up into small groups of people. When the MRE plates were all gathered and the remaining MRE's were moved to the nose section, the day's work was over. Everyone soon retired for the evening.

CHAPTER TWELVE

PLEASURE AND PRESSURE

The seventh morning on the island began just as the sun was beginning to rise. Marah's daughter, Arianna, woke her up asking to go to the restroom. Marah got up, grabbed one of the solar lights and led her out of the nose section. This was the second night they had slept inside. As they approached the restroom at the beach, they could hear moaning or someone crying. Curiosity drew Marah to the source of the sound. It was Jack, obviously having a nightmare. He was crying, saying, "I was asleep and so many dead. Oh God, please forgive me." She told Arianna to stand back a few feet and wait a moment. Marah reluctantly reached out to touch Jack's arm to shake him awake. She was a bit frightened as she remembered her husband would occasionally hit her when being woke up.

Jack jumped being startled into alertness. When he opened his eyes, there kneeling over him was the most beautiful woman he had ever seen. Marah said, "I am so sorry for waking you, Captain Wellington. You were having a bad dream about the crash no doubt. You were crying and talking about having been asleep when it happened."

Jack answered, "Oh, I'm sorry. Did I wake you two?"

Marah said, "No, Arianna woke up needing to."

Arianna interrupted shouting, "Mommy I really have to go potty, now."

Jack replied, "Say no more. Thanks for waking me and oh, you can call me Jack." Arianna then grabbed Marah's hand pulling her toward the restroom. Jack arose feeling like he had been touched by an angel. He marveled at the fact of his nightmare being of importance to such a perfect creature.

It was soon apparent that Marah wasn't the only one who heard Jack talking in his sleep. Several people were sitting up on the beach and beginning to stir. Chun and Su Li had camped near by next to Nigel French and his wife Elizabeth. Chun Li asked Nigel to see if Jack was alright and to let him know in one hour coffee would be available. Breakfast would be served sometime afterwards. Jack thanked Nigel French and waved a thumbs up to Chun Li.

At least ten other castaways came over to ask if Jack was okay. Ophilia Parker warned him about blaming himself for the crash. "The Lord works in Mysterious ways," she told him. "We are here in His time and of His making. You must forgive yourself or else you will never truly see the beauty of this island. We have all been blessed to have you to lead us. I would like to say thank you for trying to keep us all safe since the crash," she added.

As she walked away, Nigel French said to Jack, "Whenever you are ready, I will help to load the crate holding the fishing equipment onto one of the skids. The other skid will need to be saved for Mr. Patel to be transported to the cave. The fishing crate was quite heavy when Sanjay and I moved it into the storage shed. The entire crate would be better housed at the cave for convenience purposes. Besides the promise of my first cup of coffee in a week is calling my name."

Jack agreed asking for ten minutes to "clear the morning brain fog". He sat there offering a silent prayer of thanks that his sleep talking did not reveal the truth of his involvement in the crash. Realizing the possibilities of this happening in the future, he decided that by nightfall he would find a more private place to camp. He could be risking his life if the wrong people ever learned the truth. His insides shook at the thought. Soon he was ready to go, secretly hoping inner peace would come from fishing today. In his memories from childhood, fishing always worked that way. When they were leaving the beach, Sanjay told them that he would wait for Doctor Goodson and Mr. Patel to go to the cave. He and the doctor could easily pull Mr. Patel's sled to the cave. Jack thanked Sanjay and he and Nigel were off to the storage shed.

Before long the two of them were nearing the cave lured by the familiar aroma of fresh coffee brewing. Even the fragrance was delicious. Upon arrival they would enjoy at least one cup before beginning to examine the available fishing equipment. The past week had been so complex, Jack could not exactly remember the types of tackle they had brought along. It would be to Jack's benefit to appear surprised at the crate's contents.

Even though the coffee was instant and the creamer non-dairy powdered, it proved to be one of the best cups Jack ever had. There were even sweetener packets available in abundance. However Jenny Parker asked when handing them their cups, "I realize the cups are disposable, but we plan to wash them and reuse them as long as possible. There are barely enough to go around so please be gentle with them."

Nigel said, "My wife, Elizabeth, runs a ladies club just west of London called Something from Nothing. The ladies meet and create things from materials otherwise discarded or overlooked. She has been one of the ring leaders of the grass weaving team. Just last evening she was talking about trying to make clay pottery dishes for the cafeteria. We will let her know there is an immediate need for coffee cups." Nigel French then turned to Chun Li, speaking in Chinese he asked Li to help him build Elizabeth an oven of her own outside the cave to fire the pottery dishes in. They agreed to build it the following day. Su Li was overjoyed to hear they would soon have real dishes to eat out of.

Soon Harold walked in, shirtless, carrying his shirt filled with fresh picked bananas. He said, "I saw these bananas just hanging there invitingly. After I had picked all I could reach, I couldn't carry them all." He unloaded the bananas onto the natural counter and put his shirt back on. There were 42 of them.

Jack said, "Good morning. The bananas were a great idea. Thank you. Where is Janie?"

"Apparently exhausted. When I woke her, she said she was so tired that she longed for a snooze button. I told her to go back to sleep as she was not responsible for breakfast anymore starting today. She smiled, rolled over and instantly resumed snoring," chuckled Harold. "I understand from Marah that you had a rough sleep as well."

"I did indeed," answered Jack. "It is hard enough to bear the responsibility of being on sleep duty at the time of the crash. Now that some are wondering about my participation in it, my nightmares seem to have magnified. Speaking of Marah, do you know if she will be coming for coffee this morning?"

Harold replied, "When I spoke to her, she and Arianna were putting the solar lights on the beach for recharging. She said the two of them would wait for Janie and then come to the cave. In the meantime she was planning to empty the sand bags from the restroom and tidy up the lower level of the nose section. That's where she sleeps, you know." Harold couldn't keep from grinning when answering Jack about Marah. Having been his best friend for many years, he could recognize Jack's growing attraction for the lady. Harold and Janie had discussed their hopes for Jack and Marah becoming a couple in the future. Harold had watched for years as Jack was belittled and taken advantage of by his wife Janet, and always felt his friend deserved a better life than that. He was hopeful this better life would be found here on this island.

Back at the camp, Marah had changed out all the solar lights for freshly charged ones shedding new light inside the cargo hole that she now called home. In the corner of the wreckage was a clip board with paper still attached. Having found an ink pen earlier, Arianna wanted the paper to draw on. Being wedged between the ceiling and the cliff, Marah had to work the clip board back and forth to free it. She was soon successful. As she examined the documents held by the board she learned they were multiple copies of sign in sheets for the crew members. Only the top copy had been used. Marah removed the used copy and gave the clip board to a very demanding Arianna. Staring at the log in sheet, Marah stopped and rubbed her eyes. Having looked at the journal on a number of occasions over the past week, she kept starring at Janie's signature on the paper in front of her realizing they were in the same handwriting. There was no doubt about this fact. None of the other signatures even came close. Obviously, Janie, her new friend was involved in crashing the plane. Just then she heard Janie climbing down from the level above her. She quickly folded the paper she was holding and put it in her pocket. She was unsure what to do about this unexpected discovery. Her life was so much more peaceful not having to deal with her very abusive husband that she liked it here. She decided to keep it to herself for now. She called out to Janie to wait for her and Arianna and they would walk to the cave together. Janie entered the lower level and asked Marah if they could wait a few minutes to leave. She had seen Sanjay and Doctor Goodson helping Mr. Patel onto the sled to be moved to the cave. She did not want to walk with them. Instead she would prefer for Marah and herself to move at their own pace considering Arianna was with them. Marah agreed.

Later on the path to the cave, as they reached the quicksand pit, Mr. Patel began sobbing uncontrollably. He suddenly became very frightened of his surroundings. Sanjay and Doctor Goodson immediately ran back to his side to attempt to calm and console him. Once they finally got him to stop punching at some invisible target and hear them, he soon regained his composure. Doctor Goodson explained to Mr. Patel that flashbacks were normal after any snake attack not to mention everything else he had been through. He told his patient that this too would heal with time. Then the three resumed their journey.

At the cave, Jack, Harold and Nigel French began to unpack the large crate of fishing materials. They had just started when Habib and Guillaume Rotge arrived carrying a large armload of perfectly sized bamboo shoots to make cane fishing poles. Jack smiled and said, "You're just in time guys. Those poles should produce a lot of happy fishermen today. Thank you so much." The five men were all pleased with every layer of equipment they uncovered. As they neared the half way point in the crate, ooohs, wows, and shouts of joy rose from their group. They had just uncovered five guns of various calibers along with an arsenal of ammunition.

Habib said, "You all do realize this insures our ability to provide fresh game and protect ourselves from predators for a long time to come. I had so worried over having only one gun available with less than one magazine remaining to protect ourselves. It's hard to believe how fortunate we are."

The five decided to place the crate still containing the guns and ammo inside the only cavern inside the cave/cafeteria. They would place it just beyond where the light from the main room illuminated for safe keeping. Today was a day for fishing. They all worked together to equip all the fishing poles and the few available rods and reels with the necessary string and tackle. Their efforts were well underway when Nigel French looked up and said, "Ut Oh, here comes trouble." The other men looked up to see Sanjay and Doctor Goodson pulling the sled with Mr. Patel their way. Jack and Harold lept into action, going to relieve them of their pulling. The two men were appreciative of the help.

After a very shaken Mr. Patel was helped inside the cave, he was seated close to the entrance and given coffee. Doctor Goodson advised him to face the opening to the outside and to try to take in the beauty of his surroundings. The doctor took some coffee and walked outside to give Jack and Harold the details of their trip here this morning. Sanjay soon joined them in conversation. He said, "It is my belief, and I believe the good doctor will agree, that Mr. Patel may be suffering from Post Traumatic Stress. None of us know his mental state prior to the plane crash. Add to that everything that he has been through since then and we have all the ingredients of a perfect storm. I fear he may become a danger to himself or those around him. We all need to keep an eye on him."

Doctor Goodson replied, "I agree totally. I feel we need to attempt to calm his mind. Fishing is great for stress relief. If we could let him use one of the better rod and reels, I will stay close by him. I will go in and stay with him through breakfast and then set him up fishing, assuming he feels healthy enough." Everyone agreed and Doctor Goodson accompanied by Nigel French returned to the dining area of the cave.

Soon after taking their seats, French, the doctor and Mr. Patel were approached by a smiling Ophilia Parker. She said, "I believe after eating breakfast this morning, you gentlemen will agree that we are all in the hands of a culinary genius. I have watched Mr. Li this morning as he turned dry evaporated milk into a creamy sweet nectar by mixing it with dry non-dairy creamer and an ever so small amount of sugar. It is the best milk I have ever tasted. Part of it he mixed with dry cocoa for hot chocolate. But that's just the start of it! I'm sure you are all familiar with the bland taste of powdered scrambled eggs. Well that evidently is not the Chun Li style. Gentlemen, I will have you know that he used powdered popcorn butter and bacon bits in the eggs to produce a delight to the taste buds. We also have a sweet buttered rice dish to offer. Until we run out, anyone who wants can add a half of a banana to their order. There is fresh water, coffee, tea, milk, and hot chocolate to choose from to drink. So in down home restaurant fashion, may I take your order please?"

Being wowed by her vocal menu, all three men requested a little of each along with some of the milk she had so deliciously described. Three bites into his food, Nigel French excused himself from the table momentarily to speak with his friend Chun Li. One could tell Li was appreciating the praise being heaped upon him. Nigel returned to his breakfast. Doctor Goodson asked what Nigel had told Li. "I told him he's a bloody genius. This is the best food I have had in months, not just the last week," French answered.

Even Mr. Patel agreed saying, "It is good." When he had finished eating, the doctor went to the cave entrance and yelled to Jack and the others to come and eat some good food.

Just then, coming up the path was Janie, Marah and Arianna. Hearing someone yelling about food, Arianna asked, "Mommy, is that where we are going? I'm hungry."

"Yes, baby, we are almost there and I will get you something to eat," Marah answered.

Jack laughingly looked at Harold and said, "Now there comes trouble." They both giggled as the ladies approached.

Harold greeted Janie with a kiss and said, "Hello sleepyhead, how are you feeling?"

Janie answered, "Still a little tired but looking forward to a good cup of coffee." They all entered the cave together.

Arianna, being an outgoing and curious child, immediately pulled away from her mother's hand and ran up to Mr. Patel. She poked him on his arm and asked, "Hey, mister, does your boo boo feel better yet? I hope so. My mommy says that some boo boo's don't get better. Then you have to go to heaven. But if your boo boo's do get better you get to stay here and go fishing. They both sound like fun to me." The child tarried a moment waiting for a reply then ran back to her mother's side. She looked up and told Marah, "Mommy, I don't think that man can hear anymore."

Mr. Patel was starring in Jack's direction with total hatred beaming from his eyes. He turned toward the doctor and loudly announced, "I see they don't mind feeding mass murderers here. I would like to go outside and sit by the water for awhile if you don't mind helping me get there."

Harold walked over to help Doctor Goodson walk Mr. Patel outside. Mr. Patel yanked his arm away from Harold and yelled, "Take your hands off me. You know you were involved in the crash as well."

Doctor Goodson calmly said, "I've got this Harold. It's okay." The doctor then led his patient far enough away from the entrance to the cave that he could neither see nor hear what was going on inside. He then got a rod and reel and handed it to Mr. Patel. He then told Mr. Patel that he should attempt to catch his own dinner as he wasn't making many friends here. After days of dealing with this irate individual, the good doctor's patience was wearing thin. The doctor then told Mr. Patel to stay put while he returned to the cave for another cup of coffee. He advised him to shout if he caught any fish and he would return to help him. Then Doctor Goodson returned to the cave.

Jack was visibly shaken by the sudden turn of events. He once again stated, "I cannot turn back time and change the fact we are all here. I think about it all the time, even in my sleep. Again I apologize to you all, but my only involvement in the crash was being on sleep duty." The lie was so deeply rooted in Jack's heart, it had become his new truth. The words now flowed so freely even Jack, himself, now found it believable. His table was now surrounded by well wishers.

Jenny Parker patted Jack on the back and said, "There's one in every crowd. It's pretty obvious that Patel is going to be the "one" among us. We have all seen his type. Don't let it bother you. The majority of us believe you and believe in you. Now eat your breakfast and get busy fishing. Our dinner will not catch itself."

Just as Doctor Goodson rejoined the group seated at Jack's table, Chun Li came over and asked Nigel French to get the translator from Jack so he could say something. Li then voiced his annoyance at Mr. Patel's outburst. He called their attention to his wife who stood next to the natural counter frantically beating and mashing on some unknown substance wrapped in a towel. He explained to the group that Su Li's OCD rendered her incapable of tolerating drama of this sort. When asked what she was doing, he explained she was grinding corn into corn meal for the bread to be served with the evening meal. He requested that Mr. Patel's actions be answered with temporary exile from the cave until such time as his attitude had improved. Chun Li's first concern was obviously with his wife. Doctor Goodson agreed to serve Patel's meals elsewhere hoping that his attitude would soon improve.

In an effort to change the subject, Doctor Goodson complimented the Li's expertise for creating meal from corn. He said, "I don't know if you would be interested, but in my chosen line of medicine, I have learned that Coconut Flour is quite healthy. In the next few days, I would be happy to make the effort to create some of it for you to try." Chun Li agreed saying he was familiar with the product.

Nigel French asked, "Exactly what is your chosen line of medicine, Doctor?"

The doctor smiled and answered, "I am an OB GYN by trade. Due to poor dietary habits, many American women develop Gestational Diabetes. I actually had courses that taught about the existence and the benefits of using both coconut oil and coconut flour. It is quite healthy."

Harold joined in asking, "Being an OB, how did you know how to treat Mr. Patel's injuries?"

Doctor Goodson answered, "A physician is trained in all fields of medicine prior to choosing which field they plan to specialize in. My brain seemed to retain most of the original training on emergency medicine. I have always been good at it. However I prefer to deal more with the beginning of life rather than the ending of it. But I do know how to treat other ailments."

Having finished her breakfast, a fidgety Arianna walked over and tugged on Jack's sleeve saying, "Sir, can we go fishing now? I catched a fish before and it is fun. Come on and I will show you how." A chuckle rose from all who heard the child's request.

Marah began to apologize, explaining Arianna's personality, "Please excuse Arianna. She has a very nurturing heart and is apparently concerned for you."

Jack turned to the precious child and replied, "Why yes ma'am, young lady. I would love for you to teach me how to catch a fish. We will do that very thing as soon as I finish my coffee."

Being highly intelligent and a little bossy, Arianna said, "Okay, but hurry up. Time's a wasting." The group again burst into laughter.

Moments later people who were yet to have breakfast arrived at the cave. Some had arm loads of firewood, others carried bananas. Realizing that seating was incomplete, all who were finished eating exited the cave to make space for the others. They all gathered around the fishing equipment to choose their pole. Marah then convinced Arianna the fish would be more likely to bite her hook if she took a bath first. Marah, Janie, Elizabeth French, and Iva Rotge gathered 4 large pots of water along with 2 large cups to use in bathing the children. They would ask all mothers to take turns cleaning up their children. Arianna was delighted to go first.

Suddenly they were startled by frantic shouts coming from the fresh water lagoon outside the cave. The men were running toward the spot where Mr. Patel had been fishing. The women watched as Jack quickly removed his shirt and shoes and jumped into the water. Jack soon surfaced pulling an unconscious Mr. Patel behind him to the shore. Due to his prior injuries, Patel had been unable to reel in a large fish he had snagged and had fallen into the deep water. After being helped to get the victim ashore, Jack immediately began CPR before Doctor Goodson could reach the fallen man. Mr. Patel soon began to expel the water from his lungs, coughing and spitting until he could again breathe normally. When he looked up and saw Jack had been the one who had helped him, his eyes again filled with hatred. After deliberately spitting in Jack's face, he screamed, "Get away from me you murderer."

Jack, still out of breath and hurt at Patel's statement said, "I think he will live. He seems to be back to normal." Jack then pushed his way through the gathering crowd and walked back to the fishing equipment.

Jack was soon joined by Harold, Habib and Sanjay. Habib said, "You should have let the trouble maker drown. I can not believe how ungrateful he was. You could have died saving him."

Jack answered, "There's been enough death here already. I did what I had to do."

Harold said, "Well the jerk lost the rod and reel I wanted to use. I wish the fish had left the rod behind and took him instead. The rod would have been of more benefit than that guy ever will." The men all laughed at Harold's statement.

The ladies had not left the area chosen to bathe the children 30 feet away from the fishing equipment and the four men. Having witnessed everything that had just occurred had a profound effect on Marah. Being neither a stranger nor a fan of drama, she excused herself from the group of ladies. With her voice shaking, she asked Janie to keep an eye on Arianna for a few minutes while she walked away long enough to gain control of her nerves. Janie agreed unable to hide her concern for her friend. Marah assured her she would be alright soon but didn't want to upset Arianna. After everything else, this place did not need a crying child added into the mixture.

Marah turned and walked toward the campfire burning just outside the cave entrance. As she stood watching the flames dance, she attempted to put into perspective the events of the morning. She thought of how Mr. Patel's actions were just what she would have expected from her husband, Ragish. She thought of Jack risking his life for someone who was obviously a sworn enemy, something that Ragish would have never done. The lack of selfishness Jack had displayed was like nothing she had ever personally witnessed. After a few moments she reached into her pocket, removed the flight crew log and tossed into the middle of the fire. She had decided to let the proof be devoured by the flames rather than adding fuel to the firestorm that Mr. Patel had tried so hard to ignite. She stood there watching until the paper had been completely been turned to ash wanting to be sure that every trace of it's existence was erased. She felt a wave of calm engulf her and returned to the ladies and her child. Inside she knew she had done the right thing.

Guillaume Rotge told Jack he would prefer to fish upstream from the cave. He felt his soul required the peace and quiet of separating himself from the many people gathering there. He said he was also curious as to the origin of the lake. Habib asked to go along to help with avoiding unknown quicksand pits and to have a pistol to keep them safe from threatening wildlife. Rotge agreed this was a good idea and approached the ladies group to ask if his wife wanted to go fishing. Iva Rotge declined the offer, choosing to stay behind to help with the children. Meanwhile, Habib asked that Nigel French would check with Chun Li about what kind of fish were suitable for the evening meal. French returned smiling, saying that Li answered all fish were edible so that kind was needed. Habib and Guillaume Rotge grabbed two cane poles and a pocket full of tackle and were off.

As the morning progressed, twenty-four children were bathed by their mothers. As the last two of the children were being washed, an elderly French lady, whose shirt bore the name Claudette approached with a little boy. She told Janie and Marah the child had been with her since exiting the plane the morning after the crash. He had been calling her Grandma. She had not been approached by the child's parents as of yet and had felt the need to care for the child thus far. The little boy named Pierre heard what Claudette was saying and immediately pulled a photograph from his front pocket. With a tearful voice he said, "Grandma don't you remember, when Mommy put me on the plane she said when I got off in France, you would be waiting for me. She even gave me this picture of you so I would get it right and not get picked up by bad people."

Surprised by this revelation, Claudette took the picture from the boy. As the ladies each examined the photo, it became clear Claudette resembled the child's grandmother. With tears streaming down Janie's face she said, "Oh no, I had forgotten there was a child traveling alone aboard the plane. There were two other flight attendants assigned to see that the child was handed off to his family member in France. This poor child is here alone. Please excuse me for a moment." Following Marah's lead from earlier, Janie knew it was best to walk away from the children to cry. She had totally forgot about this little boy and was unsure of how to handle it.

Claudette sweetly said to the child, "You are right, Pierre. Grandma is old and forgetful." She looked over the top of his head at Marah and winked. Then she continued, "You stay here and let this nice young woman give you a bath. I will be right over here when you are done." Claudette walked over to an upset Janie and quietly said, "Ma'am, I would be happy to continue caring for Pierre. He is a very calm and sweet boy. Actually I have grown quite fond of him already. I am sorry that I didn't already know his story, but this is the first time he has shown me the photograph of his Grandma. I guess he thought his Grandma knew what she looked like." Janie agreed and hugged this wonderful lady.

Unaware of what was going on with the ladies, Jack and Harold were threading large bamboo limbs through the top and bottom of the large fishing net. It had been decided the net would be placed in a small semi-circle mini lagoon outside the cave entrance to serve as a live well for the fish caught today. With about fifty people currently fishing, it was hoped there would be more fish than enough for one meal. In an effort to make things easier for Chun Li and his crew to prepare meals, the men planned to always keep one or two meals of fish available for the chef. They also decided to use one of the empty wooden crates placed at the water's edge inside the live well to chill drinks in. After entering the water, Jack had said the water was nearly as cold as ice. With no form of refrigeration available they took advantage of this Heaven sent cooling system.

Jack was glad he had removed his shirt before entering the water earlier as he took the translator from his pocket and went to get Chun Li. He explained the plans for the live well and crate cooler to Li asking his preference for the placement of the crate. A very pleased Chun Li chose the spot and told Jack he would have Su and the Parker ladies empty the largest crate of supplies available. Unfortunately most of the other crates had been disassembled and used as shelves inside the cabinets the day before. Mr. Li then returned to the cave and his work.

Suddenly everyone's attention was grabbed by squeals and shouts of joy ringing out from down the river bank. All were watching as Nigel French reeled in a fish as long as his leg. Sanjay ran to his side with the hand held fish net and helped land the monstrous creature. Arianna shouted, "Look Mommy, that man caught Free Willy." The child's assessment caused all who heard it to burst into side splitting laughter. In an instant, the tension of the morning seemed to have been lifted.

Harold said to Jack, "See, in spite of evil's best efforts, I believe God will grant us a great day or at least a great dinner tonight."

Jack answered, "I do believe you are right." The two men went to help Nigel and Sanjay move the still fighting fish to the cave to be cleaned and cut up for cooking later.

Upstream and out of sight, Habib and Guillaume Rotge were still walking the river bank. The body of water was surrounded at all angles with fruit trees. Mango, pineapple, banana, avocado, peach and coconut trees were in abundance as far as the eye could see after they turned the corner at the river's bend. The two men were amazed at the sight since there were no fruit trees near the cave entrance. When they came upon four passion fruit trees clumped together, Rotge joked that he would pick Iva an arm load of those on the way back to the cave later that day. Iva had been so busy with all the projects led by her new friend Elizabeth French that he had barely received so much as a kiss on the forehead lately. The two men laughed aloud.

They couldn't help but notice the further they got upstream, the louder the sound of the water's flow became. Seeing another bend in the river bank, they pressed on expecting to find rapids ahead. Instead they were surprised and delighted to discover a small water fall coming out of the side of the hill. It was about twice the size of a large dinner plate and landed on a shallow area of bedrock. Habib and Rotge discussed the possibility of the bedrock being slick but could not resist the idea of the first shower in a week. The water was cold. It turned out the rock floor beneath the fall was free of slime and algae making it an easy surface to stand on. Each man turned his back on the other while he stripped and bathed in the water fall. The feeling was breathtakingly refreshing. Guillaume Rotge said, "Next time we should bring soap." Again they laughed. The two men walked half way back to the cave and started fishing feeling invigorated. They planned to gather two shirts full of fruit when they finished fishing. Hopefully they would have fruit and fish to haul back at that time.

Back at the cave, fish were being caught in abundance. The live well had proven to be a good idea and now held ten fish of various sizes, none of which were even close to the size of Nigel French's large fish. Mr. Patel had finally settled down and was sleeping peacefully underneath a tree next to the water allowing Doctor Goodson the chance to fish as well. Noticing the doctor was using a cane pole to pull in one fish after another, Harold approached him and asked what he was doing so differently than everyone else.

Doctor Goodson answered, "As a kid, I used to fish with my Grandaddy. He never believed in artificial baits. He only used earthworms. I was lucky enough when searching for a place for Mr. Patel to lie down to move a dead limb off a nest of night crawlers. Grandaddy always chewed tobacco and would spit the juice onto the worm before casting his line into the water. I don't have the tobacco, but to honor his tradition I have been spitting on the bait prior to casting my line. Evidently it is not the tobacco but the spit they are so attracted to."

Harold, having not caught a single fish yet, decided to test the doctor's theory. He borrowed two night crawlers and headed a small distance up stream. Thirty minutes later a smiling Harold was walking back toward the cave with four fish hanging from a stick he had used as a stringer. "Your Grandfather was a brilliant man obviously. Using his idea I caught four good fish with only two large worms," a thrilled Harold exclaimed.

Doctor Goodson replied, "You're right. I have known it all my life." The two men shook hands. Harold walked on to happily add his catch to the live well.

While placing his fish into the well, Harold smiled as he noticed Jack sitting nearby with a fishing pole in his hand. Jack seemed oblivious to the fact a fish had taken his bobber to the water's bottom. He instead was mesmerized watching as Marah taught 25 children to play hop scotch in the sand. Once again Marah was deeply enjoying playing with the kids, laughing as she taught them to play a new game. Harold walked over and sat beside his friend and asked, "Are you going to catch that fish or should I?"

Jack answered, "Oh, wow. I didn't even see it."

A laughing Harold said, "You know, fishing is not exactly child's play. I saw what you were looking at."

Jack replied, "I can't help it. I find that woman captivating, not just for her looks either. Her fun loving nature is entrancing. Look at the way she is playing with those kids. She is like no other woman I have ever seen. Aside from your wonderful mother, I have never met a woman like that anywhere. As you know, my mother and my wife neither one had an affectionate bone in their bodies. I can only imagine what it would be like to have a woman of that caliber to walk by your side. I picture it as being like a bit of Heaven on Earth."

Harold said, "You should ask Janie to put a good word in for you. They have become good friends already." Jack said he preferred to give it some time citing the fact that she had so recently been widowed. Harold reluctantly agreed, all along planning to speak with Janie that night on the subject. He would honor Jack's wishes but would ask Janie to investigate whether Marah shared Jack's interest. In the event she did not, he would try to keep his best friend from getting hurt.

The sun had traveled half way down to the horizon when Gilliaume Rotge and Habib returned to the cave. They did not return empty handed. They were carrying a string of six fish, all nearly one foot in length. They were both shirtless, each holding shirts full of a variety of the fruits growing next to the river. Jack and Harold went to meet them and help with their cargo. The fish were added to the live well which already housed enough fish for two more meals for all. The fruit was immediately seized by the very eager Jenny and Ophilia Parker to transform into a lovely fruit salad to be tonight's dessert. The four men were soon joined by Sanjay, Nigel French and Doctor Goodson, all eager to hear what sights lie beyond the river's bend. The aroma of dinner cooking surrounded the cave's entrance.

Habib had proven himself a sufficient marksman by killing the snake earlier this week. Now for the second time since arriving on this island, he would prove himself a poetically descriptive reporter of the sights they had encountered today. He said to all who would listen, "Today I experienced a further confirmation that we are stranded in Paradise. Approximately 1000 feet past that river's bend right up there the water widens. Both sides are bordered by a 15 or 20 foot sandbar of beautiful polished multi-colored shiny pebbles about twice the size of pea gravel. Oh but gentlemen, it gets better. Those river beaches are then bordered by various kinds of fruit trees, not in the forest density but right there on the river bank for easy picking. I counted seven different kinds of fruit just in what the two of us brought back! Walking up the river's edge, with every minor turn in the bank's direction the water's sound got even louder. We discovered a magnificent small water fall just inside the first cove we came to. It pours a stream the size of a common beach ball down onto a flat bedrock that is free of slime. The water it produces is cold and refreshing. I highly recommend this fall to any adult wishing to shower. Oh and I must add, it's beauty is as breath taking as it's temperature."

"Here, here, bravo. An exact description of everything I saw as well," said a smiling and excited Guillaume Rotge, finally getting an opportunity to speak. Rotge added, "On the other side of the cove which has the water fall is a large jagged cliff. There were at least 50 Albatross nesting on the side of the cliff and on the sandbar below it. I also saw three turtles while we were gone each the size of the average automobile tire. You never know, the albatross may be like everything else and taste like chicken and I have heard there are seven kinds of meat in a turtle. If Mr. Li is as good a cook as he appears to be, I think we are in good shape. I am sure Iva and Elizabeth French will make good use of the bird feathers and turtle shells. Until we are rescued, this place has a lot to offer."

Chun Li approached the group and asked Nigel French to spread the word that dinner would be done in about an hour. Then Li walked to the other side of the cave entrance where the bedrock was very flat. Su Li and her husband were discussing where to build the oven for Elizabeth French to fire the pottery dishes she planned to make for the kitchen. French told the group it was obvious when Su Li made a decision, her husband was happy to follow it to the letter. He said he understood Chun's actions as his wife was also a stickler for detail. He felt the two ladies would get along fine aside from any language barriers they might encounter. When the Li's had finished their discussion, Nigel called Chun Li back over to the group. Nigel asked what the foods were that smelled so delicious. Li explained using the translator. There was 150 fish filets baking in the oven accompanied by 3 large pots of white beans seasoned with bacon bits and both garlic and onion powder. This was to be accompanied by rice and corn bread made from freshly stone ground corn meal, powdered egg, his milk mixture and onion powder making the bread taste like hush puppies. The drink menu would be the same as this morning, and the ladies had prepared a fruit salad for dessert. Li was excited about finding a package of fifty disposable aluminum sheet cake pans in the cabinets from the plane's kitchen. The find had made him feel like good fortune had been heaped upon him. His kitchen crew would wash and reuse them for as long as possible. Then he asked for someone to refill the water tank and excused himself to go and check on dinner.

Almost exactly one hour later, Chun Li exited the cave carrying a plate of food and a bottle of tea. He motioned for Nigel French to accompany him to give the food to Doctor Goodson. Through French's translation he told the doctor the food was for Mr. Patel. His wife's nerves would not be exposed to the trouble maker again today. Li said Patel was not welcome inside the dining area until he had shown a change in attitude from what had been displayed today. Leaving no room for discussion, Li turned and went back inside the cave. Doctor Goodson delivered the food and drink to a very disgruntled Mr. Patel who chose to rant about his exile from the cave rather than offer a thank you. Following the chef's lead, the doctor turned and walked back to the cave.

Just as expected, dinner was as though it was being served in a five star restaurant. Everyone ate until they could hold no more. There were numerous hugs and hand shakes given to the kitchen staff. Many of the ladies pitched in to help with the clean up and to make the kitchen ready for tomorrow morning's coffee and breakfast. Chun Li asked that Nigel French and Jack would put the remaining half pot of beans and rice inside the crate with the guns hidden inside the cave's lone cavern. If the temperature there was cool enough, the food could be added to a gumbo he was planning for tomorrow's dinner.

While they were eating, Janie had informed Jack and Harold of the disturbing news of the child, Pierre, and the lovely lady named Claudette. She told them Claudette had volunteered to care for the boy for the duration of their stay here. Also the lady had brought up an important point she herself would not have thought of. There were twenty-five children here. These children were sure to grow as time past. Claudette, being a seamstress by trade, had requested the opportunity to cut down and re-sew the clothing brought here by the dead passengers into clothing for the children as they out grew what they had. "She knows how to rip the original seems out and reuse that thread. We need to provide her with at least half of the unclaimed baggage for this task. Our stay here may last months, years or may even be permanent. We must provide clothing for this growing group of children," Janie told them. Jack and Harold agreed to help out as much as possible.

Soon all had made the slow, full bellied walk back to the camp. Sanjay had helped Doctor Goodson get an ever complaining Mr. Patel back to his quarters. Janie and Harold, being concerned for his safety, convinced Jack to sleep in the upper part of the nose section where they would be. Harold had told Jack, "Always remember there's safety in numbers. We are here together. We have got your back, my friend, always." That night's slumber was peaceful and uneventful. The next morning would begin another week of work, surprises and adventure. Janie and Harold fell asleep feeling happy after overhearing Jack's prayer of thanks for the good blessings of the day and thanks for survival of the bad events they had experienced. Their sleep was filled with dreams of the new blessings to come.

CHAPTER THIRTEEN

FROM PLANS TO REALITY

The morning of the eighth day began with the castaways eagerly making their way to the cave for coffee and an opportunity to plan out the daily work schedule. Chun Li, his wife Su, and the Parker sisters had prepared oatmeal containing the remainder of the fruit salad from the day before. Yesterday's hot chocolate was today's chocolate milk for the children. It had been chilled in the wooden crate in the water next to the cave, exactly 25 water bottles half full of delicious chocolate nectar.

There were discussions on the building of Elizabeth French's pottery oven, the building of more shelters of various types, and alternating opportunities to shower at the water fall. Guillaume Rotge was excited to begin his attempt at reviving the dead welder, generators, push mowers, and weed eaters. The Li's were planning a shelter home close to the cave built from stone like the successful oven. Janie, after bringing up the journal entry about the vegetable seeds, suggested they be planted along the half mile trail leading from the beach to the cave. This would allow for easy harvest by all who traveled the trail. She believed they needed to start planting as soon as possible. Nigel French and Habib would gather two or three days of various fruits. Jack and Harold would resume the metal removal from the rapidly disappearing tail section. The two planned to finish the tables and benches for the cafeteria. This morning, Iva Rotge would lead a ladies hike to the water fall for showers. Her husband requested that Iva be allowed to carry a fire arm along to protect the ladies from predators. They had met while serving in the French military in their twenties, and he could guarantee her marksmanship. Many of the women, children and the elderly planned to resume the grass weaving. Two elderly gentlemen volunteered to begin whittling wooden spoons and forks citing the fact the plastic ware would not last forever. Soon all were off to perform their chosen tasks.

Harold set out to extract today's fuel supply from the wing needed for the working generator. Jack showed Guillaume Rotge where the broken machinery had been placed. When Harold had finished obtaining the fuel, Jack stopped him at the storage shed. Jack asked him, "Can you help us for a few minutes. I believe we might be able to move the supplies other than the broken things to one shed. Then this shed could be Rotge's shop. Just look, do you think it would all fit?" After checking it out, Harold agreed that at least most of the supplies would fit in one shed. Even if they had to line one wall of the second shed with supplies, it should leave ample work space. The three men worked together and within one hour their mission was accomplished.

Sanjay, followed by Janie, Marah, Arianna and two of the older children appeared from the path to the cave as Harold and Jack had just finished helping Rotge. They were each carrying arm loads of weaving grass. Janie smiled and said, "We started clearing the way for planting the seeds. The grass will keep the weavers busy for awhile." Jack noticed Arianna was not carrying grass. Instead she had a bottle of dish soap.

The child looked at her friend Jack and said, "Mommy is going to make us some bubbles. Do you like to play with bubbles? You can play with us. We won't let the mean man get you."

Touched by Arianna's words, Jack answered, "No thank you sweetheart, I need to help these gentlemen work today."

Then the child replied, "I'm not sweetheart, I'm Arianna and you're Jack. Remember, you told Mommy and me to call you that yesterday."

Jack smiled and said, "All right then, Arianna. I will try to remember." Everyone within earshot laughed at this three year old's words.

Marah shook her head and said, "Oh Arianna, what am I going to do with you?"

The quick witted child answered, "You said you were going to let me blow bubbles." Then they walked on to the beach.

After unloading his armload of grass at the beach, Sanjay headed toward the doctor's quarters to help transport Mr. Patel to the cave for breakfast. Harold asked

Sanjay to bring back from the cave the hand tools that had been used there and give them to Guillaume Rotge to use repairing the broken equipment. Mr. Patel was unusually quiet while being helped onto the sled by Sanjay and Doctor Goodson. Harold looked questioningly at the doctor. Doctor Goodson uttered one word of explanation, "Valium." Harold nodded and said, "Oh." With no need for further conversation, the three men were off to the cave.

Soon Janie returned to Harold and Jack's location followed by Marah. Arianna, along with the dish soap to make bubbles had been handed off to the babysitters for the day. This freed Marah up to help Janie with planting the seeds. With journal in hand, Janie showed Jack and Harold the entry on where the seeds would be located. After reading the entry, Jack entered the upper level of the nose section and made his way to the cockpit. He soon rejoined them carrying one of the black boxes. They opened the box to see multiple packets of seeds. There were every kind of vegetable, herb and spice currently sold on the market. The two ladies decided to read each pack of seeds to determine whether to plant that batch in the sunnier or shadier areas of the path. Marah remembered as a child helping her mother harvest the garden food. She suggested the cucumbers and squash be planted near the beach. Their vines grow across the ground and would need space to spread. Otherwise the fruit they would bear would get trampled and destroyed by people walking the path. Marah showed no sign of her secret knowledge that the journal was in Janie's hand writing. She had no desire to lose Janie's friendship or to stir up trouble. Regardless of how they got here, she wanted a good life for herself and her daughter.

Meanwhile, Nigel French and Habib were on the river bank picking fruit to stock the kitchen. They were careful to keep a safe distance from the water fall where Iva Rotge and 15 other women were currently taking turns showering. Periodically they would hear a woman squeal out loudly. Habib assured Nigel French they had more than likely just stepped into the frigid flow of the water fall. He remembered the initial shock to the system from yesterday when he, himself had showered. He felt sure the ladies were fine. An hour had past and the men had lost count of how many squeals they had heard when three gunshots rang out from the water fall area. No longer concerned with the modesty of the ladies, the two gentlemen ran in their direction. Just prior to reaching the cove which housed the water fall they saw three women each dragging a dead albatross. Iva Rotge, still leading the group with albatross in tow, smiled at the men and said, "I hate gumbo so I thought we would offer Mr. Li an alternative meat source for dinner. With any luck, I can have these birds cleaned and ready to cook in half an hour. We can save the feathers to make pillows at a later date." Habib and Nigel took the heavy birds from the ladies. They asked them to each help to transport the fruit that had been harvested. The men suggested the women could use their dirty clothes to wrap the fruit in for transport reminding them all the fruit would be washed before consumption anyway. They were all proud to be returning to the cave with such a large bounty.

As they neared the cave, it became quite obvious there was a large disturbance going on. They first heard shouting followed by screams. Both Habib and Iva Rotge dropped their cargo and ran toward the cave with guns in hand not knowing what to expect. Upon reaching the entrance they saw Mr. Patel lying on the floor with his right arm cut from wrist to elbow. Next to him on the floor was a large bolder. A shirtless Doctor Goodson hovered over Patel tearing his shirt into strips to tie the wounded arm together. A shaking Chun Li stood just feet away holding a bloody meat cleaver. Three men stood guard between Li and Patel. Ophilia and Jenny Parker were in the corner of the kitchen attempting to console the hysterical Su Li.

Nigel French had dropped his albatross and ran to the cave as well. Elizabeth French came toward him with two bloody knees and scrapped hands. "Elizabeth, are you all right? What has happened?" Nigel asked his wife.

She answered, "I was gathering stones for my pottery oven," pointing at a large pile of stones outside the cave's entrance. "When the doctor and Mr. Patel arrived for breakfast, Chun Li requested the doctor leave Mr. Patel outside saying he did not want any trouble this morning. Doctor Goodson found Mr. Patel a shady spot to sit and brought him coffee and oatmeal. After Mr. Patel ate his breakfast, he soon began to talk to himself. He got louder and louder until he was in a full angry rant, screaming that he was not the villain here. He said he was not the one who killed over 80 people by crashing the plane. He said something about those suitcase tags on the pharmaceuticals that Captain Wellington spoke to us all about. He yelled something about the cook having been involved in the crash. Then he struggled to get to his feet, shoved me down as he went by, and grabbed a large stone. He lifted it above his head and ran inside the cave. When he tried to strike Mr. Li with the rock, Mr. Li threw his arms up to protect his head. Mr. Li had been chopping up fish for the gumbo he was working to prepare and still held the meat clever in his hand. When Patel attempted to strike Mr. Li with the boulder, he cut his own arm wide open and collapsed to the floor. It was awful Nigel, just awful."

Nigel French was instantly furious over the injuries his wife had sustained. With anger now beaming from French's eyes, he said, "I'll kill him. He had no reason to shove you down."

As he tried to push past his wife, Elizabeth grabbed his arm. She said, "Nigel wait. You don't understand. Think about it for a moment. Mr. Patel obviously believes his version of the truth so deeply, he is willing to do anything to convince others. It is understandable after all he has been through, the snake attack, the collapsed lung and broken ribs, the near drowning, not to mention the crash itself. The poor man has evidently had a mental breakdown. While he was just talking before the rant began, he was weeping over the possibility of never seeing his family again. He is alone here."

"Are you saying you believe him?" asked Nigel.

"No. I am saying he believes it to be true. Think about it Nigel. In the same position, would you act any differently?" said Elizabeth.

French answered, "I would never have pushed an innocent woman down onto a bed of jagged stone. The man is obviously deranged."

During this conversation, Habib and Iva Rotge had exited the cave and joined them. Realizing the situation at hand could escalate rapidly, Iva Rotge interrupted the discussion. "Nigel and Elizabeth, please could the two of you help me to clean these birds and cut them up for cooking. They probably will not have time to get done if cooked whole. Have either of you ever cut up a whole chicken?" asked Iva.

"I know how," answered Elizabeth.

Nigel asked, "Do you plan to scald them and remove the feathers?"

"No. I doubt there is a pot large enough to dip them into. Instead they will need to be skinned, gutted, cut up and washed before being handed off to Mr. Li," answered Iva. She then looked at Habib and asked, "Please go back inside and ask Jenny Parker to give you 6 of the disposable aluminum cake pans and 4 sharp knives. Tell her what we are doing, and ask her to use the translator to convey the message to the Li's once their nerves have calmed."

Habib, understanding Iva Rotge's unspoken concerns said, "Yes ma'am," and immediately walked back into the cave. Five minutes later he exited once again carrying the requested items. He was pleased to see Iva and the French's had moved some twenty feet away from the entrance to speak to the group of 15 women still holding shirts full of fruit. They were explaining to the ladies what had occurred inside and asking them to wait to deliver the fruit at least for a few minutes. Habib quickly joined the group intentionally positioning himself to see the cave's entrance. He soon began talking to Nigel French attempting all the while to keep French turned away from the cave. His plan worked as French was distracted when Doctor Goodson and Sanjay silently loaded a bloody and unconscious Mr. Patel onto the sled and headed down the path out of sight.

Forty-five minutes later just as the last albatross was being cut into manageable pieces, they were joined by the entire kitchen staff. A much calmer Chun Li with translator in hand thanked each person individually. All helped to transport the 6 trays of fresh meat and the enormous bounty of fruit into the kitchen. Both Habib and Iva Rotge were surprised at how fast the kitchen had been cleaned and brought back to normal. There was no visible sign of the large puddle of blood that had surrounded Mr. Patel after the earlier incident. The boulder was gone and the tables and benches were back in their original positions.

With their mission accomplished, the group scattered out to perform their chosen daily tasks. Nigel French, still shaken and concerned for his wife's safety, chose to stay and help Elizabeth gather the remainder of the stones needed to build her pottery oven. Iva Rotge was asked via translator by Chun Li to save any hair lost by combing after showers to put in the mortar needed for building the oven. She then headed to the beach, along with the women who had showered, to gather the next 15 women interested in showering today. Jenny Parker had stopped Iva when she was leaving the cave and given her the tool belt forgotten by Sanjay. She told Iva, "These were supposed to be taken to your husband. Sanjay said they set him up a shop inside one of the storage sheds. I don't know which shed, but he shouldn't be hard to find." Iva thanked her and was off.

Guillaume Rotge was excited to see Iva when she reached the shed. He hugged her and took the tool belt she had brought him. He was talking so fast she decided to let him finish before telling him of her experiences this morning. He showed her his new shop and promised to have everything picked up each night if she would agree to live there with him. If everything was moved to one side, there would be plenty of room to sleep inside. As his small engine repairs were completed, even more space would open up. Iva found his childlike fascination with his new surroundings endearing. When Guillaume was threw speaking and Iva had agreed to live there, it was her turn to talk. Her husband found humor in the fact she had shot three albatross. He had wondered what she would do for dinner knowing her hatred for the scheduled gumbo. He became immediately concerned, however, when Iva told him of the episode at the cave with Mr. Patel. The couple made a plan to build a door that could be locked from inside for their new home. He would design, construct and install it before nightfall. This structure was very close to the doctor's quarters where a possibly dangerous Mr. Patel would be staying. Guillaume Rotge found it doubtful that anyone was safe around such a deranged individual. He told Iva to watch her back, and the two again split up to continue with their plans for the day.

When Iva had first reached the beach, she saw Janie and Marah planting cucumber and squash seeds next to the wood line. She stopped and told them about the events at the cave. She said she was sure that Doctor Goodson and Mr. Patel were back by now at the doctor's quarters. She advised the ladies to remain aware of their surroundings. She asked if they would like to be among this group of ladies to go to the falls to shower or wait until the next group later this afternoon. Janie and Marah chose to continue planting until the next group left. Soon Iva Rotge was off followed by 20 ladies carrying fresh clothing. Along the way she had told two other groups of ladies of the occurrences at the cave. Janie and Marah marveled that five minutes after Iva was gone, the whole beach was alive with chatter. Everyone seemed to be talking at once. It was amazing to see how fast gossip spreads.

An hour later as Janie and Marah were finishing this area's planting, Harold and Jack stopped by. The two were dragging a sled of four table tops for the cave. Guillaume Rotge had informed them of the events at the cave. The two felt it important to check on the Li's and the Parker ladies. Janie suggested they take along the large piece of woven grass the ladies had created this morning to be seat bottoms for the benches.

"I suppose this means you want to be able to sit at these tables," Harold joked.

"Unless you plan to get on all fours and let me sit on your back," Janie answered laughing. Harold and Jack told Janie they had just helped Guillaume Rotge install one of the plane's interior doors on the front of his shop. The door had previously been detached from the tail section and was lying in the remaining cargo area.

Harold said, "Rotge thinks there's a possibility of building a small shrimp boat from part of the tail section cargo hold. Man if that guy is as smart as he seems to be, Heaven only knows what we can achieve here." He leaned over, kissed Janie's forehead and said, "See you later. We will be staying at the cave to build these tables and chairs. If there's time we will help with the pottery oven." With that, the two men headed to the cave.

When Jack and Harold reached the cave all seemed normal. The delicious aroma of meat beginning to smoke filled the air. Nigel French was adding boulders to a large pile of stones that had already been gathered. Chun Li was examining and prestacking the stones just as he had done on his own oven. Jack asked Nigel, "How big is this oven going to be? Looks like an awful lot of stones just for that."

Nigel French answered, "Chun has decided to build he and his wife a home right over there out of stones and homemade mortar." French pointed to a spot near the corner of the bedrock where it appeared there were already four corner stones placed. "Mrs. Li has requested a metal roof with the windows left intact to act as sky lights. Do you think there will be a chance we can make this happen? We need to keep our cooks healthy and happy."

"Honestly, I see no reason this can't happen tomorrow. I will make salvaging the metal for their roof my first priority. The rest of this afternoon I plan to help Harold build four more tables with the benches to go along with them," Jack replied.

"I'll let them know you said you would help them out with a roof. Thanks old man," French said with a firm handshake for Jack.

Chun Li asked with the help of Nigel French if Harold would try to build the ladder planned for the water tank this evening. The tank was nearly empty again after having to clean up the bloody mess left after the episode with Mr. Patel. Li had tried to fill it with Su Li atop his shoulders. She was not strong enough to lift the bucket high enough to empty it into the tank. He felt sure he did not possess the upper body strength to lift anyone else on his shoulders. Harold and Jack would push the ladder to the top of the list right after they filled the tank for the use of the cooks.

Back at his shop, Guillaume Rotge was having rapid success. He had managed to obtain enough fuel to fill one of the push mowers from the pan placed under the drip from the hole in the wing. Harold had told him it leaked about one half gallon of fuel daily. The three mowers had been mostly crushed and mutilated, but he was able to piece the three together to build one. However there were no handles that survived. Rotge instead ran rope through the holes the handles would previously have been bolted to. At least now the machine could be pulled along and used. He started the mower and began pulling it along the path to the cave. Janie and Marah were busy planting corn seeds at the beginning of the path. As the pleased Guillaume Rotge approached their location he yelled, "Excuse me ladies, but I have created the world's first and only pull mower." The ladies stepped aside as Rotge passed by. His excitement spread to them as they watched him and the mower disappear down the path. They wondered if he would mow the entire pathway to the cave.

Suddenly their discussion was interrupted by the blood curling scream of a child. "Oh no, that sounded like Arianna," Marah said as she jumped up and ran in the direction of the beach. Claudette, followed closely by Pierre, was running toward them carrying a very distraught Arianna with a large thorn sticking all the way threw her hand.

"Quickly," Claudette stated, "The child must see the doctor." The three ladies and two children fearfully approached the doctor's quarters. Recognizing the child's cries as being those of pain, Doctor Goodson ran toward them as well. While attempting to console the child, Doctor Goodson was also examining the thorn. He told them the thorn would need to be pushed the remainder of the way through her hand as it had burrs that would make taking it out the way it went in too painful. By then, Marah feeling her child's pain was weeping as hard as Arianna.

Doctor Goodson said, "Please wait here for a moment while I go get my medical bag. I don't want any of you to go inside my office around Mr. Patel. He is too unpredictable." Within a few seconds the doctor was back by their side.

Surprisingly the doctor reached first for the tooth numbing gel which had been used on Mr. Patel's Pneumothorax. He placed some on both sides of the child's hand and along the part of the thorn which would have to pass through Arianna's hand. Doctor Goodson said, "Now we wait 60 seconds to allow the hand to numb." He looked at his watch and then back at the ladies. During that one minute wait was the first time Arthur Goodson had noticed the beautiful Marah's perfect facial features. He wondered how it could have taken him eight days to realize someone so beautiful was also on this island. He looked back at his watch and said, "Okay, is everyone ready?"

Suddenly Janie covered her mouth and said, "Oh no." She then ran a few steps away and threw up. By the time she had finished, the thorn was removed and Arianna had nearly stopped crying.

The always nurturing child asked, "Janie are you okay? Maybe you ate too much candy. Every time I do, I get sick. I hope you feel better now."

Janie answered, "Yes Arianna, I'm okay. I think I just got upset because you were hurt."

Arianna replied, I'm okay now too. Look." Arianna moved her fingers back and forth making a fist to show her hand was alright.

Janie looked at her friend Marah and said, "I'm so sorry I couldn't help. My stomach is not usually so weak. As a matter of fact, I don't recall this ever happening before." Meanwhile Doctor Goodson reached back into his bag and produced two bandaids, some medical tape and a tube of antibiotic ointment. He placed a bandaid on each side of the child's hand after treating it with the ointment, and wrapped the tape around her hand to hold the bandages in place. Hearing moaning from inside his office, the doctor then excused himself to check on Mr. Patel.

Marah suggested she and Janie conclude their planting for today and make their way to the cave. She feared Janie might have gotten too hot and may be getting dehydrated causing the nausea. Claudette along with the two children helped the ladies place a string tied to bamboo sticks along the line of planted corn seeds. They would need for the row of corn to be marked so Guillaume Rotge would not mow it down the next time the path was mowed. The corn would surely be growing by that time. Afterwards, while on their way to the cave they ran into Rotge sitting next to his mower at lookout cliff. It was plain to see his return trip with the mower had ended there. He had a plastic cup filled with water from the pan still sitting beneath the drip coming from the cliff. He pointed to a stack of cups next to the pan in case they needed a drink and informed them his mower had ran out of fuel. When he cooled off he would make his way back to the shop and refill the machine and finish this row of mowing. He promised the path beyond him was much more easy to navigate. The women told him of their marking the row of corn. He agreed to be mindful of the corn's existence and not mow it down next time. After having a drink, the ladies continued on their journey.

The cave was alive with activity when the three ladies and two children arrived. As they walked inside they were surprised at how much different it looked. Jack and Harold were finishing up the benches for the four tables they had added to the dining area. There were small grass woven bowls on each table containing various condiment packets. The bowls were separated into two sides. One side held salt, pepper, sugar, artificial sweeteners, and non-dairy creamer. The other side contained ketchup, mustard, mayo, and barbeque sauce packets. The tables were lined up neatly and there was a new ladder built and attached to the water tank stand. Su Li was stirring two large pots of gumbo and placing the pieces of albatross meat that were done onto large aluminum cake pans. Ophilia Parker told them dinner would consist of gumbo, albatross meat, cornbread, and a fruit salad containing peaches, pineapple and mango.

Outside Iva Rotge was just getting back to the cave with the twenty women she had led to the shower. Janie watched as she gave Nigel French a shirt which had a large amount of shedded hair from the ladies brushings. He in turn took the hair to Chun Li who was stirring a large pot of mortar he was making for the pottery oven construction. He was surrounded by the large stones he would build it with. It was an interesting process to watch as Chun Li seemed to know the exact stone to grab each time. Within twenty minutes of preparing the mortar mix, the stone pottery oven was complete. Mr. Li returned inside, washed his hands, and took Su's place at the grill. Ophilia Parker came back over and said, "Just look at that. Mr. Li thinks no one can run that oven like he can. To tell the truth as good as his food tastes, he's probably right." Then she walked away giggling.

Upon entering the cave, Iva Rotge joined Janie, Marah and Claudette's table. She asked them if they would wait until after dinner to go shower. She knew already that the Parker sisters and Su Li wanted to go at that time and Iva hoped to make the trip only one more time today. The ladies agreed this was a good idea. Janie informed Iva of her husband's success with the mower and the door for their new dwelling. Iva then excused herself to go see for herself.

As soon as Jack and Harold had finished the last bench, they joined the ladies. Arianna got off her mother's lap and walked over to them. She held up her hand and said, "Look Jack, I got a boo boo. Something loud happened and I falled on a horn." Marah immediately corrected her child, "No Arianna. Not a horn, a thorn." Arianna continued, "It went in this side and commed out that side. I had to go to the doctor but I didn't get a shot."

Saddened by the child's accident Jack replied, "Oh I'm sorry you got hurt. I hope it will feel better soon." He looked at Marah and asked what had happened. Marah explained the mower being started the first time had startled Arianna who thought she could run through the undergrowth to where she and Janie had been working. Marah was touched by his concern as well as by her daughter's growing friendship with this kind gentleman.

Harold, who had been looking at Janie since he sat down asked, "Sweetheart, are you okay? You look very pale."

Janie answered, "I think so. I am just tired, and I got sick when Arianna got hurt. I have become very fond of her and I think that must have been a contributing factor. It is unlike me to be sickened by the sight of an injury. But on a lighter note, Marah and I finished planting the squash and cucumbers. Then we planted probably 80 feet of corn along the pathway here. Don't worry about me. After dinner and a shower, I will be as good as new."

Habib soon joined the group. He asked Jack and Harold, "What do you think about helping me after dinner shoot some coconuts down from their trees. They are the only kind of fruit we have very little access to. Sanjay told me Doctor Goodson talked a lot about being able to make flour and cooking oil from them. Nearly the whole trip back to his office with Mr. Patel this morning, the doctor spoke of the multiple benefits of this healthy fruit, not to mention the promised coconut cream pies afterward. There's a good sized grove of coconut trees about half way to the falls. Come on guys, it would be fun. Will you help?"

Jack and Harold nodded at each other. Jack said, "Sure we will help. But what will we do with the coconuts that we shoot holes in?"

Habib said, "We will take a cake pan to sit the damaged ones in pointing the holes upright. We can take a couple of the heavy duty trash bags to carry the undamaged coconuts to Doctor Goodson to begin his process. We can leave the damaged ones here at the kitchen for the ladies to use however they choose."

"Sounds like a plan," replied Jack.

At this time the group was joined by Iva and Guillaume Rotge. Iva thanked Jack and Harold for helping her husband install the door on his shop. Then Guillaume began telling Jack and Harold of the successful day he had. He told them he fixed one of the mowers and had mowed the pathway. He believed by noonish the next day he could have one of the generators pieced back together. There was a possibility he would be able to finish fixing the gas powered welder by tomorrow evening. He wondered if the LED lighting from the planes' wreckage could be installed inside the cave and run off the repaired generator. Rotge quizzed Jack and Harold as to their thoughts on a mixture of jet fuel and hydraulic oil being even closely related to gasoline and 2 stroke oil. It might be the only way to power up the weed eaters. He hoped to modify one of the weed eaters by adding one of the lawn mower blades to the shaft and using it for a trolling motor. They would need that when they finished the small shrimp boat he was planning from a small portion of the tail section cargo hold once the section disassembly was complete. He reminded them the boat would only be a dream if he could not repair the welder but the possibility intrigued him. All within earshot agreed his ideas were exciting.

More people began to pour into the cafeteria. Chun Li was beginning to dish up tonight's dinner. Many got both gumbo and albatross. All got cornbread and fruit salad. Again the meal was as though it came from a five star restaurant with the perfect amount of herbs and spices. The kitchen was equipped heavily with all the spices imaginable in quantities that should last for years. Sanjay was served first. He walked away with two water bottles full of sweet tea strapped around his waist. He carried two plates full of gumbo, albatross meat and cornbread. He also held two pint sized freezer bags full of fruit salad. Jokingly, Jack said, "Hey man, save some for us."

Sanjay laughed aloud and answered, "These two dinners I am taking back to the camp for Doctor Goodson and Mr. Patel. I will be back to eat my dinner here after I make my delivery."

"Thank you Sanjay. I didn't even think about them," said Jack. Habib said, "Li's a better man than I am. After Patel tried to kill him this morning, if it were me, I would have let him go hungry." No one commented on Habib's statement.

After all were served their meal and a few had seconds, Ophilia Parker announced the kitchen would close for the day once everything was cleaned up. There were no left overs to store. The staff planned to place all the solar lights outside for recharging and place the firewood for tomorrow morning's cooking inside. Her bones could feel rainy weather coming. She claimed her aching joints could predict the weather better than a meteorologist. Some of the ladies who had already showered pitched in to help so the Parker sisters and Su Li could join the last group of ladies to shower for the day. Twenty minutes later Iva Rotge led 12 more ladies to the water fall to shower.

While the ladies were making their way to the fall, they were passing where Habib, Jack and Harold were trying to shoot the coconuts out of the trees. After watching them miss with five shots in a row, Iva approached the men and asked, "May I?"

The men looked at each other and agreed. Jack said, "Sure." He handed her the semi-automatic 22 caliber rifle he held.

Iva said, "Everyone watch your heads." She lifted the gun to her shoulder and emptied the magazine. When she had finished, around 50 coconuts lay on the ground. Habib sat next to the fruit rubbing his head. After asking if he was okay, the whole group erupted into laughter.

Before the ladies moved on to the shower Jenny Parker said to the men, "As you gentlemen head back toward the camp later, there is a trash bag half full of albatross bones just inside the cave entrance. Please throw the bones into the quicksand pit. We don't need to draw wildlife to our kitchen, and you need to find someone capable of climbing the coconut trees rather than using up the valuable ammunition. You will never be able to replace the wasted bullets you know."

Feeling like a scolded child, Jack said, "Yes ma'am. We will." The ladies then walked on. Before Jack, Harold and Habib got all the coconuts loaded into the bags they were already hearing squeals coming from the shower area. They decided to take the coconuts to the cave. They would also place the guns back into their hiding place. Then after the ladies returned from the fall, they would go and shower.

Back at the cave, Chun Li and Nigel French were already making progress on the first wall of the Li's home. Amazingly the wall was already waist high and this time they were mortaring as they went. Jack complimented them and asked if they needed help. Nigel translated and Chun Li accepted the offer. Li then began spreading mortar all across the top of the wall they were building. French then translated that Li would point to what stone went where when brought to the wall. He, himself, would control the mortar. By the time the ladies had returned 45 minutes later, the first wall was 7 feet tall in the front and 6 1/2 feet tall at the rear. This was intentional to make water drain to the rear of the structure during rain storms. Mr. Li had cleaned out his mortar pan and the men sat on the river bank resting. Su Li instantly walked over to her husband, pointing in the direction of the wall and hugged him. Then she began speaking again in Chinese to him pointing him toward the shower. After two more times of her tapping him on the shoulder and pointing, Chun Li stood up and got Nigel French to ask if the guys were ready to go and shower. Understanding what Li was not saying, French, Jack, Harold, and Habib all got up to follow Chun Li. As they were leaving, Guillaume Rotge and Doctor Goodson shouted at them from the path asking where they were going. They joined the group. The doctor said Sanjay had offered to stay with Mr. Patel for an hour or two so he could have a badly needed break. A shower would be just the breath of fresh air that he needed.

When they returned one hour later, the cave was empty. Everyone had gone back to the camp. Jack and Doctor Goodson had decided to leave half of the coconuts at the cave. They would bring the other 25 to the doctor's quarters for him to work on tomorrow. Along the way they would dispose of the Albatross bones. Harold and Jack asked Chun Li for he and his wife to sleep in the upper nose section where they were. Doctor Goodson felt sure Mr. Patel could not get to them there in his current condition. Everything had been decided and soon all were in their chosen nightly quarters feeling it had over all been a successful day.

CHAPTER FOURTEEN

PASSION AND PROGRESS

The following morning, Chun Li woke Jack and Harold early. Using the pocket translator now in his possession, he asked the two men to accompany him to the cave. They could start the coffee and relax for a bit before breakfast had to be prepared. A soft yet soaking rain had fallen over night. The three men were grateful for the mowing efforts of Guillaume Rotge from the day before as the path barely wet their shoes. They all remembered the foot care instructions given them by Doctor Goodson just days before.

Upon arrival, Chun Li asked Jack and Harold to use the bucket to draw enough water to fill his largest four pans to be boiled for usage. He would go inside and replace the newly charged solar lights and start the fire. After placing the lights back in their original spots, Chun Li noticed the metal shield which covered the front of the grill had been moved about six inches at the bottom. Having been married for many years to a detail oriented woman, Li was bewildered at the displacement. With his instincts telling him to beware, he removed the top cover of the grill. He jumped back in fear and drew a deep rapid breath at what lurked inside.

From outside, all Jack and Harold heard was first the sound of metal crashing followed by the sound a martial arts expert would make prior to delivering the fatal blow. Moments later, Chun Li exited the cave carrying the shovel he normally used to move the coals from the fire pit to the grill. The shovel held the approximately eight inch head of a large Boa Constrictor. Jack and Harold listened closely as the translator helped Li explain that dinner for today had delivered itself. The snake had curled up inside the grill over night. He would need them to help him stretch the snake's body out for cutting into steak sized portions. The head needed to be thrown into the quicksand pit. These tasks needed to be moved to the top of the list to avoid instilling terror into his kitchen helpers. When stretched out the body measured some 16 feet in length. Ten minutes later the snake had yielded 75 salad plate sized steaks. Once cut in half, there would be 150 New York Strip sized meat portions, the perfect amount for tonight's dinner. The steaks were placed into a large pan and sat down in the wooden crate submerged in the water just outside the cave for chilling until dinner time.

Then the fire was built. The water was boiled for coffee, tea, and to prepare today's milk mixture. The day's food menu had been decided as breakfast: sweet buttered rice and fruit, dinner: snake steak, mashed potatoes, and corn. Chun Li had planned to use the majority of his day to work on his house. The simplicity of the day's chosen cuisine would allow him the free time to do so.

The three men had time to enjoy their first cup of coffee before Su Li and the Parker sisters arrived to begin work. Jack, Harold and Chun Li had discussed the roof for the Li's home. One piece of the roofing material was already detached from the tail section. Jack felt confident the other piece could be ready by mid day. They planned to furnish the home with two passenger seats and two over head cabinets . Chun Li had requested they also provide the metal to finish Elizabeth French's pottery oven. He would need one slotted piece for the middle shelf, a solid piece for both the top and the front. Li would ask Nigel French to help him with the home construction when he arrived.

Back at the camp, Janie, Marah, and Arianna were just exiting the nose section cargo hold. Doctor Goodson had been sitting outside his office waiting for them to emerge. He said, "Good morning ladies. How is her hand doing? If you don't mind, I would like to check it and change the bandage."

Marah answered, "She hasn't complained about it hurting since just after the accident, but yes, I would like for you to recheck it." Doctor Goodson could barely take his eyes off Marah while examining the child's wound. While trying to strike up a conversation with them, the doctor commented on how lovely they were even upon just waking up. Nigel and Elizabeth French walked by and smiled at the doctor obviously stumbling over his own words revealing his growing crush on Marah.

"Good morning doctor, ladies," Nigel said as he tipped his hat to them in passing. Then he and Elizabeth disappeared down the path to the cave. After the bandage was changed, the ladies and Arianna would visit the restroom before making their way to the cave. This meant Nigel and Elizabeth were about 20 minutes ahead of them.

Jack and Harold, having already eaten, ran into the French's at lookout cliff. They told Nigel Chun Li wanted him to help with his house and about the snake this morning. Then Nigel French told his friend Jack, "By the way, old boy, you may want to step up your game. I have noticed the way your face lights up when you are around the young Marah. I thought you might want to know the doctor is showing the same kind of interest in her. You may already have the upper hand as the child seems to have taken a shine to you. All I can say old chap is may the best man win."

Jack let out a concerned giggle and said, "I will certainly keep that in mind." Jack shook Nigel's hand and they all went on toward their destinations.

Ten minutes later Jack and Harold met up with Janie, Marah and Arianna. As soon as she saw them, Arianna jerked away from Marah's hand and ran, jumping into Jack's arms, hugging his neck. She said, "Hi Jack. Look I got new bandaids on my boo boo. It don't hurt much. Look." She moved her hand back and forth making a fist.

The very surprised Marah was soon by their side offering her apologies. "I am so sorry Jack," she said as she tried to take Arianna from him.

With the child's arms now in a death grip around his neck, Jack said with a smile, "Really, it's okay. Arianna, I am glad you are feeling better. I was wondering how you were today. Now you mind your manners and be a good girl for your mother today." He put the child down after returning her bear hug.

"She has never been so open to a stranger as she is with you. Honestly, I don't know what has come over her," Marah stated.

"Apparently she sees me as a friend, and that's just fine with me," Jack said, smiling.

Harold told them about the Boa this morning and reminded them to be mindful of their surroundings. Janie asked Harold to bring a trash bag full of sand back to the cave when they transported the metal for the Li's roof later in the afternoon. She wanted to clean the sandbox toilets at the restroom next to the cave. They would need more sand than she and Marah could carry. Harold promised to fill the order and they were off in separate directions.

As Janie, Marah and Arianna continued down the path to the cave, Janie's curiosity got the best of her. She said to Marah, "It looks like after your bereavement period, you will have suitors waiting."

"What do you mean?" asked Marah.

Janie answered, "Well, Jack is obviously taken with you and Arianna, and the doctor could barely complete a sentence this morning when talking to you. It shows badly that he has a big crush on you."

Marah laughed and said, "Well, I have plenty of time to choose a mate. It is my family tradition that a widow or widower spend one full year honoring the memory of their past loved one. After that time they are free to resume life as a single individual. Therefore I am in no hurry. Besides that, Jack is clearly a married man. He wears his ring of marriage showing he is clearly attached."

Janie immediately felt panic and desperation spread over her. She had already imagined that she and Harold would raise their future children along side their dear friends, Jack and Marah. She felt it would not be the same if Marah married anyone else. She began her plea to Marah with a lie. She said, "Jack and Janet have been separated for some time now." Then Janie followed the statement with the truth. "Janet is a cruel hearted individual. She has never been affectionate to Jack or their children. She has taught her children that their father is only their provider and doesn't allow them to hug him or anyone else. She is so determined to use her children to climb the social ladder that she has been having an ongoing affair with an Olympic soccer coach for over a year now. The only playing the children are allowed is when Johnny is on the soccer field or Amy is seated at the piano. Janet is nothing like you and me. Over the years I have wondered if she was born without an emotional heart. Jack is only still married to her for moral and religious concerns."

Marah replied, "Oh how sad. He seems like a very kind man. I was taught if your spouse commits adultery against you, one may submit a writing of divorcement and be restored once again to the life of a single person. Do his beliefs prohibit that?"

Janie said, "I believe it is allowed. He just hasn't done that yet. She has broken his heart many times during their relationship. I have wondered through the years if her constant abuse has robbed him of the ability to take up for himself. I would love to see him walk next to a lady with such a beautiful heart as yours. Joy and kindness are evident in all you do. I hope you will at least consider my dear friend as a candidate in the running for your hand in the future."

"If he finds a way to divorce the monster you described, I will at least consider it," Marah stated. Feeling as though she had laid the necessary ground work for Jack's future happiness, Janie changed the subject. She asked Marah if she had ever eaten snake before. The question launched a conversation which would last until they arrived at the cave for breakfast.

As they approached the cave entrance they could hear lots of chatter. They were surprised to see upon entering that nearly all the tables were full of people. There was food, drinks, laughter and conversation everywhere. As they made their way to the serving area, Janie heard different conversations about how nice the dinning hall was, how the food was again delicious, and people talking about the snake. It felt as though they were back in the city in a fancy popular restaurant of some sort. After gathering their food, Janie, Marah and Arianna joined the French's for breakfast and conversation.

Before long Iva and Guillaume Rotge entered the dining area and approached their table. Guillaume carried what looked to be the bottom base of a push mower with things attached to it. He said to Nigel and Elizabeth, "We are proud to present you with this very low tech semi automatic pottery wheel. I believe you will find it helpful in your efforts to create enough dishes for a crowd this size."

The French's stood to examine the contraption. It consisted of the base of a mower with the shaft still attached that would have held the missing blades, a pair of vise grips, a large number of thick rubber bands, several plastic ties, and two round thick plastic pan like spheres. Before Guillaume could explain, Iva declared, "First you should know my husband refuses to travel without a gallon bag full of thick rubber bands and an equal amount of plastic strip ties."

Guillaume said, "It is my belief that a man can survive anything if he can provide himself a sling shot. So other than the stick handle and the rock ammo, I go prepared. That being said, your pottery wheel comes equipped with it's own table. Beneath the table begins the shaft. Inserted into the slots in the shaft which formerly held the blades you will notice multiple layers of rubber band which has been stretched tightly. Above the rubber bands there is a thick plastic plate. Clamped onto the plate you see vise grips that are attached via plastic strip ties to the table base. Two inches above table top there is the plastic pan to create the dishes upon. Granted the device won't turn for long, but it is free rolling and will turn longer than you would expect. The vise grip tips you will note have been covered with our very own tooth brush covers to add resistance to the lower plastic pan. This will make it take longer for the rotation to finish. You should at least be able to shape the circle for the outside of a cup or plate by using it. I hope it will be useful." Nigel French shook Rotge's hand and Elizabeth hugged him and Iva. Then the Rotge's went to get their breakfast and returned to join them.

Iva asked Janie and Marah what their plans for the day were. Janie answered, "We were going to continue planting today and clean both restrooms."

Iva asked, "Do you want some help? Elizabeth, do you want to help me. You and I could team up and Janie and Marah could as well. We could work on opposite sides of the pathway and see how far we could get before Captain Wellington gets the metal for the pottery oven cut out. I promise to help you gather the materials for the first dishes this afternoon."

Elizabeth said, "It sounds like a plan to me." The four ladies ate and were soon on their way to the camp to gather seeds. They would ask Claudette to keep Arianna so she and Pierre could play together.

Back at the camp the ladies were surprised to see Mr. Patel sitting on the beach with Sanjay. Doctor Goodson was outside his office working to open some of the coconuts he had volunteered to turn into flour and oil. He was pouring the coconut milk into water bottles. He had one of the aluminum cake pans from the cave nearly half full of fresh coconut. Elizabeth French asked, "Excuse me Doctor Goodson, but after yesterday's encounter with Mr. Patel I have to ask what is his demeanor today? Also what are you going to do with all that coconut?"

The doctor answered, "He seems much calmer today and maybe a little more coherent. He has been better after Sanjay stayed with him yesterday evening while I went and showered. Sanjay told me he explained to Mr. Patel his beliefs on our whereabouts and that rescues of that magnitude can take weeks or months. He also told him we have to live here together until that time. Only then can he have his concerns about Captain Wellington addressed by the authorities. It has helped greatly to calm his nerves even more than any medication I had tried. As far as the coconut, it needs to be placed in the sun on the aluminum pan to dry out to be crushed into coconut flour."

Elizabeth French stated, "I nearly needed nerve medicine for Nigel yesterday after he realized Patel had shoved me down. But it's like I told him, Mr. Patel wept uncontrollably for a period before trying to hurt the chef saying he would never see his family again. The man is grieving terribly as are many of us but we must try to stick it out until we are rescued. And in the event that we are never found, well I am pretty sure we could have crashed in a much worse place with worse people. We need to make this paradise our home, be it temporary or permanent."

"Honestly, Mrs. French, I couldn't have said it better myself," replied Doctor Goodson. He continued, "Personally I disagree with Mr. Patel's take on the circumstances surrounding the crash. I believe our esteemed pilot had nothing to do with our whereabouts. I truly do believe him."

"So do I," replied Elizabeth as she went on to rejoin the other three ladies.

The ladies chose to plant beans across the pathway from the corn that was planted yesterday. Iva Rotge suggested they add sweet pea seeds to the row of corn already planted. She said, "If I know Guillaume, he will keep the pathway mowed. We don't need him mowing our crops down, so we need the peas to run up the corn stalks instead of across the pathway."

About three hours later they had just finished tying a string above their 80 feet of newly planted vegetables when Jack and Harold came along. They were pulling a sled full of metal for the Li's rooftop and the metal to finish the pottery oven. They also brought along two airplane seats, two over head cabinets and a large trash bag of sand. Harold smiled at Janie and said, "Most of the sand will be for the restrooms but I feel sure Chun Li may need some of it for his mortar mix. He won't need very much though. Oh and Mrs. Rotge, your husband will probably be along shortly behind us. He was finishing the repair on the welder, or at least he was hoping so. Jack and I helped him to load it onto the other sled in case he is successful. If so we will weld the Li's roof together and tomorrow we will weld the roofs of the shed, the doctors office and you guys shop/quarters."

Iva Rotge answered, "Oh that's good. I will go and see if he needs any help. Thank you." She then disappeared down the path back to camp.

Jack had stopped to talk to Marah. After what Nigel French had told him that morning about Doctor Goodson showing interest in her, he now planned to talk to her at every opportunity. He began by saying, "Marah, here is a picture that Arianna asked me to deliver to you. When we were coming down the beach to the path, she ran up and gave it to me after asking Claudette's permission. It's like I said earlier, I believe she sees me as her friend."

Marah thanked Jack and looked at the drawing. It appeared to be two stick people, one large and one small, with a pile of circles between them. Marah said, "Wow, I wonder what she was drawing."

Jack smiled and said, "She told me the drawing was of you and her with a pile of snow balls between you. She says you two have only seen snow on TV or through windows but never got to play in it. According to her this is a someday picture. I thought it was sweet. We all need those someday dreams. Don't you agree?"

Marah held the drawing to her heart and said, "Yes absolutely. I, too, have many of those someday pictures etched into my mind. With proper faith and hard work sometimes those someday pictures can come to life. Thank you so much for bringing it to me."

Harold, fearing Jack would talk all afternoon given the chance, said, "Janie, if you are finished with them for now, may I take the claw hammer and screw driver you have been using. We may need them while installing Mr. Li's roof." Janie, Marah, Iva and Elizabeth had been clipping the grass away from the planting areas and then using the screw driver and hammer to make individual holes for the seeds. The ground was hard and difficult to deal with otherwise.

Janie smiled and said, "Just don't forget where you got them from."

Then she handed Harold the tools and he said, "Come on Jack. I bet when we get there the Li's will give us a cold glass of tea for our efforts." Jack nodded his head and said, "Very well then. Ladies, until we meet again." Jack and Harold continued on their journey to deliver and use the materials they had in tow.

Janie, Marah and Elizabeth French headed back toward camp to clean that restroom. The sand bag toilets would need to be dumped. The plates of sand to cover the waste needed to be refilled. The wiping rags currently soaking in bleach water needed washing out and hung out to dry, and new bleach water needed to be made. Once completed, they would head to the cave to repeat the process at the other rest room. Marah would relieve Claudette and take Arianna along with them to the cave.

Meanwhile, Jack and Harold were surprised to see how much progress Nigel French and Chun Li had made on the Li's house. To go along with the wall built yesterday now stood a second completed wall which included a window opening and a third wall about 70% complete. Chun Li was pleased to see the sand. He asked Nigel to convey the message that he needed to stop and mix more mortar. He needed the three of them to gather a few more stones while he prepared the mixture. It shouldn't take more than fifteen minutes. There was no shortage of available stones to bring back to the construction area. By the time Chun Li was finished, there were more than enough stones to finish the wall and build two 4 foot mini walls on each side of the front. Su Li had told Chun to put the door in the center of the front wall. He felt a four foot opening was a good start while he figured out how to build a door for the house.

As they were finishing all the stone work on the front walls, Guillaume and Iva Rotge arrived with welder in tow. Chun Li excused himself to go and start dinner. Guillaume explained that he had run into a minor problem with the welder. After going through his own trouble shooting routine he had discovered the carburetor was malfunctioning and the fuse had blown. Luckily, the parts were available on the best of the two generators he had tried to piece together. The welder was now usable. However to be able to provide the kitchen with a working generator, both parts would have to be on the generator rather than the welder. In finishing, Rotge said, "So today a welder, tomorrow a generator."

Jack, Harold, Guillaume Rotge, and Nigel French decided they should be able, with enough man power, to lift the entire roof onto the house after the metal was welded together. After the welds were complete, they would find Habib and Sanjay to help. They were sure Chun Li would help, and they could ask any of the other men to join them as well. They couldn't have timed it better. By the time the welding was done, the aroma of dinner cooking had begun to draw a crowd to the cave. There was no shortage of manpower to help set the roof. Knowing the rock would be too hard to drill into, Chun Li had built rope into the walls. Two feet from the top of the walls in multiple places he had placed a six foot section of rope. Using the drill, holes had already been made in the metal to put the rope through to tie it securely to the structure. As they were tying the last knot, Chun Li came to let them know dinner was ready. He was followed by his wife. He was elated to see his home now had a roof. Su Li, however being a stickler for detail noticed a spot in the ceiling where daylight shined through one of the seams. She patted Jack on the shoulder and said in broken English, "You eat, then you fix!" She pointed toward the crack in the roof. Jack nodded as he said, "Yes ma'am," having no clue if she understood or not. Then they all went inside the cave to eat.

Dinner was delicious once again. Even though many had never eaten snake meat before, no one complained about anything. Some compared the taste to chicken, others pork. Jack and his group of roofers had barely swallowed the last bite when Su Li approached their table and said to Jack, "You fix now!" as she took the plate from in front of him.

Jack said, "Well gentlemen, I think we have just been invited to leave." As they got up to go back to work, they were discussing the roof repair. Being unsure of the roof's weight bearing capabilities, the men decided the smallest among them should go up to do the repair. Due to his size, Habib drew the short straw.

There was a lot of movement in the area. Being still short on table space in the dining hall, the hungry were entering and the full were exiting. Jack's crew felt since the home was set off to the side, it would still be safe to complete the repair now. After the men hoisted Habib up onto the roof, they realized the hose that led to the welding rod would not reach. Guillaume Rotge and Sanjay automatically stepped in and lifted the welder above their heads to allow the wand to reach the repair area. A few moments later chaos erupted.

As Habib was finishing the repair on the roof, a hot coal flew off and hit Claudette in the head as she and Pierre were exiting the cave. She screamed as her hair began to burn. Janie and Marah, walking along side her, began instantly to beat the fire out. Her scream had startled Habib who stood up immediately to see what had happened. His feet got wrapped around the welder hose and he fell. He landed so hard on the bedrock below he cracked his head open and was rendered unconscious. Upon his impact, the pistol he still carried fired a shot hitting the child, Pierre, in the leg. Simultaneously Sanjay and Rotge dropped the welder which landed on Sanjay's foot leaving a broken bone protruding through the skin. To magnify the situation, Doctor Goodson was still at the camp with Mr. Patel. Sanjay had been supposed to take their dinner back to them after eating.

Having gone to high school together Jack knew Harold to be not only a track star but a fast long distance runner. He said to Harold, "You came in fifth in a marathon race. You are the fastest guy I know. Please hurry and get Doctor Goodson here as fast as you can." Without a word, Harold took off running down the path to the camp. Janie and

Marah were attempting to help Claudette and Pierre. Iva Rotge and Elizabeth French were providing cold wet towels to apply pressure to all open wounds. Guillaume Rotge held a compress to Sanjay's foot. Jack and Nigel French tried to hold Habib's wound closed with one of the towels to attempt to slow the bleeding. Elizabeth and Iva then took Marah's place along side Pierre as Arianna had begun to cry uncontrollably. The twenty minutes it would take for the doctor to arrive seemed like hours.

Doctor Goodson could not believe the crowd that was gathered around the wounded. He had trouble pushing through the people, many of them crying, some praying, some talking about the possibility of all the crash survivors being cursed. The one thing that no one seemed to be willing to do was let the doctor past. By the time he had made it to the accident scene, Doctor Goodson had been angered to the point of shouting. He yelled, "Everyone please step back. Ladies, please take your crying children somewhere that I can't hear them. I have four badly injured people to take care of and I can't hear myself think! Everyone please just give me some space."

Jack asked Nigel French to keep the pressure on the towel on Habib's head. He stood up and said loud enough for all to hear, "Please anyone who has not yet eaten go on into the dining hall. We will update any of you who go back to camp as to the condition of the injured. Thank you all for your concern and cooperation." Jack felt he had to try to ease the nerves of the hurt feelings caused by the doctor's words. More importantly he had to calm the tempers of those who the doctor had angered. There had been enough drama for one day without adding in fighting among the residents. Jack asked Doctor Goodson, "Where's Harold?"

Doctor Goodson answered, "He should be here shortly. He is gathering some gauze, antiseptic, bandages and pain medication for me. I brought everything I could quickly throw into my doctor's bag." The doctor did a quick check on everyone before deciding where to start. Habib was still unconscious and the towel being held on his wound was blood covered. Doctor Goodson commended Jack and Nigel on the job they had done applying pressure to Habib's head wound. The bleeding had obviously slowed. The doctor gave Nigel French four large wound bandages and asked that he now use them to apply the pressure so they could judge the current amount of blood loss. He moved on to Sanjay who was closest to Habib. He asked Guillaume Rotge to find a way to elevate the foot and keep the towel wrapped around it until he could get back to him. He made his way to Pierre and Claudette. Pierre's leg had both entrance and exit wounds through his middle thigh. From appearances sake he seemed to have no broken bones. He could stand, although painful, and had been kicking and screaming when Doctor Goodson had arrived. The doctor handed Iva Rotge and Elizabeth French antibiotic cream and two bandages and asked them to put the cream on both bandages and hold them against both sides of the wound until he could get back to him. Then he turned to the last of the injured, Claudette, now bald and badly burned on one whole side of her head. The lady was apparently in shock as she lay staring aimlessly into space as Janie slowly poured cup after cup of cold water over the open wound. Doctor Goodson thanked God and Janie aloud for Janie having not laid a towel on the deep burns. "A towel would have stuck to the wound without burn ointment to prevent it," the doctor said while clipping singed hair away from the edge of the wound. He continued, "I must clean the hair away from the outer edge so that the bandage will hold. The bandages have a smoother texture than the towels and along side the ointment we will have a much better result."

By the time Doctor Goodson had finished clipping the hair, Harold had arrived with the supplies. First the doctor gave Claudette and Sanjay a pain pill. Then after giving Pierre children's liquid pain medication, he looked at the child and said, "We may as well start with you." Harold had come over to be by Janie's side and help out if needed. The doctor began explaining what was about to happen, "Janie I will need you to hold the child's torso. Harold you will need to hold very firmly both of his legs. I saw him kicking and throwing a fit a few minutes ago and I bet he could out-kick a mule. I need to clean the wound with antiseptic first. It burns like fire and I have to pour it as deeply as I can into both sides of the wound. Then we cover both ends with antibiotic cream, bandage it and hope for the best. Oh and by the way, more than likely we will be done with the procedure long before it will stop burning so he will probably still be crying and fighting. It's going to be a rough ride, so hang on tight. Okay, let's do this." Everything went exactly as the doctor had described and he wasted no time moving to the next victim.

Iva and Elizabeth had stepped over to Claudette's side when the doctor had asked Janie and Harold for help with Pierre. The doctor addressed them saying, "Awe, but all is not lost for those whose stomachs will allow them to help. As you heard, ladies, the antiseptic burns on it's own. With limited resources I will be forced to use it to clean Claudette's burn as well. I must clip away any charred skin and wash it once again. Then I have to apply burn ointment to the entire wound and bandage it. Could you two ladies lend me a hand or do I need to look for stronger stomachs?" Iva and Elizabeth agreed to help. Doctor Goodson began to give instructions, "Mrs. Rotge, sit across Claudette's body and pin her arms to her side using your legs to hold them firmly. Mrs. French, I need you to hold her head completely still until the procedure is complete." Doctor Goodson then checked to make sure he had all the necessary supplies within arm's reach and said, "Let us begin." Claudette let out a blood curdling scream when the antiseptic was applied. Harold had to jump in and help hold her down. Five minutes later when he had finished, the doctor apologized for the pain he had caused her and told her that he no longer believed her to be in shock.

Next Doctor Goodson asked Jack to retrieve for him 5 or 6 ten inch pieces of cigar sized bamboo for splints for Sanjay's foot. He suggested Jack bring what ever he used to cut the bamboo back with him so the pieces could be better sized when working on the foot. He would recheck Habib while Jack was gone. The doctor went over to Habib. He asked Nigel French to help him roll Habib onto his stomach so he could better examine his head. While doing so Habib never even moaned. Immediately afterward, Nigel French was sickened at the sight of a gaping wound across the entire back of Habib's head with bright white shiny bone showing in it's center. Doctor Goodson seemed annoyed at the turn of events and barked out, "Can I get someone over here to help me please! Nigel, really man, good God." Harold and Iva went to help the doctor while Elizabeth rushed to her husband's side who was still vomiting. The French's soon walked over to Claudette and Pierre and sat down. Doctor Goodson stitched up Habib's head leaving an opening for any further drainage.

Jack returned with the requested bamboo splints. He helped the doctor measure and cut each one to the needed length to hold Sanjay's foot in place after they set the bone. They would wrap it in gauze around the splints until the swelling had a chance to go down. At that time it could be casted as there were four casting kits among the medical supplies.

When all the patients were tended to, Chun Li approached Nigel French and asked him to translate. Li offered to bring four of the table benches into his new house for the wounded to lie down on. Su Li was blaming herself for wanting the crack in the roof fixed and it causing so much pain. Chun Li said it would please them very much for the injured to recuperate there. The doctor agreed that was a good idea and went inside to eat leaving the recuperation area set up to the others.

Soon the benches were moved and the wounded made comfortable. Pierre was small for a five year old and fit nicely on one of the smaller benches from the ends of the tables. There were three longer benches installed for the adults. Along with two plane seats and two over head cabinets stacked to be a table between the seats. The Li's 12 x 12 foot house was full yet not crowded. Iva Rotge and Janie decided to watch over the wounded until the doctor returned.

Jack, Harold, Guillaume Rotge, Nigel and Elizabeth French went into the dining hall to join Doctor Goodson. Nigel's stomach had settled and at Elizabeth's request he got a bowl of fruit salad. Jack told the doctor the patients were now resting inside the Li house. Doctor Goodson seemed much calmer now after eating. He said, "Thank you all for your help. I could not have done it without you. I worked as an emergency room physician during my residency so I am no stranger to treating multiple patients at the same time. But in this setting with no trained medical personel to assist me, I kind of freaked out at first. With that being said, we have a lot to be concerned with. These people will need round the clock care and obviously I cannot do it all alone. Not to mention Mr. Patel. I cannot be in two places at the same time and bringing him here after he attacked Chun Li is no option. I need someone to volunteer to take him his meals and see to it that he gets the medication necessary to keep him calm while his multiple wounds heal." No one said a word so the doctor continued, "I fear that Habib may have bleeding on the brain or it could be coma or maybe even a severe concussion. He lost a great deal of blood but if there is no internal bleeding, I believe he stands a strong chance of recovery. Pierre is young and healthy and should heal nicely barring any complications from infection. Infection complications are an across the board worry with them all but especially Claudette with the burns she sustained. Then there's Sanjay. With no x-ray equipment available, chances are his foot will not heal properly and his walking could be altered permanently. That's the way it is. I still need your help. Who can I count on to do what?"

Harold spoke first, "I will take what ever shift needed up here, but I am not doing anything for Mr. Patel. He blames Jack and anyone associated with him for the crash. Even while I was gathering the supplies he said if I wasn't trying to help his only friend, Sanjay, he would kill me right there for my involvement in the crash. I plan to try to stay away from the psycho."

Elizabeth French said, "We will take care of Mr. Patel."

An instantly angry Nigel French jumped to his feet and yelled at his wife, "WE MOST CERTAINLY WILL NOT! Dear Lord Elizabeth have you taken leave of your senses? When that monster knocked you down yesterday, did you learn nothing? No we will not be caring for Patel, but we will help with the injured. We will take care of them during the morning tomorrow and will take responsibility of the child until Claudette recovers, assuming she ever does. That is my final word on the subject." The look she gave her husband went from disgruntled to relief by the time his final words were spoken.

Guillaume Rotge then said, "Iva and I will take the grunt job. We are both trained military personel and have no fear of the demented. I will stay in the doctor's quarters with Patel and Iva can hold down the home fort. But all of you should know ahead of time I will be sleeping with a large wrench in my hand. If he starts anything, I plan to take him out."

Doctor Goodson said, "Well good. It's settled then. I need to speak with whoever of you has a great memory. I need a list of medications from my office to tend to the wounded here. Mr. Rotge can stand guard while the listed meds are gathered. Then Harold, if you would since you are fast on your feet, you can bring me the supplies and still have time to make it back to camp before dark. So if we are all in agreement, we should all start heading home for the evening. By the way, Mr. Patel will need to have dinner delivered and I have medications for him to take. I will tend to the injured over night and see you all in the morning." Doctor Goodson gave his list to Ophilia Parker who claimed to have a perfect memory. As a test he waited five minutes and asked her what he had said. She recited the list perfectly and all were off to the camp. Doctor Goodson moved five solar lights into the new hospital ward and sat down to watch over the injured.

Upon arrival at the doctor's office, Guillaume Rotge and Ophilia Parker wasted no time going in while Harold waited outside. Ophilia Parker seemed to take charge. She handed Mr. Patel his dinner and told him to eat while she raised him up on the bed and fluffed the duffle bag he was using as a pillow. Patel was grouchy and unappreciative. He asked, "Just what part did the pilot play in the injuries today?"

She answered that Jack had no part in the chain reaction accident. Then in the firm voice of a parent correcting an unruly child, she told him, "You may as well just calm down. Accidents happen. You know in this life you play with the hand that's dealt you. Win, lose, or draw but one thing is for sure, folding is not an option. Now eat!" Ophilia turned and began to fill the list of supplies requested by the doctor. Patel continued to complain about the crash. Ophilia Parker, trying unsuccessfully to think because of his constant talking, said, "Mr. Patel, I realize that most men are cranky when hungry. I am trying to gather the supplies Doctor Goodson needs to help four badly injured people. I have to think. It would help both of us out if you would shut up and eat!"

Mr. Patel being very annoyed said, "No one wants to face the facts."

Ophilia Parker interrupted, "I really don't have time for this right now. Even your only friend, Sanjay, is wounded and needs these medical supplies. So from you, I need less talking and more chewing."

Mr. Patel seemed saddened by her statement and said, "Oh, that's right. Only for Sanjay's sake, I will shut up." She had soon finished filling the order and she quietly recited the order one more time checking the stack of supplies while doing so. She grabbed an empty suitcase from the corner of the room and placed everything inside, exited the room and handed the suitcase off to Harold for delivery.

Guilliam Rotge who had been standing in the doorway watching Ophilia Parker work her magic stepped inside and took a seat. He introduced himself and said, "Mr. Patel, I will be staying with you at night to take care of you until such time as the doctor can return to you. Please finish your dinner and let's try to get some rest. If you need anything just ask." Rotge played with the wheel on the large crescent wrench he planned to hold all night. Mr. Patel apparently understood the unspoken meaning behind the wrench and chose to not speak another word all night.

Jack checked his wrist watch when Harold returned to the camp. He said, "Fifteen minutes, huh, man you're slowing down in your old age."

Harold laughed at his friend's teasing and said, "I could have made it in eleven but the doctor wanted to talk too much. Anything happen while I was gone?"

Jack answered, "No other than me filling everyone in on the condition of the wounded. They were pleased it wasn't any worse." The two men kept talking while they made their way into the upper nose section where they now resided. Janie was waiting and handed her beloved Harold a bottle of water accompanied by a kiss. Out of respect for the Li's and the French's who shared the living quarters, they all settled down for the night feeling overwhelmed by the day's events.

CHAPTER FIFTEEN

THE UNEXPECTED

The following morning Jack, Harold and Chun Li again decided to go to the cave early. As they exited the upper nose section, Marah was sitting outside the entrance of the lower section crying. She was holding a pointed stick about the length of a baseball bat. Jack asked, "Marah, are you okay? What's wrong?"

Through her tears Marah answered, "You are not the only one having night mares. I had a warning dream last night and I must protect Arianna." Harold immediately went back up to tell Janie her friend was in distress. They soon returned. As Marah hugged Janie and held on she continued, "It was awful, Janie. Ragish was chasing me, he was going to kill me. Only his head was on a snake's body. As I ran from him in the dream, I looked back to see how close he was. The snake had now developed a second head, and when the head turned toward me it was Mr. Patel's head. My guardian angel is telling me that Mr. Patel and Ragish are cut from the same evil cloth. Janie, I cannot live in fear like I did for years under Ragish's rule. I cannot allow him to kill me and leave Arianna behind unprotected. I swear Janie, if he comes anywhere near me I will spear him through his wicked heart! The past nine days have been the most peaceful I have ever experienced and I can't live afraid any more. I just can't."

Janie looked Marah in the eye and said, "Marah it was just a dream. Starting tonight, if you are scared, you and Arianna can sleep up there with us. Even with the Li's and the French's there's still plenty of room for the two of you. I promise if we all stick together we will be fine." Harold and Jack both agreed and excused themselves to go help with the coffee and check on the wounded.

At the Li house by the cave, Doctor Goodson sat on a seat asleep, holding Habib's pistol for protection. He was startled to alertness by Habib. For the first time since the accident he had regained consciousness. He sat up, grabbed his head, and said, "Oh God." Rubbing his eyes, he looked around and asked, "Where am I? What happened and why does my head hurt so bad? Why do I have on a turban?" Painful moans of relief that Habib had finally woke up came from Sanjay and Claudette. Habib sat up, complained about being dizzy and said, "Doctor, I need your help. I have to go to the restroom NOW. I am not sure I can walk right now without falling. Please, I need help now."

Doctor Goodson helped Habib to his feet and began to explain what had happened while they walked to the nearby sand box restroom. By the time they got there, Habib was in tears feeling a great deal of responsibility for the injuries to the others. The doctor told him, "You don't need to be getting upset. Accidents happen and that is exactly what this is, a messed up group of accidents. No one could have seen this coming. I believe all of you stand a good chance of recovery." With his upset growing, Habib said, "What do you mean, chance of recovery? Are you saying because of my stupidity someone could die?"

The doctor answered, "Listen to me Habib, you had no control over the direction the welding coals would fly or when anyone would exit the dining hall. No one bears any responsibility for what happened yesterday. It was a chain reaction accident, period. Now if you are finished, I need to get you back in bed." The two then returned to the Li house.

As they entered the ward, Habib's weeping woke Pierre. The child was angered at the sight of Habib and shouted, "Mister, why are you so mean? You set my Grandma on fire and shot my leg? Why did you hurt us? We didn't do nothing to you? I hate you."

Habib sobbed uncontrollably at the five year old's words and said, "I'm so sorry Pierre. I would never have hurt you or your Grandma on purpose. I am so so sorry."

All the wounded were now awake. Claudette sat up and said, "Pierre, that's enough. It was an accident that we were all hurt."

The distraught child replied, "But Grandma, you told me that accidents only happen once, and he hurt three people. How can that be an accident?"

Sanjay spoke up and said, "Pierre, Habib did not hurt me. I dropped the welder on my foot myself. He did not throw fire on your Grandma. The wind did that."

Pierre, still crying said, "Then why did he shoot my leg? I hate him."

Claudette repeated, "Pierre, I said that's enough." After being called down for the second time the child quieted down. Doctor Goodson gave each a dose of medication to help ease their pain and calm their nerves. His patients were again resting by the time Jack, Harold and Chun Li arrived.

Doctor Goodson walked outside to greet and talk to the gentlemen upon their arrival. He believed his patients to all be asleep at that time. As they stood next to the cave entrance discussing the morning's events and today's menu, a gun shot rang out from inside the Li house. The men ran toward the structure as the bullet ricocheted out the doorway. Pierre stood in the middle of the floor on one leg holding Habib's pistol that Doctor Goodson had left lying on his seat. Harold having got there first, grabbed the gun from the child's hands, and said, "Pierre, what have you done?"

Pierre answered, "My daddy says an eye for an eye. That means he shot my leg so I shot his."

Doctor Goodson pushed past Harold and the child to check on Habib. Luckily the bullet had missed Habib's leg by inches from the hole that had been shot through the bench he lay on. The doctor said, "This one's on me. I helped Habib to the restroom earlier and left the pistol lying on my seat. I can assure you all, it will not happen again." He picked Pierre up, set him back on his cot, and said, "If you get up again young man I will whip your bottom good. Do you understand me?!"

With fear in his eyes, Pierre answered, "Yes sir."

Back at the camp all were beginning to stir. Su Li and the Parker sisters headed to the cave to help with breakfast. Elizabeth French told Nigel, "I will be along in a bit. I want to help Marah and Janie to relocate. If you don't mind, we may just trade spaces with her and Arianna. Their spot has been at the deepest area of the lower level. I like the way it has been set up and there is more space down there. May I Nigel, may I move us down there and give them the area we have been using?"

"Whatever you desire my love," Nigel answered.

As French exited the nose section, he was approached by the two elderly gentlemen who had spent the last few days whittling forks and spoons. The two men shook Nigel French's hand and introduced themselves as Sherod and Butch. Butch held out a shirt wrapped around something and said, "So far we have 10 each of completed forks and spoons. We feel we can make crutches for the man with the broken foot and for the child. We have found the perfect small tree trunks with shallow v-shaped branches at the top. They each even have a branch located in the right area to be a handle. If we can get some help to cut them they would probably help."

Sherod added, "Yes and we could tie cloth around the top to cushion the under arm."

Nigel French replied, "What intellect gentlemen. That's a marvelous idea. Follow me and we will retrieve the hand saw from the storage shed and I will cut the small trees for you."

Iva Rotge was walking by at that time to go check on Guillaume. She said to French and the gentlemen, "Just inside our dwelling to the right, my husband has a gallon sized bag of plastic zip ties. Feel free to obtain a few of them to attach the cloth cushioning to the crutches when you are ready."

Nigel French answered, "Why thank you and good morning Madam."

Iva said, "You're welcome," and walked on.

Janie and Elizabeth tossed down the French's three pieces of luggage as they began relocating Marah and the French's living arrangements. They found Marah in her quarters still holding the pointed stick while Arianna played nearby. Janie asked her very shaky friend, "Are you okay? That dream must have really disturbed you. Elizabeth and Nigel have agreed to swap living spaces with you and Arianna."

Marah answered, "I hope I am okay. I have spent Arianna's entire life trying to protect her from cruel individuals. Even Ragish's mother was horrible to her. She used every opportunity that Arianna was disobedient even for a moment to slap her hard across the face. In answering all of my protests she would say Arianna may as well get used to the abuse. She said women were nothing more than mere slaves in this world and the child didn't need to believe otherwise. I will never allow anyone else to harm my child. Thank you Elizabeth for switching places with us."

As the three women began gathering Marah and Arianna's belongings the child held up her teddy bear and asked, "Mommy, can I give my bear to Pierre? I'm sure Barry can make him better. He always makes me better when I am sick."

Marah answered her daughter, "If you are sure you want to give Barry up because once a gift is given, it no longer belongs to you. Now that you know this are you still willing to part with him?"

The sweet child answered, "Maybe I will ask Pierre if he wants to share Barry with me. He can keep it till he gets well and then give it back to me."

Marah replied, "We will ask Claudette if that will be all right with her first and take it from there."

Elizabeth French then asked Marah and Janie, "Can you tell me anything about the boy Pierre? Nigel says we are going to care for the child until his Grandma recovers. We have been unsuccessful in our efforts to have children. I am both excited and nervous at the prospect of taking care of him."

Janie replied, "Claudette has been caring for Pierre since the crash as a result of mistaken identity as you know. He seems quiet as a rule of thumb stopping just short of being clingy. He has no clue that she is not his Grandmother. She has fallen in love with the child."

Marah added, "Arianna has too fallen for him I suspect. They play well together and she has never even offered to let me have her teddy bear."

Elizabeth asked, "Marah if I need you, will you please help me with him? I have watched you and your parenting skills far exceed today's normal. I have a lot to learn and you are just the person I would like to teach me."

Marah's nerves were calming from the dream as they discussed the children. She told Elizabeth, "Yes, of course I will be happy to help in any way I can. I have found children like to try to do what the adults are doing. He would probably enjoy trying to help with the pottery after the clay mixture is prepared. You might try that first."

Janie said, "If you think about it, trading dwellings will benefit you both. Marah and Arianna will no longer be alone at night, and you and Nigel will not have to figure out how to get Pierre into the upper section with an injured leg. Once again, God knows just what we need." Both ladies agreed.

They finished switching out the belongings and headed to the cave for breakfast. Elizabeth said she would sit with the wounded for a bit after breakfast. Janie and Marah made plans to plant more seeds. They would begin this time at the cave side of the pathway planting herbs and spices making them easy to harvest in small amounts as needed by the kitchen staff. Upon arrival at the dining hall they were shocked to hear of the shooting that morning. As they were entering the dining hall Doctor Goodson walked up to Marah and asked, "How is Arianna's hand this morning?"

Arianna climbed Marah like a tree and held her neck tight. Marah had been angered at the doctor's attitude the evening before when he asked all mother's to remove their crying children. In a combative tone she answered, "She is fine. I'm sure you have others to worry about." Without another word, she turned and walked away.

Elizabeth French told Doctor Goodson, "The two elderly gentlemen, Butch and Sherod, have Nigel helping them build crutches for Sanjay and Pierre. We will teach

Pierre to use the crutches and take him off your hands until Claudette recovers."

Doctor Goodson answered, "That's good news. You will have your hands full. Can you ladies sit with the wounded for a few hours today? I need to go to my quarters and get a few hours of rest so I can watch them tonight."

Elizabeth answered, "I am sure we can arrange that. Please don't leave without giving us medicine and instructions." Doctor Goodson seeming annoyed at her request said, "I wouldn't think of leaving you empty handed. After all, I am the doctor here." He then returned to his seat to finish his scrambled eggs and fruit before exiting. Elizabeth gathered her breakfast and went to the Li house to relieve Harold who had been sitting with the injured since the shooting.

As Elizabeth entered, she saw that Claudette was the only patient awake. She took this opportunity to talk to Claudette about Pierre. Elizabeth said, "My husband and two other gentlemen are currently building crutches for Pierre and Sanjay. If you do not object, Nigel and I will take care of Pierre for you during your recovery."

Claudette replied, "That would be a big help. He could have killed someone this morning, and I was too weak and slow to stop him. Even though the boy is only five years old, from the stories he has told me he has had a difficult upbringing so far. As you know my relationship with him stems from a mistaken identity. He told me his father used to beat his mother, but the last time his mother sent his father to Heaven. He said his mother now has to go live at the jail and he gets to grow up with me, well you know his grandmother. He even explained his actions this morning as coming from his father's teachings, an eye for an eye. It is important for him to learn better values than that."

"I promise to do my very best," said Elizabeth. She noticed Claudette had developed a deep cough over night. She would mention it to Doctor Goodson before he left.

Claudette asked, "If you would ask Janie to bring me some unclaimed clothing and my small sewing kit, I will attempt to stay somewhat busy during my recovery resizing them for the children. My sewing kit is in the lower level of the nose section. My area is two aluminum curtains from the back where Marah and Arianna stay."

Elizabeth answered, "Either Janie, Marah, or I will see that you have it by this afternoon."

Claudette said, "Thank you. If you don't mind, I would like to rest a bit now." She appeared to be asleep before her head hit the pillow.

After about an hour, Jack and Doctor Goodson appeared in the doorway of the Li house. With both men shirtless and with wet hair, Doctor Goodson said, "Excuse our lack of upper body attire but I didn't want my blood stained shirt back on after showering. How have they all been?"

Elizabeth said, "Everyone has slept the entire time except for Claudette. She and I talked for a while about Nigel and I caring for the child until her recovery. Doctor, I am concerned about her cough. I don't recall her being congested before she got burned."

"May we step outside, Mrs. French," requested the doctor. As the two of them stood a few steps away from the entrance, he continued, "I am very concerned about Claudette. All too often burn victims develop pneumonia. Honestly, I am unsure if she can survive her injuries. I will do the best I can to save her but I just don't know. I plan to wait until I return this afternoon to change everyone's bandages. We may know more then."

With tears now streaming down her face, Elizabeth replied, "Thank you doctor for letting me know."

With breakfast finished, Jenny Parker approached them and asked, "Would it be okay if I sat with the wounded for awhile. I am not needed for a few hours to help with dinner. Sanjay and I have enjoyed chatting over the past few days and I would like to sit with my friend for a bit."

The doctor answered, "That would be fine. They have all been medicated and may sleep for two or three more hours. If anyone needs pain meds after waking up, give them one of the pills in the green bottle from the cabinets by the seats. Thank you ladies. I am going now to the camp to check on Mr. Patel, deliver his breakfast and take a nap. I will see you both later and thank you for your help." A few moments later he exited the dining hall with Patel's breakfast and disappeared down the pathway.

Nigel French, Butch, and Sherod arrived as the doctor was leaving. Each man had their hands full, two carried crutches and the other had the flat ware that had been carved already. Doctor Goodson found the crutches acceptable upon inspection. Sherod who carried the flat ware also brought along a hand saw to do any necessary adjustments to the height of the crutches. Jenny Parker thanked them for the flat ware and took it to the kitchen. She returned immediately to the Li house.

Nigel very soon recognized his wife had been crying. He asked, "Elizabeth, what is wrong. Has Pierre's condition worsened?"

"Not exactly. This morning he shot at Habib in an effort to gain revenge for yesterday's accident. No one was hurt, but there is bad news. The doctor fears Claudette may not recover. My heart finds that possibility unacceptable," Elizabeth said as tears once again began to flow down her cheeks.

Nigel hugged his wife and said, "The situation is in God's hands my darling. All we can do is pray for her and take the child so she can rest. Now dry your eyes. I will go eat breakfast and afterward you and I can gather the needed materials for your pottery dishes. When Pierre wakes up, if he feels up to it, we can begin our relationship with him by letting him help with the first of the dishes. Little boys love to play in the mud and the first dish he creates will give him a sense of accomplishment. That may be the first step toward his rehabilitation. I love you. Would you care to join me?"

She answered, "I have already eaten, but I will come and sit with you." As they were walking into the cave she explained how Pierre got the pistol and that the child would need constant supervision.

Jack and Harold were standing near the entrance to the dining hall when Janie, Marah and Arianna exited. Arianna ran over and hugged Jack and said, "Mommy, his hair smells good. Hug him so you can see."

Embarrassed again at her child's actions, Marah smiled and said, "I will just take your word for it." When Arianna was ready to let go, Jack handed her to Marah.

Then he smiled and asked, "How is your hand feeling this morning, little lady?"

Arianna answered, "It's almost better. Look." She moved her hand back and forth to show Jack.

"Well, I couldn't be happier to see that," Jack stated. Then he turned his attention to Marah and said, "I certainly hope you are feeling better after your bad dream."

Marah answered, "Yes, thank you. As it turns out, you and I are now neighbors. Arianna and I changed dwellings with the French's, partly to help me keep Arianna safe and partly to make it easier for them to take care of Pierre with his leg injured. Anyway we now reside two curtains away from you. You were very kind this morning when I was out of sorts. Some nightmares reveal messages and are quite unnerving."

Jack replied, "Well I owed you one. It's only been a few days since I was awakened from a nightmare myself by your gentle hand. Sometimes just knowing someone cares can calm the soul of even the savage beast so you are welcome and thank you too."

Harold asked Janie, "What are your plans for today?"

Janie answered, "I believe Marah and I are going to plant the herbs and spice seeds right over there." She pointed to a clearing just beyond the end of the bedrock surrounding the cave's entrance. Janie added, "That would make them easily accessible to the kitchen. First we have to go back to camp to get the seeds and Elizabeth said Claudette requested some material and her sewing kit. We will bring that back as well."

Harold said, "Jack and I are going to meet with Guillaume Rotge to make some sort of plan for his proposed shrimp boat. If we are successful in the quest, the kitchen's menu will be expanded. We will be along in a bit. First we need to make sure Chun Li has everything he will need for the dinner meal. Then Nigel, Jack and I will gather Elizabeth's clay pottery materials. I will see you in awhile."

As the ladies were about to leave, Ophilia Parker stopped them and asked them to take the Rotge's breakfast with them. She said, "They are the only people who have not yet arrived for breakfast. Considering they were taking care of Patel over night, there's no telling what has kept them away this morning. I just want to see they have breakfast." She handed them two prepared and covered plates and they were off.

Meanwhile, Doctor Goodson was nearing the camp and his office. He could hear what sounded like periodic hammering. It was Iva and Guillaume Rotge finishing up his coconut project. There were several bottles of coconut milk and only three remaining untouched coconuts left to deal with. Mr. Patel sat on one of the plane seats which had been placed just outside the office doorway with a disgruntled look on his face. When Guillaume saw the doctor approaching, he said, "Good morning doctor. I hope you don't mind that we are finishing your coconut disassembly. Iva and I have a problem being still. We knew you would be spread pretty thin with the additional patients to care for."

"To be honest with you, I had completely forgotten about the coconuts," replied Doctor Goodson as he handed Mr. Patel his breakfast.

Mr. Patel asked, "Doctor, how is my friend Sanjay this morning?"

The doctor surprised at Patel's concern for another said, "He is as well as can be expected and rested most of the night. It will take some time for his foot to heal and it is unsure as to whether the bone will set properly with no xray machine to check it. I believe he will recover but he may develop a limp afterwards. I will let him know you were asking." Then Patel's normal demeanor returned as he complained about cold eggs for breakfast and the fact he was the only resident not allowed to go to the dining hall.

Iva Rotge spoke up and said, "Considering you tried to kill the cook, you should be grateful they are even feeding you at all." Mr. Patel gave her a mean look, shut up and began to eat.

As soon as the Rotge's finished the remaining three coconuts and Mr. Patel finished eating, Doctor Goodson addressed his patient. He asked, "Mr. Patel, may I ask you a favor, sir?"

The puzzled gentleman replied, "I suppose so, but why me?"

The doctor answered, "If I give you my wrist watch, can I depend on you to wake me in four hours? I was up all night tending to the other patients and have to do the same tonight. I must sleep at least for a while. I have taken care of you through everything you have been through. Now it's your turn to return part of the favor. Please will you do this for me?"

Patel's attitude changed instantly having been trusted to do anything. He answered, "Yes sir, doctor. It would be my pleasure to help the only person on this island willing to help me. If you don't mind, I will continue to sit here and enjoy the day."

Iva Rotge said, "Mr. Patel, you should be aware, I will be nearby all day if you need something. But be advised, if you start any trouble, I will finish it!" She raised the hammer they had been using showing Patel she meant what she said. She added, "This may be your only chance to prove yourself trustworthy. Don't blow it." Mr.Patel never uttered a word.

It was then that Janie, Marah and Arianna emerged from the path carrying the Rotge's breakfast. Marah drew a startled deep breath upon seeing Mr. Patel sitting outside. Her mind immediately went back to the nightmare she had. She told Janie, "Arianna and I are not going over there!"

Janie said, "It's okay, Marah. Iva, we brought you and Guillaume breakfast. Could you please come over here?"

Iva walked toward them saying, "Oh thank you so much for thinking of us. We have been busy with Mr. Patel and the coconuts and time got away from us. Now that we have food I realize how hungry I am. Thank you again." Guillaume joined her and they both sat down outside the nose section to eat where they could keep an eye on Patel. Janie, Marah and Arianna got busy gathering seeds, unclaimed clothing, and Claudette's small sewing kit to take back to the cave. Arianna brought along her teddy bear to offer to share with Pierre. Then they were off.

Once they were back at the cave, they first took the sewing kit and unclaimed clothing to the Li house to give to Claudette. She was again awake when they arrived. They explained they had found three burkas and brought them to cut into clothing patterns. They had also brought one outfit each of Pierre's and Arianna's to start out with. Jenny Parker was very interested in learning the craft of tailor making clothes. She would help Claudette with the sewing while she talked to her, Sanjay and Habib. Janie, Marah and Arianna went on to start planting the herbs and spices. Arianna laid her teddy bear next to Pierre who was still asleep and said, "I'll tell him we have to share Barry when he wakes up." Then she ran out to join her mother.

Jack and Harold were about to head to the camp. Harold asked Janie, "Let me check out the area you are planning to plant in before you go over there. I need to be sure there is no quick sand or wildlife to harm you."

Janie said, "Thank you sweetheart."

When Harold was checking the vegetation around the clearing, he jumped back and yelled, "Wo, Jack, there's two big turtles over here."

Jack asked, "How big?"

Harold said, "About as big around as a car tire."

Jack said, "Hold on a minute while I go ask Chun Li if he wants to prepare turtle for tonight's dinner. Then we will know whether to kill them or shoo them away." Soon Jack returned followed by Chun Li holding his biggest meat cleaver and his shovel. Harold pointed him in the right direction and soon he had both turtle heads on the shovel. He asked Nigel French to take the heads to the quick sand pit for disposal and for French to ask Jack and Harold to help him move the turtle bodies to the kitchen for preparation. Once finished, Harold did one more check of the planting area and gave Janie the all clear. Then he and Jack headed to camp to meet with Guillaume Rotge.

Iva Rotge was sitting outside Guillaume's shop weaving grass when Jack and Harold arrived. Guillaume was inside trying to piece together at least one of the badly damaged weed eaters. They shouted their greetings before entering. They were instantly puzzled by the fact Rotge was placing a lawn mower shaft complete with blades onto one of the weed eaters. Jack asked, "Guillaume, what on Earth are you building?"

Rotge answered, "I am trying to design a trolling motor of sorts for the shrimp boat I was telling you about."

Jack asked, "Do you think it will work?"

Rotge replied, "By the time I get done with it yes, but I don't know if it will be this design or another one. I have three currently floating around in my head."

Jack stated, "Well that's encouraging. About the shrimp boat, can you come with us to the tail section and physically show us what you are talking about doing? I am having a little trouble visualizing it and don't know where to start because of it."

Guillaume Rotge said, "Why yes, I would be delighted to help with the design." He stepped out the door and asked his wife, "Iva, are you going to be alright watching Patel while I am gone?"

Iva lifted up the hammer shaking it in Patel's direction and said, "Yes I believe I have the situation handled." He kissed his wife and the three men headed to the tail section.

As they walked around the entire outside of the remaining tail section wreckage, Guillaume Rotge began to explain. He said, "I believe we will need at least 30 feet of the farthest back part of the cargo hold. From the floor of the cargo hold to the rim of the boat needs to be four feet deep to prevent anyone from going overboard. The end of the plane needs to be the bow of the boat due to it's pointed shape. We will use metal from the rest of the cargo area to close in the rear of the boat. Once closed in, I will drill a hole in the stern of the boat to insert the trolling motor through. I will develop rubber gaskets to put the shaft through to prevent the vessel from taking on so much water as to sink itself. The boat will still more than likely take on some water so we will need a bucket aboard at all times incase bailing is required. When finished, it won't exactly be a cruise ship, but we should be able to do some shrimping and still make it back to shore safely."

Jack asked curiously, "Where will you get the rubber to make gaskets?"

Rotge answered, "From the wheels of the plane. They may be buried in the sand now but I can dig one out far enough to cut enough rubber away from it to make gasket material for both sides of the connection."

Jack asked, "How do you plan to connect the stern of the boat to the rest of it? Do you plan to add sails to the craft?"

Guillaume answered, "We will weld the metal together very carefully trying hard not to leave any cracks. But realizing no weld is perfect, again we are taking a bucket along."

Harold giggled and said, "Maybe we should get Su Li to check it for cracks. Nothing gets past her." Knowing what he meant, all three laughed.

Jack said, "Thank you for the brilliant idea. Harold and I will spend the next few days finishing cutting away the upper section so we can access our new boat."

Rotge replied, "Iva and I would like to call dibbs on enough metal to roof a 12' x

24' structure. We want to, as a surprise, build the French's a two room dwelling. They are going to be taking care of Pierre. We thought by the time Claudette has recovered, they will have likely grown very fond of the child. Iva suggested we provide them with a two room shelter so Claudette could reside on the other side and they could share in rearing the boy."

Jack said, "What a thoughtful venture. We will be glad to help with the roof. What about the sails?"

Rotge answered, "I haven't thought that far ahead yet. I will let you know in plenty of time."

Harold said, "We need to get some fuel from the wing to refill the generator. Let's get with it." The three men headed in the direction of the middle section.

There seemed to be work going on everywhere. Some of the families were beginning to build structures of various kinds along the pathway to the cave. Everyone had embraced the art of grass weaving. Some were even adding bamboo stalks into the grass woven wall material to strengthen them. Some were gathering stones to build structures in the Chun Li style near the cave. Li had asked some of his Chinese friends to help him provide a home on the opposite side of the cave entrance from the Li house for the Parker sisters to reside in. All together there were four homes under construction. Jack and Harold would try to provide roofing material for all of them in the next few days. They would also remove the flooring between the upper and lower levels of the tail section as they went to add more tables for the cafeteria. They still needed approximately ten more tables to completely provide enough seating for all to eat at the same time.

Progress was being made at the cave also. By the afternoon, Janie and Marah had successfully planted all the herb and spice seeds. Nigel French was working the Rotge turn table while Elizabeth laughed at Pierre's first effort at making a cup from the clay they had mixed. Arianna stood nearby watching, holding the teddy bear she now shared with Pierre saying, "Don't get any of that icky stuff on Barry." Jenny Parker had helped Claudette disassemble one shirt and use it as a pattern to cut out a size or two bigger shirt from the burka provided. They were ready to begin sewing the new shirt together. Claudette had suggested they soak the new clothing in bleach. Once the material was white or gray from the bleach it might be fun for the children to decorate the shirts with dye they could make from different color berries. Jenny Parker worried about Claudette as she asked that they stop for the day. Her cough had deepened throughout the day, and her head was beginning to put off a strange odor. Parker gave Claudette a pain pill and stepped outside to ask Nigel French to move the two plane seats outside the Li house for her and Sanjay to sit and watch the water. Habib and Claudette could sleep uninterrupted then and the two of them could talk freely.

Inside the kitchen, Chun and Su Li, along with Ophilia Parker were busy. They had both the turtles butchered, cut up, and separated into the seven kinds of meats. There were bowls containing meats that resembled pork, chicken, beef, shrimp, veal, fish or goat. Li planned to serve mashed potatoes and corn with the turtle meat. He would make accompanying gravies for the pork, chicken and beef portions of the turtle. Ophilia Parker worked on the fruit salad for desert and the drinks for the evening. Su Li worked to clean the turtle shells completely to use the shells for huge bowls for various dishes like the fruit.

When it was time to head to the cave for dinner, Jack and Harold had two pieces of roofing for the Rotge's surprise home for the French's. Tomorrow they would cut the other two needed pieces out. They had also removed enough of the flooring between the two levels of the tail section to take to the cave for three more tables. They would build the tables after dinner. As they passed by the Rotge shop, Jack asked, "Iva, Have you and Guillaume picked a spot yet for the French's house? If you have, it would probably be a good idea to drop the metal off at the home site. We can transport your grass weavings too if you would like."

Iva Rotge said, "Yes actually I was thinking of a spot just this side of lookout cliff. It looks like some of the fire wood for the cave has been cut from there already and the site is pretty clear. I would appreciate you taking the weavings too. I have 36 feet long already that's 7 feet wide. That will cover two of the walls, but it is heavy. Thank you for offering. The site is flat and nice. They will even have nearby access to a cold drink of water from the pan at the cliff. I believe they will be pleased." As Iva had woven the grass wall, she had rolled it up like a rug making it easy to load on top of the sled. Jack and Harold both agreed they would appreciate a home.

Guillaume Rotge said, "Iva, I will go with them and show them where you are talking about. Please don't let Patel forget to wake the doctor in about 30 more minutes. Do you mind if I go?"

Iva answered, "No, I still have my hammer. Besides, the natives have been friendly today." The three men entered the pathway to the cave with sled in tow.

As they walked away, Guillaume Rotge said, "I am having trouble with my weed eater trolling motor idea. The blades from the mower are too heavy for the motor to turn. It barely moves. Tomorrow will you please help me to use the plasma cutter to cut the blades down to a more acceptable size. I believe we might be successful if they were smaller. However, after giving it more thought, we need to consider asking the two gentlemen who made the crutches if they will whittle us some orrs for the boat. We will need 10 of them so they may need to get some helpers. We will affix them to the boat, five on each side and row ourselves back to shore if necessary. We will need to study the tides every evening to know the safest time to go shrimping. I have seen it done in canoe racing. We will need man power, at least ten men aboard at all times to handle the nets and the orrs if necessary."

Jack said, "Wow. You have given a lot of time and thought to this already. We have just been concentrating on disassembling the tail section so you could have a roof for the French's home. You are way ahead of me. We still have probably a week's worth of metal removal just to be rid of the upper level. Then we have to remove enough metal to get the tub only four feet deep from the cargo floor. You said you wanted it 30 feet long so that will probably take nearly another week considering how slow the cutter is. So we are at least two and a half weeks away from a completed vessel."

Rotge replied, "That will be a good amount of time. Meanwhile, I will take on your roof assembly detail. I assume many structures will be erected during that amount of time, so I will get some help and roof them as you two cut away the metal sections. Iva said Janie told her there were four different shelters being built already, one stone and three grass huts. She said they were weaving grass to cover both the walls and the roof. Then they were going to cover the roofs with thatch grass to water proof them. Before long there will be a regular community of homes along this pathway. I will install the metal roofing on any of them that request it until there is no more metal to use. Then everyone else will have to use the thatch roofs. Crazy thing is it will probably work good with the layer of woven grass beneath it. That was a wise choice."

Harold said, "I have been thinking about the net for the shrimp. We will have to take the fishing net back that we are using for the live well at the cave. It has small holes which is what we will need for shrimp. We have seven or eight nice cargo nets. We can put the cargo nets together with plastic ties and shrink the size of the holes in them to a smaller size to hold the fish. That way we can have our fishing net and still provide a sufficient live well for Chun Li. I will ask Janie to get some of the ladies to help her combine the nets."

Guillaume said, "I am sure Iva would like to help. It sounds like a plan." The three men arrived at the spot where the French's house was set to be. The roll of woven grass was taken off the sled first. Then they unloaded the two pieces of metal and walked off the perimeter of said house. It seemed the fates were for them as there were trees in the exact four corners with a somewhat straight line of wall sturdying trees. It would be a good house. Then they proceeded on toward the cave.

They arrived at the cave half an hour before dinner was ready. Jack asked Janie and Marah, "Ladies, if we gather you enough grass, could you make the seat bottoms for the benches we will need for the three new tables after we eat?"

The two ladies looked at each other and answered simultaneously, "Sure." They both broke into laughter at having answered together.

Sanjay, who was still sitting outside the Li house said, "Jack, I want to help with the weaving. It is something I can do and I am feeling quite useless at this point."

Jack replied, "The more, the merrier. How do you like your crutches, Sanjay? Do they fit you properly?"

Sanjay said, "They will take some getting used to. I won't attempt the trip back to camp yet, but I am sure there will be time to get used to them before I am fully recovered. Doctor Goodson says 6 weeks to two months if I am lucky. To tell the truth, it is my first experience having to use crutches, so I am unsure how they would compare with the manufactured version. However I am pleased with having been awarded some sort of mobility."

Janie spoke up and said, "Why thank you Sanjay. We would be glad to have the help."

He then stated, "It will help me as well. I am not used to having so much idle time on my hands. I almost resorted to sewing today. I really need something to keep me busy."

Jack teasingly said, "Lots of gentlemen become tailors and clothing designers."

Sanjay laughed and said, "Not this gentleman.

Soon Doctor Goodson arrived. He checked on his patients, both the two who were still sleeping and the two who were currently outside. He asked the French's how Pierre had been? Pierre answered for himself, "I'm good doctor. Look, I made a good cup. I messed up on the first two, but then I made this one." He held up a slightly crooked coffee cup complete with the handle. He continued, "My friend Sanjay showed me how to use these sticks (crutches) to walk with." Pierre got to his feet and took two or three steps with the crutches to show Doctor Goodson. Then he got a little dizzy, sat down and scooted back over to the French's.

The Doctor said, "Good job. Just be slow and careful when you are standing up. You don't need to hurt your leg any worse than it already is." Doctor Goodson then asked the French's, "After dinner will the two of you help me with changing everyone's bandages and tending to their wounds? I really will need your help." The French's agreed to help when it was time. However, after eating the doctor once again approached the French's. He told Nigel, "I have been thinking about my request for you and Elizabeth to help me with the patients. I decided I will change Pierre's bandages and check on his wounds first. Then I would like for you two to use the sled and take him on back to the camp. I fear what it will do to him to hear Claudette crying while I change her bandages. It will be awful for her and there is nothing I can do to change that. We don't need Pierre to feel the need again to protect his Grandma. It would probably be better if he was out of ear shot."

Nigel answered, "What ever you think is best doctor."

Doctor Goodson then turned to see Guillaume Rotge exiting the dining hall with Iva's dinner and drink in his hands. He said to Rotge, "Guillaume, I can not thank you and Iva enough for helping with Mr. Patel. He seemed to be quite calm today for the first time since the crash."

Rotge answered, "You're welcome, doctor. I believe Iva has scared Patel straight. She can be no nonsense when necessary and has explained over and over to Mr. Patel that his actions will determine his fate, good or bad. Time will tell how long it will last."

Doctor Goodson asked, "Would you please be so kind as to take dinner back to camp for him as well? I will be staying here again over night to care for the others and would appreciate it if you two could watch him again tonight."

Rotge replied, "Oh how thoughtless of me. Of course I will take it, and Iva and I knew taking care of him was not just for last night. We are prepared to help throughout the duration."

The doctor said, "Thank you," and walked outside to get started.

Upon his arrival, Doctor Goodson had awakened both Habib and Claudette. He had ushered Sanjay back to bed. Then he had got Jenny Parker to bring them each their dinner. Now that they had eaten, he gave each one pain medication and promised to return in half an hour to begin changing bandages once the meds had taken effect. Meanwhile, Pierre asked the doctor to let him show his grandma the cup he had made for her. Elizabeth carried the cup while Pierre made his way inside the doorway of the Li house. Once inside he said, "Look Grandma, I made you a cup. They still have to cook it tomorrow in the oven before you can use it. I love you." Then the child made a face and asked, "What is that stinky smell in here?"

Knowing the odor was being emitted from her wounded head, Claudette answered, "Sometimes sick or hurt people just stink, Pierre. Thank you for my lovely cup, sweetheart. When the doctor finishes checking your leg out, you go home with the French's tonight. Behave yourself and remember that I love you too."

Pierre answered, "Okay Grandma. They said I get to ride on the sled to the camp. Can Arianna ride on it with me?"

Claudette said, "If her mother doesn't mind then I don't see why not."

Pierre stepped outside the Li house and sat on the plane seat that was located there and said, "Okay, doc. I'm ready. Fix me so I can go sledding." Doctor Goodson wasted no time doing just that. Then he gave Elizabeth some medication for the child in the event he started hurting during the night and sent them on their way. Nigel and Elizabeth pulled the sled with the two children aboard while Marah and Jack followed a few steps behind. It crossed Arthur Goodson's mind that Jack was gaining ground with the lovely Marah while he was busy caring for the patients. He found this fact internally annoying as he watched the two walk away together. Under his breath he grumbled, "How many wives does one man need?" referring to the wedding ring Jack presently wore.

Harold had stayed behind at the cave to construct the three new tables. Janie sat nearby the cave entrance weaving grass for the benches to accompany the new tables. Doctor Goodson asked the two of them if they would help him with Claudette after he finished the bandage change on Habib and Sanjay. They promised to help when the time came. He then went on to begin with Sanjay's foot. He was pleased that neither Sanjay's or Pierre's wounds showed any signs of infection. However, this was not the case when it came time for Habib. His head wound showed signs of redness and inflammation. Upon checking his temperature it was evident that he had a high fever. Doctor Goodson cleaned the wound, added antibiotic ointment and applied a clean bandage. He gave Habib a fever reducer, pain medication and antibiotics. Then he walked outside to get Harold and Janie. He told them both of his concern for both Habib and Claudette. He told them of a case he had worked on during his medical training as an ER physician in which an infected head injury had caused temporary brain damage and sudden death to a patient. Habib had been so distraught over the accident and all of the injuries he felt responsible for, Doctor Goodson felt he could be a suicide risk if the infection should reach his brain. Then he warned them of the sight they would see once Claudette's bandages were removed. The odor being emitted from her head was one he recognized as the onset of gangrene. Her deepening cough had magnified his fear of Pneumonia. Her prognosis was not good. He would need to clip away any tissue that the infection had killed throughout the day. It would be awful for them all especially Claudette. Having listened closely to the doctor's instructions, the three of them entered the Li house to begin.

As soon as the bandages were removed from Claudette's head, the odor of rotting flesh filled the room. Janie immediately covered her mouth and ran back out the door. She vomited profusely. Sanjay got to his feet and said, "Doctor, allow me to hold her legs still. I can at least lie across her lower body and hold it still. Harold will have to control her upper half. Please, I can do this and keep my foot out of the way all the while."

Harold said, "Doctor I am surprised at Janie's weak stomach lately. She usually can stand up to anything."

Doctor Goodson replied, "Yes this is the second time I have seen her sickened by the sight of wounds. It would probably be a good idea for her to have a pregnancy test tomorrow. Now back to the task at hand. Everyone take your places." Habib watched in horror as the procedure took place. Claudette's shrill screams of agony could be heard throughout the valley which housed the cave and river. After the bandages were replaced on the poor woman's head, Doctor Goodson gave her the same medications he had given Habib, fever reducers, antibiotics and a double dose of pain medication. He apologized to Claudette for the pain she had been through and exited the Li house. He sat on the airplane seat outside the entrance.

Harold went and checked on Janie. He hugged her and asked, "Sweetheart, are you alright?"

Janie answered, "I guess so. I don't understand what is going on with my stomach. I have always been able to stand up to the sight of blood. This makes twice since we arrived here that I have gotten ill when I was asked to help."

Harold replied, "Yes, even the doctor has noticed. He wants you to take a pregnancy test tomorrow."

Janie appeared stunned and said, "Well it may be too early to tell if I am. My cycle is only five days late."

"What?" Harold said, "You haven't mentioned being late."

Janie answered, "As you know, our physical relationship began after our arrival here. I am not completely sure what can be expected in the early stages of pregnancy. I am new to all of this."

He hugged his love again and stated, "I am so excited. I hope it turns out to be positive, that is if you want it to."

"I will have to figure out how I feel about the idea after we get the results of the test tomorrow. But for now, can we finish the seats for the new tables tomorrow. I am very tired and would like to go back to camp and relax for awhile," said Janie.

Harold said, "Absolutely my love, anything you want." The two wished Doctor Goodson good luck, and said their goodbyes. Harold promised to relieve the doctor the following morning.

Doctor Goodson said, "Harold, in my office, in the top cabinet you will find three early pregnancy tests. When you arrive at camp, go ahead and get one out and give it to Janie. For best results the test needs to be taken during her first morning urination. Let me know tomorrow what the results show. If we get a negative and the symptoms persist, we will retest her in two weeks."

"Yes, doctor. Thank you sir," said Harold. Then Janie and Harold headed toward camp.

Once they arrived at camp Harold wasted no time going to the doctor's quarters to retrieve the pregnancy test. As he neared the entrance, Mr. Patel sat on an airplane seat next to the doorway eating his dinner. Iva and Guillaume Rotge sat nearby eating. Mr. Patel looked up and said loudly, "Well if it isn't the accomplice. Have you helped crash any planes lately?"

Iva Rotge immediately lifted the hammer she had kept at her side all day and said, "Patel I told you already, if you start anything, I plan to finish it."

Guillaume added, "She is serious Patel. I'd listen to her if I were you." Harold never said a word as he entered, grabbed the test from the cabinet, and exited. Mr. Patel mumbled under his breath something about Harold not even attempting to defend his actions as Iva put down her plate and moved to sit near Patel with hammer in hand. Mr. Patel threw his dinner on the ground and asked for his sleeping and pain meds. He looked over at Guillaume and asked if he would help him to get back to bed. "I seem to be upsetting the ladies," said Mr. Patel as he looked toward the nose section wreckage and saw Marah starring daggers through him while holding her pointed stick from that morning.

Iva Rotge had no patience for trouble makers and said, "You seem to be determined to ignore the fact that we all need to pull together to survive until we are eventually rescued. What if no one had helped you with the injuries you have suffered, even the one you deserved when you attacked Chun Li. You would be dead by now and yet you continue to try to stir up trouble. Guillaume please help him to bed. I am sick of looking at him."

With tears streaming from his eyes Mr. Patel answered, "It's easy for you to ignore the obvious when your spouse is standing next to you. You are not alone here!

My wife and two children were waiting in France for me to arrive. They still wait today, 10 days later for my arrival which will almost certainly never occur! Who will take care of them now? Who will teach my four year old son to be a man, and who will be there to walk my two year old daughter down the aisle when the time comes? It was supposed to be me. It was supposed to be me." By the end of his statement, he was sobbing uncontrollably. Iva had to help Guillaume get Patel to bed. His words had softened her opinion of him. Even Marah laid her spear aside and had to dry her eyes. Then she picked her weapon back up and walked inside the nose section to join the French's where Pierre and Arianna played. Her sympathy for Mr. Patel was only surpassed by her determination to protect her daughter.

Harold had taken the pregnancy test to Janie who had gone to their quarters to lie down. She had complained to him that she was unusually tired and still felt sick at her stomach. By the time he went to join her she was already asleep. He put the test next to her and exited for a while to join Jack at the beach to discuss their plans for the following day as the sun was setting. Before long everyone would be arriving back at camp to retire for the night. It had been a long day.

CHAPTER SIXTEEN

THE CIRCLE OF LIFE

The morning of the eleventh day began with Chun Li and Jack exiting the nose section to find Harold sitting outside. Jack asked, "Are you ready to go have coffee this morning?"

Harold smiled and said, "No. If you would please take my place relieving Doctor Goodson for a while, I want to wait for Janie to wake up. The doctor recommended for her to take an early pregnancy test this morning. I really want to be with her when she gets the results."

Jack replied, "Oh, that's great news. Why didn't you tell me?"

Harold answered, "Well you were a little busy it appeared. You were sitting on the beach with Marah watching Arianna and Pierre build sand castles. I didn't want to disturb you guys. Besides we haven't learned the results yet so there was really nothing to tell."

Jack asked his best friend, "Are you excited? How would you like the test to turn out?"

Harold answered, "I have loved Janie for as long as I can remember. I would be thrilled to become the father of her baby. He or she will absolutely be a love child born in paradise. I cannot think of anything that would make me happier. If the test is negative, I pray for a positive one in the future. I want a family."

Taking a line from their favorite movie, Jack said, "Then may the force be with you my friend." The two smiled and shook hands. Jack joined a very patient Chun Li who had been reading the conversation on the pocket translator that he now kept with him. He too smiled and shook Harold's hand. He and Jack then entered the pathway to the cave and disappeared from view.

As they made their way to the cave, Chun Li asked Jack about the building site for the French's. Jack explained the Rotge's were building a surprise two room dwelling for the French's, Pierre and Claudette. That way the three adults could share in the upbringing of the child. Chun Li agreed it was a good idea. They also saw two grass huts that would be finished today or tomorrow. Li asked Jack to help his two friends put the roof on the home he had them build for the Parker sisters next to the cave. He reminded Jack that he had already delivered the roofing material for that structure. Jack promised to help.

When they were nearing the cave, they first thought they were hearing an animal of some sort barking or choking. As they got closer they could see Doctor Goodson sitting outside the Li house with his head in his hands. Jack asked, "Doctor, are you okay?"

Doctor Goodson answered, "It would depend on your definition of okay. I have anxiety issues when I feel myself loosing the battle on one of my patients. As you hear, Claudette is showing all the signs of developing pneumonia. The type of cough is clearly recognizable to the trained ear. I will not be changing the dressing on her head today. I see no reason to put her through such agony as cutting away the dead skin which has been taken by Gangrene. I doubt if she will survive the day. I can't even get her to wake up this morning. I find the situation emotionally painful every time I have experienced loosing a patient which has only happened four other times in a twenty-five year career. Aside from that, I suppose I am okay."

Jack stated, "I am so sorry to hear that." Being at a loss for words Jack immediately started to gather water for Chun Li and to fill the water tank. Sanjay and Habib were still sleeping thanks to the medication.

Back at the camp, Janie had woken up. She exited the upper nose section with pregnancy test in hand. She was delighted to see Harold waiting for her when she reached the ground. "Good morning, my love. How are you feeling this morning?" asked Harold.

Janie answered, "I'm okay, just a little queasy. It may be my nerves because of this test."

Harold stated, "I am not nervous, I'm excited. I look forward to such a time when we have our own family. No matter how this test turns out, I want you to know I love you Janie and I am with you all the way."

Janie smiled and said, "Well then be with me all the way to the restroom. I can't wait any longer so let's go find out if we have a bun in the oven." They both broke out in nervous laughter and headed toward the restroom. A few moments later she rejoined him outside the ladies room with the pregnancy result stick in hand. She handed it to Harold and said, "Here, you look at the results. I'm scared to look."

Harold looked at the result and said, "I didn't read the box so you tell me." He held it out for Janie to see the plus sign knowing they were pregnant, smiling all the while.

Janie took a quick deep breath right after she looked and said, "Um Harold, I seem to be expecting a baby."

He took her in his arms and said, "Yes, I saw that." Right that moment, it felt as though they were in a perfect world with the promise of a bright and happy future. It was the first of many emotions they would experience as the day went on.

People were beginning to stir when they walked back to the nose section. Marah, Arianna, Elizabeth French and Iva Rotge were all standing there talking. Before Janie could say anything, Harold went up to them dancing around and singing, "We're gonna have a baby, we're gonna have a baby."

The three ladies and Arianna immediately encircled Janie, each awaiting their turn to hug her in delight of this news. Janie asked Elizabeth how Pierre had faired overnight. Elizabeth answered, "He slept through the night. We haven't had a minute's trouble out of him. Nigel is dressing him now, he wasn't ready for me to see his bottom yet."

Arianna asked, "Janie, when you get your baby, can Pierre and me be it's sister and brother?"

Janie answered, "Well Arianna, I guess you will be more like cousins, but I promise you we will all be like family. I love you sweetheart." She then hugged the child.

Marah and Arianna accompanied Harold and Janie as they headed toward the cave for breakfast. They were excited about the baby as they walked along attempting to choose a spot for their home. Janie asked, "Harold, when we build our house, can we have a sand box and maybe use a turtle shell for a wash basin. Oh and can you ask the elderly gentlemen, Sherod and Butch if they would try to build a cradle for the baby?"

"Yes, my love, anything you wish," Harold answered.

Arianna said, "I'm gonna ask my friend, Jack to build me and Mommy a house close to yours and Pierre's house."

Harold said, "I think that's a great idea, Arianna. I will help Jack to do just that. I know that he likes you and your Mom very much, and I am sure he will help."

As the group neared the cave, they too began to hear Claudette's cough. Marah said, "Oh no, that cough has the sound of death. I have heard that sound before when my Grandfather died. I was just a child but the deep rattling cough is a sound I will never forget." She picked up her child and walked much faster for the rest of the journey.

As the path opened up to the cave area, they saw Jack standing outside the cave entrance talking to the Parker sisters and Su Li. They had arrived just prior to Harold and company. Jack was in the process of telling them the news about Claudette's grave condition. It was obvious the ladies were fighting back tears as Marah, Arianna, Janie and Harold walked up to them. Marah shushed Arianna as she began trying to talk to Jack. Doctor Goodson sat outside the Li house still with a distraught look on his face. He tried to speak to Marah and Arianna to no avail as Marah still harbored anger toward him for his outburst toward the children two days ago.

Once they had finished discussing Claudette's prognosis and the group had scattered, Arianna asked Marah, "Now, Mommy? Can I ask Jack about our house now?"

"I suppose if you need to speak to your friend, now is as good of a time as any." She put the child down. Arianna immediately ran to Jack who automatically hugged the child.

"Good morning young lady. How are you this morning?" Jack asked.

Arianna started, "I'm okay. Hey Jack, did you know Janie and Harold are gonna get a baby? They're gonna build a house. Will you build me and Mommy a house close to them? Me and Pierre get to be the baby's cousins. We are all going to be a family. Can you be family too?"

Jack answered the child, "That's all wonderful news and yes, I will help to build you a house. It will be a few days though. First we are going to build a boat."

Arianna said, "Okay. I understand. That's what Mommy was talking about when she said for me to be patient. I know I have to wait my turn."

Soon they were all having breakfast, Oatmeal with peaches. Chun Li had made plans to make fish, beans and cornbread for dinner. Ophilia and Jenny Parker had brought with them from camp two of the trays of coconut. They planned to try to reduce the dried coconut to flour today in an effort to produce coconut cream pies for everyone's dessert tonight. Su Li currently was working to make meal from the corn for tonight's bread.

With all the conversations going on, even Doctor Goodson failed to notice when the silence began from the Li house. He had busied himself with getting Sanjay and Habib into the dining hall to eat for the first time since the accident. A maximum of thirty minutes may have past between the last time he had checked on Claudette and when he heard Pierre crying at the top of his lungs. He was shouting, "No Grandma. Wake up, please just wake up. You can't leave me here all alone. Grandma, please."

Doctor Goodson jumped to his feet and ran out of the dining hall. Nigel and Elizabeth were hugging Pierre just outside the doorway of the Li house. Nigel shook his head at the doctor and uttered, "She's gone, doctor. She has already started getting cold."

Doctor Goodson burst into tears himself and said, "I only stepped away for a few minutes to get the others breakfast and to eat myself." He checked Claudette for a pulse hoping the French's were mistaken. The result was confirmed death.

The weeping was contagious as many had followed the doctor to see what the commotion was about. Harold, Janie, Jack, Marah, Iva and the four members of the kitchen staff now surrounded Doctor Goodson, the French's, and the heartbroken Pierre. With tears continuing to flow, Doctor Goodson said, "Her injuries were so deep and seviere that pneumonia set in very rapidly. I treated her with the strongest antibiotic I had and still, I couldn't save her. She was such a sweet lady. Even after treating her wounds would cause her tremendous pain, she would still thank me for trying to help her. I am so sorry. I tried so hard to save her but I just couldn't. I'm sorry."

Ophilia Parker said, "I would like to speak at her funeral. In the days prior to the development of the kitchen, I spent several hours next to her weaving grass. We talked for hours on end about every subject imaginable. When will her service be so I will have my statements ready?"

Doctor Goodson answered, "Unfortunately it should be done later today if possible. Some forms of pneumonia can be contagious. To be on the safe side I will scrub down the Li house with bleach water. It is about 10 am now. We will need to prepare the body for burial and dig her grave. We could probably have her service around 2 pm today if that is agreeable with all of you?" Everyone agreed to do their part. Marah and Jenny Parker volunteered to bathe and dress the body. Janie would return to camp to gather Claudette's best outfit to wear on her trip to Heaven. Iva would show Jack and Harold a place next to the river bank where Claudette had told her she would like her dwelling to be built eventually. It would be an appropriate spot for her final resting place. Nigel and Elizabeth French would devote their attentions to the heartbroken Pierre. Arianna would stay with the French's also to try to take Pierre's mind off the loss he so deeply felt. With heavy hearts the group separated to perform their tasks. By noon all the preparations were complete.

By one o'clock it seemed the entire population of the island had ascended upon the cave area. With each dressed in their finest attire, one by one they all lined up to enter the Li house to view the body and pay their final respects. At 1:30 Jack, Harold, Nigel, Doctor Goodson, Chun Li, and Guillaume Rotge acting as pal bearers lifted the bench Claudette laid on and carried it to the grave site. Guillaume Rotge had even brought Mr. Patel along and told him to stay with Sanjay, the one person he called friend. The two men seemed pleased to see one another inquiring about the progress of the other's injuries. At two o'clock, Ophilia Parker stepped to the front of the group to stand next to Claudette and deliver her eulogy.

Ophilia began, "Hello everyone. We are gathered here this afternoon to say goodbye to one of our own. Since our arrival here eleven days ago we have dealt with a great deal of death. The bible states that it is appointed to each of us once to die. It is a fate that no one will ever escape. Claudette spoke of this fact during the early days here while we sat weaving grass. It saddened her to think of the people who had died in the crash and never experienced the beauty of this island. She spoke not only of the beauty of the island itself, but also of the beauty of a community of people who were pulling so hard together to survive. She felt there was a possibility of true happiness being achieved here due to this fact, a fact that civilization no longer offered. She stated she would be happy if she never had to return to civilization because of it. She hoped her newly adopted grandson, Pierre, could be taught the love of others, a love he had experienced so little of thus far. So it is in her honor that I ask each of you to continue pulling in the same direction of survival. But it is through the things I learned by spending time with this lady that I ask that you would take time to laugh, to taste the sweetness of the fruits growing here and to take time to smell the flowers along the way. Very few flowers along the path of Claudette's life went unnoticed. It is now that I ask each of you to offer a silent prayer that her path to heaven will be straight and uninhibited. Thank you all for your attention."

After all had observed a moment of silence, Doctor Goodson stood and asked all women with children return to the dining hall during the burial. As soon as all were out of sight, Claudette's body was lowered into her grave. Then the grave was covered and wild flowers of every kind available along the pathway and river bank were laid atop it. No sooner was it complete than multiple screams were heard coming from the cave. Nearly a stampede of people ran toward the cave to see what had happened.

The women and children who had been sent away during the burial had stumbled upon the unimaginable when they reached the cave's entrance. In the water splashing up against the fishing net live well was a man floating face down. With his head still bandaged, it was obvious even from behind that it was Habib. Jack, being the first man to arrive on the scene, threw off his shoes and dove in to save him. Just as he had done days before with Mr. Patel, he drug Habib back to shore and started CPR. Soon Harold and Doctor Goodson joined him. The three men tried for at least 20 minutes to revive their friend. Their efforts were fruitless. Habib had been without oxygen too long for them to save him, he had drowned. Finally, Doctor Goodson said, "Okay, stop. Time of death: 3:02 pm. Cause of death: Drowning. Unknown origin whether accidental or intentionally due to a broken heart. May God rest his soul." Jack and Harold sat back on the ground on opposite sides of Habib's body and stared at each other. They were silently communicating some sort of guilt feelings that had began only when Claudette had passed away. Somehow they had avoided such feelings with all the other death that had occurred. Maybe those people had been collateral damage; acceptable in some crazy way to allow them to be here. But Claudette, possibly because they had come to know her had hurt them both. Now Habib was gone.

Habib in the last eleven days had become their comrade leaving behind a vast array of memories. His vivid reports of discoveries made on the few explorations to date had given them picturesque details of the discovery of the quicksand pit, the snake attack, lookout cliff, the cave which was now the dining hall, and most recently the natural water fall shower now enjoyed by so many.

Jack and Harold were snapped out of their deep thoughts by Sanjay. He said, "Oh no. This is all my fault. Just this morning Doctor Goodson told me he was afraid the infection in Habib' s wound might be trying to effect his thinking. I said it was probably just lack of sleep from Claudette coughing all night. I knew he was worried about her but I don't remember seeing him after hearing she had expired. I thought he might have needed some time alone. But I never expected this. I should have stayed with him."

Doctor Goodson said, "No Sanjay. Neither of us could have predicted what happened. The infection spreading to his brain caused him to be unable to clearly process his role in Claudette's death. Now don't you start doing the same thing, because as you can see I am unsuccessful at treating such ailments. It is important for all of us to remember that in the course of human events unfortunate things happen that are completely out of our control. We all need to accept the unacceptable and attempt to go on. There's nothing else we can do."

Sanjay said, "While we were having breakfast this morning, Habib told me a story. He began by asking that if anything happened to him would I see he was laid to rest in the quicksand pit. He said when he boarded this flight in Malaysia he was accompanying his two elderly parents to live with him in the French countryside. They both died in the crash. He said he was not grieving because the two of them were inseparable. They had been married over 50 years and were in very bad health. He felt it had been God's mercy to take them both to Heaven together. They had been among the first load of bodies laid to rest in the quicksand pit. He wanted to follow the path they had taken to Heaven. I didn't realize what he was thinking. I thought he was just examining his own mortality because of all the death since the crash. Even if it's not my fault, I still wish I would have known."

Jack said, "Very well then. It is only fitting that we honor our friend's wishes. Forgive me ladies, but I ask that all of you and the children remain here at the cave.

Currently the entrance to the quicksand pit is blocked and camouflaged by tree limbs and debris to avoid sparking the children's curiosity. After the burial we will replace the blockade. Therefore I ask for this funeral possession to be gentlemen only."

Doctor Goodson said, "If you will all excuse me. I am going to escort Mr. Patel back to my office at the camp. I believe he has had enough excitement for today and I am unsure how much longer the nerve medicine I gave him before we left will last. We don't need him acting out after the day we have had."

The doctor then went over to where Mr. Patel was standing next to the pathway home and asked, "Are you ready to go?"

Mr. Patel answered, "Please sir." The two men then began their journey back to the camp. Ten minutes later Jack and Harold led the way for the island's male population to bury one of their own at the quicksand pit. One hour later the men would reappear at the dining hall having completed the task at hand. Most everyone sat on the river bank drinking tea or coffee for the rest of the afternoon. Still the area was very quiet as all were lost in their own thoughts. The splashing of the river on the banks always has a soothing effect and by the time dinner was served that evening, periodic bursts of laughter could be heard from this group or that.

Dinner that night was later than usual. At the time of Habib's discovery it had not even been started. It was well worth the waiting. The fish, beans and cornbread were a delicious combination. The coconut cream pies were as though they had come from the finest bakery on the planet. The children were given fruit salad instead of the pie. Once everyone had finished eating, many pitched in to help with the clean up effort at the dining hall. Soon all made their way back to camp. Sanjay knowing his foot would not allow him to make another trip after attending both funerals stayed behind. He took a pain pill for his foot and was sleeping before the last of the people had left. Olivia Parker rolled her eyes as she waited for her sister, Jenny, to step inside the Li house and kiss the sleeping Sanjay on the forehead before leaving. Teasing her younger sister, she said, "I double dog dare you to do that tomorrow while he is awake." They entered the pathway home laughing and bickering the way that only siblings can do without it coming to blows.

The French's asked Marah to let Arianna stay with Pierre that night. They found it amazing she had such a calming effect on the boy. The two children had talked to each other at length that day about both having lost a parent and now sharing in the loss of Claudette. She had represented a grandparent not only to Pierre but to Arianna as well. Arianna had explained to Pierre her ideas on Heaven and that Pierre's Mom had been right about his father being sick causing him to be mean. Pierre had been worried that his father would be mean to Claudette in Heaven because he had hated her so much. Arianna explained, "My Mommy says in Heaven no body is sick or mean. They are well and happy there. It's okay. Everybody likes everybody there." Her childlike take on the situation had calmed Pierre like no other words had been able to. Marah had agreed to let her stay for the night.

The evening contained a pleasant breeze blowing along the beach. The island cast few shadows as the sunset from the other side of the island reflected it's beauty across the sea water. The sun always rose on this side of the land mass but sunsets were evident. Some how tonight Heaven's painters were presenting their entire color selection. Jack joined Marah who was sitting alone staring at the masterpiece before her. Jack asked, "Could you use some company?"

Marah said, "Sure. Have a seat. Look out there. The sky is beautiful this evening. I bet they put on an especially nice party to welcome Claudette and Habib home. I don't think I have ever witnessed a more beautiful sunset. The only way it could be more breathtaking is to see it from the other side." It was as if she had reached inside Jack's chest and massaged his heart. Her words instantly had calmed his mind and soothed away the guilt feelings that tried so hard to rear their ugly head.

Jack said, "You know this world would be a much better place if there were more people like you in it."

Marah seemed surprised and asked, "Why would you say that?"

Jack answered, "You hold a different perspective on life in general than most people. You, despite having had a difficult existence thus far, have managed to grasp the true meaning of happiness. You exhibit faith beyond the norm. You are beautiful both inside and out. I realize we have been stranded here for only 11 days, but there's something about you Marah. I feel very drawn to you. With everything that has taken place today, I can find no reason not to tell you about it. Few times in my life have I felt more delight than I did this morning when Arianna asked me if I could be family with you guys. Maybe some day her request could become reality."

Marah said, "Thank you very much for the compliment, but it is you the world could use more of. I have seen you more than once in the last eleven days risk your life in an effort to save others. I have watched you both laugh and cry and never before have I seen the personification of what I think a man should be stand before me. But in you Jack Wellington it all seems to be wrapped up in one handsome package with the exception of one minor flaw. The ring on your finger says you are already taken."

Jack felt the need to explain. He began, "Unfortunately both my wedding ring and my marriage should have been eliminated more than three years ago. My wife has been involved in an ongoing affair with a pro soccer coach for the whole time. We were married for five years before I learned of her infidelity. Our physical relationship ended then. She has turned my two children completely against me. They will barely even speak to me. It has honestly been years since either one of the three of them have so much as hugged me. I should have divorced her years ago. I guess I just wanted a family. But thanks to Janet, that will never happen. If I had known we would ever wind up here I would have ended the marriage years ago. I never dreamed a woman like you existed in this world. Otherwise I would have spent my time searching for such perfection."

Marah answered, "I assure you I am far from perfect. Just this morning I harbored murderous thoughts toward Mr. Patel. But aside from that, it was my mother's belief the wedding vows were law. She especially preached the importance of one of the vows, 'Abandoning all others, clinging only to one another'. She taught me once that vow was broken by your mate biblical law allows for one to give a writing of divorcement to the adulterous party. Only then can you return to the life of a single person and seek out a new mate. Her beliefs are permanently imbedded in my soul. My father was not a good person, much like Ragish. As a matter of fact he gave me to Ragish when I was fifteen as payment of a gambling debt. I was the pot in a lost poker hand. I never saw my parents again. I found out a year ago his gambling addiction cost both their lives. They were found shot to death inside their home. When their killer was captured he turned out to be a hit man for a bookie. But still my mother's teachings have been the guidelines for the life I have lived. I don't see that ever changing. However, I too feel drawn to you. In light of today's events I am reminded we never know when our lives might end. Somewhere inside I feel my Mother would approve of you. We both need to think on this subject, just not too long. But enough for now. Tomorrow begins the rest of our lives. I am tired. Will you walk with me back to our quarters? Arianna will wake up before the French's and Pierre. I will need to be awake and available at that time."

Jack replied, "I would love to." As they walked toward the nose section, Marah slipped her hand into Jack's. The two were silent on the walk. A simple Good Night was exchanged as they separated prior to entering the wreckage.

As Marah quietly climbed up the tree limbs into the upper level of the section, she smiled. She overheard Janie and Harold talking about the baby. Janie told Harold, "If the baby is a girl, we will name her Claudette."

He answered, "Yes and if it is a boy, he will be called Habib." She drifted off to sleep that night realizing the circle of life continues.

CHAPTER SEVENTEEN

BUSY BUILDERS

The next three weeks were filled with work with the exception of Sunday's. Every Sunday had been set aside for the purpose of replenishing the fish in the live well and gathering fruit for the following week. Thanks to the island's own Annie Oakley, Iva Rotge, albatross had become the preferred Sunday dinner. Iva likened it to going to Grandma's house on Sunday after church for fried chicken. This seemed to have become their first island tradition.

Two of the three weeks had produced ten dwellings complete with metal roofs. Meanwhile five additional homes had been constructed with roofs made of a combination of woven grass covered with thatch grasses. Delightfully the grass roofs had proven themselves nearly water proof during the three rain storms they had experienced during that time. The final week of the three, the efforts of the entire community were steered toward the construction of the shrimp boat. Every available man worked under the supervision of the elders, Sherod and Butch to carve out some twenty oars. It had been decided by Guillaume Rotge they would need ten oars on each side of the boat to ensure they could make the trip safely back to shore. Per his design, the oars would be connected in pairs allowing one man to work two oars simultaneously. This would give them a way to have more mobility with less man power. Rotge had also been successful in converting the weed eater to a trolling motor capable of moving and steering the boat as well. Excitement spread through the community as the boat neared completion. Everyone looked forward to adding shrimp to the island's main menu.

Fourteen of the new dwellings had been built along the pathway to the cave. The remaining house was the stone home on the opposite side of the cave entrance from the Li house. That home had originally been intended for the Parker sisters. Jenny Parker now resided there with her new beau Sanjay. His foot was beginning to show signs of healing. Ophilia Parker had taken up residence in the extra room of the French's new home. The Li's had finally been able to move into their dwelling. Harold and Janie had moved to the lower level of the nose section once occupied by Marah and then the French's. Harold had promised Janie a home by the time the baby was born.

The upper level of the nose section was now occupied by Marah, Arianna, Jack and another couple. Francois Savage and his wife, Rita, shared the residence. Francois was the man pulled from the quicksand pit on the maiden island expedition. He had spent most of his time on the island clearing home sites by gathering fire wood and grass for weaving. He was a man of few words, highly intelligent, an observer by nature. As Elizabeth French and Iva Rotge had moved on to other duties, Rita had become the leader of the grass weavers. It had become a friendly competition between Rita and her husband as to whether he could supply the grasses needed before they ran out every time. The two kept tabs as to the daily winners. The winner of the day received a nightly back massage given by the loser along with daily bragging rights .

The ladies had completed their task of planting the vegetable seeds. They were already seeing the fruits of their labor as the squash, cucumbers, beans and corn were now 2 or three inches tall. It appeared every seed of anything planted the first week had been successful. Everyone on the island had been very careful not to trample the young plants while both traveling the path and building dwellings along the way. The entire population of the island recognized the importance of the success of these crops. They planned to waste nothing from the fresh produce. Even the corn cobs would be used to make corn wine from. Ophilia Parker planned to deliver on her promise to make wine from left over fruit salad in just one more week. She believed there would be enough for all consenting adults to indulge. There had already been meetings on, and people appointed to recover all seeds from the vegetables harvested prior to cooking to insure future crops. Everything from squash to tomatoes. A certain amount of beans, peas, rice and corn would be put aside to be used as future seeds. The corn would be put to a number of uses, corn, corn meal, corn oil, corn syrup, and finally the wine. The production of coconut oil, milk and flour had become a great success. Survival efforts promised to continue to please the pallet.

All the home construction had the upper middle section nearly unoccupied. Janie, Marah, Iva Rotge and Elizabeth French had made plans to turn it into a school for the children to all learn to speak English. The language barrier had proven to be a problem in them all being able to play together. Any adult interested would be allowed to attend as well. Many of the passenger seats had been removed to furnish the homes and build the restrooms. They would leave forty seats and some space in the front for the teacher to stand. Currently they were all working to help Elizabeth finish the last of the 150 plates she was crafting. Once finished she would be available to help with the English lessons.

Marah had told Janie two weeks after the crash about her growing feelings toward Jack. She had said, "Considering our current circumstances being unsure of our life spans more than ever before, if Jack wasn't married I would have to consider him for a mate. Accidents happen quickly here. You just never know."

Janie had told Jack about the conversation. Jack had said, "I too have undeniable feelings for Marah. She has told me if there was some way for there to be a writing of divorcement between me and Janet, she might consider me for a husband. Janie, how does she expect me to accomplish that?"

Janie answered, "I know one of the other flight attendants I have worked with was granted a divorce from her estranged husband by running an unanswered ad in the classified ad section of the newspaper. Considering our current location, you could send Janet's 'Dear John' letter as a message in a bottle. If an unanswered newspaper ad was sufficient in a court of law then a message in a bottle should work from a dessert island I would think. Shall I speak with Marah and see if that would be satisfactory?"

Jack replied, "Actually, I had never even thought of that. I am willing to provide the document if Marah thinks it would be sufficient. Yes please speak with her for me. I don't want to be the one to hear her say no if that is the stance she takes on the subject.

Thank you Janie for helping me."

Janie had spoken to Marah and all the terms had been agreed upon. Now on this afternoon before the maiden shrimping voyage, Jack had invited those closest to him to join him at the beach for some unknown reason. He stood next to the water's edge surrounded by Janie, Harold, Marah, Arianna, the French's with Pierre, the Rotge's, the Li's, the Parkers and Sanjay. He began, "Thank you all for joining me today. During the four weeks and three days we have been on this island, we have both lost loved ones and learned of the coming of life in the near future. The realization of unknown life spans have become reality. For years now I have been in a marriage with a woman who was actively engaging in an affair with another man. Even after my discovery of this fact, I really had no reason to terminate the marriage. Her affair continued. Since our arrival here I have met a woman of such virtue that I now have a reason to believe once again in love. This love will not be allowed existence without the prior severing of the of the soiled marriage vows I am currently bound by. Inside this bottle is a document of divorce addressed to Janet Wellington. It is signed and dated by me and has witness signatures of Harold and Janie Renolds, and one Nigel French. As I release this bottle into the ocean, I pray that it will be sufficient to Almighty God in Heaven. I pray that he will bless me with the ability to be soon joined in life by the beautiful Marah. I ask for all of your blessings on this possible new relationship. Again thank you all for coming." He then threw the bottle as far as possible into the ocean. They all stood in silence watching the bottle float away with the waves. The men all shook hands with Jack and the women all hugged him. He and Marah walked away from the sea shore with Arianna holding both their hands. A new relationship was about to begin.

Doctor Goodson and Mr. Patel sat outside the doctor's office. From their vantage point they could see Jack and his friends. Thanks to the fact that voices carry, they heard every word. As the agony of defeat set in on Doctor Goodson, Mr. Patel began to speak. He said, "Well, my good doctor, it appears you are loosing the competition for Marah's affections. They are not married yet. Are you going to just sit by and let such a beauty be taken by a mass murderer? I thought the doctor's solemn oath included protecting the innocent from unnecessary harm. Looks to me like you better get busy."

Arthur Goodson responded, "She will barely even speak to me. When everything came down at the cave accident, there were 25 crying children with crying mothers standing around the scene. I lost it man. I couldn't even hear myself think, and I yelled for the mother's and children to leave. Marah obviously was very offended at my melt down and has hardly spoken to me since. She wouldn't even allow me to do a recheck on her daughter's thorn wounded hand. At this point, I don't even know how to approach her much less the subject that I too am interested in a relationship with her. It's probably too late now."

Mr. Patel said, "If it were me, I would start tomorrow. After those idiots leave in their so called shrimp boat, there is no guarantee they will ever return. When they are no longer in sight of the lagoon, you should present her with a gift basket of sorts. I would include fruit, coconut milk, and flowers. Explain you were under enormous pressure with so many patients to care for at once accompanied by the premonition for disaster. Offer your deepest and most sincere apologies for your rude outburst. It wouldn't hurt if she saw you cry during your request for her forgiveness. You never know, when you are done, you once again may be in her good favor."

Goodson looked at Patel with shock. The doctor said, "Patel, you may be on to something. Maybe it's still worth a try. Actually that is the first rational thing I have ever heard you say. Could it be possible that your body is not the only thing that has begun to heal? Your mind is showing signs of recovery as well. Thank you for the advice. I think I will try it. Even if she refuses to accept my apology, I will still feel better having made it."

Mr. Patel added, "If you are successful, I too will win. I will get to watch as the good Captain Wellington has to fight for the heart of his new love. I want to watch as that snake slithers on his belly in agony as he sees you win the affections he has tried so hard to earn. Go get him doc." Doctor Goodson was once again startled by the deep look of hatred to the point of insanity in Patel's eyes when he talked about Jack. He wondered momentarily if he should even act on Patel's suggestions. He chose to take the advice of a crazy man rather than allow Marah to slip away without putting up a fight.

With Sanjay's lingering lack of mobility to deal with, Harold and Nigel French were happy to pull him back to the dining hall on one of the sleds. Sanjay had been using his time in recovery wisely. He had taken over Claudette's clothing alterations. In the last three weeks he had cut out and sewn three new shirts each for five of the island children. The other twenty child residents were at growth stages to grow into hand me downs from older children. Sanjay's goal was to next sew pants to go with the shirts. Currently he had the new shirts soaking in bleach water to change the black burka material into a lighter cooler color. Per Claudette's plan for the clothing she had planned to create, the children would soon be allowed to decorate their own shirts. His new life partner Jenny Parker had gathered five bowls of various colored berries and three stacks of different colored flowers to design their shirts with. Sanjay told Harold, "Hopefully my shirts will dry by the time dinner is over. I am actually looking forward to seeing what kinds of designs the kids create on them. Who knows, we may discover a new Davinci in our midst."

Nigel French, being proud of his new son, said, "You know Sanjay, I wouldn't be at all surprised if you are right. Our Pierre is sharing a large coloring book with Arianna. Elizabeth and I have been delighted at the results of the pictures he has colored. He is perfect at staying within the lines. On two of his masterpieces he has drawn a small face in the upper right hand corner of the pages. It is unmistakable the face has a single tear on the cheek of a smiling face. Just yesterday I asked him about the faces he drew. He explained it to me as being Claudette watching over him. The smile represents her happiness at currently being in Heaven. The single tear he says shows that 'Grandma misses me as much as I miss her'. The boy's words were both touching and heart wrenching. Never the less, my money is on him being the island artist."

Sanjay replied, "Spoken as a true proud father. Nigel you seem to have taken to parenthood well."

French answered, "Oh yes. It is the happiest time of mine and Elizabeth's marriage. Pierre has filled the hole in our lives that being childless had created. I would not trade this opportunity for the world."

After delivering Sanjay back at the cave and refilling the water tank for Chun Li, Harold and Nigel French returned to the beach to join the men. They were all working on the finishing touches for the shrimp boat. Guillaume Rotge was completing the final welds attaching the end of the boat to the sides. Rotge planned next to install the make shift trolling motor he had built. He asked Harold upon his arrival to go to the middle section wreckage and bring him a one foot square piece of tire rubber from the landing gear. While making his request he apologized for the level of difficulty involved in obtaining the rubber needed. The landing gear was currently buried in the sand thanks to the first bad storm they had endured on the island. However the rubber gaskets would be necessary to prevent leakage around the rolling motor once installed. Harold borrowed a knife from one of the men whittling and asked Jack to come along to help him. Within an hour the two returned with the rubber in hand. Harold told Rotge, "We had to go to your quarters to get wire cutters to remove the rubber. Luckily the tire held no air, otherwise it would have been dangerous to puncture it. Anyway, be careful and don't cut yourself on the protruding wires." By the time they all had to go to dinner the trolling motor was installed and all but one pair of the oars had been created. All involved in this huge accomplishment were bubbling with excitement. The boat would be complete by night fall. Tomorrow morning would be their maiden voyage.

CHAPTER EIGHTEEN

SHRIMP TODAY, GONE TOMORROW

The entire community seemed to rise early in anticipation of the first shrimp boat voyage. There were last minute tasks which had to be performed. The fishing net used to create the live well had to be replaced with the combined cargo nets. Jack and Harold had spent much of the night before reworking four cargo nets into a large net to hold the bigger fish only in the live well. The original fishing net's holes were much smaller and would work much better for shrimp. The live well had been emptied of fish the night before to prepare dinner. Just as they were about to install the new net, they were stopped by Sanjay. He said, "Hey Jack, I still have five burkas left. What do you think about us using fishing twine to connect them to the new net. The water will still go through it and the smaller fish will not. Also it will allow for a place to store any excess shrimp you might catch. Considering the stitches can be large, it would take about an hour to sew it all together. Is there time to do that?"

Jack answered, "Sanjay, you are an absolute genius. What can we do to help?"

Sanjay said, "One of you can bring me the fishing twine. The other one can help me gather the burkas, the scissors and three embroidery needles. We will need to cut the burkas off just below the arm openings. Then there will be large pieces of material to sew together. After that we attach them to the net and install it into the live well. If we try we can have it completed by the time breakfast is served."

Harold said, "I'm going after the twine." He was gone in an instant. The twine was in the storage area inside the cave just beyond the kitchen/dining area. Jack and Sanjay went to Sanjay and Jenny's house to retrieve the rest of the needed materials. Five minutes later the three men were again next to the live well, this time sewing.

Soon Janie, Marah, Arianna, and Elizabeth French accompanied by a rapidly healing Pierre arrived at the cave. Upon seeing the men sewing, Marah laughed and said, "Well I never knew you were so domestic, Jack. Do you clean too?"

Jack laughed too and answered, "Lately I have been cleaning up my act for you, so I assume the answer is yes. Ladies feel free to pull up an embroidery needle and join us. We are reinforcing the replacement net for the live well as the holes are too big to hold any thing not baby whale sized."

Feeling the freedom to openly flirt with Jack now, Marah jokingly said, "After seeing the minnow sized fish you have caught so far, it may be the only way to save your catch for me to use as bait." They all laughed loudly then remembering the Sunday before when Jack and Marah had simultaneously caught a fish each. Marah's was about 8 pounds while Jack's would hardly be 8 ounces. Marah and Janie then sat down to help. Elizabeth took the children inside the cave and sat them each up with crayons and a page torn from the coloring book they shared. Prior to heading to the dining hall this morning the kids had decided to color pictures for the kitchen staff. Even at their young age they appreciated the work being done by the staff. With the extra sewing help of the two ladies, the job was done in a few minutes with time to spare prior to breakfast.

The entire community arrived early and ate quickly. All wanted to witness the departure of the shrimping vessel. Many gathered supplies for the fishermen. Ophilia and Jenny Parker prepared 12 individual sized baked peach pies along with some assorted fruits. Jack said, "Why thank you ladies but we should be back long before dinner."

Ophilia answered, "One can never be over prepared, Captain. Please take these along."

Jack said, "I couldn't agree more," as he took the food. Chun Li brought 12 bottles of water. Harold brought the net. Jack carried a bucket to bail any water leakage, a large piece of rope to attach to the net and a butcher knife to cut the rope and net if necessary. Guillaume Rotge filled two water bottles with fuel from the plane's wing to refill the make shift trolling motor while on the trip. Francois Sauvage provided a beach ball sized rock which had a hole all the way through it to act as an anchor if necessary. Nigel French quickly threaded rope through the hole and tied knots in it. Early on in their island habitation it had been discovered he was an expert at knot tying. As Butch and Sherod proudly presented the last of the oars, it was realized the time had come to load and launch the boat.

Moving the boat into the water from forty feet away from the water's edge they knew would be quite the task. During the ship's construction they had filled the space between the bottom of the plane to the floor of the cargo hold with sand. Then they had welded the end of the ship to keep the sand dry. They had done this to keep the ship upright as the plane it was made of had a rounded bottom. Otherwise it would surely tip over if too many men were tossed to one side by the waves. This way it was weighted evenly on the bottom. However necessary, it would make moving it that much more difficult. Once the supplies were loaded, it was time to choose the crew. With all island residents surrounding the ship, Guillaume Rotge announced they needed 10 male volunteers at least 6 foot tall of medium build to staff the voyage. The walls of the ship measured nearly 4 feet tall. The crew had to be tall enough to maneuver the oars and work with the shrimp net. Within minutes the crew was assembled and shaking hands. Then the real work began. It was decided all men who were not retired would work at the same time to move the ship. The community who had pulled together to stay alive once again came through. When the ship caught it's first wave the crew scrambled to go aboard as a rope attached to the front of the ship was held by those on the bank. Once the entire crew had chosen their spots, Jack shouted it was alright to release the rope. He pulled the rope into the boat as they began to float into the lagoon. Many sat on the beach watching as they managed to stay close enough to the coast line to be seen during their entire trip.

Janie, Marah, Elizabeth French and the two children stayed close to the sea shore hoping to witness the first net full of shrimp be hoisted into the boat. With their nerves on end, together they wondered if their mates along with the other brave men would be able to ever return to shore. Janie asked Marah, "Have you and Jack had your first kiss yet?" The two women had developed a deep and honest friendship.

Marah blushed at the question and said, "Well he did kiss Arianna and me both on the cheek before they moved the ship to the water. Does that count?"

Janie said, "Well I don't know if it counts as the first kiss, but it definitely matters."

It was then that they were interrupted by Doctor Goodson. He was carrying a grass woven basket filled with flowers, fruit and one bottle each of coconut milk, juice, and sweet tea. He laid the basket in front of Marah. Then he said, "Hello ladies. Marah, I feel we may have got off on the wrong foot. I fear I hurt your feelings with my minor melt down the day of the accident at the cave. I am here now to offer you my sincerest apology. Please accept this gift basket as proof of my regrets for having offended you. That is not my true nature." Arthur Goodson's stomach seemed to climb into his throat as Marah stared at both him and his peace offering in silence. Tears were welling up in his eyes while he awaited her reply. To his surprise they were real tears, not stemming from Mr. Patel's advice.

Finally, Marah said, "Doctor, your apology has been noted and I am not closed minded to considering it. However, it has been my past experience the actions taken by one under enormous pressure in most cases reveal that person's true nature. I will let you know if and when I decide whether your reaction that day was your normal or if it was a public panic attack. Time will reveal if your apology is merely topical or deeply felt. Thank you for the gift basket though. If you have no objections, I will share it with Janie, Elizabeth and the children."

Goodson answered, "You may do with it what you please." With tears now streaming he turned and walked away.

Nearby in the shadows of the vegetation, Mr. Patel listened. For nearly the whole duration of the ship's construction he had been lurking close by. He joined the doctor as he returned to his quarters. The always disgruntled Patel said, "That was the most pathetic effort to gain a woman's attention and affection I have ever seen. I mean really doctor, did it not cross your mind even once to say 'I am interested in you and I am not a mass murderer'. If you don't start reminding her of Wellington's guilt, he will win her hand."

Goodson replied, "Unlike you, I do not believe Captain Wellington had anything to do with the crash. Since the beginning of time men have competed for women's hearts. I am not closed to a little friendly competition. However I find no benefit in being chosen as the lesser of two evils. Again unlike you, Jack has worked tirelessly trying to take care of us all. But, in the sense of the saying 'May the best man win', I am in this for the long haul. I must stay focused on proving to her that I am indeed the best man."

As a now angry Mr. Patel was walking away, he said, "If you proceed in that manner you will be the best man, alright, at their wedding." His words hit like a stone right to the heart. Doctor Goodson would spend the rest of the day considering the advice of a mad man.

As Janie, Marah, Elizabeth and the two children sat enjoying the contents of the doctor's peace offering, Elizabeth asked Janie if she and Harold had chosen a name for the baby yet. Janie answered, "Yes, if it's a boy, Habib. If it's a girl, Claudette."

The children giggled as Pierre added, "Yeah, if it's a girl, I'm gonna call her Grandma." The three ladies found both humor and pain in the boy's take on the situation.

Janie continued, "With all the moving I have misplaced the journal. However I do remember reading in it there are six dozen cloth diapers somewhere, probably deep in the storage shed. Sometime soon we will need to locate them. There are three diaper aged babies here already. The supply of disposable diapers my colleagues brought along is nearing depletion and the cloth replacements will soon be needed. When found, I plan to save one dozen for our baby."

For some unknown reason, the mention of the journal sent Marah's mind reeling. She had been so busy she had all but forgotten about the time sheet she found in the early days on the island. She remembered the handwriting. Deep down she felt it had been in Janie's penmanship. She looked briefly at Janie, the first true friend she had ever known. Momentarily she wondered if she could have been involved in the crash. Suddenly she shook her head hard. Simultaneously, Elizabeth and Janie asked, "Are you okay?"

After forcing the thoughts out of her mind, Marah answered, "Yes, I think the fruit has made me sleepy. I was just trying to clear the cob webs away."

Just then, Arianna began to jump up and down shouting, "Mommy, Mommy look. Jack's coming home." The preoccupied ladies looked up to see the oars of the ship working tirelessly to bring them back into the lagoon. It appeared the ocean's current wasn't allowing them full control of their landing spot. They were coming in to some point around the bend of the beach beyond the edge of a large cliff. The child's shouts had gained the attention of all waiting the return of the ship. Everyone began to migrate toward the cliff trying to see where the ship came ashore. It was impossible. The cliff was too large and smooth to get past. All feared for the safety of the crew. Some thirty minutes would pass before their worries were relieved. Suddenly two men appeared in the water. They both had ropes tied to their waists. As they got further past the cliff, it became obvious the two were pulling the ship to a more friendly docking location. There were ten men rowing the oars as the boat rounded the bend. Cheers rose from the crowd as the boat turned the corner and was brought safely to shore. It was then apparent that the two swimmers were Jack and Harold. As they walked onto the beach they smiled and boasted, "Man that was fun." Jack announced, "Everyone should know we have probably three meals of shrimp to look forward to. The trip was a huge success. If someone could bring both sleds to us, it will take both to transport all this shrimp to the cave. Thank you all for your support."

When Jack had untied the rope from his waist, he handed it off to be tied to nearby trees. Arianna ran and jumped into his arms with a bear hug following. She said, "I was scared you couldn't come home. I couldn't see over that big hill. I am so glad you came home." Arianna was crying as she held on tight to his neck.

Jack softly said, "It's okay sweetheart. I am here now."

She released her grip, dried her eyes, and said, "I told you already, I'm not sweetheart. I'm Arianna." Her dislike of nicknames had not crossed his mind.

Jack said, "You sure did. I forgot. But anyway, I am here with you now so no more tears, okay?"

"Okay," she answered.

He handed the child to Marah who said, "We were all worried when the ship landed beyond the cliff. All of us are glad to see all of you."

Jack said, "Believe me, we're glad to be here. For a moment out there we wondered if the tides were going to cause us to miss the island all together. We have a few adjustments which will need to be made to the boat before our next trip sometime next week. But just wait till you see, at least a third of the boat is nearly knee deep in fresh shrimp. I think I could eat a bucket of them by myself. I really love shrimp. Let's go help get it loaded."

The sleds had been positioned. Iva Rotge had gathered ten aluminum blankets to load the shrimp onto to contain them until they were moved to the cave. An assembly line had formed from the front of the ship to the beach where the sleds lay. The bucket used to bail water was now being used to move the shrimp to the sleds. By the time the last of the shrimp were loaded it totaled 32 buckets full, a fine haul by any standard. The subject was all the rage for the rest of the afternoon as all looked forward to tonight's dinner. Happiness seemed abundant.

The kitchen staff were ready and waiting when the crew and the shrimp arrived at the cave. The shrimp would need to be separated and cleaned for cooking. The smaller shrimp would be boiled for peel and eat. The larger ones would be grilled, with some so large they would be butterflied. They would serve rice and corn as the sides. There was fruit available for dessert. As a special treat tonight, Ophilia Parker would serve the first of her wine made from the leftovers of fruit salads she had prepared over the past month. After taste testing it earlier this afternoon, a smiling Chun Li had asked his staff to wait until the work was done to indulge. He uttered two words in English, "strong, good", before using the translator to request that they wait. The news of the wine spread quickly among the community who had all gathered at the cave. Janie told Harold, "Oh I can't wait to sip a couple glasses of wine after dinner."

The nearby Doctor Goodson said, "No young lady you may not. No expecting mother in my care is allowed to consume alcohol. The way I see it, you have about eight months to wait for your first glass of Parker wine."

Janie smiled and said, "Oh doctor, you're always such a stick in the mud."

Goodson, still saddened by Marah's rejection earlier said, "That seems to be the popular opinion, but I mean stay out of the hooch."

Janie noticing his demeanor answered, "Yes sir, Doctor. Thank you for your concern."

With all the excitement at the dining hall about tonight's dinner, everyone had forgot to keep an eye on Mr. Patel. No one would have ever fathomed what he was up to back at the camp all alone. It wasn't until darkness had begun to take over before everyone headed back to camp with bellies full. Many returned with heads swimming from the strong sweet wine. To add to the confusion, thick fog was beginning to set in on the beach. As Jack and Marah began their evening stroll on the beach, it was Jack who first noticed the ship was missing. He released Marah's hand and ran to the place the boat had been docked. At first he thought the tides had untied the ropes that had secured the vessel. With the fog so thick across the surface of the ocean, the boat was nowhere in sight. Marah watched closely as Jack reacted. He sat down on the beach and said, "Well, I guess that was three weeks of hard work for nothing. It stinks, but it may be God's way of keeping us from getting lost at sea. We did almost miss the island on our return. Besides that the island itself is abundant with food. Loosing the ship is disappointing, but it is nothing we won't survive. I trust that God knows what He's doing."

Marah's heart was filled with love that very moment for this kind hearted man. She sat down next to him and hugged him tight saying, "It's going to be fine." The two looked deep into each other's eyes. Marah felt they were experiencing the mirrored images of two identical hearts. They were about to have their first real kiss when the moment they were having was interrupted by shouts from up the beach, back at camp. People were shouting for Mr. Patel. Jack and Marah both got up and hurried toward the voices. At daybreak it would be confirmed that both Patel and the ship were nowhere to be found.

There were mixed emotions that morning over the loss of the boat and the disappearance of Mr. Patel. Jack, Harold and Guillaume Rotge walked to lookout cliff to get a better perspective of the sea as soon as the fog had lifted. Mr. Patel and the ship were nowhere in sight. It had been approximately eight hours since the discovery of the missing boat and man. Jack said, "I'm not surprised the ship is out of sight since it's been gone so long. How far do you think the trolling motor will last?"

Guillaume said, "Patel currently is floating aimlessly in the Indian Ocean. I noticed yesterday as we were fighting to make landfall the salt water was rapidly corroding the small engine components. I had made a mental note to self after each trip I would have to disassemble and clean each engine part before the next voyage to keep it running. I had planned to do the job today. That poor fool is on a suicide mission. He just didn't know it ahead of time."

Harold who had been the recipient of Patel's verbal attacks and threats on more than one occasion said, "Good riddance is my opinion all the way around. He was a trouble maker. Besides that, it could very well have been the twelve of us yesterday who wound up floating aimlessly as you put it in the Indian Ocean. I'm not going to miss him or the boat."

Back at the camp, several of the ladies were standing around talking. Iva Rotge said, "I'm not really surprised that Mr. Patel left with the first opportunity. He was a tortured soul. He had no faith that we would be rescued. Two or three weeks ago I watched as he sobbed uncontrollably over his wife and children being left in the modern world without his protection. He evidently saw life as being not worth living without them."

Marah said, "I was terrified of him. He had a hatred for anyone associated with Jack, Harold and Janie. I'm ashamed to say I am glad he is gone."

Janie said, "I wonder if he even took any food or water with him?"

Doctor Goodson was sitting nearby, outside his office. He joined in the conversation, "I am pretty sure he took about ten or twelve bottles of water with him. I keep a few bottles stored here in case I need to wash a wound out. This morning all of them are gone along with some assorted fruits I picked extra yesterday while fixing the basket for Marah. He even took his suitcase with him. Personally, I wish him all the luck."

Guillaume, Harold and Jack returned as the doctor was speaking. This was the first Jack had heard of the fruit basket offering to Marah. He chose to investigate that fact later. Jack said, "You know, Patel could survive indefinitely if he is smart. He could use the net to provide fish for food. If he's not opposed to sushi he can feed himself that way. As for fresh water, the heavy dew that falls on the ocean at night will condensate on the inside of the ship. If he tries he can probably use it to stay alive, even if he has to use a piece of clothing to dry it up and then squeeze it into water bottles. I hope in time he finds what he's looking for."

Doctor Goodson still feeling the impact of the probability that Jack and Marah would wind up a couple said, "Awe our dear Captain Jack, nothing if not noble. I find it interesting to hear such well wishes for someone whose second largest wish in life was to watch you suffer and die a horrible death. His only larger wish was to rejoin his family." Rather sarcastically he added, "Tell me Captain, how do you do it?"

Jack bewildered at the doctor's strange attitude toward him answered, "I harbor no ill feelings toward Mr. Patel. Although his beliefs about my involvement in the crash were mistaken, they were obviously his truth. If I were in his shoes, I'm not sure how I would have reacted."

Harold recognizing an oddly resentful tone growing in the conversation said, "Is anyone else ready for coffee?" A chorus of affirmative answers rang out and the group dispensed. They all left the grumpy physician sitting alone outside his office. When they were out of ear shot, Harold asked Janie, "What do you think is the Doc's problem? Do you think he is actually going to miss Mr. Patel or what?"

Janie answered, "I don't know if he will miss him or not. It may have something to do with Marah. Doctor Goodson likes her too. I think he may be jealous of her and Jack. He came up to us on the beach yesterday bringing her a fruit basket complete with drinks and flowers. He offered her the basket along with his apologies for having offended her a few weeks ago. She rejected his advances and he walked away with tears flowing. If I was a betting person, I would put my money on that as the reason for the attitude."

Harold said, "Well that sheds a new light on the situation. Later today, I will let Jack know what's up."

Jack, Marah and Arianna had stopped at the French's house to wait for them to finish getting Pierre dressed for the day. Arianna had requested that she and Pierre get to walk together the rest of the way. In the days prior he had graduated from using the crutches to walking freely again. Nigel and Elizabeth were shocked to hear the news about Patel and the boat. Elizabeth echoed Iva's words on Patel being broken hearted over his family. She recalled in great detail his grief which proceeded hia attack on her and Chun Li a few weeks ago. She ended her recollection with the words, "That poor crazy man."

As they walked to the cave for breakfast, Nigel French echoed Harold's earlier remarks, saying, "Actually I feared the next shrimp expedition would prove fatal for all aboard. We almost missed the island on our return. Personally I am happy here. I feared I might never see Elizabeth and my new son again. I'm glad the boat is gone, and Patel may be better off at sea than here with me. He hurt my wife. Karma had me imagining many ways to get back at him. Good riddance is all I have to say to that."

Nigel's words sent Jack's mind reeling over the unpredictability of life here. He wondered what he would have regretted had the ship missed the island. He looked at Marah. He wondered how the love he felt already for her could have grown so deep. He searched his memory for any remnants of such affection ever existing for Janet. He found none. He had always been skeptical of 'love at first sight' but felt the moment he first laid eyes on Marah to be etched deeply in his memory banks. He knew he would never forget hearing her laughter while playing with children. Jack realized that moment he would have missed Marah and Arianna most of all had they have been lost at sea. His longing for a life with her became overwhelming that instant. He decided to waste no more time. This evening he would ask for her hand. If she accepted, the most wonderful era of his life was about to begin.

Jack ran into Harold in the serving line at the dining hall. Simultaneously, they both said, "I need to talk to you after while." They both laughed and as if in formation said, "Okay." Harold followed Janie to the table with their food while Jack, Marah and Arianna waited their turn. Jack and Harold knew each other well enough to know they both meant they should speak in private about some unknown subject sometime after breakfast. For now they would join the Rotge's and the French's along with Harold and Janie. The ladies made plans to help one another with chores today. Together they would clean the restrooms and wash clothes. They could borrow an additional big pan from the kitchen for the kids to play in. It would be fun. The kids could take turns playing in the pan and not even realize they were getting a bath.

Jack, Harold, Guillaume and Nigel decided after the grueling day they had shrimping yesterday, today was the perfect day to fish all day to replenish the live well. They would ask the other eight crew members from their one and only shrimping trip yesterday to join them again today. This fishing trip promised to be a lot more relaxing. It would also give Jack and Harold a chance to talk privately.

About an hour after they had started fishing, Doctor Goodson was walking by where Jack was sitting on the river bank. Jack said, "I trust you're feeling better now than you were earlier, doctor?"

Goodson replied, "You can bet I'm not doing as well as you are, so if you will excuse me." He held up a towel, a change of clothes and a bottle of dish soap.

Jack smiled and said, "Oh, say no more sir."

As Goodson walked away he was mumbling to himself, "I'll say no more all right cause I'm sure you don't want to hear what I have to say. Say no more indeed."

Harold saw this as the perfect time to talk to Jack about what Janie had told him. He said, "Jack, Janie said the doc has a thing for Marah. Dude if you really want her as much as I think you do, you don't need to wait long to make your move."

Jack asked, "Do you think that is why he is acting pissed at me?"

Harold answered, "Absolutely. Man while we were gone yesterday he gave her a basket full of flowers and goodies. He made a tearful apology for having offended her when Claudette and the others got hurt. He is after your woman and he doesn't even know it for sure yet. I'm telling you, you need to lay your claim. I have never really seen you happy before you met her and I have known you nearly my whole life. I hope you don't let her slip away."

Jack said, "I hope she will do just the opposite of slip away. I plan to ask for her hand in marriage tonight at dinner. Life and death move so fast here. I don't want to waste what time we have. I want to make her mine if she will agree."

Harold giggled and shook his friend's hand. He said, "Way to gain control of a sticky situation."

Jack said, "No it's not because of having competition. I have never felt this way about a woman in my life. I am hopelessly in love with both Marah and Arianna. She and I have talked. I believe she feels the same way. Today is the day my friend."

Harold said, "From what Janie says I believe you are right. I am happy for you. You deserve it."

Sanjay was sitting within ear shot and came over to join them. He sat down, threw out his fishing line and said, "Guys, I couldn't help overhearing. Congratulations Jack. Man there must be something in the water here. I too am experiencing the europhic state of finding that perfect mate. The feelings I find myself having toward Jenny Parker are like none before. I will wait till tomorrow so not to steal your thunder. But I plan to ask Jenny to marry me as well. Maybe we can arrange a double ceremony."

Harold said, "Make that a triple ceremony. Janie and I have been in a prearranged relationship nearly since birth. But now with the baby coming, I would feel better if we said the vows." Then he shook his head, giggled and said, "Just look at us, three guys standing around the river bank planning our wedding. Thing is, we ain't asked the girls yet. How about we do the asking and let them handle the planning?" The three men agreed and continued to fish. By the time dinner was to be served that evening, the live well had been somewhat replenished by the twelve crew members and Sanjay.

Chun Li would prepare a few of the fresh fish, but tonight's main course was a coconut and pineapple shrimp dish accompanied by rice and corn. The Parker sisters had prepared juicy and delicious coconut cake and pineapple upside down cake for dessert. There were juices, milk, coffee, tea and water to drink. There would be no more wine for about a week as all they had ready was drank last night.

Now the time had come. Jack had butterflies in his stomach the whole time he was eating. Jack and Marah were sitting among their friends who were nearly finished eating. The ladies had made plans to relieve the kitchen staff of their clean-up duties for this evening. Jack knew the time was upon him. He stood and asked for the attention of all at his table. Then he asked Marah to stand. It seemed that he gained the attention of the whole room when he dropped to one knee. You could have heard a pin drop when he said, "Marah, first of all I ask that you will forgive me if you do not see the world through my eyes. But since I first laid eyes on you a week after the crash, you have been the primary thought in my mind. I love you Marah. Yesterday our ship nearly missed the island upon our return. I realize because of all that has happened here I don't want to miss being with you. So with that being said I humbly beg you my love to be my wife. Will you marry me Marah?"

With tears flowing, Marah said, "I too remember the first time I saw you. It was the day Arianna went missing. Your kindness was overwhelming. I have watched you on a number of occasions risk your life for others. Under ordinary circumstances I would be required to morn Ragish for an entire year. But as we all know we are not living under ordinary circumstances. Had I been endowed with the ability to create the perfect mate for myself, it would have been you. I love you too Jack. Yes I will marry you."

The entire dining room erupted in applause and shouts of approval. Many came up to shake hands with Jack or to hug Marah. Harold was the only one who seemed to notice the look on Doctor Goodson's face. He was the only person not joining in the celebration, his expression was one of disapproval and pain. He sat there staring in their direction as he pushed away his half eaten dinner. Harold was unsure as he lacked the ability to read lips, but it appeared the doctor had mouthed the words, "We'll just see about that." He watched as the green monster of jealousy reared it's ugly head in the disappointed doctor's heart. He decided to stay close to Jack for the next few days to watch his back as he knew jealousy can kill.

Harold was startled back to the conversation by a hand touching his shoulder. He looked up to see a smiling Ophilia Parker standing next to him. She said, "Captain Jack, I would be honored to perform the wedding ceremony if you would allow me to. I am an ordained youth minister in the Baptist Church back home. May I be part of this union?"

Jack answered, "I would be delighted for you to guide our nuptials as long as it is acceptable to Marah." Marah nodded in approval.

Ophilia Parker said, "Now there's a man who knows how to treat a lady. It already matters what you think." She patted Marah on the back and said, "I think you have found a keeper young lady."

Marah answered, "I believe so too."

Once all were finished with dinner, Janie, Marah, Iva and Elizabeth began to clean up. Ophilia and Jenny Parker stayed to help and begin planning a wedding. Jack, Harold, Guillaume, and Nigel decided to head back to camp to clean up what was left over from the final disassembly of the tail section. There were a few seats left along with four pieces of metal and six pieces of wood set aside to complete the tables for the dining hall. Everything would be moved to the storage shed. The tables would be brought to the cave in the morning to complete the dining room furniture.

As the final load was delivered to the storage shed, Doctor Goodson sat nearby just outside his office. Nigel French yelled to the doctor, "Hey doctor, no need to sit there all alone. Come on and join us." They had placed four seats in a circle and were gathering enough wood for a small fire to put in the center. As he invited the doctor over, Nigel added a fifth chair to the circle.

Doctor Goodson sarcastically answered, "No thanks. I think I will pass. I wouldn't want to crowd the new groom."

Harold said, "Oh boy, here it comes."

As Jack walked toward the doctor's office he asked, "Arthur, have I done something to offend you sir? I had so hoped for the blessing of all the Islanders for mine and Marah's relationship."

Goodson got to his feet and answered, "Well I cannot offer my blessing for a union which goes against all that is good and right. I mean honestly man, how many wives do you need at one time. Did you ever once consider the possibility that Patel could be found by some ship floating around out there. And if by some stroke of luck we are rescued in the next few months, what then? If faced with the choice, which wife would you choose? By law it would have to be the woman you left behind, would it not?"

Jack stated, "I suppose you were not aware that I offered a writing of divorcement from my adulterous wife a few days ago severing the relationship."

Goodson shouted, "What court of law will uphold such a charade? I can tell you from experience that not everyone who is accused of adultery is guilty of the crime. What would become of Marah and her child should that happen?"

Jack yelled back, "The court of God's law is the only one I am truly concerned about. You can take your blessing and stuff it! Marah and I love each other and I will never let her go, not to please you or anyone else. Besides that, Marah's child has a name. My future daughter's name is Arianna."

Doctor Goodson shoved Jack down saying, "Get out of my way you bigamist!" He then ran face to face with Marah who had arrived moments before unbeknownst to him.

Marah said, "It is my decision and I choose Jack. I am sorry if you are hurt but I never gave you any reason to believe otherwise."

Doctor Goodson looked at her and said, "Just shut up." He then disappeared back down the path to the cave. Marah went over to check on Jack.

Jack was embarrassed. He was unaware of how much of the argument she had overheard. He quickly got to his feet. She asked Jack, "Are you alright?"

Jack, who had already stood back up said, "Yes, I'm fine. Where's Arianna?"

Marah answered, "She is with Elizabeth and Pierre. They will be along shortly."

He asked, "How long had you been here when I noticed you?"

She answered, "Long enough to hear you tell that jerk off. Long enough to hear you say you will never leave me. Long enough to hear you say you love Arianna like she is your own. I'd say I have been here just long enough."

Jack still worried about her reaction to the situation said, "I guess I don't look like much of a protector. I didn't fight back when he pushed me down."

Marah said, "There was nothing besides you to protect. Don't worry, I have seen what you do when others are in danger. You are far from being a coward. The fact is you are a selfless individual. I love you Jack. Now go join your friends and stop worrying about it."

Jack smiled and said, "Yes ma'am. Anything you say."

Harold wanting to further calm the situation added, "Jack, you are learning fast. The key to a happy life is answering every request your woman makes with a simple 'yes ma'am'." Within minutes the four men were seated around the small camp fire laughing, telling stories about their wives. All agreed that 'yes ma'am' was the go to phrase. Nigel joked that Elizabeth had lost some of her 'yes ma'am' leverage when they arrived on the island. Before she would pout and refuse to cook for him if she did not get her way. Now he had Chun Li to keep him from starving. But he added he still said 'yes ma'am' to keep the peace. The four men sat and talked for two more hours before retiring.

Meanwhile, Janie, Iva and Marah were going through the unclaimed luggage. They hoped to find some garment which could be used as a wedding dress. Sanjay had promised to do any needed alterations. The ladies decided the color didn't matter because they would bleach the garment to a crispy white before the wedding. Very little of the unclaimed luggage had been gone through yet. Early on it had been decided the extra clothes would be kept to replace the things that would eventually wear out. An hour into the search, they hit the jackpot. It was a large suitcase which took two of the three women to move. When they got the suitcase outside the storage shed and opened it all three gasped. Inside they found three ball gowns, all of different styles but all breath taking. They put one up to Marah. It looked like it would fit. Janie ushered her into the lower nose section to her quarters to try the dress on. Iva said, "We mustn't let Jack see." The dress looked like it had been tailor made for Marah fitting her like a glove. Janie wrapped the dress in one of the aluminum blankets and laid it aside. Then Marah asked if Janie would stand up with her at the wedding as her maid of honor. Janie accepted. Iva said, "Janie you need to pick one of the other dresses to wear for the ceremony."

Janie laughed, patted her stomach and said, "Well okay, but they don't need to wait too long to get married. This little guy is growing already."

Marah said, "Oh do you think it's a boy?"

Janie answered, "Well Harold hopes it is. I just want a healthy baby."

Later that night before going to their separate quarters, Jack and Marah would experience their first kiss. Both secretly felt the electric bolt of true love shoot through their bodies as Jack took this beauty into his arms and pressed his lips to hers. The single, long, lingering kiss was followed by a simple, "Good night beautiful. I love you and can't wait to see you in the morning."

She answered, "I love you too. Good night." Then the two went their separate ways. They each fell asleep knowing the world stood to look much brighter in the days to come.

CHAPTER NINETEEN

The following morning Harold woke up early. Not wanting to miss the opportunity to jump aboard the matrimony train, he had wandered around picking just the right flowers. By the time Janie emerged from the nose section he had arranged the perfect bouquet. There were five varieties of beautiful purple flowers, purple being her favorite color. The Islanders were beginning to stir. As she walked out of the wreckage, Harold handed her the flowers. She looked surprised and delighted by the gift but had no idea what was about to happen. Immediately after she took the bouquet, Harold dropped to one knee. Startled, Janie asked, "Oh, are you alright?"

Harold answered, "I will be alright only if you agree to my request. Janie I have loved you for my whole life. I realize we have been married in our hearts since early childhood. But now with a child on the way, I feel it necessary to make the bonds even tighter. I ask you my sweet love now, will you marry me?"

With tears flowing down her cheeks, she answered, "Yes. With every fiber of my being I would love to make our lifelong love official. Yes, I will marry you." Janie had no expectations of a ring of any kind. After getting to his feet, Harold removed the wallet from his back pocket and took out a single gold wedding band.

He showed Janie and said, "I bought you this wedding band shortly before my father was arrested seven years ago. I have carried it with me every day since waiting for just the right time. Now is the right time. I had it specially made and polished to perfection. There is no visible sign of where the band starts or ends, no line means no end. I want to spend the rest of my life with you no matter where we are, no matter if we get rescued or are here forever. All I really need is you." They then embraced, unaware of the crowd that had gathered until they erupted in applause. The two looked around and burst into laughter.

Jack and Marah approached them with hugs and handshakes. Marah asked Janie, "Instead of you standing with me when Jack and I marry, can we please all take our vows together? I mean can we have a double wedding?"

Janie replied, "I would love that. Besides we found great dresses yesterday. Come on, lets go see what else we can find."

As the two women were running off like excited school girls, Marah stopped suddenly and turned to Jack and asked, "Will you please let Elizabeth know what I am doing. Please tell her I will be along shortly to get Arianna or if she prefers, she and the kids are welcome to join us."

A still smiling Jack answered, "Yes of course I will. You two have fun."

Marah smiled back and said, "Thank you. Now you and Harold get out of here so we can look at dresses. Everyone knows the grooms must not see the bridal gowns before the wedding. So get."

Both men giggled and simultaneously said, "Yes ma'am." As Marah joined Janie the two men headed down the path to the cave.

As Jack and Harold reached the cave they saw Sanjay standing on the natural three step stair way to the water outside the dining hall. He was on the second step down holding Jenny Parker's hand. She was standing at the top of the steps. Jack and Harold looked at each other and stopped in their tracks. They listened as Sanjay said, "Miss Jenny Parker, I am but a portion of the man I was in my younger days physically. However, you, my dear, have made my heart feel young and free. It's almost as though my life began when I met you because I have trouble remembering life before you. I long for you to be more than my mistress. Therefore I stand here before you, because I cannot get on one knee to ask for your hand in matrimony. I have already secured the blessing of your sister who offered this lovely ring to make our engagement official. She has informed me the ring was your grandmother's and was to be used by who ever married first. Please Jenny, will you be my wife?"

Jenny answered, "Sanjay, there is nothing in the world I want more. Yes, yes I will marry you. I love you too." As soon as she had said yes, Ophilia Parker, the Li's and a few residents stepped out the entrance to the cave applauding. Jenny cried as she hugged her sister and said, "Thank you so much. I know we were planning to live together for the remainder of our days. I promise you will not be alone, and Grandma's ring, are you sure?"

Ophilia said, "Grandma made the rule and we will abide by her request. Don't worry about me being alone. I have my eye on a couple of eligible gentlemen myself. God only knows what the future holds."

Jack and Harold joined the group then. They shook Sanjay's hand as they heard Ophilia say, "Maybe I can hold a double wedding."

Jack spoke up and said, "Make that a triple wedding. Harold and Janie want to make their lifelong commitment official, he proposed as well this morning."

Ophilia said, "Very well, a triple ceremony it is."

Jack added, "Miss Jenny, Janie and Marah found some ball dresses in the unclaimed luggage. They are looking through them now at the storage shed if you would like to join them."

Before she could answer, Ophilia said, "Go on Jenny if you want to. I'll handle things here. But leave the dress with Janie and Marah so Sanjay doesn't see it. After dinner I will accompany you to the camp, and we will take the dress to my house. Who knows, maybe my house can served as a dressing room for the three brides. I love you sis."

An extremely happy Jenny said, "Oh thank you. I love you too. I will be back as soon as I can."

As Jenny Parker disappeared down the pathway to camp, Nigel French accompanied by Francois and Rita Sauvage arrived at the dining hall. As the three smiling faces approached the group, Nigel said, "Oh no, I don't think he would be offended at all. Rather I believe he will be delighted with your gift."

Rita then said to Jack, "Pardon me Captain, but Francois and I heard you have no ring to offer your young bride. If it would not be offensive to you, we would like to offer you one for her. My father was a jeweler and I an only child. I was therefore the apple of his eye and showered with jewelry. As you see, I have rings on every finger. I only really need one, my wedding ring. Because I feel so strongly about that, I would love to see Marah have one on this blessed day. Please will you choose one." She held both hands out in front of him. The rings were lovely.

A very surprised Jack said, "Oh my, they are all beautiful. But how could you ever part with a precious gift from your father? How could I ever repay you? I don't know what to say. Besides, how would I know which one would fit her?"

Rita answered, "Many years ago I learned a secret trick to discover an approximate ring size for cases of surprise engagement. Yesterday rumors were circling about your plans to propose. After hearing of it, I went to Marah bragging on what a good mother she is and offered a high ten, you know a two handed high five. She had no idea I was checking the size of her hands. It appeared our hands are nearly replicas."

Rita then removed a beautiful ring from her right hand ring finger and handed it to Jack. It was a band with small diamonds embedded all around it. It looked like a wedding band. He asked, "How can I ever repay you for such kindness?"

She answered, "Well to tell the truth, Francois and I would love to have a house. He has still got a lot of pulled muscles and bursitis from being pulled from the quicksand pit. He hates any doctor so he refuses to let the Doc check him out. He allowed me to pick a spot and I would like to live close to the Rotge's. So tell me, do we have a deal Captain?"

Jack answered, "Yes ma'am we sure do." Jack held out his hand to shake with the Sauvage's. He added, "Construction will begin after breakfast. Thank you so very much."

Their conversation was interrupted by Sanjay who still stood on the second step down to the live well. He said, "Hey Jack and Harold, could you two help a fellow groom back up on level ground. I seem to have gotten down here fine but I cannot get back up there alone." All three men were giggling like children as they got him back up.

Ophilia Parker came up and said, "Okay boys, hand over all three rings and I will take care of them until the ceremony. I know how men are and one of you are sure to loose one of them if left unattended. Also, I see no reason to waste time. It's two days until Sunday. If that's not too soon, it would be a blessed day for the weddings. What do you say?"

Sanjay said, "Will that be too soon for Jenny?"

Ophilia said, "Not according to what she told me after Jack asked Marah last night. At that point she had no idea you wanted her hand, but she said she would marry you in a minute if only you would ask her."

Sanjay replied, "Very well then, I'm in for Sunday."

In unison Jack and Harold said, "Me too."

Ophilia said, "Good, now hand over the rings." She then placed the three rings on a thick chain necklace which hung from her neck and went back to work in the kitchen. Rita followed her to help in the place of a missing Jenny. Excitement began to build among the residents.

Back at the camp there was a ladies only dress up party going on. Elizabeth French and the children had joined Janie and Marah. Iva Rotge had sent Guillaume to join the other men at the cave so her home could be used to try on the ball dresses. Jenny Parker could hear their laughter as she approached. Jenny said to them, "I hope you ladies don't mind if I join the party. I got the surprise of my life a few minutes ago. Sanjay asked me to marry him and I accepted. Do you think there may be a dress among the ones you have that will fit me?"

Iva said, "I don't see why not. There are five very beautiful ball gowns here and you three ladies are very close to the same size. Jenny you may be a little shorter than they are so we need to compare the length of the remaining three dresses to choose properly. Janie and Marah have already chosen their dresses."

Janie said, "Oh Jenny we are so happy for you and Sanjay. Would you and Marah be opposed to a triple ceremony?"

Marah answered, "I would love that."

Jenny said, "Well that's good because if I know Ophilia, she would probably prefer to do one ceremony. She tends to be a little bossy at times. Thank you both so much for allowing us to join your wedding party. I love you all."

Elizabeth French said, "I can't believe how happy I am here on this island. You know this is the first time I have felt like I was part of a family. It feels like you are all my sisters. I have become a parent here, something I have always longed for. Who would have ever thought a place which lacked modern luxuries could provide true happiness. In my wildest dreams I could have never imagined it."

Iva said, "It just goes to show you civilization as we know has lost the true meaning of life. We are blessed by the magnitude of the values of the people we are here with. Survival with a twist of family values tossed in. Finally our lives offer time to recognize the pleasures life offers. Back home there was no time to fish or play. I never realized it when we were there. Since we have been here many times I have laughed until my sides hurt. That has never happened before. I could very happily live the rest of my life with all of you. Thank you all for including me in your lives. Now let's get to trying on those dresses. Remember ladies to stay inside once you have the dresses on so no man can tell the grooms how beautiful you all are. Also, the Americans have a lovely tradition we should abide by, something old, something new, something borrowed and something blue. It promises success in the relationships. We have work to do. But after the dresses are properly fitted we need to go eat. We don't need to hold up the kitchen staff any longer than necessary." The three brides agreed as they grabbed their dresses and went into Iva's house to try them on. Each lady looked stunning in the dresses which could have been tailored for them and them alone. God had obviously blessed the unions. All were pleased.

At the dining hall, Jack, Harold, Sanjay, Guillaume and Nigel sat eating breakfast. They made plans to gather enough flowers to have a large center piece for each table. Guillaume and Nigel promised to go into the storage shed and bring all the candles to the cave. They would place candles in every possible spot for the wedding. Nigel had suggested that only candle light should be used for the wedding and the solar lights should be removed. He felt the flickering of so many candles along with the fire pit would reflect beautifully the gold and silver veins running through the dining hall.

After the wedding plans had been decided, Guillaume Rotge took the conversation to a new subject. He said, "You know Jack, now that the tail section is no more, we should consider making an expedition to the debris field. There's no telling what kinds of materials we might find useful. We all saw it. From out there in our boat, it appeared to be very vast. We should take along rope and a few tools like a hammer, screw driver and wire cutters. We can make a sled out of something there to haul our bounty back."

Harold said, "We should probably take a saw as well in case we have to cut something to make the sleds. It looked like a lot of big pieces there."

Jack added, "I have been so consumed with the proposals and wedding plans I had all but forgotten the debris field. From out in the ocean it almost looked like there was the wreckage of a small fishing vessel there. It would do me good to see the boat up close. I can't help but wonder if my father could have survived the tsunami. If he made it here I can all but guarantee he is still alive."

Harold said, "You all would have loved Jack's dad, and he would be a great help in the art of survival. I remember him being smart, kind and always calling your attention to things in nature that were important to survival."

Nigel asked, "Like what?"

Jack sat smiling while Harold continued, "Like the fact that honey contained natural antibiotics, and that all birds could be eaten. Also that certain tree barks and roots could be used to make teas and medicines. He was super smart."

Nigel French said, "I would like to meet such a scholar someday. Maybe we will find him living somewhere on the other side of the island."

Jack said, "Actually he was not a scholar. His dad died when he was a young age and he had to go to work to help his mother pay the bills. He didn't get to go very far in school. His knowledge came from experience."

Harold added, "Yeah I remember his saying, 'Experience is the only school anyone ever really learns from'."

Rotge replied, "How true."

With their imaginations running wild, Ophilia Parker interrupted. "Captain Wellington," she said, "I would like you all to produce some type of small stage or stool for me to stand on while performing the weddings. The Li's and I have decided the ceremony should take place around 4 pm on Sunday. We have planned a special menu for dinner that night and want the meal to serve as the reception dinner. I have Sherod and Butch working on candle sticks to produce the unity candles. Also, Mr. Rotge if you have any wire left from the machinery you have been working with, Butch feels he can build a guitar type musical instrument. We need the wire today so he can design the thing. If time allows, he wants to provide music for the ceremony. Now since it's only two days till Sunday, if you all are finished with breakfast, you need to get busy." The men were just about to say they couldn't return to camp without the ladies permission when they walked into the cave smiling.

Guillaume asked Iva, "Is the coast clear? Can we go back to camp yet and where did you all hide the dresses so we don't stumble across them unintentionally?"

Iva answered, "We put them where no man has gone before."

Jenny hugged Ophilia and said, "We planned to say that sis. Elizabeth and I put them in your house. I hope you don't mind."

Ophilia answered, "You mean where no man has gone yet. I told you I have my eye on a couple of eligible gentlemen. Time will tell." She giggled and walked away. The men got up to get busy trying not to be reprimanded by the very take charge Ophilia Parker. The ladies got their breakfast and sat down.

Sanjay was the last to leave the table. As the ladies and Pierre and Arianna came to sit and eat he said, "Marah and Elizabeth, if you two agree, I will watch the children for a while today. I have been waiting for the right time to let them decorate the shirts I sewed for them. There are four different color berries in a bowl just waiting for them. There are five shirts each for four children. I have already cleared it with the other two mothers involved. I have Chun Li's pocket translator because one of the children speaks only Chinese and one only Malaysian. But I believe the delight they will all experience will cross the language barrier and show them they can all play together and enjoy each other's company."

Arianna said, "Please Mommy. I want to paint shirts."

Pierre added, "Yeah, I want to do it too. Please?"

Elizabeth said, "It sounds like fun. I will help you Sanjay. Marah you can use the free time to gather more of your wedding essentials like the ones Iva mentioned earlier if you like. Marah is it okay with you?"

She answered, "I would love to go take a shower. It sounds great."

Iva said, "Oh a shower sounds lovely. After we eat, I will grab a pistol for our protection and join you."

Janie said, "I'm going."

Jenny Parker chimed in, "Me too."

Sanjay said, "Sounds like a plan. I'll go start getting everything together." He exited the dining hall.

Upon returning to the camp, Jack found Francois and Rita Sauvage already working to clear the spot for their new home. He asked Francois to help him salvage enough bamboo from the site to build the stool/stage Ophilia Parker had requested. The two men believed there would be plenty harvested from the home site to not only build the stool but to frame the roof of the home as well. Rita thanked Jack for coming to help her husband and excused herself to return to the dining hall to help Ophilia. Jenny was busy with wedding plans. Rita had already promised to cover for Jenny. Francois told Jack, "I really appreciate your help with our house. Since the quicksand episode, my shoulder will not allow me to reach above my head. I felt it as it was pulled out of socket when I was holding on to the vine they were using to pull me out of the pit. I suppose I should be thankful I have plenty of strength still when reaching straight out or downward. After watching our doctor in action, I believe I will give it time to grow back on it's own."

Jack said, "I understand. It should only take three or four days to complete the home. Ordinarily it would be sooner, but the wedding is in two days. Tomorrow I must help with gathering the flowers and anything else Ophilia Parker requests. I promise you we will finish your home as soon as possible. I cannot thank you and Rita enough for what you have done for me and Marah. She will be so excited when she sees that ring."

Francois replied, "Awe yes, the ring. All of her rings are very nice. Her father delighted in trying to make me look bad, always showering her in jewels I could not afford to give her. He had no idea he had raised the least materialistic woman on Earth. He doesn't know it but we live in a very modest three room cabin. We were traveling to France to attend a wedding. At home she wears only her wedding ring, but she was wearing a ring on every finger because her father was to meet us at the airport upon our arrival. Otherwise he would repeat a fit he threw a few years ago on another visit in which he accused her of selling his gifts to support us. He considers me a failure because I am a laborer rather than a trained artist of one sort or the other. I am lucky to have Rita's heart. Otherwise I would have been alone years ago."

As they were talking, Guillaume Rotge heard the end of the conversation as he returned from the cave. Without hesitation, he joined the two men in their site clearing efforts. Soon they were joined by Nigel French and Harold. Nearby there was a very large piece of woven grass being added to by several ladies while their children played next to them. Surprisingly to all involved, by dinner time the walls of the home were completed and the framing for the roof attached as well. Guillaume and Nigel promised to recruit help the next morning to roof the home so Jack and Harold could prepare for the wedding.

The next day was filled with wedding preparations. The flowers and candles were gathered. The stage was built for Ophilia Parker to stand on, nothing elaborate just a simple three foot square around one foot high. The Sauvage's house was completed allowing them to vacate the upper nose section leaving Marah, Arianna, and Jack the only remaining residents. The lower level had been left vacant except for Harold and Janie. With Jenny Parker and Sanjay already living in a private dwelling, all three couples would have their own honeymoon suites. It had been decided Arianna would spend the wedding night with the French's. Butch had produced a musical instrument which held very little resemblance to any known before but with the ability to carry a nice tune. He planned only to play the wedding march as the brides entered the dining hall. That evening after dinner Ophilia Parker announced all three brides would be staying at her house over night. It was imperative that no groom see the brides prior to the wedding march. Nigel French had promised to deliver breakfast to each groom the next morning. The grooms were expected to be at the dining hall/wedding chapel at 1:30. The ceremony was set to begin at 2:00. The brides would get ready inside the Li house. All had been decided.

By 1:00 the Sunday of the wedding, the dining hall had been transformed. The tables all held flowers and candles. The natural counter top held three separate wedding cakes, one coconut, one pineapple, and one large very rare chocolate cake. An aluminum blanket had been hung behind the stage on which Ophilia would stand to deliver the wedding vows. The tables had been moved and now lined the walls of the dining hall. The seats had been arranged in rows with an aisle way down the center. The scene was breath taking to all who entered. The residents of the island had all turned out in their finest attire.

At 1:30 as Doctor Goodson was just arriving at the cave, Ophilia Parker exited the Li house looking nearly unrecognizable. He said, "My Mrs. Parker, you look absolutely stunning."

She said, "Why thank you doctor, but that is Miss Parker. I have yet to find my mister right. I am not working today so I was free to fix up a bit. Would you mind escorting me to the festivities? I have been too busy to find a date."

He stared at her for a moment and said, "It would be my pleasure." He offered her his arm and the two walked into the dining hall together. Inside he took a seat near the front. He watched Ophilia as she finalized the arrangements for the ceremony. He had never seen her with her hair down before, only up in a bun on her head. Her hair cascaded all the way down her back in blonde ringlet curls with hints of silver scattered through out. Her tall slender build had been hidden well until now by her chosen work attire. The dress she wore hugged her curves well and struck her just below the knees where her high heel boots ended. Arthur Goodson found her suddenly beautiful regardless of the fact she was a few years his senior. He was glad he had chosen to attend.

The dining hall turned wedding chapel erupted in applause when Ophilia entered. Doctor Goodson escorted her to the front of the room where he shook hands with each groom, including Jack, saying good luck with each handshake. He then took a seat nearby. Ophilia gained the attention of the grooms and very softly said, "Okay gentlemen, this is the last chance you have if any of you want to bail out. Well actually only you two have the chance. Sanjay if you hurt my sister I will beat the crap out of you." The three men laughed out loud, a needed relief from wedding jitters. She said, "Well alright then. Here, you all will need these." She handed each man his bride's wedding ring.

Harold asked Jack, "Does Marah know about her ring?"

Jack replied, "No, not that I know of. I think she will be surprised. Her deceased husband never honored her with a ring. I hope she likes it."

Ophilia said, "She will. Now on to more important things. I have arranged escorts for your brides. The ceremony may not be traditional as to any of your past experiences. All of you men will take your vow first, saying your brides name at the right time. Then the ladies will do the same, if they so choose. Then there will be a moment of silent prayer as we may not all share the same religion. Following that will be the lighting of the unity candle. The rings will be placed on the brides fingers next. I will say a few words and finally you will be allowed to kiss your new brides. Are we all clear?" The trio said yes.

Ten minutes later, Butch entered the cave carrying a stringed instrument which resembled a steel guitar and took a seat at the front next to the stage which Ophilia was to stand on. The room became quiet as he began to play the wedding march. The sound was beautiful, a mixture of the tones produced by a guitar and a mandolin. Ophilia took her place on stage. The guests turned to watch as the brides began their march, one by one, along side their escorts, Nigel French, Francois Sauvage, and Chun Li. The grooms stood at attention awaiting the arrival of their future spouses. Janie wore a pale purple evening gown with a white lace over lay and a crown of baby breath sized purple flowers. Jenny wore a beautiful deep blue shoulderless evening gown with a simple white flower pinned to the side of her hair which hung in a beautiful French braid. Marah wore a spaghetti strap off white ankle length sundress. A crown of white wild roses held a home made vale of white lace material they found in Claudette's sewing kit. The brides were utterly breathtaking. Each escort handed the brides off to their chosen grooms and took their seats next to their own brides. The service began.

Ophilia Parker cleared her throat and began to speak. "My fellow Islanders, today we come together to celebrate the love of three couples. As we have all come to realize, both life and death move at a rapid rate here at our new home. The people who stand before me began as six individuals, but by taking these vows will soon become three couples, fused together by the promises of matrimony. I ask that you all, not just those uttering the vows, will take these unions seriously. I take this opportunity to remind you that marriage is not an agreement on some paper inside a government office. It is however a commitment governed only by Almighty God. So it is without further ado that I ask you three gentlemen to repeat after me one at a time. You will need to insert your ladies names in the appropriate spots. I feel confident you will all know where. Let us begin. I blank, take you blank to be my wife. I promise to honor, protect, and provide for you to the best of my abilities. I promise to respect your opinions and only touch you with gentle hands. I promise to love you all the days of my life." The grooms held the hands of the brides and repeated their vows. Next Ophilia addressed the brides. "Now ladies it's your turn. I blank take you blank to be my husband. I promise to walk beside you not behind you in an effort to always be your best helper in life. I promise to nurture you in times of illness while never forgetting to treat you like a man, my man. From this day forward I will try to make our home the comforting cocoon that homes were intended to be and I will love you all the days of our lives." The brides tearfully repeated their solemn vows. Next Ophilia said, "Gentlemen, the rings." The three produced the rings from their front pockets. She continued, "Repeat after me. By allowing me to place this ring on your finger, I make you my wife for life." The men placed the rings on their lady's fingers. Then Ophilia said, "What God has joined together no one on Earth can ever sever. Gentlemen, you may now kiss your brides." As the three couples kissed, Butch began to play the after nuptials tune and the crowd cheered and applauded.

One final time Ophilia gained the attention of the crowd to announce the time had come to cut the three wedding cakes. Three special baskets of goodies were presented to the couples. The baskets held two water bottles filled with sweet home made wine, fruits, nuts and berries. The couples were told after the cake and refreshments were over, the baskets were to go with them to their honeymoon suites. Happiness seemed to flow like a water fall throughout the room.

Once again, Ophilia was approached by Doctor Goodson. He said, "I am both impressed and intrigued by the unconventional vows in that wedding ceremony. That was by far the most beautiful wedding I have ever attended. Did you write the vows or did they do it?"

She answered, "That was all me. I hope I covered all the necessary subjects."

Arthur Goodson replied, "I am convinced you touched on everything important. Even my heart longs for a relationship so true. Unfortunately it doesn't turn out that way for some of us."

She smiled and stated, "Maybe not always the first time, but only God knows our future."

Harold interrupted their conversation by walking up to shake the doctor's hand and thanking him for attending. Goodson answered, "I actually am very glad I didn't miss it."

Harold recognizing the doctor's new found interest in Ophilia added, "Sometimes when we accept that one door has closed, we discover the door we were intended to enter in the first place. Good luck doctor."

The doctor replied, "You may just be on to something. Now don't you have some cake to smear?" The two men laughed as Harold returned to Janie's side.

Marah stood next to Jack, starring at the beautiful ring on her finger. She asked, "Jack, where on Earth did you find such a beautiful ring?"

He told her about Rita and Francois Sauvage. "They saw that we had a need. They also had a need. They needed a home and Francois evidently suffered extensive muscle strain while being pulled from the quicksand pit. He has not regained his strength and needed help constructing a home. It worked out beautifully, don't you think?" he asked.

Marah smiled, looked back at her ring and said, "Yes so beautifully."

The two were then interrupted by a very excited Arianna. "Mommy, Mommy, does this mean we get to keep Jack? Is he now my new Daddy? Pierre says new daddy's are not as mean as old daddy's. He says his new daddy is really nice. If Jack gets to be my new daddy will he get mean or stay nice? Please, Mommy, I need to know."

With teardrops now flowing down both their cheeks, Marah answered, "Arianna, Jack has promised to always be nice to both of us. When we pray we will ask that God will help him to keep that promise. And yes, we get to keep Jack for our very own. Does that make you happy?"

The child hugged her mother and said, "Yes that makes me very happy. I'm gonna call him My Jack." She turned and gave Jack a bear hug and said, "My Jack."

Then she ran back to Pierre and the French's to discuss the answers she had been given.

Jack said to Marah, "I promise to do my very best to never let either of you down." The two embraced, said I love you and were then instructed to cut the cake in front of them.

At the table next to theirs, Sanjay and Jenny stood with bites of cake in their fingers. Sanjay very gently placed his cake in Jenny's mouth. Jenny then smashed her cake in his mustache, giggling all the while saying, "I believe my dear that you were the one who promised to be gentle."

Sanjay grabbed Jenny and kissed her deeply, transferring much of the cake mess to her face. He then laughingly said, "Okay then, but remember loving also means sharing." The crowd's laughter rose again as the other two couples smashed cake into each other's faces.

Afterward the three couples engaged in the lighting of the unity candles and the service was adjourned. The crowd enjoyed fellowship and the feast that had been prepared for the celebration. Everyone was encouraged to take fruit home with them since dinner was served so much earlier than usual. It had been a wonderful day for all involved. The remainder of the day would be taken for rest and relaxation for all.

CHAPTER TWENTY

TSUNAMI DEBRIS FIELD

The next two weeks consisted of the building of five more homes along the pathway to the cave. The middle section upper level now only housed two residents. The two had moved to one end of the wreckage to allow space for the school room Janie and Marah had been planning for. Together with Iva and Elizabeth they had set up a twelve student school. They would take turns attempting to teach the English language to the Islanders who only spoke other languages. Nigel French had promised to help Elizabeth teach the Chinese children as he was fluent in their language. Iva Rotge was to handle the French speaking children. Janie would teach those speaking the Malaysian dialect and Marah would instruct the Egyptians. If successful, all the children could be speaking the same language in a few months.

Beneath the school room, the lower level of the middle section had become the favored spot for the elderly to reside. The entrance was easily accessible and now housed sixteen aged couples. There were four other older couples who shared the lower level of the nose section with Harold and Janie.

This morning had been the subject of two weeks of discussions and planning. With the tail section of the plane no longer existing they were at a loss for conventional building materials. Even on the day of the wedding, Guillaume Rotge had been pushing for an expedition to the tsunami debris field. He strongly felt there would be usable materials among the debris. Today was the day. On this Monday morning there would be a ten man trip to the rubble pile. Rotge would replace Habib as the trigger man, becoming armed for the group's protection.

Jack and Harold had climbed lookout cliff five times during the two weeks in an effort to plan the route to be taken. Each time Jack had spoken of the wrecked ship among the debris. He and his lifelong friend wondered if the ship could possibly turn out to be Jack's father's. Just the day before, while the two were atop the cliff, Harold had said, "It would have been nice if the idiots who brought us here would have thought to bring binoculars." Unsure if and when anyone could be within ear shot, the two stood by the agreement made never to speak of being involved in the crash.

Jack answered, "Yeah really. But maybe we will get lucky and find a pair among the debris field." The two friends had looked at each other in relief when they heard someone laugh from below having heard what they said. They looked down on the ground level to see Francois and Rita Sauvage passing by.

Francois said, "Well good luck with all that. My bet is that anything among that junk pile will be too weathered to be of use. It has been years since the great tsunami."

Jack replied, "You are probably right, but that ship looks like my father's from this distance, so I must see for myself. I can't help but wonder if he is living on the other side of this island."

Francois answered, "Oh, I didn't know that. In that case, I hope the trip is a success."

"Thank you very much," said Jack.

The plan was that the expedition would begin following coffee and breakfast. They would bring along saws and hammers for material retrieval. They would need path clearing tools as well. At the request of Doctor Goodson they would also take along a first aid kit. It was undetermined if the new pathway to the debris could be cleared in one day. They would return before dark and repeat for as many days as it took to reach the junk pile as Francois had chosen to call it.

However this morning would start a little differently than expected. Jack had kissed Marah while she slept before going to the lower level to wake Harold for the trip. Just as they were exiting the plane, from above vomit poured down on Jack's head. Harold following closely behind stopped dead in his tracks. Doctor Goodson, who sat outside his office nearby, busted out laughing. As Jack jumped from under the vomit stream and looked up, he saw Marah was the one sick. Doctor Goodson, who had come to terms with Jack and Marah's marriage said, "Well, Jack, it sure didn't take long for her to get sick of you, now did it." He laughed again.

Jack said, "Apparently not. Marah, honey are you alright?"

She answered, "I guess. I'm sorry Jack. I had no idea you were there. I think I better lay back down."

Jack replied, "Maybe you should, but could you toss me down a clean shirt first? Do you need me to stay here and take care of you?"

"No I don't think so," said Marah as she dropped the shirt down to her husband. "I feel a little better since I threw up."

Doctor Goodson said, "Don't worry Jack. I will see to it that the ladies know to keep an eye on her today. I will also have Janie administer a pregnancy test on Marah. As we all know, life happens quickly here on our island. Considering she said she felt better after throwing up, it sounds like a classic case of morning sickness to me. We will let you know the results this evening when you return. Again don't worry, we will all take care of her. Now go wash your hair before the junk dries in it."

Jack looked up and said, "I love you Marah. See you later."

From inside the upper level she said, "I love you too. Be careful."

Jack and Harold hurried to join the rest of the expedition team at the cave all of whom laughed at hearing what was in Jack's hair. He quickly went to the water's edge and washed the vomit from his hair. As soon as he was finished suddenly he realized what Doctor Goodson had said. He said to Harold, "Wait a minute, did Goodson say he thought Marah could be pregnant? Do you think he was kidding me?"

Harold answered, "I can't say for sure, but I think he was serious. I hope she is, and I would love if Janie and her both had boys. Then they could grow up together as best friends just like us."

Jack said, "That would be great. I just never expected it this soon."

Harold stated, "Well you know Janie and I started our physical relationship after the plane crash and we are already pregnant too." He laughed and added, "Maybe it's something in the water."

Nigel French arrived at the cave then and asked, "Jack, have you a plan of attack as to our route to the debris field? Will we be traveling by land or by beach?"

Jack answered, "It appears the best path will be through the forest. It promises not to be too bad, there are two fields of weeds between here and there besides all the wooded areas. I believe we will be safe from quicksand going that direction. Harold and I both looked for areas that looked similar to the quicksand pit and saw no more. We will still need to be aware of the possibility of one existing and be careful. But I believe it to be the safest route."

Nigel said, "Very well then Captain. Shall we eat and get this show on the road?"

"Sounds like a plan to me," said Jack.

Their journey would begin by going around the mountain which held the cave/dining hall. Once they reached the other side, they began cutting and clearing their path. It would take some three hours before they reached the first field of vegetation. The weeds and chest high vegetation was harder to cut through than the undergrowth of the wooded areas. There would be a much narrower wooded area before they reached the second of the two fields. This time it was much different. There was a stream which ran the entire length of the field along it's outer edge. As they began to cut their path into the field, it began to smell more and more like a skunk. Knowing skunks were not native to the area, Jack, Harold and Guillaume Rotge began to examine just what it was they were cutting. They soon realized they were in a field of either Hemp or Marijuana.

Nigel French was the first to speak of the find. "Well gentlemen, I have heard that in certain regions of the world, cannabis grows wild. I had no idea we were in that region. These plants will go a long way as to creating medications for a number of ailments that we may face here in the years to come, should we not be rescued that is."

Rotge said, "Even if it turns out to be hemp, the healing qualities are enormous."

Three of the men in the group were Chinese. Nigel French began to translate to the rest of the group that the three men were making plans to cut the plants from this field. Then they could plant rice here. After planting they could dam up the stream to flood the field during the growing season for the rice. Then the dam could be removed for harvest. All involved agreed to help in the coming days to make this happen. Realizing they were now nearly six hours into the trip, the group chose to take the ten or so plants they had already cut and head back to the cave. The plants would be hung upside down and allowed to dry so they could be tested. It was the only way to discover exactly what they were. Tomorrow they would begin again to try to reach the debris field.

When they arrived back at the cave, the three Chinese gentlemen went straight to Chun Li to discuss their finding of the perfect place to grow rice. Even through the language barrier, it was plain to see the excitement it instilled in the four of them. Rice was an important staple in the diet among the Islanders. Until now they had worried about the possibility of not being able to ever replenish the supply. Today they may have solved that problem.

Outside the dining hall, Doctor Goodson sat along side Ophilia Parker. The two each held a fishing pole. Jack went over to ask about Marah and tell the doctor about the Hemp field. As he approached, Goodson pulled in a fish that was barely bigger than a minnow. Ophilia laughed loudly as she lifted a stringer from the water which held an approximate 7 lb fish. Jack watched as she teased, "How thoughtful of you Arthur to catch my fish some dinner."

"Yeah, yeah, yeah," he replied.

Jack laughed as he stated, "Be careful doc. Women who outfish you tend to steal your heart as well."

Goodson replied, "I wouldn't be at all surprised Captain. So tell me how was your trip?"

Jack said, "First, how is Marah? Do you know if she has been sick any more today? I have barely thought of anything else today."

Doctor Goodson answered, "I believe she will be fine, that is in a few months. You do fast work, Captain. Her pregnancy test was positive. She should deliver six weeks to two months after Janie. Really, congratulations Jack. Please don't tell her you already know. Ophilia heard her and Janie making plans on some special way to tell you the test results."

"Wow, what did Arianna say about it?" asked Jack.

Ophilia said, "They didn't tell her yet. They were afraid she would let the cat out of the bag. They didn't realize they had Arthur to do that for her." The three all laughed.

Jack said, "You asked about the trip today. While attempting to cut out a pathway to the debris field, we encountered an entire acre or so field of what appears to be Hemp or Marijuana. Nigel and Guillaume felt you would be interested due to the medicinal qualities of the plants either way. We had already cut some 20 or so plants before realizing what it might be and we brought them back for you to examine. If you would like to see them just give me a shout when you finish here. I'm starving and am gonna grab some dinner."

Ophilia said, "I believe you will enjoy your meal. Tonight we have the first harvest of squash and cucumbers added into the menu. It is simply delicious."

Jack said, "On that note, if the two of you will please excuse me?" He turned and entered the dining hall. He joined the other nine men of the expedition group who had already retrieved their plates of food. The group were the last of the Islanders to eat for today. Jack looked forward to going back to camp to be with Marah and Arianna. He hoped she would be as thrilled over the baby as he was.

When Jack and Harold arrived back at the camp, Arianna was sitting in the entrance to the lower level of the nose section. As soon as she saw them, she ran and jumped in Jack's arms. She hugged him tightly and said, "Mommy says we are gonna get me a little brother or sister in a few months. I can't wait to be a big sister."

"Well that is great news. I am glad that you are excited about the baby," Jack said as he hugged the child back.

Arianna added, "But is Mommy gonna be sick for a long time? She has been sick a lot of times today. I want Mommy to feel better. Can you please make her well?"

As Jack sat the child back on the ground, he said, "I don't know if I can or not but I sure will try. Where is Mommy now?"

Arianna answered, "She is inside with Janie folding clothes. They did laundry today. Mommy said they had to because I needed clean undies." Arianna grabbed Jack's hand and led him into the wreckage. As they entered Janie and Harold's living quarters, they were met by Janie and Marah both wearing shirts which read "MOM". Both ladies held out shirts which read "DAD" to their husbands. The two men gently took their wives into their arms and hugged them before accepting the shirts.

Jack said, "How are you feeling Marah? Arianna tells me we are going to 'get her a little brother or sister'. She also said you have been sick all day. Are you okay?"

She replied, "A little queasy but I will be fine in eight and a half more months." She laughed at her own statement.

Jack stated, "Thank you for my shirt and for our baby. I love them both."

Marah said, "The shirts were actually Sanjay's idea. He had the berries used to decorate the shirts. When he saw Janie and me doing laundry he told us of the idea. It was supposed to be how I told you about the baby, but I guess Arianna couldn't hold it in any longer."

Jack smiled and stated, "Well I wouldn't have had it any other way. Besides this baby will be hers as well. Soon we will be one big happy family."

Soon after, Jack, Marah and Arianna went to the upper level to retire for the evening. Jack talked nonstop until he eventually fell asleep. He told Marah all about their adventures of the day. He talked a lot about tomorrow. He had hopes of the shipwreck being his father's boat. He was very excited about the prospect that his father might somehow have survived the tsunami and might be alive on the other side of this island. Overnight he even talked in his sleep. Marah listened as he told his father in his dream about his beautiful new wife and daughter. He spoke also of having a baby boy who he would name after his father's father, Ivan. In his slumber he apologized to his father for having already used his name for Janet's son. Marah fell asleep soon after he finally shut up talking. She would tell him all about it in the morning. She had no clue the men would already be gone when she woke the next day to extreme morning sickness once again.

The group of ten men had obviously shared the same excitement as they gathered before breakfast the next morning. They chose to finish off the leftovers from the night before with their coffee rather than waiting for breakfast. Then they were off once again in an effort to reach the tsunami debris pile. After reaching the field of Hemp like plants, it would take four more hours before they chopped out a pathway to the section of the beach which held the massive pile of debris.

As they got closer to the ship wreck they could see very little of the deck remained. The hull appeared to still be intact. Jack started to yell, "Dad, Dad, Jon Wellington! Harold, look, I think it is Dad's ship. Three letters of the name are still there, look C A M. Remember he named it after Mother, Camilla. Please, Harold, help me."

Harold yelled, "Slow down Jack. We have to be careful or we could be hurt or killed trying to get to the ship. There are nails, sharp pieces of metal and other things we could get cut badly on if we don't take our time getting there. Please, we will do this together." Harold laid his hand on Jack's shoulder to regain his attention. In all their years of friendship, he had never seen Jack in such a desperate state. Jack looked at Harold, shook his head, and said, "Of course, you're right. I got a lot carried away. Let's do this." Without another word, the two men began to make their way across some thirty yards of debris, some piled waist high in the water, some floating freely. Once they reached the ship's wreckage, Jack knew his suspicions were correct. He drew a deep breath as he pointed to the name of the ship. They watched momentarily as a railroad tie bashed the boat repeatedly, forced by the waves into the very spot the name was painted. C A M was still attached perfectly to the side of the ship, while I L L A was bent inward at the site of the hole. Fearing the worst, Harold asked his friend, "Shall we go aboard?"

Jack answered through tears, "Yes, I have to know."

As they made their way onto what remained of the deck, Jack was amazed at how much of it remained intact. It appeared that a ten foot section of the forty foot deck was all that was missing. Two large fishing nets remained rolled up along one side of the deck. Jack said, "Look Harold, Dad's nets are still right there rolled up and there's a roll of rope. We can probably use that at some point if it's not dry rotted."

Harold said, "Good find. Jack are you ready to go below, or do you want me to check it out alone?"

Jack answered, "We will do it together."

As they went down what was left of the steps, Harold stopped just prior to reaching the bottom. He said, "Hold on a minute. I need to let my eyes adjust to the lighting down here. There is stuff floating everywhere." Jack did the same, stopping on the stairs leading to the two room living area of the boat. The contents of the first room was investigated with no sign of Jack's father anywhere. Harold stopped again in the doorway to the sleeping quarters. He drew a deep breath and said, "Jack the lighting in here is worse. There are only two boards missing from the deck above this room. There's only a few things floating in there but brace yourself. It looks like someone is in there too. Come on, we will check it out together." Even knowing in their hearts it was Jack's father, neither man was prepared for what was to happen next. Once inside the ten by ten room both men allowed their eyes a moment to adjust to the lighting again. They saw a body, still clothed, floating face down in the water. Together they approached the body. Together they turned the corpse over to see the name on the shirt. They both screamed out in horror when the skull of the body disconnected while they were turning it and began to float away. Jack began to cry as he read the name on the uniform shirt: WELLINGTON. Horror again filled their hearts upon realizing the shoes that floated next to them still contained the foot bones which had disconnected themselves at the ankle joints. The reality of the find was suffocating.

Jack said, "I gotta get out of here." He immediately went back on to the deck and sat down. He dried his eyes and they began to talk.

Harold's biggest desire was to comfort his best friend now in his hour of need. He tried to pick the right words, quite the difficult task at this moment. He said, "Mr. Jon always said he hoped at his time of death he would be allowed by God to go down with his ship. If you really think about it, his greatest wish was granted. You know if we were to try, we might be able to retrieve enough of the boat to build you and Marah a house out of it. You now have a golden opportunity that no one else on this island has been blessed with. There are items on this ship wreck that you can be certain were your father's. These are things that can be passed down to your children here on the island. It had to be a gift from God. He could have sent this pile of debris floating anywhere. He chose to give you the closure you have needed for many years with the knowledge of what actually happened to your dad."

Jack replied, "I'm sure you're right about all of that. It's just even in death, I never expected him to be in such a deteriorated state. When his head fell off, it was that very second I saw his name. All I could think about was that's my dad. It was awful. I thought I would collapse. The air was suddenly so thick I could not breathe. I had to get out. What do I do now, Harold, I mean with his remains? I can't leave him in there falling apart."

Harold answered, "If you would like, we can bury his remains here on this beach near his ship. Afterward I will help you to gather any of his belongings we can find to take back home. I will help any way possible. Are you in agreement on that being the plan?"

Jack answered, "That sounds like the right way to handle it. If he is buried here, I can visit the grave in private if I need to grieve. Thank you Harold. Come on, we may as well get started. Please will you explain to the other men what we found and what we are doing. I don't want to talk about it yet."

"Yes of course," he replied.

The two men then joined the others who were on the beach. Harold explained what had happened. The eight men who had already been pulling loose boards from the rubble to be used in building stopped what they were doing. Everyone began to dig with whatever they could find to use. It had to have taken them an hour or more to complete the grave, but it seemed only minutes to Jack. Guillaume produced a three foot long wooden crate he had pulled from the debris. He said to Jack, "My friend it saddens me to ask, but would this box serve as a proper coffin considering the conditions of the remains?"

Tearfully Jack answered, "Probably, but I can't do it. Will you and Harold please go get Dad? If possible may I keep his shirt?" He cried hard for a moment and added, "Harold, please don't forget his feet."

Harold patted his friend on the shoulder and said, "It's okay Jack. We got this. You wait here." In a few minutes, Harold and Guillaume returned with the closed crate covered by Jon Wellington's uniform shirt. They handed the shirt to Jack and gently lowered the crate into the grave. They then offered prayers for Jon's soul and for Jack's grief. By then it was nearing time to return to camp. Jack asked them to give him a moment. He reboarded his father's ship and returned carrying a book. Harold asked, "What is that?"

Jack said, "My father's log book. It was still in the cabinet where he always kept it. Look, it doesn't even look like it got wet at all. I want to read it. Thanks for all your help everyone. I couldn't have took it without all of you." The group then headed home for the day with a load of boards in tow. As they made their way through the Hemp field they gathered the twenty plants they had cut making their pathway.

When they arrived back at the cave, dinner was already being served. Today the menu consisted of beans, squash, okra and cornbread. The community was enjoying the fresh vegetables they had grown. In the past three days there had been one new veggie added every day as the crops were now beginning to produce. As Jack was greeted by hugs from Arianna and an unusually pale Marah, he again began to cry. He still was carrying his father's shirt and log book. He told Marah about them finding his father's remains and burying him on that beach. He asked her to be patient with him, feeling he might be able to work through his grief quickly considering he had known his father was probably dead for years now. Today had just made it a reality, hard to swallow until you get used to the fact. His lovely wife hugged him again and said, "Jack, please allow yourself to find comfort in the fact that his soul now resides here on the island with us and in Heaven as well. You hold in your hand something that he held many times and wrote his deepest thoughts in. Jack please dry your eyes and enjoy that blessing. No one else here has access to such a number of items owned by a loved one who preceded them in death. I promise you, counting your blessings will ease the pain much quicker."

Jack tried to wipe the tears away. Once he had dried his eyes he could see more clearly just how pale his bride was. He said, "I am sure you are right. How was your day, sweetheart? Are you feeling any better?"

Marah answered, "A little better than earlier today. It was at least noon before my stomach settled down. I bet this baby will be a boy. I never experienced morning sickness with Arianna even once. After the baby is born, it will all be worth it. I love you. Now go get your dinner. You need to eat."

Meanwhile, Harold had told Janie about Jack's father and the events of the day. They were both very concerned about their dear friend. They decided to talk to Doctor Goodson to see if he had any nerve medication to help Jack through his grief. Sorrow over death had already caused two suicides on the island. They were concerned if Jack slipped into a deep depression over his beloved father, he could be the third. Harold said, "You know it wasn't just Habib. There was the wife of the scout leader on the second day we were stranded. Please, I don't want to loose my best friend. Is there any way you can help?"

Doctor Goodson, joining them in their concern, answered, "This is not good. Whoever supplied the meds for this trip to nowhere obviously had no respect for nerve pills or opioids. There were a very few Valium at first. Unfortunately they were all used on Mr. Patel to keep him civil and the others helped calm Claudette, Habib and Sanjay after they were injured. I have no more. There has been some research which indicates some calming effects both in CBD and THC oils. We have yet to discover if the plants you all have been bringing back are Hemp or Marijuana. Considering Jack's current state, I believe we have found our guinea pig. I will go pull some of the buds off one of the plants from yesterday and put them on a cookie sheet to dry. I can put them on the top of Chun Li's grill. It is still hot enough to dry them in a few minutes. You two find some kind of paper to roll it up in and we will make Jack test it. I will lie and tell him it needs to be tested as it may be used to ease some of Marah's morning sickness. It is already used in some of the states to ease nausea in cancer patients undergoing chemo therapy. He will do it then."

Harold said, "Thank you doctor. I will be back soon."

Just as they were about to walk off, Ophilia Parker came up and said, "I couldn't help but hear you guys. My parents were from the Woodstock era and were big pot heads. I can make you a small pipe from aluminum foil to test the herb. Lord knows I saw them do it enough. Now you and Janie go eat so we can get the kitchen cleaned up," she said to Harold. Then she added, "Doc, are we still on for our walk on the beach this evening?"

Goodson answered, "Absolutely, as soon as our experiment is complete." Soon after, as the doctor was sitting the pan of buds on top of Li's grill, Ophilia handed the doctor the pipe she had promised. After dinner they convinced Jack to test the product. Doctor Goodson allowed Jack to take three puffs only from the pipe.

At first Jack said he was feeling no effect from the test. However ten minutes later he had a different result. Ophilia laughed as Jack started to stand and sat back down quickly. He said, "Wow, my head is spinning like a top. Is it supposed to do that?"

Ophilia said, "Well in my expert opinion, having grown up around it, I believe you are experiencing the effects of 'Creep Weed'. At least that is what my parents would have called it. It is a type of high grade Marijuana which has a delayed effect on the user. You will be fine. Just stand a little slower next time. You just had your first 'head rush' as they used to call it. Doc, it appears you have plenty of nerve meds on hand now. I will have the seed removal team add the plants to their list of work. We may need to recruit more people for the task. Chun Li has demanded that all seeds in all veggies be removed and saved for future crops. With their help, we should have veggies from here on out. Now we have a new crop to add to the list."

The doctor refilled the small pipe and handed it to Jack along with a partially used pack of matches. He said, "Your next dose is a half hour or so before bedtime. There should be enough for Marah to have one puff in the morning if you only take three. Do not fail to test the effects again before morning. We have to have further proof before Marah tests it. Are we clear Captain?"

"Yes, doctor. At least I think we are," Jack answered. Everyone left the dining hall giggling at Jack and thankful for the upgrade in attitude he was experiencing.

That night after remedicating himself, Jack read a few pages of his father's log book. It had a different effect on him than he had feared it would. Marah had expected him to talk in his sleep that night as he had on occasions of major stress. However his slumber was surprisingly silent. The next morning he would know he had dreamed of his father many times during the night. He would feel as though he had spent hours visiting with him. An unexplained calm had wrapped his broken heart in a safety cocoon. He thanked God for the relief that he had been blessed with.

CHAPTER TWENTY-ONE

ANOTHER MAN'S TREASURE

On the first day of reaching the debris field there were thirty usable pieces of lumber pulled from the junk pile. The group who made the maiden journey had spread the word of lots of usable items among the debris. Many of the Islanders chose to make the trip the next day to do a bit of shopping for themselves. As the ten original explorers prepared to return to the debris field, they were surprised to be joined by forty others. Francois Sauvage spoke for the extras looking to make the trip. He said to Jack, "A few people along with Rita and myself wish to accompany you all to the Tsunami debris. We understand there is much to be gathered there, usable materials. We respectfully request permission to accompany your group. Once we arrive, we would first like to create some sort of barrier around your father's grave. Out of respect, we do not wish to walk accidentally over his final resting place. Would that be acceptable to you, Captain?"

Jack replied, "Yes of course you all can go. I truly appreciate the respect being offered my father. Besides, I am in no position of authority. I neither decide or control the actions of any of you. We are all equals here. In the future, it would please me to be referred to as Jack rather than Captain Wellington. In my opinion, Captain Wellington is buried on the beach that we are going to. Please feel free to join us."

Iva Rotge stepped from the group and asked her husband, "Guillaume, If you don't mind, go and get me one of the other pistols. At this point, there are fifty people about to make this trip and only one armed individual to protect them from unfriendly wildlife. Even if the pathway is wide enough for them to walk two by two, there needs to be another person armed."

He answered, "Very well my dear. I shall return momentarily." He was back in minutes handing her a pistol with an extra magazine of ammo. Guillaume would lead the group while Iva would follow in the rear of the convoy. Then they were off to the debris field.

Upon their arrival, the first accomplishment was gathering some twelve boards of equal length. They were stacked three deep in a square enclosing Jon Wellington's grave. Then Rita Sauvage and Iva Rotge found a two foot square piece of tin floating near by. It was Iva's idea to find a short manageable piece of wood with a nail sticking out. The two would use the nail to punch holes into the tin. Fifteen minutes later there was a tomb stone made of tin placed on the fence around the grave. John Wellington, it read. When Jack saw the sign, he was so touched by their kindness, he never told them his father had no H in his first name. He hugged the two ladies and thanked them.

The men in the group seemed to be interested in gathering any usable building materials from the pile first. The ladies on the other hand had obviously come furniture shopping. They worked together to pull numerous small tables, chairs, shelves and blankets from the rubble. They were able to salvage multiple pots, pans, and buckets. Rita laughed as she placed one of the pots on the beach and said, "Finally, I have a pot to piss in to go along with my new window to throw it out of." Laughter erupted from all who heard. As they worked to gather items, the ladies noticed a bath tub still attached to a section of flooring floating among the debris near the shore. Rita said, "Oh Iva, wouldn't it be nice if we could get the guys to move that tub back to camp. We could set it up close to the river bank and get them to build a grill close by. We could use some of the pans we have found to heat water in on the grill. The only thing I really miss about back home is a nice bubble bath soothing my aching back. Please help me try to talk them into it."

Iva said, "We can at least talk to them about it. I know what you mean about it being something as simple as a hot bath that you miss most. I find it fascinating that last Christmas when Guillaume asked for my gift request, I had no answer. There were so many modern gadgets that I couldn't choose. My home was actually cluttered with things I thought I had to have. Life is so much simpler here. I have nearly nothing and I am currently having the time of my life. I mean look at us. We are digging through what would be a garbage dump back home, and we are enjoying it. Winding up here and realizing all we really need is a roof over our heads and enough to eat has been one of my life's biggest blessings and biggest lessons as well. This island has offered me the chance to make real friends. At this point, I don't think I would have wanted to miss it for the world."

Rita replied, "Yes it has definitely been an adventure."

Not far away, Jack, Harold, Nigel and Francois were beginning to disassemble the deck of Jack's father's boat. Janie had sent along a trash bag for Jack to bring back any of his father's belongings that could be salvaged. It sat on the deck near the rolled up fishing net. As Harold, Nigel, and Francois worked to remove the boards from the deck one by one, Jack rummaged through the two rooms below. He occasionally emerged from below with an arm load of items to place in the bag. He was especially proud to find a picture of himself and his parents taken when Jack was about five years old. From what he could remember, his mother's affair had not yet begun when the picture was taken. His parents looked happy there in the photograph, nothing like the couple he recalled. His mother had built a wall of lies which stood between them evidently soon after this photo was taken. The thought of his father clinging to the memory of a happy family saddened Jack. It was then he gave thanks to God for giving him the opportunity to be with Marah, a second chance at true love, a chance his father never got. With each new find Jack's heart gained more acceptance of his father's death. By the day's end, Jack had half a trash bag of his dad's belongings. The deck of the boat had been reduced to a four foot section which still held the fishing net, rope and the bag of belongings. The boards salvaged from the boat were stacked on a piece of metal roofing pulled from the debris. Two ropes were tied to the metal to pull it all back to camp. There were four other sleds full of building materials and furniture ready to go as well. It was decided everything saved today would be used up prior gathering anything else from the pile. Everyone involved was pleased with the bounty they had retrieved.

As they were leaving Harold and Jack turned to look back at the junk pile. Harold said, "You know, one man's trash."

Jack finished with, "Another man's treasure. Today makes that old saying ring especially true."

Harold replied, "Yes, that it does." Being last in the line of sleds, the two men grabbed the ropes and pulled their sled home.

Jack was surprisingly light hearted upon their return. It was beginning to sink in he had items that belonged to his father. He was eager to show it all to Marah. He wanted to discuss with her what to do with the beautiful wood stacked on the sled. He and Harold were met at the entrance of the dining hall by Janie, Marah and Arianna. Again Arianna ran and jumped into Jack's arms. "I missed you today, my Jack," the child said as she delivered a bear hug.

Jack answered, "I missed you too, my Arianna. I hope you have had a nice day."

She replied, "My day got a lot better after Mommy and Janie stopped being sick everywhere. It was yucky. I stepped in some of it. Then when Mommy was washing my shoe off, she got sick again. Oh, will you kill the mean turtle? I am scared of it."

Concerned, he put Arianna down and turned to Marah. He hugged his wife and asked, "Are you okay my love?"

Marah said, "I have been fine for hours now. I guess she is still mad about stepping in it."

He asked, "What is this about a mean turtle she is scared of?"

Just then Butch came over and joined the conversation. "You should have seen it Jack. It was hilarious. Marah and Janie, along with the help of Arianna and Pierre were picking cucumbers and squash there on the beach. Sherod and I were nearby whittling out some flatware when the commotion started. I heard the little girl shout Mommy, look out. Then out of the bushes near by rushed a large turtle. Next thing I know there were two woven baskets of veggies flying through the air. Those two women were screaming like little girls, running and each dragging a child who couldn't keep up behind them. We nearly died laughing at them. The turtle ate it's fill and returned to the brush. Sherod and I finished gathering the squash and cucumbers for them. Someone probably does need to go turtle hunting though. Otherwise, they may just eat us out of house and home. When you get back to camp, go look at the foot prints in the sand. I bet you will be able to visualize it. Truly hilarious."

Jack patted Butch on the back, thanked him for his help and promised to try to find the 'mean turtle' when he got back to camp after dinner. He told Marah, "I can't wait for us to get back to camp so I can show you all I found on the boat. You were right. I found things that are irreplaceable. I was amazed at the things that were untouched by the water. Oh and darling, you will need to be deciding what you would like built from the deck wood we salvaged from Dad's boat. I can't explain it Marah, but I feel so excited about my Dad's stuff."

As they stood next to Jack's sled of materials, Marah's face suddenly lit up. She said, "If you don't already have plans for both of the fishing nets, I would like to claim one of them. Guillaume built Iva a bed with bamboo posts and woven grass for the mattress area. She says it is much more comfortable than the hard ground to lie on. I would like one with fish netting in the place of woven grass. Iva and Rita gave me and Janie each a blanket pulled from the debris. If we lay ours over the netting we should have a comfortable place to sleep."

Jack said, "That sounds like a great idea."

Marah continued, "I was wondering about something. I will be satisfied with a small house, but we will need two rooms, one for us and one for the kids. Would you please be mindful while building it to insure we can use this deck wood and have a real floor in our house? If you think about it, using your father's wood to floor our house would mean our home had a bit of his taste built into it. Do you think he would approve?"

Jack answered, "He would have loved it, just like he would have loved you and Arianna."

Marah, forgetting Jack had said the name in his sleep, said, "And Ivan too."

Jack looked puzzled as he asked, "Ivan? That was my Grandfather's name. How could you have known I was considering that for a baby name should it be a boy?"

Marah replied, "Last night you were talking to your father in your sleep. I heard you when you told him about the name. For a moment I had forgotten you were asleep when you said it. Personally I love the name. If we were talking about our children, Ivan goes well with Arianna, don't you think?"

Once again Jack hugged Marah tight. He said, "Absolutely, my love, absolutely. Thank you so much. If it's a girl you can pick the name."

"Okay," she answered.

Near by Janie asked Harold, "How was Jack today?"

He answered, "Surprisingly upbeat. He told me he dreamed he had a long visit with Mr. Jon last night. I believe the dream had a lasting healing effect on him. At least I hope it will be lasting. For now we will take it one day at a time. How are you feeling? I heard Arianna say you were sick today. Do you feel better now?"

Janie said, "Oh yes. I just saw Marah get sick and I guess it was like the power of suggestion. I got sick right next to her. I believe if Arianna was bigger she would have whipped us both when she stepped in it. I have never seen that child get so mad before. I'm sure if anyone was watching, they found it comical. That along with the turtle incident was the island entertainment for the day." Harold laughed and promised he and Jack would kill the 'mean turtle' for tomorrow night's dinner. Then they went inside to eat dinner and on to camp afterwards.

As they were settling in for the night, Jack was eager to show Marah his father's things. First he showed her the picture of his family. She smiled at Jack's childhood antics as she pointed at his tongue being stuck out in the photo. She noticed how his mother was dressed in the finest of attire while her husband wore a torn uniform. Jack appeared to be growing out of his clothes as his pants hit him at mid shin range. She remembered him telling her that his mother was a lot like Janet, self serving first and foremost. It saddened her to hear him say the picture was taken before his mother started cheating. Then he showed her his father's camping knife, complete with spoon and fork. He had found Jon's comb, razor, and the brush he made his shaving lather with. There was another shirt with the name WELLINGTON embroidered into it. He produced a weathered piece of paper with a child's drawing of a stick figure man and child on a boat. They were holding a fishing pole with what appeared to be a whale on the line. In the handwriting of a young child, the message was 'Happy Birthday Daddy. I hope you catch FREE WILLY so you can come home for good. I love you. Jackie.' Jack told Marah, "I couldn't believe he still had this stapled to the ceiling just above his bed. I don't understand why so many items seem to be untouched by the water and he didn't survive. How could he have drowned when some things didn't even get wet?"

Marah said, "You are overlooking the facts. Those items have had many years to dry out if they did get wet. There's also the possibility that God kept the items safe for you to have someday. He sees the future like none of us ever will. Please enjoy the blessing and don't waste your time trying to understand it."

As Jack continued to remove things from the bag he said, "You're probably right. I mean the day before we set out for the debris pile, Harold and I were standing on lookout cliff wishing we had binoculars. Look, I found Dad's. They are full of sand and ocean water but Guillaume thinks he can fix them. God granted that wish and many others. Thank you so much for reminding me where it came from. I love you Marah."

"I love you too," she replied.

Jack sat the bag aside, leaned over and kissed an already sleeping Arianna, and said, "I'm tired Sweetheart, we can finish looking at this stuff tomorrow."

Marah said, "Sleep well my love." Marah offered silent prayers of thanks for Jack's acceptance and good nature before drifting off to sleep.

Nearby in their quarters, Iva asked Guillaume, "Tomorrow will you help Rita and I to draw enough water to wash the blankets we found? There are 12 of them and more among the debris. We need all we can get to pass out to the families. We also need water to clean the end tables and chairs we found."

He answered, "Yes I will as soon as Jack, Harold and I get through with the mean turtle. After Jack promised to kill it he asked me to do it. Says he has never killed anything other than a fish or a bee. I said if they would help locate the turtle, I would kill it but they have to take it to the cave. A deal is a deal."

"Okay, thank you," replied Iva.

CHAPTER TWENTY-TWO

THE HARVEST

By the time two more months had past, the crops had grown to maturity. It had been decided by the Islanders that every fifth ear of corn would be saved for planting the next crop. With the temperature averaging in the mid 80's year round in this region, there would be no delay in planting the next crop. The seed retrieval crew had grown to forty people who had worked to gather all seeds from the fruit and vegetables harvested. Butch and Sherod had become the spokesmen for the elder island residents. The suggestions they had brought forward had reflected the wisdom only achieved with age. Per their request, it had been decided one quarter of the seeds from all future harvests be stored rather than planted. With no way to predict the weather, the wrong storm could take out an entire crop of vegetables. Sherod's words were, "It has been suggested that we don't put all our eggs in one basket. A portion of all seeds should be stored for the 'what ifs'."

Rice was the only crop not yet ready for harvest. It had gotten a late start. The rice field had been designed and built by Chun Li's right hand man and helper, Kim Wang and his wife Lin. After the Marijuana had all been harvested that field had been prepared and planted with rice. Then they, along with the help of many of the Islanders, had dammed up the stream that ran the entire length of the one or so acre field. The field would remain flooded until the rice reached maturity. Then the dam would be broken allowing the crop to dry out for harvesting. As of yet, Kim Wang believed the crop to be half way to harvest time.

Doctor Goodson had been put in charge of the fate of the Marijuana harvest. Harold and Guillaume Rotge had designed and built five wooden barrels for dry crop storage from tree bark and wire. On this, the first morning of the major food harvest, the doctor approached the two gentlemen. He said, "Is there any chance the two of you would be able and willing to create more of these storage barrels? Three of the barrels you provided have already been filled and we are only half way through the seed retrieval process. It is amazing just how much this one acre has produced. Even with no way to get a proper weight, I would estimate there will be more than two hundred pounds of the herb at the end of processing. Please, we're running out of places to put it."

Harold repeated, "Two hundred pounds of pot, really. Doc, what are you planning to do with all of it?"

Doctor Goodson answered, "I have been making plans actually. Once the processing is complete, I will retain possession of one quarter of the herb for the purpose of developing vital medications for future needs of the Islanders. I plan to use the CBD and THC oils to treat a number of ailments. My patients are currently running out of previously prescribed medications that were their treatments. The oils promise relief to joint and muscle pain, stomach, heart and blood pressure issues. The next one quarter will be passed off to the kitchen crew who plan to create edible Marijuana products. Sanjay has in his possession a book found in the unclaimed luggage which identifies the trees and plants from this region. Together we believe we have found Maple trees from which to get sweet syrup. It is also our belief that the Stevia plant is native here. We can develop a natural sugar substitute from that plant. If we are successful the kitchen crew will be able to produce Marijuana infused hard candies which could prove beneficial for years to come. The final one half of the harvested herb will be available to any and all who would like to indulge recreationally. It is a great stress reducer for anyone who feels they are spread too thin with daily tasks. As a matter of fact, Butch and Sherod are eagerly awaiting enough corn cobs to produce pipes made from them and bamboo for the smoking of the herb. Their plan is to build 120 usable corncob pipes and give every adult one of their own. That way anyone who so desires may indulge freely. That gentlemen is the plan."

Harold said, "It seems you have everything thought out." He looked at Guillaume and said, "We better go get busy on those barrels."

Rotge replied, "I agree. However I have a previous assignment so Jack will have to assist you with the barrels."

In the past two months, Rita Sauvage and Elizabeth French had worked tirelessly to produce 100 woven grass baskets to make the harvest easier. There seemed to be an endless stream of people bringing baskets filled with produce to the cave. Beans and peas of any kind were treated as the corn was with every fifth pod set aside for future crop seeds. No sooner was a basket emptied until another resident grabbed it eager to join in the harvest. A portion of certain crops, such as onions and carrots, were left growing. Their fruits may grow underground, but the seeds are harvested from the plants above ground at the end of the growth period. All seeds and produce would be stored inside the cavern beginning at the dining hall.

Jack, Marah and Arianna were enjoying the first week in their new home. The dwelling had been constructed 50 feet from the camp end of the pathway to the cave. It had two 10'x10' rooms with woven grass walls. The roof was made of metal sheeting salvaged from the debris field. Per Marah's request, the deck from Jon Wellington's ship provided a nice floor. One room had a full size bed with woven grass hammock style mattress, the other a twin size similar bed. Both rooms had multiple woven baskets stored under the beds holding clothing and other stored items. Per Arianna's request, Jack had cut a window flap in the wall of their bedroom for Marah to vomit out of. The child had lost all sympathy for her Mommy's constant morning sickness. As luck would have it, Arianna seemed to always step in the vomit piles accidentally, no matter where they were. The child had grown increasingly angry with each repeated mishap. Marah agreed Arianna would have a better chance of avoiding the mess if she had a window nearby rather than just a door. While Janie had experienced maybe six bouts of morning sickness total, Marah's stomach provided near volcanic style eruptions five or six times a day. Jack was truly concerned for her health.

Harold and Janie had built a dwelling directly across the pathway from Jack and Marah's house. Their home was a 12'x12' one room wooden building. Harold had pulled nearly petrified partial sheets of plywood from the debris pile to make the walls from. His roof was plywood covered with woven grass, then topped off with thatch grass. He had salvaged several skids from the debris, disassembled them and used them to floor the one room shelter. They too had a full size hammock bed along with a small crib built by Butch as a gift for the baby. Underneath their bed sat a number of storage baskets as well. In one corner stood a small table Harold had built to hold a medium sized turtle shell used as a wash basin. A small mirror salvaged from the plane's restroom hung above the turtle basin. Next to the shell sat Janie's hair brush and Harold's very dull razor. They had all the comforts of home.

The past two months had improved the life of Doctor Goodson as well. He and Ophilia Parker had fallen in love, and he had moved in with her. His former office/residence now only served as an office. Still, Jack couldn't help but wonder about his motives. Just days before, he had asked the doctor about Marah's severe nausea. Goodson's answer was harsh, "Some women have major morning sickness throughout their pregnancies. However I wonder about how far along she really is. Supposedly she is at least 4 to 6 weeks behind Janie on gestation. Even with the extreme vomiting her baby bump is much larger than Janie's. Jack, have you considered the fact this may not be your baby? There is a possibility this child may have been conceived before the plane crash. Only time will tell, but if I were you, I would keep track of how long she is pregnant before delivery. Without modern equipment like ultrasound, it's really the only way to tell."

Jack answered, "Well at this point I don't guess that really matters. My mind goes back to high school, studying 'Romeo and Juliet', the passage about would not a rose be as beautiful if called by any other name. As much as I love Arianna, the biology behind this child's conception truly doesn't matter. My prayer is that after the birth my wife and new baby will be happy and healthy for many years to come. I need them in my life. Please, Doc, help me take care of her."

Doctor Goodson said, "I promise to do my very best. Honestly Jack, I wasn't trying to rain on your parade. I just felt you should know about my suspicions. We will all hope for a good outcome." Jack chose not to even tell Marah about the Doctor's words. He wondered if somewhere down deep the doctor was still jealous of Marah and himself. He would put these negative thoughts to rest, stored somewhere inside a chest of hard memories to be dealt with at a later time nestled deep within his psyche.

In an effort to take care of the two pregnant women, Janie and Marah had been asked to join the seed removal team and leave the harvest to the other people. It was proving to be an enjoyable task as the two sat at a table next to Jenny and Sanjay's house next to the river bank. Their table had the two of them along with Rita Sauvage, Iva Rotge and Elizabeth French all working together. No one was exempt from work on harvest day. Arianna and Pierre helped Sanjay keep the ladies stocked with untouched veggies to de-seed. The plan was to remove the seeds from whatever foods were chosen for that night's cuisine. There had to be enough prepared to feed one hundred and fifty people. Tonight's planned meal was vegetable soup and corn bread. Chun Li had requested some of every vegetable available to be provided for the meal.

For three days now, Nigel French and Francois Sauvage had been working to provide shelves in the cavern leading off the dining hall inside the cave. They had used boards retrieved from the debris piles stacked on large stones. The two men had successfully erected shelves twenty feet long, four shelves high on both sides of the cave walls. The plan was to store the vegetables along the shelves until they were needed. They were to be single layered and laid so they were not touching. Ophilia Parker had suggested this method. That way if one piece of produce rotted it would not spread throughout the whole bunch. She remembered her parents storing potatoes in that fashion during her childhood after their yearly harvest. Every five feet along the shelves on both sides of the hallway, they had placed a candle. This would provide light for the cooks when the veggies were needed. It had been decided that any excess beans and peas would be placed on trays and allowed to dry in the sun. This would extend their shelf life tremendously. Guillaume Rotge had taken on the task of protecting the beans and peas from birds while they were drying. It had proven to be a hard job all day as the birds tried to devour them. At one point he shouted and told Iva, "Tomorrow before we start this work, you and I are going bird hunting. We can get rid of some of these pests, provide 150 birds the size of cornish game hens, and make me a feather pillow all at the same time."

Iva smiled and answered, "Awe Guillaume, how sweet of you to make plans for me to have a feather pillow."

He replied, "But I said the pillow was going to be... oh never mind. I guess I should just say yes dear and go on."

Iva laughed and said, "Yes dear, you should."

"That's what I thought," Guillaume said as he went back to shooing birds away.

All five ladies laughed heartily as Sanjay stated, "You guys are just mean." Arianna and Pierre didn't hear any of it as they were busy singing 'Row, row, row your boat' as they worked. Elizabeth had taught them the song and suggested it would be fun for them to sing while they helped with the veggies.

That night as nearly all the Islanders were having dinner, Doctor Goodson stood and asked for everyone's attention. He said, "As all of you know, in a very few months I will be delivering two babies, God willing that is. The accidents and injuries that have been sustained while we have been on the island have all but depleted my small supply of pain medications. As all of you know, child birth is a long, painful experience. Now with that being said, I was wondering since we have corn available, do any of you know how to build a still to produce corn whiskey? While Ophilia has produced some great wine, wine lacks the ability to become pure grain alcohol. Corn whiskey possesses that ability completely. Whiskey has been used for centuries for pain killers and instrument and wound sterilization as well. If anyone has the knowledge, we really need to address the issue soon to allow for aging purposes. Please if anyone can help, see me after dinner to discuss it. Thank you all for your attention." The doctor again took his seat.

From the other end of the table, Janie jokingly asked, "Doc, you mean you're gonna get me drunk when I have the baby? Or did you mean you are going to get drunk when I have the baby?"

Marah joined in the game saying, "Do Janie and I need to start a club for our little lambs called B A A?" You know, baby alcoholics anonymous."

Iva chimed in, "We will need to begin rehab before they reach crawling age for the path of least resistance."

Elizabeth said, "That's right, because if they are still drinking when they start walking, they might get early admission to the school of hard knocks."

Sanjay said, "Watch out Doc, these ladies have been nothing but down right mean all day. They have picked on Guillaume and I all day. Suddenly you seem to be the one in their cross hairs."

Guillaume added, "Yeah, be careful or it could cost you a feather pillow."

Goodson asked, "What? A pillow?"

Guillaume laughed and said, "Never mind."

After dinner Doctor Goodson was approached by Sherod, who said, "Doc, I doubt very seriously that we have all the mechanical components to build an actual still. However I know how to make corn cob wine. I guarantee the toxicity will be much greater than any normal wine made by your intended. I don't know, maybe whatever is in corn that causes it to be capable of turning into both whiskey and biofuel causes the strength to be much greater. I am no chemist. But I have always desired two or three good stiff shots of liquor to relieve the stress of a hard day's work. When my wife was alive she was all about image, so I wasn't allowed in a liquor store. We compromised and I was allowed to drink all the wine I wanted as long as I was the one who made it. After experimenting for years with fruited wines, I learned of a stronger type developed from simple corn cobs. The effect was much more satisfying. My dear wife never knew the difference. If nobody else has any better ideas, maybe that will work."

Goodson answered, "That's an amazing idea, Sherod. I would appreciate any help you can give me. Oh and about your statement on my intended, Ophilia and I are only boyfriend and girlfriend."

Sherod replied, "Well you are living with her, kissing her and sleeping with her. Need I remind you that you are not the only eligible bachelor here on the island." Sherod stood up a little straighter and continued, "You need to be intending something before some old fart beats your time and marries her right out from under you. I mean no offense but she is still a very pretty girl."

Goodson smiled and said, "Yeah and until she changes her mind she is my pretty girl so hands off old man. I assure you I have the best of intentions for my lovely lady. Currently we are enjoying our courtship. There will be time for everything else on down the road."

Sherod giggled and said, "Well you can't blame a fellow for trying." He then patted Arthur Goodson on the back and shook his hand before walking away.

The main harvest would last three days while the seed removal would be an ongoing daily task. With no real way to preserve the vegetables, cutting them up to retrieve the seeds would have to be done on the day of preparation. Otherwise the veggies would surely rot before they could all be used. Many of the plants were expected to continue to produce even after the main harvest. The tomato plants for one were still refilling themselves with ripe tomatoes every three days. The beans and peas were still offering a new batch at least once a week. The corn plants had been stripped of all the ears they had produced as the silks which extended from their tops had all turned dark, a signal that it is time to harvest. The volcanic soil on the island had provided key nutrients causing the seeds planted just months ago to offer an unbelievable amount of vegetables. That night just as dinner had begun, Chun Li with the translation of Nigel French had praised the efforts of the harvesters. He had made special mentions of the hard work in the beginning of Janie, Marah, Iva, Elizabeth and not forgetting Claudette for planting the crops they were now enjoying. He suggested that Claudette upon her arrival in Heaven had asked a special blessing be bestowed upon this crop for a huge harvest. Her blessing request had obviously been granted from the amount of vegetables that had been picked today. Nigel's final translation of the Chun Li speech was replanting would start three weeks from today. Janie and Marah would be excused from that task due to their current physical condition. Then he thanked the Islanders for their attention, shook Nigel's hand in thanks for the translation, and returned to work. Any time Chun Li offered speech to the Islanders, it was followed by applause. Every resident of this island had the utmost respect for this gentleman now thought to be one of the world's best chef's. His efforts were appreciated by one and all.

It was the hope of the Islanders that a harvest of this magnitude could occur two, possibly three times a year. The climate was perfect to grow crops year round. The keepers of the rice patch, Kim and Lin Wang, suggested they prepare an actual garden spot for the next round of planting. Kim Wang believed the first field of weeds and bushes encountered along the way to the debris field could be cleared and prepared for planting before time to replant the vegetables. It would take a large amount of manpower and some time to clear the field, but Wang suggested they had plenty of both available. He mentioned some of the corn stalks had been nonproductive due to being planted along the pathway. They had been unintentionally trampled by home construction and occupation. He reminded the people that every stalk of corn mattered. By the time he was finished with his suggestion, the island's entire population was in agreement. The field clearing would begin in three days after the harvest had been completed. That would allow two and one half weeks to finish the clearing before Chun Li's scheduled replanting was to take place. No one shied away from the tasks ahead as it was common knowledge survival in such an environment takes working together.

CHAPTER TWENTY-THREE

Four months later, Doctor Goodson approached Jack one morning at breakfast. He said, "Captain Wellington, I'm sorry, Jack, I need you to please gather your best designers, engineers, and construction workers for a meeting this afternoon around two. The meeting will be held at my office back at camp. I truly need your help, for the good of all the Islanders. I will keep the subject matter private until then. Will you help me?"

Jack answered, "Yes of course, doctor. You make this sound serious. Is there something wrong?"

Doctor Goodson answered, "Yes and no. Yes it is serious, and no there's nothing wrong presently. But that could all change if we don't address a few issues."

Jack said, "Consider it done."

At 2 pm a group of men gathered outside the doctor's office. Among them were Jack, Harold, Guillaume Rotge, Sanjay, Nigel French, Chun Li, Butch, Sherod, Kim Wang, and Francois Sauvage. Arthur Goodson thanked them all for coming and began to explain the urgency behind this meeting. He said, "Gentlemen, we all know the amount of lives that have been lost since our arrival. With major injuries I currently have barely over a fifty fifty success rating. Now that being said, I feel anxious about the upcoming births of the wives of Jack and Harold. Even with Obstetrics being my chosen line of the medical field, I am extremely concerned about delivering newborns in the facility I currently have available. I am worried about infection. There is no way to sterilize the room. I fear it may be a disaster waiting to happen. I have no access to the machinery which helped me do my job. I talked to Ophilia about my thoughts, my fear of impending doom. Now from here on out, everything I am requesting was by her suggestion and design. How such a brilliant mind stayed tucked away inside the head of a cafeteria service worker all these years is beyond me."

Sherod interrupted saying, "Doc, you gotta quit dogging her for not being a college girl. That don't mean she's dumb."

Goodson continued, "I totally agree, and if you will let me finish I will prove it to you. Anyway, Ophilia says we still have time to build a hospital before the babies come, providing they are not early bloomers. By her design, we will need four rooms, 12' x 12' each connected by a hallway with two rooms on each side. The hospital should be built somewhere close to the cave so it can have a floor from the rock slab. She wants the walls to be stone like Sanjay and Jenny's house. She wants each room to have a turtle shell wash basin like Harold and Janie's. Three rooms will have two beds each for patients. Those three rooms will also have two seats and a table for the use of the caretakers. The forth room will house the bathtub she saw in the debris pile. Outside the room with the tub she wants a grill built to heat water for the tub or other sterilization purposes. The tub will be for purposes like hot baths for pulled muscles or cold baths if needed to reduce fevers from any infections that get out of hand. There should be one stretcher sized bed in this room along with a wash basin shell and a bench to store one's clothing while receiving water therapy. But wait gentlemen, there is more. Per her design, not mine, the lighting that was salvaged from the tail section of the plane and installed in the kitchen, she has a plan for it. As you all know, it was by unanimous vote that we chose not to use the lights in the dining hall. Remember the exhaust from the generator was overpowering inside the cave. Well the spot she has measured out and chosen for the hospital will allow the cliff itself to serve as one exterior wall. Strategically her plan has the generator placed behind the hospital as in association with the entrance to the cave. It should reroute the directions of the exhaust fumes to not be bothersome. We should be able to run the machine all night to provide lighting for all four rooms of the hospital. There's probably plenty of blow dryers and curling irons here that we can gather enough cord to make plugs, keeping them individual for each room. The generator has four outlets available. She has honestly thought of everything down to counting pieces of metal roofing still among the debris pile to be sure there was enough to roof the place. However time is of the essence, gentlemen. There's babies a comin'. I know it's a lot to ask but please will you all help me? I don't think I can keep infection out of this place." He pointed to the office he stood in front of.

The entire group answered yes in various ways. Chun Li and Kim Wang held the pocket translator between them and had followed the doctor's speech in real time. They too were aboard the construction train. Chun Li said he would provide breakfast for a few days and allow the ladies to cook dinner so he could help. The stone homes constructed here had originated from his design. He felt the rock work would go faster if he were in charge of that task.

Butch said, "What do you guys think of building the interior walls from wood? The doctor might like a place to hang things. You can't do that on stone walls."

Guillaume said, "The walls that separate the two rooms on each side of the hallway would be fine built of wood. However the walls on each side of the hall need to be stone to ensure the integrity of the roof, I would think."

Harold said, "Guillaume is right. We don't need the roof to cave in during a storm on the patients inside."

Then Butch said, "Francois and I will take the responsibility of providing enough reasonably sized logs to build the walls. It would be pretty if you stone workers mortared between the logs to give it that rustic cabin feel, don't you think?"

Goodson replied, "Oh my, that would be nice."

Jack said, "I believe I can provide you with a black board of sorts for each room and chalk to write on it with. Just down river on the way to the shower, there are some pretty smooth pieces of slate rock that have fallen from the side of the cliff. I believe I can find four of them that will be suitable. We have such a limited amount of paper and pencils here, the black boards may be the best long term solution."

Doctor Goodson said, "That sounds nice too. But where on this island are you going to get chalk to write on them with?"

Jack answered, "Oh that's the easy part. You missed it because you were still babysitting Patel. Marah is the type of Mom who goes prepared with a bag of toys for the children. A few weeks before we were married, one day she arrived at the cave and offered the children sidewalk chalk to draw on the bedrock outside the dining hall."

Chun Li, still holding the translator, burst out laughing and said, "I remember that day. I thought Su would have a stroke when she saw all the writing on the ground. She took all the chalk and put it away while scolding the children for the mess they had made. I am sure she will hand it over for adult use only."

Jack laughed too and added, "Yeah I remember it too. Marah shares Su's dislike of messes. She was glad when Su took the chalk. She told me, 'the masterpieces had gotten out of hand'. You should have been there. It was hilarious. But anyway, there were sixteen colors of chalk to choose from in the box. They were barely used when confiscated."

Goodson said, "Chalk boards would be great. Thank you."

Sherod said, "If I can find some help gathering materials, I will take charge of providing the furnishings for the hospital. I have already built beds for all the homes that have been constructed here. What's a few more."

Nigel French said, "I would like to help you Sherod. I am interested in learning the art of furniture building."

Sherod replied, "Very well then. I have found my first sucker." Everyone laughed and he continued, "However, I am no killer. I will build the tables for them, but I ain't killing no turtle for the shells. Nigel don't you think Elizabeth can make them some pottery wash basins instead? Seems to me they would be much easier to sterilize." Then looking at Guillaume and Francois he continued, "Could you two fellows please ask Iva and Rita to make the woven grass mattresses for the beds and the seats for the chairs? That would really help me." All three men promised to ask their wives to perform the tasks he had requested.

Doctor Goodson said, "There's still one thing I need help with. The deceased flight crew members who organized our extended stay-cation provided very little in the line of antibiotics and pain meds. I believe we have addressed amply the issue of pain medications with the discovery of the Marijuana and the promise of very strong corn cob wine. However we need to do something about the antibiotic issue. Sanjay, I would like for you to be in charge of this matter. You live next to the dining hall. From now on, any left over breads that are prepared I need you to take. The bread needs to be allowed to mold. That mold I will need you to save. You and I will attempt to make penicillin from it."

Sanjay said, "Anything I can do to help I will be glad to do. But just FYI, last week Jenny and I were walking down the river bank sightseeing. Not far beyond the shower area we noticed a hollow tree with a lot of bees buzzing around it's gaping hole. Jenny said we should tell you about it because honey contains natural antibiotics that might prove useful. I completely forgot about it until now. We need to get someone to rob the bee hive of it's honey."

After reading Sanjay's words on the pocket translator, Kim Wang spoke up. He tapped Nigel French on the shoulder so he would translate for him. Wang said, "I'll do it. My father was a bee keeper. I will do as I have seen him do and smoke the bees out of the hive and steal their honey. With enough layers of clothing, I may be able to do it without even getting stung. It's actually one of my lines of expertise." Nigel thanked Kim before translating his statement.

Doctor Goodson thanked him as well and said, "If you guys are interested, I would like to show you where I am talking about putting the hospital. Bear in mind, I am open to any suggestions if someone knows of a better spot. I really can't thank you all enough. I feel quite fortunate to be part of such a community. So are you all ready?" Goodson lead the way followed by the rest of the men in two single file lines. The hospital was the topic of conversation on the trip to the building site.

When they arrived at the dining hall, they were surprised to see a group of women at the very site of the hospital. They had an eight foot 2 x 4 board salvaged from the debris pile and a piece of sidewalk chalk. The group consisted of Janie, Marah, Elizabeth French, Iva Rotge, Jenny, Ophilia, Rita Sauvage, Su Li, and Lin Wang. Iva Rotge seemed to be the leader as the ladies were drawing out the outline of where they believed the hospital should be built.

Jack and Nigel rushed to the group of women first as Pierre lay appearing to be lifeless inside the chalk drawing of the perimeter of the future hospital. Thinking something had happened to him, they never even noticed Arianna standing above him holding a coloring book and crayons. Nigel asked, "Oh my, what happened to Pierre?"

Arianna spoke up and said, "Pierre is in the hospital and I am the doctor who is gonna make him better."

Nigel answered, "Very well then, carry on."

Jack said, "That's a relief. I thought something bad had happened."

Nigel replied, "Yeah, me too."

Then Guillaume Rotge asked, "Iva dear, what exactly is it that you ladies are trying to do?"

She answered, "Let me explain. As this 2 x 4 has what appears to be factory cuts at both ends, we believe it to be a full eight feet in length. That means if we lay it end to end three times we get 24 feet. If the hospital is 24 x 27 feet we should get a pretty accurate reading from this measurement. At her last doctor's visit just prior to the plane crash, Marah said Arianna was two inches shy of being three feet tall. We used her to get the extra three feet."

Guillaume asked, "But why did you need the extra three feet? I thought the hospital was going to have four 12 x 12 feet rooms. Oh wait a minute, you added in the hallway that I forgot. All those looks and brains too... I am a lucky man."

She teasingly replied, "You are a smart man too, smart enough to talk his way out of the mess he just talked his way into." She laughed and kissed him on the cheek.

Ophilia Parker asked Doctor Goodson, "What did the guys think of my ideas on the hospital?"

He answered, "Surprisingly so, they all appear to be on board. Granted they changed a couple of things, but over all they found it doable."

She replied, "Oh I don't find it surprising at all. It's a great plan and it will be a great hospital."

Goodson asked, "How did you get the ladies on board so quickly?"

Ophilia answered, "We started out talking about the babies coming and concern for preventing infection. When I mentioned the hospital idea, Su Li was the first aboard. You know her English has gotten a lot better. She truly hopes there will be a hospital for the births. She had been both dreading and prepared to offer their home up again to serve as a hospital. However she is certainly hoping that won't be necessary now. Then when I told them about the bath tub being part of it, the rest of the ladies jumped aboard so quickly, had it have been a boat it would have sunk. The place we have measured out will leave ample space to walk past it and on down the river bank. We ladies feel we have chosen the perfect building site, don't you, Arthur?"

"What ever you want, Sweetheart," he answered.

Guillaume and Iva Rotge stood next to them talking. Guillaume said, "Actually Doc, they have chosen a good spot. You see how the cliff hangs out several feet over this edge of the proposed building?" Guillaume picked up the 2 x 4 and stood it on it's end and continued. "Look, there is approximately 2 inches left above the eight feet. If we build the structure here, allowing the cliff to serve partially as walls, partially as roof, we can all but insure the exhaust from the generator will not reach the dining hall. There may be occasions when it will blow inside the cave as we don't control the wind, but for the most part it will defer the fumes. It may not be the spot originally chosen, but I do believe it will work better."

As Doctor Goodson inquired how they would attach the rest of the roof, Chun Li and Kim Wang stood nearby discussing something in Chinese while pointing to the roof. Nigel French spoke up and said, "Good idea." Then he repeated it in Chinese before telling Goodson and Rotge, "These two gentlemen have the roof issue solved. They plan to build a two foot wooden frame next to the cliff's edge strong enough to hold two layers of softball sized stones. As the layers are mortared to the edge of the cliff's rock, they will place a sheet of metal roofing between the layers. The mortar will prevent any water leakage during rain storms. Then after allowing 24 hours for that mortar to dry and harden the remainder of the roof can be constructed. Truly brilliant."

That night during dinner Jack gained the attention of the Islanders informing them all of the plans to build the hospital. He said, "Any of you willing to help in the construction should be aware the first task will be to gather the stones needed to erect the walls. After that we will need a great deal of pebble gravel from the river bank, sand and volcanic soil to make the mortar. There are logs to cut for the interior walls, and metal roofing to retrieve from the debris pile, along with any boards still remaining among the debris. Last but certainly not least, there is a bath tub still connected to flooring among the debris which must be retrieved. We will also need help building the furniture and running the lighting system inside the hospital. We have all worked together since we arrived here and achieved what many would deem impossible. I humbly request your help once again as my wife is one of the women soon to give birth here. My best friend's wife is the other new mom. Please, anyone willing to join the team, we will be starting the work in the morning after breakfast."

It was at that very moment Marah jumped up and ran outside to be sick again. Up until now her morning sickness had been a constant companion daily until around noon. Previously the 12 o'clock hour had been miraculous at calming her nausea. But not today. This would be the beginning of round the clock sickness that would last the remainder of her pregnancy. As Jack followed his wife outside in concern for her safety, Janie approached Doctor Goodson and said, "Marah has been sick the whole time she has been pregnant. Is that normal, Doc?"

He answered, "It is not unheard of. I have seen it occasionally during my practice, but it isn't very common. It makes for an unpleasant pregnancy for sure. I don't have anything that will ease it. Unfortunately she may have it until birth."

Janie said, "What I don't understand is how she could be showing so much more than me when I am further along than she is. It worries me. She has become like a sister to me and I don't want to loose her."

Goodson replied, "The size difference could be attributed to a number of things. Some women carry their babies more in the back making them appear smaller during gestation. Another reason could be that she is retaining a lot of fluid due to the extreme nausea. Or her child may be bigger at birth. No one really knows all the secrets of pregnancy, we just try to treat the symptoms. That's why it is called the practice of medicine, the script is always changing. I too worry about her. I ask for everyone's prayers for a positive outcome when both of you deliver. I'm sorry I cannot be of more help." Janie thanked him and returned to Harold's side to finish her dinner. Jack returned just long enough to make arrangements with the French's to let Arianna spend the night with Pierre. Then the two of them went home so she could lay down.

The next day 75 people assembled after finishing breakfast to begin gathering materials to build the hospital. Five rock wall homes had been built since their arrival at the island. The search site for properly sized stones would have to expand since the majority of the nearest ones had been used already. By 2 o'clock a pile of rocks four feet high waited at the building site. Chun Li requested they begin gathering the materials for the mortar mix. He and Kim Wang were eager to get started on the outside walls. Both men seemed to share the ability to know which stone would fit best where. By the time dinner was announced, the back wall of the hospital stood four feet tall by 24 feet long. Even though the stone gathering had continued while they were building, nearly all the supply had been used up. Work would cease after dinner so the crew could rest up and begin again tomorrow. The next two days would be nearly carbon copies, but by their end, all the outer walls along with the center hall walls would stand four feet tall. Doctor Goodson praised the men for their work all while teasing that they did realize he was 6'1" tall and would appreciate the ability to stand up straight inside the hospital. He was after all the doctor on staff. He laughed heartily and shook their hands. After reading the translator, Chun Li laughed and said, "I had never noticed what a giant you were. We will work on that next." Chun Li and Kim Wang had stopped the walls at that height so they could ponder how to start the roof. They had decided to build five stone columns to hold a wooden tray to lay the two layers of stone that would have the roofing material between them. The layers of stone would be mortared to the cliff side to prevent water intrusion. Then the stone walls could be built up to meet the roof as it was installed. The metal would be retrieved from the debris pile the following day and installation would begin.

Sherod and Nigel had worked tirelessly in an effort to provide furniture for the hospital. Four of the seven requested beds had been finished, complete with woven grass mattresses. They were working next on the chairs and tables requested. Sherod had no tolerance for too much repetition. His decision was to finish all the furnishings for two rooms first and then build the rest.

Elizabeth French had, at Nigel's encouragement, successfully produced four nice and unique wash basins, one for each hospital room. The very request of the basins had sent her mind into actions. Upon the completion of the basins she tried her luck at making pitchers to go with them. She remembered her mother having an antique bowl and pitcher set and explaining it was a wash basin and water pitcher formerly used to bathe in during years past. Elizabeth knew it would be a nice addition. Pierre had been by her side for the duration of her efforts. On the first day of her tasks, Pierre had asked for a ball of clay 'to make Grandma out of'. Nigel and Elizabeth had already noticed Pierre had artistic abilities from his drawings. Elizabeth had barely had time to pay attention to what he was making as she worked to produce usable products. He had worked quietly nearby seemingly engulfed in what he was doing. On the third day, just as she was putting the final pitcher into the pottery oven to be fired, he approached her. Pierre said, "New Mommy," as he had chosen to call her, "Can we put Grandma's head in the oven too so it can last forever like the cups and stuff?" This was the first time Pierre had allowed Elizabeth to view his creation. Until now when not working on it, he had kept a shirt draped over it. Elizabeth gasped deeply as she viewed a bust which began as a softball sized ball of clay. It felt as though she was looking at the shrunken head of her friend Claudette. The shock of it's likeness rendered her barely able to speak above a whisper.

She asked, "Pierre, did you create this from memory? My goodness, it's perfect! How did you do this?"

The proud child answered, "Well kinda from memory and kinda from my picture of her." The boy pulled a wrinkled photo of a lady bearing a great resemblance to the bust he had just handed her. Elizabeth remembered being in the background when the story about Claudette's mistaken identity had come to light. That had been the first time Pierre had shown the photograph. She had forgotten it existed. She was surprised he still had it.

She said, "Yes we will bake this as well. I am very proud of you Pierre and your Grandma would be too. I can't wait to show everyone!"

That night at dinner, Elizabeth brought the bust wrapped in Pierre's little shirt to the dining hall. She had yet to show anyone, even Nigel the beautiful work of art. As the Islanders sat eating involved in their own conversations, she stood and asked for everyone's attention. She said, "First of all I wanted everyone to know I have started making wash basins and pitchers from clay pottery. I will make anyone one who wants me to. There are four already prepared for the hospital. But while I was making them, my son, Pierre, created this remarkable work of art. I wish that each of you when exiting the dining hall would stop by our table and look at this. It is hard to believe a five year old child could possess such an ability. Thank you so much for your attention." Then she sat down and uncovered the bust. Wow's, awe's and oh my's began to ring out from all seated with them. The name Claudette was repeated many times as people looked on through tear filled eyes.

"Simply incredible, I can find no words. Elizabeth how much did you help with this project?" asked Nigel.

She answered, "The only hand I lended was to fire it in the oven. Other than that it was all Pierre." Before everyone left the dining hall, it was decided the art would stay at the cave. There was a small ledge that stuck out just next to the entrance to the cavern hallway that was now used for storage. The bust sat on the ledge perfectly.

Pierre said, "Good, now Grandma will always be able to see that I cleaned my plate just like she always wanted me to." The situation was both sad and sweet to all involved.

The next morning after breakfast, it was off to the debris pile to gather more building materials. Many stayed behind to finish gathering the rest of the stones to finish the walls. Once the roofing metal had been pulled from the debris and counted to ensure there was enough, they had to try to find enough usable boards to build the frame. By mid afternoon, they would return to the building site with all needed materials in tow. Jack had stayed behind to help Chun Li who had added one foot of wall all the way around the structure already. The walls now stood at five feet tall. They were planned to end up at seven feet on the back side and seven feet six inches on the front side. This would allow the water from rain to run away from the cave's entrance. Once the roof and the stone walls were complete, the wooden log wall dividers could be added. At this point it had only been five days since the doctor had called the meeting asking that a hospital be built. Everyone was eager to get as much done as possible since tomorrow was Saturday. The Islanders had come to look at Sunday as being their fun day of rest, relaxation, and private worship time. No one intended to work on the hospital this Sunday either.

By Sunday morning the outer walls were complete and the roof only lacked three pieces being fully installed. Sanjay approached Jack at breakfast and asked, "Jack, what are your plans for today?"

Jack replied, "It's Sunday, I really don't have plans. Why do you ask?"

Sanjay said, "Well up until now, I have stayed away from the hospital. My leg as you know doesn't work so well anymore and I didn't want to get in the way. But this morning I went inside of it. I didn't realize before how many nail holes are in that roof. We gotta fix that to prevent leaking. Luckily I have been studying that book I have about trees native to our region. You know I told you guys about the honey bee tree? Well that is not all that Jenny and I have discovered on our walks by the river. I believe I have identified a tree which may be a rubber/tar producing tree. If we can take a pan and a knife or spoon along, maybe we can fill the holes with that to prevent leaks inside the hospital. Would you be interested in helping me? Jenny won't do it because it is very close to the honey bees."

Jack answered, "Of course I will help. We can either do it today or first thing tomorrow morning. When would you prefer?"

Sanjay said, "Early tomorrow morning to do the actual substance removal would probably be best, you know while the dew is still heavy. The honey bees are not very active in the very early hours, and the tree is very close to theirs. Jenny is not the only one afraid of those bees. Later today if you are going fishing, we can walk down there and I will show you."

Jack said, "It sounds like a plan."

During this first few days of construction, Butch and Francois had been very busy cutting and preparing logs for the divider walls in the hospital. The task had proven both harder and easier than expected. They had chosen tall straight trees in an effort to keep the diameter as close as possible for the twelve foot needed length. By Saturday they had gathered enough logs to build one wall, keeping to the 'no bigger than a soft ball size' theme of the stones in the outer walls. They expected to have all the logs ready by no later than Thursday of the following week.

Sunday proved to be as relaxing as ever. The gentlemen had enjoyed a day of fishing, hunting and gathering the following week's fruit. After breakfast most of the women had returned to camp. During the mid-afternoon, Jack and Harold returned to camp to check on Janie and Marah. Upon arrival, Harold said to Jack, "Uh oh, look at that. When those women get together it usually means work for us." Janie, Marah, Elizabeth, Iva and Rita sat in a circle around the fire pit their husbands used nearly every evening. They were laughing and talking while the children played near by.

Jack replied, "Maybe we should go back to the cave." When he and Harold both laughed, their presence was discovered.

Arianna shouted, "My Jack, my Jack, did you catch any fish?" as she ran to his side.

Jack answered, "I sure did. I caught two."

Marah laughingly said, "Were they real fish this time or just minnows again?"

Still laughing, Harold said, "Hey now. I didn't give you my best friend to have you pick on him about his fishing handicap. Today his two fish were as big as a hand,

Pierre's hand that is. But he is getting better at it."

Jack said, "Harold, exactly whose side are you on anyway?" The group laughed heartily.

Janie said, "Since you two came here to give Marah a hard time for giving Jack a hard time, it is my privilege to ask when is the bath tub going to be installed? You all have yet to move it to the building site."

Harold exclaimed, "See Jack, there's that work I was talking about."

Jack replied, "I told you we should have gone back to the cave."

Chuckling, Harold answered, "As soon as the hospital construction is completed, we will try to get the bathtub installed. But it has to wait until the thing is totally built to keep it from getting in the way. Rest assured when Chun Li and Kim Wang were designing the entrances they made the doorway big enough to get the tub inside when the time comes."

Janie said, "Well the time can't come soon enough for all of us."

Harold said, "You do realize this is a hospital, not a bath house, right?"

Iva spoke up and said, "Ophilia said she will handle Goodson. When there are no patients, it will be a bath house."

Harold said, "Very well then. Jack it looks like our mates are doing just fine. Let's abandon this hen party. I guess we could hike to the debris field and make our plan on how to get that tub. Obviously our future happiness depends on it." The ladies laughed as the two men re-entered the pathway to the cave.

By the end of the work day on Monday, the roof and rock walls had been completed. Kim Wang had volunteered to handle the mortaring of the log walls the following day. Chun Li was pleased to be released from construction duties to return to his post as head chef. Although there had been no complaints, the food during this project had lacked a certain pizzazz that only Chun Li had the knack of providing.

Jack and Harold had been asked by Doctor Goodson to build a door for the front of the building and to provide shutters for the one window installed in each room. Harold had a plan for them to return to the middle section of the plane wreckage on Tuesday. There they would remove the doors from the remaining over head compartments. If possible, they could be used as shutters. Otherwise they would remove the hinges from the doors and use them on new doors they would build themselves. Afterwards, they planned to go to the remaining nose section. One half of the cockpit still remained intact with a door still attached. They hoped to remove the door along with the petition wall which still stood behind Jack's pilot seat. Upon examination Harold said, "I think this is going to work. Measurements don't lie and I believe we have two inches to spare." Harold noticed Jack didn't answer and his face offered an expressionless stare into space. He asked his friend, "Jack where are you at? Never mind, I know where you are at and you need to come back right now."

"I am all right," said Jack. He continued, "I have only entered the cockpit a couple of times since the crash. I was just remembering."

Harold said, "I understand what was happening, but Jack I need your help. Our wives need your help. This is no time to go there. Always remember, we live in the present not the past. In life there are no do overs. Now shake it off and help me. We can do this together."

Jack said, "You are right my friend, I'm sure." The two got busy and within an hour were lowering the petition to the ground with ropes tied around it. Their efforts would be successful right down to the over head compartment doors working for the shutters.

Still Jack remained quiet, obviously lost in his own thoughts. That is until Arianna saw him climb down from the nose section. As usual the child ran to him with a hug. This time she said as she jumped into his arms, "I love you so much, my Jack. Is it okay with you if I was to start calling you Daddy. I want to be able to say I love you Daddy because you are so nice to me and Mommy. My first Daddy was never nice to us. So can I, can I please? I didn't love my mean Daddy, but I really do love you."

With tears now streaming down his face he said, "Yes I would like that very much, my Arianna."

She added, "You can say my little girl Arianna if you want to." The child hugged him again and got down and ran off to play with Pierre as it was Marah's day to watch them both.

Jack looked at Harold and said, "Thank God for little girls."

Harold realizing Jack was back in the present now said, "I fully agree."

At dinner that Tuesday night it was announced by Guillaume Rotge the roof was to be welded first thing the following morning. All the Islanders were asked to try to stay away from the cave during the process for their own safety. Rotge said, "In honor of Claudette's memory, I humbly request as all of you begin to arrive for breakfast that you would stop at the end of the pathway. Please check to see if we have completed the weld before entering the open area outside the dining hall. I realize we all enjoy our morning coffee. However, we haven't had rain for ten days now. Therefore the welds must be made while the dew is heavy on the ground to prevent the chance of fire. We believe we can do the welding in one to two hours. Also as you all can see we have an entrance door for our hospital now leaning against the wall over there. It can only be installed after the bath tub has been transported and permanently placed as it won't fit through the doorway once installed. We, the gentlemen builders, feared a lynch mob of angry women if we didn't get that tub in there first. But really, I believe the welding will be complete by 9:30 or 10:00 in the morning. Thank you all for your attention." As Guillaume then sat down to eat, all through the dining hall translations were taking place. Some of the Islanders had been attending English classes. They were eager to spread the message to stay away and be safe the next morning.

Sitting nearby, Sanjay said to Jack, "Since they are going to be on top of the roof tomorrow morning anyway, it might be good if we get the rubber/tar for patching the holes in the morning too. Then someone can patch the holes when the welding is complete."

Jack replied, "Good idea. I will be at your house just after daybreak and we will head out."

Sanjay said, "Sounds like a plan."

The next morning seemed to play out like a well written script. Just as Guillume Rotge and his crew were finishing the welding on the roof, Sanjay and Jack arrived back on site with the patching material. Jack climbed the ladder to the roof as soon as the welders got down and began filling nail holes. Nearby, Butch and Francois eagerly waited his completion so they could start erecting the two petition walls needed to separate the hospital rooms. Butch told Guillaume, "We should be able to complete one of the interior walls today. Maybe tomorrow while Francois and I move the logs for the other one to the site, Kim Wang can get the first wall mortared. We believe we can have the other wall put up by Thursday afternoon."

Rotge replied, "If I hadn't already promised Harold I would help to move the bathtub, I would help you and Francois."

From atop the roof, Jack said, "As soon as I am done patching holes up here, I can help you guys. Meanwhile, see if Sherod and Nigel would like to take a break from building furniture and join us."

Francois said, "We really need an even number of people instead of an odd number, you know, someone at each end of the log."

Just then Arthur Goodson emerged from the end of the pathway, overhearing their conversation. Jack saw him and said, "Hey Doc, would you consider joining us in hauling a few logs in a bit?"

Surprisingly Goodson answered, "Actually, I would be honored to be included as one of the guys. Yes I would be glad to help you guys."

Francois said, "Good, now we have a logging party of four."

Butch said, "I am going to find Sherod and Nigel to see if we can make that a party of six. I know they were planning to build two baby beds for the hospital and four tables for the water bowls and pitchers. I still think they will help us. With enough help we should be able to bring the remaining logs here plus have enough time left to put up one wall today. Thank you guys so much. I shall return."

Doctor Goodson said to all of them, "I find it amazing that a week and a half ago this hospital was merely a vision in mine and Ophilia's minds. You people are just simply amazing. It looks as though it will be a completed reality by two weeks later. You do realize this will even allow me time to get everything set up prior to the births. I find myself pinching my own arm to be sure I am not dreaming. Ophilia says that all things happen by the will of God. I am eternally grateful for the brilliant minds he placed on that plane and in turn here on our island. Together this seems to be an unstoppable community. I can't say it enough, thank you all so much."

Jack replied, "Actually Doc, it's you who deserves the thanks. You have shown honest concern for Marah and Janie and the babies. Harold and I both feel that our wives and babies could not be in better hands. Oh and I suppose we really owe you an apology for not including you in the physical labor of the build. I guess we all just thought you worked with your mind considering your profession. I know we haven't always seen eye to eye. But to tell the truth, you have my utmost respect sir."

Just then Butch, Nigel and Sherod appeared at the end of the pathway. Butch had found them heading for the cave not far away. Due to his attraction to Ophilia, Sherod held a certain dislike for the doctor. Hearing the compliments being tossed back and forth between Jack and Goodson annoyed him. Sherod said, "Why don't you two girls just kiss and get it over with. I have too much to do today to be delayed by this nonsense. Butch, didn't you say there were logs to move?" Butch and Sherod were best friends, having spent many hours together whittling flatware. Butch couldn't help but giggle at his friend's childlike protest.

Butch said, "We should all grab a bite of breakfast before we set out on our log hauling quest. We don't want to hold up the kitchen staff. Breakfast is already late due to the welding this morning. I, for one, am hungry. I don't know about you fellows." Butch knew Sherod could be a real grouch when he had an empty stomach. He knew the log transfer would go much smoother if Sherod wasn't grumpy. Butch said, "Jack, are you coming?"

Jack answered, "In just a few minutes. I have about ten or so more holes to patch and I will join you guys." The men would enjoy a delightful bowl of oatmeal with peaches and hot coffee before heading out.

While they were eating, Guillaume and Harold decided they would join the log transfer team. Afterward they would have plenty of time to attempt the moving of the bathtub. It would take the four pairs of men five trips to haul the logs to the hospital. Within two hours the team had completed the task. Guillaume and Harold went on to begin the bathtub retrieval. Jack, Nigel French, Francois, Sherod and Butch decided to work together in an effort to get both petition walls in place. Doctor Goodson chose not to join them for the building. He had quickly grown tired of all the sly remarks Sherod had thrown at him. Instead he went to join Sanjay in his efforts to turn molded bread into a Penicillin type product.

By mid afternoon, the five men exited the hospital and sat down on the river bank. Sanjay approached the group and said, "It's about time you guys took a break. You've been at it for hours now."

Jack said, "Oh we're not taking a break, we're finished. Both petition walls are now in place awaiting mortar."

Sanjay said, "Well then, today has been quite successful for us all. I do believe Arthur and I have made a usable antibiotic from the molded bread. I do realize only time will tell, but we feel good about the result. You know that Goodson is a smart cookie. His memory of the chemistry he studied in medical school is remarkable."

Jack replied, "Then there were two brilliant minds working to produce the medication. You are no dummy yourself, you know."

Sanjay smiled and said, "Thanks man."

Sherod, annoyed again by the praise being given to Doctor Goodson stated, "Awe, here we go again. I suppose in modern society it is acceptable for grown men to display such feminine lovey dovey affection for each other. Can't you girls just shake hands and act like real men for a change."

Then Butch got up, walked into the dining hall, and returned with a banana which he handed to Sherod. Butch said, "Here eat this. You are getting grumpy again."

Sherod grunted, took the banana, and said, "Yes Mother, if you insist."

Suddenly, an angry Kim Wang exited the path to the debris pile. Rapidly he stomped into the dining hall and began yelling something in Chinese to his friend Chun Li. Nigel went and stood in the doorway to the cave while he translated Wang's words. Nigel said, "Kim seems to be furious with Harold and Guillaume. He says they along with their helpers are currently dragging the bathtub through the center of his rice patty. There was no clear path otherwise. Oh boy, he is angry. Says a path around the patty could have been created if the logs for the petition walls had been cut from that area. Chun Li told him to get over it, that we are all subject to make mistakes. Oops, here he comes." Nigel rushed back to the group and sat down on the river bank. Wang immediately walked over to Nigel. Again in his native Chinese, Wang pleaded his case to him. The nearly always calm Nigel French seemed to always have a way with words in any language. After a five minute conversation he had calmed Kim Wang who walked into the hospital. As French got to his feet to join Wang he explained the conversation to the rest of the group. Nigel said, "Guys can you help gather some mortar materials right quick. Wang is angry still over the damage to the rice patty, says the plants were half grown and starting to bloom already. I called his attention to the fact that sometimes storms damage crops, knocking their plants over. Many of them will straighten themselves back up given time. He says that probably won't happen considering the rice is grown under water. Knowing he was right, I did the only thing I could think of. I told him that once the hospital construction was complete, we all would help to drain the rice patty and prop up the plants that were still viable. His reply was 'Then the building will be completed today and tomorrow morning after we drain the patty the destroyers will help repair their damage'. He and his wife have worked tirelessly to grow that field of rice. His grief and anger is understandable. I hope you guys aren't mad for me volunteering all of us, but I didn't know what else to do."

Jack said, "Of course we will help. We have got this far by all working together, and we will all benefit from the rice grown. In the spirit of community, today we finish the hospital, tomorrow we fix the rice plants, assuming that's alright with all of you." Jack, Francois and Butch stood to go gather mortar materials while Sherod sat still.

Butch looked at his friend and asked, "You coming Sherod?"

Sherod answered, "No, I ain't going in there with that irate China man. You can't understand nothing he's saying, and what if Nigel missed the part where he said he was gonna knock somebody in the head. Nope I ain't going in there with a mad man. I heard them Chinese men if they get mad at you they will cut your head clean off. We already saw when his buddy Chun Li cut a huge turtle's head off with one chop. I'm sitting right here."

Shaking his head, Butch said, "You go right ahead, I'm not a bit surprised." Then Butch turned to go and join the others helping Kim Wang.

Barely over an hour later, the log wall petitions inside the hospital were mortared. As the men were exiting the hospital, Guillaume and Harold, along with their crew arrived on site with the bath tub in tow. A still angry Kim Wang again began yelling and pointing at the tub and then the hospital. Nigel French translated to all, "Kim wants all of us to help get the bloody tub in it's final resting place. Says he doesn't want to look at the destructive piece of junk. Please, let's help our friends complete the task." Once Jack, Nigel, Butch, Francois and Kim Wang joined Harold's six man crew, the tub and six by eight piece of flooring it was still attached to was easily lifted rather than dragged. Within minutes the eleven man crew had moved the tub some eighty feet into the hospital and sat it in place. Kim Wang had raved the entire time. As soon as they were done, Nigel said, "Will anyone who still has the energy please help with installing the door. Wang is right, if we do it now, the construction will basically be complete by dinner time. Then after we eat we can do the finishing touches like adding the furnishings and shutters. Please, I don't think he's going to shut up until he is sure we are available to help with the rice patty tomorrow morning. Please guys. Just a little longer."

Jack said, "Harold, Guillaume, are you in?" They nodded. Jack added, "Okay then, come on Nigel. The four of us will install the door. Send Wang on his way. I'm starting to feel like Sherod. I have heard about all the ranting I am going to listen to. Wang is starting to remind me of my ex-wife."

While Nigel explained the game plan to Kim Wang and sent him on his way, Harold asked, "How long has he been carrying on like that?"

Jack answered, "At least an hour and a half, and I for one am sick of hearing it. Hanging the door panel will go much smoother if he goes somewhere out of hearing range. He is getting on my nerves." Satisfied the door installation would complete the hospital freeing his help up for the following morning, Kim agreed to go home until dinner. The installation was over twenty minutes later.

Just after finishing the door installation, the four gentlemen turned to step away from the hospital. Behind them they saw Doctor Goodson standing next to Ophilia Parker, both with tears streaming down their faces. Goodson said, "It's just unbelievable. We the Islanders now have a hospital. It's crazy how all of you took Ophilia's idea and made it reality in eleven days. Really, I just can't find the words."

Ophilia said, "Arthur, it wasn't only my idea. There's Doc Goodson written all over that place. Gentlemen, it's just beautiful. Now if you will all excuse me. Oh, I almost forgot. I guess Kim Wang's ranting has got Su Li riled up. She said to tell you all to shower before dinner, that you are all to filthy to enter her dining room. Sorry guys, but she is on a roll. Dinner is in an hour." She returned to her work in the kitchen.

Jack said, "Well I guess we are all cruddy. Let's all meet back here in 20 minutes or so with clean clothes and we will all go get cleaned up." His suggestion was agreed to by all and they were on their way.

The ladies were thrilled to learn the hospital had been completed. They were all working to weave enough grass to mattress four beds and eight chairs. There was one noticeable absence from the group. Marah was missing from the mix. Jack asked and Janie told him that Marah had been vomiting so much she had chosen to go home and lie down. The ladies were watching Arianna so she could get some rest. Janie asked if Marah was sleeping that he leave her be. Jack reluctantly agreed to Janie's request. He informed the ladies dinner was in one hour and went to gather his clothes being ever so careful to not wake his sleeping wife. Meanwhile, Iva, Elizabeth and Rita gathered a homemade broom, mop and dust rags and headed to the cave to clean the hospital before dinner. Janie agreed to keep an eye on both Arianna and Pierre while they built a sand castle city and bring them to dinner when the time came. By the time dinner was served, the hospital had been cleaned and wiped down with bleach water, even down to the stone walls.

By nightfall the shutters had been installed and part of the furniture was in place. Twenty four hours later all furnishings were in place right down to the doctor's cabinets from his original office which held all the meds available. Other than four chalkboards, the lighting system, installing the generator and building the grill for heating the bath water, this project was a done deal.

The completion of the hospital couldn't have come at a better time as Marah's condition continued to worsen. Janie had woken Marah up to join them for dinner. Her nausea had severely increased over the recent days. Her pregnant belly had grown to one and a half times the size of Janie's baby bump. However with her sickness being so intense, the rest of her body seemed reduced to merely skin stretched over bone. Although she had told Janie she still felt tired, weak and a little nauseated, she chose to accompany them to the dining hall. Upon arrival, however, the aroma of the food stopped her outside the cave for another round of vomiting. Once finished, she took three steps, said, "Oh no," passed out and fell on Arianna. Luckily, the child was not hurt and prevented her mother's head from hitting the bed rock below them. A terrified Pierre ran inside the dining hall and yelled, "Help, somebody, my Aunt Marah is dying."

Instantly Jack, Doctor Goodson, Harold, followed by a herd of Islanders rushed to Marah and Janie's side. Doctor Goodson checked her pulse and breathing. Jack quickly took his shirt off, wet it in the river and began bathing his wife's face in an effort to help her regain consciousness. Harold had picked up a crying Arianna, and he and Janie were in an effort to check her for injuries and calm her. The doctor sent Ophilia to her quarters to get a Coke. Unbeknownst to anyone he had early on stashed the last available case of soft drinks for occasions such as this. He believed they had a stomach calming effect and had saved them to help fight any dehydration faced in the future. The future had arrived. He asked Jenny Parker to go in the cave and get a bowl of the left over oatmeal from breakfast and remove any fruit in it. If left bland he believed Marah could stomach it. Thirty minutes later her condition had greatly improved. He handed Jack a small amount of Marijuana, instructed him that she was to take three puffs every two hours to help reduce her nausea, and he wanted to recheck her before breakfast the following morning. He suggested Jack go finish eating and take his wife home. What she needed most now was rest. Finally he instructed Jack to stop along the way home by his and Ophilia's house and grab one more soda from underneath their bed, and to remember it was medication as well. Jack shook the doctor's hand, and followed his instructions. As he fell asleep that night, he wondered what the next few weeks held in store for his family. He prayed and asked God's help and blessing on whatever surprises were to come.

CHAPTER TWENTY-FOUR

BABY, BABY, BABY

Four weeks later, on a Wednesday just prior to daybreak, Harold awoke to Janie saying, "Oh no, I really gotta go." She was trying unsuccessfully to get her shoes onto her swollen feet. She said, "Harold I am sorry for waking you up, but I gotta go to the bathroom right now. Please help me with these shoes. My stomach is so big I can't get them on. Really Harold hurry."

Sensing something was not normal, first he asked, "Are you sure it's not the baby?"

Suddenly annoyed she snapped, "Right this minute all I am sure of is that if you keep laying there doing nothing I am going to shit all over creation. Now get up and help me, now please." Harold immediately jumped to attention and shoed his wife.Then he followed Janie who had wasted no time getting out the door. Half way to the restroom facility, Janie doubled over in pain.

Harold grabbed her fearing she would fall and asked, "Janie, are you okay?"

"No, I am not. I really gotta go. Please just help me to the toilet. I think I will be okay after I go." With no hesitation, Harold scooped Janie up into his arms and carried her to the restroom. He stood her in front of one of the toilets and she asked him to go away. Harold stepped outside the doorway and immediately found himself pacing back and forth.

With Jack living nearby, he overheard Harold and Janie. He soon joined Harold outside the restroom. As he was asking Harold if everything was alright, Janie let out a loud and painful scream. In the split second that it took the two men to respond to the scream and run to her side, a baby's first cry filled the air. They ran to Janie who was trying to lift the baby from inside the toilet. Janie's shrill scream had brought Iva and Guillaume to the scene. As they heard the baby's cries, Guillaume said, "You go help Janie, I will go get Doctor Goodson." Guillaume then took off running down the path like his life depended on it.

Iva rushed to Janie's side and took over. She began barking orders at Harold and Jack just like she was still commanding a military platoon. She needed a blanket for Janie, a shirt or something to wrap the baby in, two pieces of string, and a pair of scissors or a knife to cut the cord. She smiled as the first rays of sunlight began to peek through the clouds and shine on the newborn. Unnerved by the early morning arrival, Iva rudely scolded both Jack and Harold for taking what she perceived as too long to bring the supplies she had requested. Iva had just finished cutting the cord and wrapping the baby up when Doctor Goodson and Guillaume arrived. Doctor Goodson said, "Well, I guess I just found my new head nurse. Good morning all. Iva, you take care of the baby and I will tend to the mother. Jack, will you and Guillaume please get the sled to transport my two patients to our new hospital." Everyone did as they were told.

A very nervous Harold asked, "Doctor, Iva, somebody please tell me, are they alright?" Doctor Goodson was working on Janie.

Iva answered, "Harold, I believe your wife and new son will be fine. He appears to be perfect. Ten fingers, ten toes, and lungs that allow him to scream and cry. Pretty much perfect."

Harold repeated, "New son...oh wow, I have a son! Please Iva, may I see him?"

Iva answered, yes but only for a moment. As soon as the doctor is done with his mother, she will get to hold him first." Iva unwrapped the newborn to show his father.

Harold, through tears said, "You are right, he's just perfect. Have you ever seen so much hair on a new baby's head. He's so cute." As he reached to touch his son, the baby grabbed Harold's index finger. Harold giggled and said, "Look, he wants to shake hands and introduce himself. It's like he's saying, 'Hello Daddy, I am Habib. Pleased to meet you'."

Surprised, Iva said, "How very sweet. I was not aware you were going to name him after Habib. I like it."

Harold replied, "Yes, it is a decision we made the day of his and Claudette's funeral."

She stated, "It is a very special name for a very special baby. He is the first official natural born Islander, you know. Soon he will be joined in his class by Marah and Jack's child. This begins a new era. I am grateful to have been a part of it."

Harold said, "Yes I am thankful for everything to do with it."

It was then that Guillaume and Jack arrived with the sled. They were accompanied by Marah and Arianna. Marah rushed inside the restroom to check on her best friend. "Janie," she said, "Are you alright?"

Janie seemed groggy as she answered, "Yes, I think so. I am just so tired. I have had a stomach ache most of the night. I have never gone through this before and I had no clue it was really labor. Honestly it wasn't all that bad. I really thought I just had to poop. My poor little baby. I hope it never knows of it's stinky arrival in this world."

Marah asked, "Hasn't anyone told you it's a boy yet?" Janie said, "A boy, I had a boy? Well that means I will have to do this again because I wanted a little girl. I wanted her to be like my own Arianna. But I had a stinking boy." Just then, Iva overhearing Janie's words, walked in and laid the baby in his mother's arms. Janie fell in love at first sight. Marah, Iva, and Doctor Goodson watched in awe as the new mother and child bonded instantly upon first laying hands and eyes on each other. Janie's entire demeanor changed right in front of them.

After a few moments, Doctor Goodson exited and asked, "Harold, Jack and Guillaume, could you all help me lift mother and child onto the sled? I am uncomfortable with the idea of Janie standing just yet." They answered with a trio of 'yes and of course'. Twenty minutes later, the first two patients were admitted to the new hospital facility. Doctor Goodson told Harold he wanted to keep them for at least two days for observation. Harold thanked him and shook his hand. He offered to sit with his family and allow the Doctor and Iva to have breakfast before beginning their tasks. Doctor Goodson said, "No Harold, you go eat. I am not yet finished working on Janie. By the time you have finished eating, we should be done and then we will change places."

Harold, very concerned asked, "Is she alright?"

The doctor answered, "Yes, I believe so. There is just a few stitches and some tidying up to do. Now please, get out of here and let me do my work."

"Yes sir," replied Harold as he exited the hospital.

Harold entered the dining hall, gathered his breakfast and joined Jack, Marah, Arianna, Guillaume Rotge, and the French's including Pierre. He smiled as he listened to Arianna recounting the events surrounding the birth to Pierre. She said, "Mommy told me the other day that when nobody is looking, God sends an angel to hand you your new baby. She was right! But when the Angel handed Aunt Janie new Habib, she dropped him in the potty. You should have seen him. He had poopoo in his hair and gooey stuff all over him. It was really icky. I hope Aunt Janie will give him a bath quick cause he stinks."

Pierre replied, "Did you see the Angel? I think I saw her. When new Mommy and me were coming out of our house for breakfast, I saw her fly over. New Mommy said it was just an Albatross but that was before we knew Aunt Janie's baby was here. I think it really was the Angel, don't you?"

Arianna said, "I bet it was. I wish I would have seen her too. Uncle Harold, can we hold new Habib after they get the poopoo off of him?"

Harold said, "Today or tomorrow sometime, if the doctor says it is alright."

In unison, the two children said, "Yaaa."

Then an unusually up beat Chun Li came over to Nigel and asked him to translate for him. He said to Harold, Jack and Marah, "To all you new parents, Su and I have surprise. For six months now we save powdered milk. We grind rice into fine particals to make rice baby food. We save till babies need. If mother's no can feed, we feed. No worries." As Harold and Jack offered their thanks to Chun Li, Marah burst into tears, jumped to her feet, hugged Chun Li and then went to where Su was working and hugged her too.

Jack followed his wife, curious as to her reaction. He asked, "Marah, are you okay?" With her tears now uncontrollable, she hugged Jack and held on.

She answered, "Actually, yes thanks to these two wonderful people, for the first time since I learned I was pregnant, yes finally I am okay."

Jack said, "Marah, I am sorry, but I still don't understand."

Through tears Marah said, "I didn't tell you because I didn't want you to worry. When Arianna was born, my body refused to produce milk. She nearly starved the first two days before my doctor demanded I bottle feed her. I have been worried sick that our baby would starve if the same happened again. To tell the truth, every time I have thought of it, I threw up. Unfortunately, it is never far from my mind causing me to vomit all the time. Thank God for these two wonderful people. Janie had promised to feed them both if she could, but I have been so worried. I can't wait to tell her now she doesn't have to worry about it."

With tears now running down his face, Jack hugged his very frail, yet very pregnant wife tightly. He said, "Marah, I love you, and we are in this together. You don't have to protect me, sweetheart. You should never again suffer or worry in silence over any subject. You can always talk to me. We will always work together to fix what we can. Next time don't be afraid to tell me. Okay?"

She said, "Yes, thank you. I love you too."

Marah's gestation period would last another four weeks. Incredibly, during that time she would experience not one bout of nausea and vomiting. For months prior to Chun Li's announcement, she had been sick multiple times a day. With the sickness behind her, her appetite returned. Her already oversized baby bump grew to enormous proportions. Doctor Goodson had secretly told Jack to be mentally prepared for twins, a revelation he had kept to himself. Although she was eating twice the normal amount, her stomach was the only place that had gained weight. With her arms and legs now skin and bones, she could barely stand without falling over forward.

On the morning of the eleven month anniversary of the plane crash, Marah woke Jack to say, "We have to go to the hospital. The baby is coming!"

Jack, very excited and nervous, sat up, threw his shoes on, went in the other room, picked up a sleeping Arianna and ran out of the house. A few steps down the pathway, he remembered Marah. He turned and ran back to the house. He said, "Oh Marah, I am so sorry. I am not thinking. Can you walk? Oh of course you cannot walk that far in labor! What am I doing?"

Harold and Janie heard the commotion and came to help. Janie said, "Arianna can stay here with me and little Habib. Harold, run and get the sled so you and Jack can take her to the hospital. How are you doing, Marah?"

Marah answered, "My pains started during the night. From the best I can tell I think they are at every ten minutes now. The last one was very hard. Please make them hurry, Janie. For some reason, I feel very uneasy, almost like something is wrong."

Janie said, "Got ya. I will go wake up Iva so she and Doctor Goodson will be ready. I love you my friend."

Janie ran out the door, yelled at Jack for him and Harold to hurry and ran to Iva and Guillaume's door. As she knocked, she yelled, "Iva, Iva please wake up. Marah's in labor and thinks something is wrong. Please, please wake up."

Iva answered the door as Janie finished her statement. She said, "I am on my way. I have to put my shoes on. Then I will go wake up Doc Goodson and we will meet you guys there. Guillaume will you go help transport the mother to the hospital?"

He answered, "Yes, of course I will," all the while putting his shoes on.

Just then a very out of breath Harold returned to the scene with the sled in tow. He said to Janie, "I think that must be a record. The sled was still at the hospital from us taking you and Habib the day he was born. I guess we had not thought of everything while getting ready for Marah to deliver. How long did it take me to get back?"

Janie answered, "I just hope it wasn't too long. Marah said she feels like something is wrong. Please Harold, you guys need to hurry."

Having overheard, immediately following her statement, Jack ran to his wife's side. With tears flowing uncontrollably now he dropped to his knees and began to pray. He said, "Oh dear merciful God, please grant your blessings on the birth of our baby and keep my wife safe. Oh please, dear God, please."

Harold laid his hands on Jack's shoulders and said, "Pull yourself together buddy, we gotta get her to the hospital as quickly as possible." Jack got to his feet, wiped his eyes, and he and Harold helped Marah outside and on to the sled.

Guillaume said, "Jack, me and Harold will pull the sled. It would probably be better if you follow behind so Marah can see you. I think it will help keep her calm. Marah hang on sweetie, it's probably gonna be a bumpy ride." With no hesitation, they headed out.

Not far down the pathway, they met Nigel French and Pierre. He said, "Not to worry folks. Iva has informed all of us about you being in route to the hospital. She will be waiting there along with Doctor Goodson, Ophilia and Elizabeth. I am taking Pierre to Janie to help keep Arianna occupied, then I will join you. Good luck Marah. God speed gentlemen." The three men along with Marah thanked Nigel for his well wishes and continued on their journey.

Along the way Marah had one contraction. Upon their arrival she had another, this one so intense she let out a shrill and painful scream. Doctor Goodson, Iva and

Elizabeth met them at the hospital door.

Goodson said, "Good morning. From the sound of things, we need to hurry and get you into bed." The gentlemen helped Marah to her feet and Iva and Elizabeth disappeared with her to the designated delivery room. Doctor Goodson stayed behind intentionally to speak to Jack and the others. "I need you guys to stay close by. I may need your help at some point." The doctor's brow showed deep lines of concern not normally visible on his face. He turned to Harold and Guillaume and said under his breath, "For some reason, I have a bad feeling about this. Please I will need you to keep Captain Wellington calm. Thank you both, and if you will excuse me?" He went to check on Marah.

As they waited for word on mother and child's condition, Jack paced back and forth between the entrances to the hospital and dining hall. He said to Harold, "How long do you think it took to bring Marah here this morning? She told Janie she thought the pains were about ten minutes apart when we left."

Harold said, "I really don't know man. Probably fifteen minutes max."

A nervous Jack replied, "Well they must be closer than ten minutes apart because she had two along the way and we have heard her scream three times since she has been in there. I wish Goodson would let us know something."

No sooner were the words out of his mouth than Arthur Goodson appeared in the doorway holding a baby wrapped in a towel. With Jack's back to the doorway, a smiling Doctor Goodson asked, "Jack would you like to meet your son?" Jack turned and ran the few steps to the doctor's side. As Doctor Goodson uncovered the baby's head to show his father, Marah screamed from inside again. It was followed by Iva yelling for the doctor to get back in there. The doctor handed the baby to Jack and said, "Here take this. We may have been right about twins. I will be back."

Having seen the baby being handed off to a very shaky father, Ophilia appeared from inside the dining hall with a seat for Jack. She sat it next to Jack and said, "Here Papa, sit down before those shaky knees give out on you."

"Thank you Ophilia," Jack said. "I am just so scared for her."

She answered, "You're welcome. You are all in my prayers. Please remember, God's will will be done. It is our job to be accepting of his decisions no matter what they may be." She patted Jack on the back and said, "Now let me see that good looking boy." She reached down and uncovered his face saying, "Hello there little guy. I am your Aunt Ophilia. We are going to be great friends." Then she covered the baby back up and returned to her work.

It would be ten minutes before the doctor would return, carrying another baby wrapped in a towel. It was immediately evident that his demeanor had changed. His face showed a deepening worry. He handed this baby to Harold and said, "Jack, this is your daughter. I have to go. We may have problems." Harold then walked over to Jack and uncovered the baby's face to show her father. Meanwhile they had been joined by Nigel, Sanjay and Jenny.

Jenny took the baby from Harold who had already let the three of them know about the doctor's request for help if needed. She told Harold, "I will take the baby. You could be called on for help at any time. You need to be ready if needed." Sanjay retrieved a seat for Jenny and placed it next to Jack. At this point Jack seemed to be in shock, staring silently at the hospital door. Concern spread as Marah's screams were becoming more frequent and obviously weaker each time.

Inside the hospital chaos was erupting. The second baby had been followed by yet another round of mucus, rather than the placenta. Upon examination a third child had been confirmed. The first two births had been nothing out of the ordinary coming head first as normal. The third baby was in a breach position, however. It was trying to arrive feet first. Doctor Goodson, who always seemed to loose his bedside manor in dire emergencies, barked his orders to Elizabeth and Iva. "Elizabeth," he said, "Go now and get me four men. I need them to hold her down while I try to turn the baby. What ever you do, don't let Jack in here, and by all means, leave Nigel out there with the other women. He has the stomach of a woman and I don't want vomit to contaminate this room. Stop giving me a dirty look and go get me some help now! We are going to lose mother and baby both if we don't hurry. The baby's head is stuck. We have got to work fast. NOW GO!" Suddenly worry and concern replaced the anger Elizabeth initially felt at the doctors hateful words about her sweet husband and she ran to get help. Panic struck Elizabeth momentarily as she ran outside to realize no one else had arrived at the cave for breakfast yet. Quickly she counted, Harold-one, Guillaume-two, Sanjay-three, Nigel-no, Jack-no. Oh God, she thought, there's only three.

Then it dawned on her. "Nigel, quickly go in the cave and tell Chun Li we need his help." Nigel, realizing he had no stomach for injuries of any kind, offered no argument. Instead he ran and got Chun Li who joined Harold, Guillaume and Sanjay as they followed Elizabeth back into the hospital.

Doctor Goodson met them at the doorway of the room Marah was in. His tone was direct and to the point. Inside the room Marah lay covered with a sheet while Iva took her blood pressure yet again. She said, "Her pressure is dropping. Please, Doctor, we have to hurry."

Instantly Goodson said, "Listen closely gentlemen, you will be holding Mrs. Wellington down while I attempt to turn a breach baby. Those holding the arms will face her head. Those holding the legs will face the feet. Her privacy must remain private during this procedure. Someone make our cook understand and we must begin now!" While the four gentlemen were taking their places, the doctor handed Elizabeth a vial with an eye dropper inside it. He said, "Drop four drops of this in her mouth every time I tell you to."

Elizabeth asked, "What is it?"

"A mixture of the last of the liquid valume and THC oil I extracted from the Marijuana plants. I am hoping it will disconnect her brain from the pain," replied the doctor. Everyone was now in place.

Iva said, "Doctor, her pressure dropped again, now 98 over 50."

Doctor Goodson, now positioned on his knees underneath the sheet at the end of the bed asked aloud for God's help. Then he said, "Elizabeth four drops now. Then bring me the solar light from on top of the cabinets in the corner. Hurry, I can't see under here." Elizabeth rapidly did as she was told. As Doctor Goodson began the procedure, Marah began trying to thrash and fight as expected from the pain. Goodson shouted, "Elizabeth, four more drops, hurry! Iva, pressure check?"

Iva yelled, "I can't get a reading. She is moving too much."

The doctor removed his head from beneath the cover and screamed, "Harold, you gotta hold her arm still. I have to know that blood pressure at all times!"

He returned to his task underneath the sheet and Iva soon said, "Not much change, 94 over 48." Three minutes later, the doctor's head emerged once again. He said, "Gentlemen, if you will, please step into the next room and await further instruction. I think I have turned the baby. Now we must wait for the next contraction to be sure of the outcome."

From the other side of the wall the men waited for instructions in silence. Approximately three minutes later, Marah screamed in pain. Goodson's voice sounded relieved as he said, "Thank God, I see a head. I think we got this. Now come on baby, be okay." They could hear a trio of voices yelling, "Push, Marah, push." Then the doctor said, "Oh no. The cord is wrapped." With one more hard push, the last baby was born, already blue in color from the lack of oxygen. They heard the doctor say, "Elizabeth, help me. Iva, mother's BP?"

Inside the hospital room this scene played out. Doctor Goodson handed Elizabeth the baby while he quickly unwrapped the cord from the neck. He then clamped and cut the cord.

Iva said, "BP improving, now 100 over 62."

He said, "Good, give me the stethoscope." As he tried to get the baby to draw it's first breath, he stopped several times to check for a heartbeat. He tried everything from CPR and mouth to mouth resuscitation to the traditional slap on the behind. Nothing worked.

After 20 or so minutes, Iva patted the doctor on the shoulder and said, "Arthur, it's over. This baby is still born. It's time to call TOD. You have to attend to Marah and the placenta. Now come on Doctor." He picked the baby up and handed him to Elizabeth. She asked, "Shall I inform the father sir?"

With tears flowing he said, "No unfortunately that's my job as well. After the mother is stable, I will break the bad news. Please just wait."

"Yes, doctor," she answered. After the stitches and clean-up were completed, he asked Elizabeth and Iva to take the live babies and bathe them. He informed Iva of some baby formula and baby bottles in one of the cabinets and requested she get sterilized water from Ophilia to mix it. The babies would need feeding right away. Then he went to tell Jack and allow him in to visit his very groggy wife.

Doctor Goodson stopped in the doorway of the other hospital room and told the men who were awaiting instruction that they could go. He asked that Harold stay in the room with Marah while he talked to Jack and while the ladies cleaned and fed the babies. The gentlemen preceded Doctor Goodson, Iva and Elizabeth when they exited. The doctor asked Jenny to take the baby she held in the hospital. Then he asked Jack to give the other baby to Elizabeth to take inside. He asked Iva to go get the sterilized water and handle the formula. Jack recognizing the doctor's grim expression began to cry and asked, "Please doctor, please tell me my wife is still alive?"

Now sobbing as badly as the father, Goodson answered, "I am so sorry, Jack. I tried hard to save them both. But after trying everything the last baby was still born. Marah is still alive, but she has been through so much, honestly without proper medical equipment, only time will tell if she is going to survive. I promise you I will do everything in my power to get her well. Please forgive me. Marah and the other two babies desperately need our prayers. Now it would probably be good if you switch places with Harold. Right now he is sitting with Marah until you get there."

Jack only said, "Thank you sir. Please excuse me." Then he rushed inside, checked all four rooms before finding Marah and Harold.

Harold met him in the doorway and said, "Good, you're here. You okay Man? She has been asking for you."

Jack said, "I am scared to death, happy and sad all in one big ball of nerves. Could you ask Janie to try to feed them, they are so small they won't need much. I don't see how she will manage them all. Oh God, what am I going to do?"

Harold said, "Easy Jack, the doc has your back. He said he found some baby formula he had stored and forgot about right after the crash. He ran across it while sitting up the hospital. There were even a few baby bottles in with it. The ladies are mixing formula in a few minutes. We all have your back. You go visit Marah. Tell her we are feeding the babies so she won't worry. I am sure you have much to discuss."

"Thank you Harold," said Jack as he entered Marah's room.

As Jack entered the room, he noticed it was brightly lit. He looked around and saw not only the lights which came from the plane, but also twenty or so solar lights. The room smelled like antiseptic and rubbing alcohol, the setting being as close to a real hospital as possible. Marah lay still until she saw him. She lifted her arms in a request to be held. He hugged her and she held on with no words, only tears at first. Then he asked, "How are you feeling, my love?"

She answered, "Kinda like I stepped in front of an oncoming bus. This is such a mess. I can't believe I had more than one baby. Jack, what are we going to do? Janie can't feed them all. Are the other two going to join their brother in death? The last of the three had such a horrible time coming into this world, it is no surprise he chose to return to Heaven so quickly. Oh Jack, I am so sorry."

Jack said, "Marah, sweetheart, please listen to me. We have two beautiful surviving babies. The doctor stored baby formula, a whole case of it, just after the crash, forgot about it, and found it the other day. Iva is currently fixing them each a bottle."

Marah said, "A bottle, where did they get baby bottles?"

Jack answered, "I don't know, I just know they have them now. Please try not to worry. Everyone wants to help."

She asked, "Where is Arianna? Does she know what happened?"

Jack answered, "She is with Janie and Pierre. Harold just left to go check on them. I know he will protect her from learning of the last baby's outcome. I think we need to name our children. I don't like saying the last baby and the other two. They all deserve names. So what do you want to name them? After what you have been through, you should be allowed to choose. So tell me, who are these beautiful kids?"

Marah was quiet for a moment. Then she said, "Okay I got it. The boys will be named Arthur Jackson Wellington and Ivan Amal Wellington. The baby girl shall be called Claudia Jane Wellington. You must decide which son is which. I have done my part."

Jack asked, "Claudia Jane? Don't you mean Claudette Jane?"

"No," said Marah, "I don't want Pierre to have the constant reminder of her. He has said if we had a girl he was going to call her little grandma. I do not want that. You said it was my choice and I choose to name her Claudia instead. Please honor my request."

Jack said, "Yes, my love, of course I will." He walked over to the blackboard slate hanging on the log petition wall and began writing. He wrote 'Baby #1'. Underneath that he wrote 'Baby #2 Claudia Jane Wellington'. Under that he wrote 'Baby #3' leaving the first and third names blank at first. He asked, "Any further instructions, ma'am?"

She answered, "If you would find it pleasing, I would rather the living son to bear the names of both our grandfather's. I feel as a matter of respect one of the boys should be named after the doctor, but I really don't want to spend the rest of my life yelling 'Arthur you get back here, or Arthur stop hitting your sister'. Ivan is much easier to say quickly. Would that be alright with you?"

He replied, "That would be perfect with me." He then placed the names in their designated spots.

Then Marah said, "Later today after I have met the babies, I would like to attend Arthur's burial. He shall be buried at the debris field along side his grandfather. He should be with family. I don't want him laid to rest for an eternity in the quick sand pile where Ragish is, and I don't want a constant reminder as I would have if he is placed next to Claudette. Can you make this happen?"

He answered, "Yes, absolutely. If that is what you want."

Just then, Iva and Elizabeth both entered, each carrying a baby. Jenny followed with two baby bottles. As they handed each parent a baby and bottle, Doctor Goodson entered also. He said, "These two children are very healthy and very hungry. I would like for Marah to attempt to nurse each baby five minutes on each side prior to the bottles. This may help her milk to come in. Any mother's milk at all will help them and then we can supplement with the bottles. So enjoy these two cute kids." As he was about to exit he noticed the chalkboard, burst into tears and left the room. At that point there was no need for words.

Jack and Marah did exactly as the doctor had instructed them to do, passing babies back and forth during the process. They both giggled about the fact Ivan had a head full of hair while Claudia only had hair around the bottom without a single strand on top of her head. Jack told Marah that his father was bald on top as well and looked a lot like Claudia. As they finished the nursing process, they noticed both babies fell asleep afterward, barely touching the bottles they were offered. Suddenly Marah looked down and saw she had milk dripping. She began to cry and say, "Oh thank you dear God, thank you."

Immediate concern flooded over Jack as he asked, "Marah, are you alright? Are you in pain? Do I need to get the doctor?"

She answered, "Everything is fine. No it's better than fine. Look, Jack. I have milk. We can feed our babies. This never happened when Arianna was born, I never saw even one drop. Now just look, I am a sticky, soaking mess. Isn't it wonderful."

He happily replied, "Yes it is so wonderful. What a blessing."

Just then from the doorway, Janie said, "Knock, knock, can I come in?"

Marah, thrilled her best friend had arrived said, "Yes, Janie. I have some good news, I have milk and formula for my babies. God has allowed us to keep two of them while he reclaimed the last of the trio. I feel very blessed. I will miss my last son, but I know he has already re-entered his Heavenly home. I feel it in my heart. He is fine. Later today we will lay his little body to rest next to his grandfather at the debris field. I may need your help from time to time if you are still willing."

Janie answered, "I will do whatever you want me to. But in the dining hall, we have a very excited little girl who is anxious to see her Mommy and meet her little brother and sister. Is it okay for me to bring her in after she is finished eating?"

The new parents both answered, "Yes, definitely."

Janie continued, "You should have seen it. Arianna had slept the whole time she had been with me. Pierre had wanted to wake her many times, but did as I asked and sat quietly drawing while we waited. But when Harold came to tell me about everything, Pierre followed me outside while we talked. As soon as he heard there were two babies, he ran inside and woke her up. It was so cute. He told her, "Arianna, you have to wake up. You are a big sister now and I have two more new cousins. Wake up or they will be big before we get to see them."

Marah said, "We don't want the children to know about the last baby."

Janie said, "We were careful to not let them hear that part. Your secret will be kept."

Marah said, "Thank you. Come, look at the babies. They are beautiful. I can't wait to hear what Arianna will say to them and about them. Both she and Pierre are so funny most of the time, just like two shrunken adults. You know, you have seen them."

Janie said, "We are going to have so much fun with all these babies. I will be glad when you get well and get to come home."

Marah said, "Yeah, me too. Please see if Arianna is finished yet. If Pierre wants to join her he is welcome."

By the day's end, Arianna fell asleep still talking about her new babies. The third baby had been laid to rest. Marah was stable and on the road to recovery. She would be released from the hospital three days later with a clean bill of health and instructions to take it easy until further notice.

CHAPTER TWENTY-FIVE

Eleven months later, Janie and Marah organized a birthday party for all three babies, Arianna, and Pierre. They chose the day which landed directly in the middle of Habib and the twins, as they were now often called, which coincidently was Arianna's birthday. No one had any clue as to when Pierre's birthday was. It was Arianna who said one day, "Mommy, if Claudia and Ivan can have the same birthday, why can't I share mine with Pierre."

Marah had said, "Arianna, I think that is a wonderful idea. I will ask his Mom and Dad." When Marah spoke to Elizabeth about it later that same day, tears of joy streamed down her face.

Elizabeth French said, "Oh what a lovely idea. Arianna is so smart, and for a child her age, it is such a selfless idea."

Marah said, "We are all family here. We need to make sure Pierre doesn't feel left out. I don't think any of us could have come up with a better solution."

Janie, Marah, Elizabeth French, Iva Rotge, Rita Sauvage, Jenny, and Ophilia Parker had formed a sisterhood of sorts, always helping one another and spending leisure time talking and laughing. Iva suggested to Marah and Elizabeth, "After the party for these five children, we should call a Women Islander meeting. There are twenty-three other children on this island, many of whom have been attending English classes. All of the children here need to have a celebration for their birthdays as well. Maybe we could have four birthday bashes per year, one every three months. That way we could celebrate whoever just had or is about to have a birthday all together. At one time, the Americans adopted a saying 'No Child Left Behind'. We need to follow that concept as far as the birthday parties are concerned." Both Marah and Elizabeth agreed.

By this time, some twenty-two months had past since the night of the plane crash. Life here on this island paradise had become the new normal to all who lived here. Soon they would all be involved in the fourth crop harvest. Some of the foods, such as the powdered eggs had all been used. The egg deficit would soon be balanced, thanks to the planning of Chun Li. He figured out the Albatross flock could be treated as chickens. One day he had asked Nigel French to help him take two gallons of dry corn to the shower area where the Albatross nests were. The two were joined by Kim Wang and his four children, ranging in age from 5 to 11 years old. They were going to rob the nests of their eggs. Carefully while the children stood in the shadows of the tree line, Chun Li poured a small stream of corn that led to a pile of corn a safe distance away from the nests. Their plan worked famously. Virtually all the adult birds made their way to the large pile of corn. While they fought and pecked at each other eating the corn, Chun Li and Kim Wang climbed the sides of the jagged cliffs. They threw the eggs down to Nigel French who handed them off to the children to be taken a distance from the flock of birds and laid in a basket. Long before the corn had been finished, the basket was full. After Chun Li and Kim Wang had climbed down, Li asked Kim and Nigel to join him in making a mental note as to which nests should remain untouched for the next egg harvest. They would rob the same nests each time to allow for the next generation of Albatross to flourish. The eggs were much larger than chicken eggs and would go a long way as to feeding the Islanders.

During the past months, the two remaining sections of the plane's wreckage had become the favorite residences for the elderly community. All the younger families among the Islanders had built homes, allowing for the elders among them to expand their living quarters to fill the lower level of the middle section and both levels of the nose section wreckage. All the dwellings had become quite comfortable with the additions of new furnishings being built along the way. Half of the upper level of the middle section was now a functioning school. Nearly all the children on the Island had learned basic English. The other half of that section had turned into a sewing factory of sorts. All of the unclaimed clothing from the crash had been moved there for storage and alterations. Lin Wang and Rita Sauvage had gathered enough silk worms to produce approximately two yards of fine silk material. The process had been extremely time consuming as they had by hand woven the fine string into usable cloth. Literally hundreds of hours had been invested in their project. They felt it necessary to begin producing new fabric to start making clothes from as the atire of the Islanders was becoming worn out.

Sherod had taken over the original doctor's office which had become a barber and shaving center. He shared the business with Iva Rotge who was the island's hair dresser for the ladies. Sherod worked the shop on Monday, Wednesday, and Friday. Iva ran the business on Tuesday, Thursday and Saturday.

The remaining supplies originally stored in the storage shed had been moved to various places. The shed itself had been transformed into a woodworking shop for Butch. Sherod helped Butch with projects on his days off from the barber shop. Lots of days there were many others who joined in to learn more about the art of woodworking. In recent days they had all been working on secret birthday surprises for the children. Standing in one corner of the wood shop were three very pretty rocking horses. Various berries from the island had been used to paint the horses. Ivan and Habib's horses were a shade of blue, thanks to hundreds of blue berries being mashed and rubbed on the wood. Claudia's horse was a reddish pink from red berries. Their manes were made from small strips of cloth from the sewing shop. Their eyes were black rubber washers saved from the extra gaskets and rubber seals brought along to be used in the small equipment on the island. Elizabeth had created the noses for the horses from the tops of an old pair of boots she had, stuffing the leather with strips of cloth. The nose holes were created with the screws that attached them to the heads. The finished products were amazingly beautiful. As for Arianna and Pierre, gifts had been designed for them as well. Corncobs had been used to produce three dolls each, girls for Arianna and boys for Pierre. Lin Wang and Rita Sauvage had sewn clothing for the dolls, silk for the girls and fabric for the boys. Tiny holes had been drilled through the heads of the dolls allowing real hair from the barber shop to be ran through the holes and styled to perfection. Arms and legs for the dolls were made by wire run through the corn cobs and then covered with small straws of bamboo with knots at each end of the wire to be the hands and feet. Currently the wood workers were designing a doll house complete with a few furnishings for the children to share.

In an effort to make all the children of the island feel included, wood had been attached to ropes which would become ten swings. They had also designed three see-saws from wood salvaged at the debris field. The planned playground area had been chosen close to the dining hall. They had already built a ten foot square wooden frame to be filled with sand from the beach for a sandbox. The chosen playground had plenty of shade being surrounded by big trees from which to hang the swings. The final addition to the new playground was a wooden tray filled with 100 square 2 inch blocks of wood with the alphabet carved into them. The blocks had been provided by Nigel French who had taken a real interest in woodworking.

It had been a busy year for Jack, Harold, Guillaume Rotge, and Francois Sauvage as well. It had been by Guillaume's design that they had been working on a sidewalk which spanned the entire distance between the camp at the beach to the cave/dining hall. In the beginning Guillaume had been mowing the pathway. However the airplane fuel they had been using had long since ate away at the mechanical components in the mower rendering it useless. Since then, they had been using a mixture similar to the mortar mix designed by Chun Li, adding gravel which had turned the mortar to a concrete like substance. The project was nearing an end as they now lacked only forty feet having reached completion. The sidewalk was actually quite pretty, resembling pea gravel concrete but much more colorful. The stones retrieved from the river were multicolored. When mixed with the glass particles from the volcanic soil and the crystal particles in the sand itself, the sidewalk glistened and glimmered in the sunlight.This had proven to be quite the task. The four men were delighted it was nearly finished. The news of the big party had spread. Sanjay had heard Jack and Harold saying they wished it could be finished before the large gathering and he had spread the word. Their four man construction crew grew to 23 men on this final day of mixing and pouring the concrete sidewalk. The task which could have taken three more days was complete by 2 o'clock, leaving plenty of time for it to dry before the party.

The birthday bash was scheduled for the next day. Ophilia and Jenny had been making the preparations to provide special treats. The babies would be having rice cereal with crushed pineapple, mango and peaches. For Arianna and Pierre there would be pineapple upside down cake, which was their favorite. They would prepare enough for everyone, along with coconut cream pie for the adults in attendance which was expected to be all of the Islanders. Excitement was in the air everywhere.

Iva Rotge had come to help Jenny and Ophilia. She told them, "I really appreciate you letting me help. I do believe my name sake, Ivan, has stolen my heart."

Ophilia said, "Iva, you do realize that baby was named after Jack's grandfather, don't you."

Iva replied, "So I have been told. But when I hear Marah next door saying, 'Ivan, don't do that, or Ivan, stop hitting your sisters' I always wish I had a sister I could clobber." The three ladies burst into laughter.

Ophilia said, "I hear you, huh Jenny."

Jenny said, "Yeah, remember Mom used to say she needed a tape recorder to say 'Stop hitting your sister' to the both of us so she didn't have to repeat herself. Iva, did you only have brothers?"

"No, I was an only child. I never had brothers and sisters until I arrived here and met you all. Now I feel like a part on one big family. I really love you all," answered Iva. Iva's words seemed to vocalize the general opinion of the Islanders. Everyone had developed lives here and were always willing to help each other, a camaraderie which had grown to family proportions.

Doctor Goodson and Sanjay had done their part, small as it was, to help prepare for the party. Together they had tied string to trees around the edges of the planned play ground. Then using some of the remaining aluminum blankets and tape to drape the small compound, hiding it from the view of any children who might pass by. In the days leading up to the party, the two men had taken pleasure in hearing many of the island children discuss 'the huge birthday present' which must be hidden behind the shinny drapes.

Arthur Goodson and Sanjay had become the best of friends, along with now being brothers in law six months before. Doctor Goodson and Ophilia Parker had married six months ago. They had planned a small ceremony performed by Jack in front of the water fall shower. Their intention was to only have a few people in attendance as Arthur was nervous about saying their vows in front of a large crowd. However, word had spread about the wedding and the entire population had turned out in their finest attire. Doctor Goodson had been wrong on how a large crowd would affect him and had managed to declare his undying love for Ophilia with no mistakes. It had been a beautiful ceremony.

On the day of the party while doing the set up, Lin Wang and Rita Sauvage arrived carrying huge smiles and a large trash bag. When asked about the bag, Rita said, "Lin and I have special gifts for all 28 children of the island. We have been very busy making rag dolls for them, both boy and girl dolls. Every child needs a friend to hold on to while falling asleep. It was Lin's idea. She couldn't stand for the others to feel left out. Being the mother of four of those children she knew they could be hurt and jealous otherwise." It had been quite the undertaking just keeping her children from finding out about the dolls as a curtain was all that separated the school from the sewing area. They had been forbidden to look behind the curtain, a rule which had been hard for the teachers to enforce. Finally that rule could be reversed.

Plans had been made to first bring all the children to the dining hall for their treats before presents would be passed out. It was during this time that the men would quickly assemble the playground. Once finished, the men would join the others in the cave to watch as the children received their gifts. By this time the drapes were to have been removed from the perimeter of the play area. After the gifts were given, then all of the children would be taken to their new playground.

Once the gentlemen had arrived, Ophilia took center stage and asked that the three mothers of the birthday children say a few words before the gifts were given. This event had been at Marah's request. First Elizabeth and Janie would speak and then she had a poem she wanted to read. Ophilia called Elizabeth to the stage. Elizabeth began, "Hello, everyone. Today we come together to celebrate the birthdays of five of our children, my own son being one of them. To my precious Pierre I would like to say Happy Birthday son. I know this will be the first of many amazing birthdays we will spend together. I love you all. To our dear Arianna, thank you so very much for wanting to share your birthday with Pierre. It was a delightful idea. Happy birthday to you, your little brother and sister and to Habib as well. Again, I love you all." Elizabeth then returned to her seat next to her family.

Janie was next to take the stage. The room was soon to erupt in laughter at her light hearted antics. She said, "My fellow islanders, thank you all for coming today. First of all I want to say Happy Birthday to my little Habib and his cousins, Ivan, Claudia, Arianna and Pierre. To Habib, I would like to say I know you may have entered this world into a real mess, but I promise to never again drop you in such a pile again. The world over all really doesn't smell like that. You have brought me and your father much joy in your first year of life. We all love you, our little stinker. Thank you all again." Then she returned to join Harold and their son.

Marah's mood was one of mixed emotions. She was obviously both enjoying the fact of the children's birthday party while still grieving the death of one of her babies. At first, the birth of little Arthur Jackson Wellington was to be kept secret from his older sister, Arianna. That was successful until one day three months after the birth of the triplets when Arianna had found her mother crying uncontrollably while trying to hide behind their house. Marah had chosen not to lie to her daughter anymore at that time. She had explained to Arianna that one of her brothers now resided in Heaven and her tears stemmed from missing his presence. The very compassionate Arianna, being wise beyond her years had said, "It's okay Mommy. Don't worry, God will keep my baby brother safe. He won't let my first daddy hurt him. He will probably let Claudette take care of him until we get there. It's going to be all right Mommy." The child's words had done a wonderful job of easing the pain of Marah's partially broken heart and helped her to regain her focus on the children she still had, Arianna, Ivan and Claudia.

Marah began her speech, "Thank you all for coming today. I want you to know that I feel you are each one a part of my family. It is only since arriving on this island and meeting all of you that I have ever truly been part of a family. Arianna and I both feel each of you to be more valuable than all the riches the modern world has to offer. I would like to say Happy Birthday to my nephews, Pierre and Habib, and to all of my children, Arianna, Ivan and Claudia. I also would like to send special birthday wishes to my other son in Heaven, little Arthur Jackson Wellington. I ask that you will all help me to honor his memory each year in the future on this date as well. In modern society often we are so busy trying to make a living, at the end of the day we are left wondering 'where did the time go'. If you will all please indulge me, I would like to read a poem I have written. I hope this poem will leave you all with a new appreciation for our current location and lifestyle. Here we have the opportunity to enjoy our lives realizing the important things in life have no connection what so ever to how much money we can make. Here we have the time to enjoy our families, friends and a sense of community like I have never experienced anywhere else on Earth. Hopefully we will never be left with the question 'where did the time go'. So here goes:

WHERE DID THE TIME GO

Where did the time go? Seems I just learned you were on the way,
Says the mother to her newborn child.
Where did the time go? It seems you just arrived,
Says the mother on her child's first birthday.
Where did the time go? Seems like yesterday you turned one,
Says the mother as she tucks in her first grader the night before
        School's first day.
Where did the time go? Seems you just started first grade,
Says the mother to her twelve year old as she dries her child's tears
        Over the first teen aged breakup.
Where did the time go? Seems impossible you could be graduating today,
Says the mother who still sees this young adult as her baby.
Where did the time go? Seems like you just finished school,
Says the mother about to witness her child's wedding.
Where did the time go? Seemed like there would be time to visit later,

Says the over worked young adult at the mother's funeral.
Where did the time go?

Thank you all for coming and for listening. Remember to enjoy your time with family for in the end, it is really what mattered most." Marah then rejoined her family.

Ophilia then retook the stage and said, "I think Marah brings a valid point to all of us. I believe our time here on this island has brought a lot of us a new outlook on life. Upon our arrival here, we were all just surviving. Now I believe we are all living our lives. All of the efforts put forth by all of us Islanders has produced true happiness like never before to many of us. Now speaking of true happiness, I do believe we have some happy birthday gifts for the children. Shall we?"

It had been previously decided since so much work and effort had gone into building toys for the children, the toy creators along side the parents would give out the gifts. Sherod, Butch, Nigel, and a host of other helpers took the stage and began uncovering many the presents which had been hidden on the stage behind the speakers. Momentarily the three babies were sat on the rocking horses. They were soon removed at the request of Doctor Goodson saying, "Sorry, but the bedrock floor in here is unsuitable for a one year old's possible landing spot should they fall off. So I recommend you parents take the horses to your homes to be placed on the ground or wooden floors. Consider that Doctor's orders." Jack, Marah, Harold and Janie immediately did as he had asked and sat the rocking horses aside until after the party to be taken home then. Afterwards Arianna and Pierre were called to the stage. The two children squealed with delight when given the three corn cob dolls each. Immediately they named each doll after people here with them. Then they were presented with the doll house complete with some furnishings. After they had both hugged the doll house, together they carried it back to their seats.

Rita Sauvage and Lin Wang took the stage next and asked that all the Islander children line up in front of the stage for a special surprise. They were each then given one rag doll a piece. There were no two dolls alike to avoid getting them mixed up later. This way they could trade them around at any time. All the children were very happy with their new toys. After returning to their seats, Ophilia announced that all parents, children, and anyone else who wanted to should follow her for one more surprise. She led the crowd to the new playground and directed them to surround the drapes which were about to be removed. Very few of the Islanders were in on what was behind the aluminum curtains. Next to every tree to which the curtains were tied stood one of the playground's creators. Ophilia asked for quiet. The creators counted to three and dropped the curtains all at once. The 28 island children let out a squeal that could have been compared to that of a crowd at a basketball game in which the winning basket had just been made. The children swarmed the playground in delight. Jack laughed and told everyone in ear shot, "It's a good thing they weren't bigger people or we might have gotten trampled."

The entire birthday bash was a major success. All of the children were happy which made all of the parents and extended families happy as well. Everyone looked forward to the next scheduled birthday celebration in three months. Throughout history it has been said that home is where the heart is. With the passage of time this beautiful island had become a true home for these people. They were not the only thing which resided here. The true meaning of happiness resided here too.

CHAPTER TWENTY-SIX

STORM ON THE HORIZON

One morning some seven months after the first birthday bash, Jack woke just before daybreak with a very uneasy feeling. He had become known as the weather man, seeming to possess some sort of sixth sense in times of trouble. He quietly dressed and walked outside and on to the beach. There was an eerie stillness in the air. Off on the distant horizon was a very well defined squall line of storm clouds. It seemed to be moving toward them at a much accelerated rate compared to the other storms he had seen rolling in before this morning. The ocean's waves were taller, more busy than ordinary. As he stood there momentarily trying to assess the situation, suddenly he felt as though he had been hit by a wave of sorts. Only his was a wave of impending doom. As panic began to rush over him, he turned and ran back to the camp. He began by waking his neighbors, knocking on doors shouting, "Wake up, hurry, we must get to the cave. There's a bad storm coming. Now, we have to go now!"

After alerting the Rotge's, Sauvage's, the elderly residents of the plane's wreckage, and Harold's family, he rushed inside his home to help Marah with their children. On the way to the cave they stopped at all the residences, banging on doors and shouting warnings of the storm which would soon arrive. Upon arriving at the dining hall, Chun Li was shocked at the sudden swarm of people. He had the coffee started and was about to begin preparing breakfast when Nigel French, directed by Jack, told him of the coming weather. Li had been unaware other than noticing the wind had made his fire building more difficult than usual.

Recently Jack and Harold had decided to examine how far back the cavernous hall off the main dining room of the cave extended. The storage shelves which had been built just inside the cavern's entrance were thirty feet long on each side. The two men had gone at least fifty feet further inside before deciding that was far enough. Up until that point the floor seemed to gradually go up. Just past that there was a definite declining floor that led to God knows what. After a brief discussion between Jack and Harold, the two decided they had to quickly make preparations as time was running out. Jack rushed outside to grab the basket which held many solar lights that were fully charged and ready for use. Meanwhile Harold had grabbed half of the solar lights that were inside the dining hall. They called for some of the Islanders to help them. By that time the wind was beginning to blow the lighter items in the cave around.

Together Guillaume Rotge and Francois Sauvage grabbed the crate of cold drinks out of the live well just outside the cave entrance and took it to the cavern. Chun Li and Doctor Goodson took the made coffee and cups into the cavern as well. The Islanders were going to try to ride out this storm inside that very cavern. Jack had a feeling they would all be safer there than inside the lower level of the Nose section of the plane's wreckage. They had ridden out bad storms there before, but the sick feeling in the pit of Jack's stomach told him this storm was different, much different. Jack shouted for everyone who was not holding a frightened child to quickly help grab the seats from the dining hall. If this storm turned out to be a hurricane, they could be there a long time. The seats would be much more comfortable than the rock floor.

They had barely gotten everything in place when the storm arrived. First the wind began to blow the remaining dining furniture around the dining cathedral. All the while the sky was darkening to the point of being nearly as dark as night outside. Then the rain began. It looked as though the cave entrance had magically transformed to Niagra Falls with hundreds of gallons per minute pouring over the doorway. Luckily very little of the rain was making it's way inside at first due to the gradual decline in the bedrock just outside the entrance. However the wind had no problem getting inside. At times the dining hall appeared to have a small tornado inside as it's contents was blowing around in circles as it was busted and destroyed.

Inside the cavern the Islanders huddled together. Many offered prayers asking for God to keep them all safe from the storm. All of the mothers had placed their seats in a circle enclosing their children, forming a human play pen of sorts. Almost magically all of the mothers had grabbed their children's beloved rag dolls for them to hold onto to comfort them during the storm. As the children, ranging in age from one to eleven, sat on the floor they were telling stories about their dolls, some true some made up. The mothers and the dolls did what they could to keep the children calm. However the loud sounds from the storm, the thunder, the wind, the extreme pouring rain and the sound of trees breaking outside numerous times interrupted their calm. The emotions of the children seemed to be racing from one end of the spectrum to the other time after time. The situation would span the entire time the storm lasted.

Nearly every adult Islander inside the cavern at one point or another thanked Jack for alerting them to the coming storm. His split second thinking had led them all to the safety of the cave's extended hallway. It wasn't until they had been hold up for some two hours that someone noticed there were absentees from their group. Instantly startled by the revelation, Jack suggested a head count of all who were present. Everyone knew currently the population of the island was 150 souls. At the end of the first headcount there were 138 residents inside this cavern. Jack, being overcome with fear and grief, requested a second count. Again 138 was the last number called. Guillaume and Harold had to grab Jack as he attempted to run out into the storm to try to find the missing Islanders. Hysterically Jack shouted as they held him back, "I thought I had warned everybody. Oh God, who is missing? Who did I not tell? They could die out there. Please, I gotta go find them." By now he wept uncontrollably.

Marah had handed her children over to the other mothers and run to her husband's side. "Jack," she said, "Please don't leave us. Sweetheart, I was with you when we were coming here this morning. I know you knocked on every door and warned each family. All of the children are here and accounted for. You don't know how many of the 12 missing people chose to take shelter in the nose section as we have all done in the past. Please don't leave me and our children, Jack, we need you. We will find our people when the storm is over. Please Jack, listen to me. Don't go." When Marah had finished speaking, Jack stopped trying to pull away and collapsed into a weeping pile. Together they prayed for the dozen missing Islanders. Her efforts had been successful. Finally he agreed to wait the storm out before trying to check on the missing people.

At least another two hours would pass before there would be a break in the storm. By now it was nearing noon and for the first time since the wind and rain began, there was a ray of sunshine beginning to peek through the thick clouds. Harold said, "Finally it's over. Sanjay, do you still have the binoculars, by any chance? I want to use them and go to lookout cliff and check out camp. Maybe I will get lucky and see what happened to the others."

Jack interrupted and said, "Harold, I believe this storm to be a hurricane. Remember if I am right, the calm we are experiencing now will soon return to the storm. Please hurry as best you can. We don't know how long the break will last, but we do know it will not last long."

Harold said, "Point taken. I really hadn't thought about it. Now Sanjay, where are those binoculars?"

Sanjay said, "I keep them under our bed in a basket. I will go get them." As Harold followed Sanjay outside the cave, both men were shocked at what they saw. The storm damage was wide spread already with another round on it's way. There were downed trees and debris scattered everywhere. There was metal roofing, furnishings, clothing all over the place. Half of Sanjay and Jenny's roof was missing and their house was tossed about. It took a few minutes to locate the binoculars and Harold left immediately.

Harold waded flood water that hit his mid thighs to get to lookout cliff. Reaching his destination had been made even more difficult by numerous trees that had fallen along the pathway. Once atop lookout cliff, he turned the field glasses toward the camp area. It appeared every home had sustained damage. The beach looked to have been reconstructed to include a tall ridge of sand against the tree line. The ridge seemed to prevent the flood water from draining back into the ocean. He stared at the scene in shock, all the while seeing no sign of life. Just as he was about to give up, he began to hear voices below him. As he quickly climbed back down the cliff, he heard Sherod saying, "Don't let go of each others hands no matter what. Remember there's safety in numbers. But hurry as best you can. The second half of the storm is coming right behind us. Come on everyone." As Harold rounded the corner of lookout cliff to meet them, he saw 12 very wet, very tired elderly individuals trying to get to the cave before the storm restarted. The group was pleasantly startled to see Harold appear out of nowhere and stopped to tell him what they had experienced. Just as they began speaking, a loud clap of thunder alerted them the storm was returning.

Harold said, "Come on you guys. We can discuss this at the cave. Time is running out to get there before we get blown away." The people offered no argument as they made their way the remaining quarter mile to their destination. They barely made it there before the storm began in earnest once again. The rest of the Islanders were thrilled that the cave now held the entire population of the island safely.

When the excitement of their arrival had subsided, Jack asked Sherod what caused their group to not go to the cave when alerted earlier. Sherod answered, "Well there are those of us who don't move as quickly as some of you younger folks do. Besides that in the nearly two and a half years we have lived here we have always weathered storms inside the basement of the nose section. By the time our joints loosened up enough to make the trip the wind was so bad we chose to take cover in the original storm shelter. It wasn't long until it got very hairy in there. Fellows I am here to tell you we were holding onto any part of the plane that we could. Honestly if the eye of the storm had not arrived when it did, we probably could not have held on much longer.

It was crazy. The water was rushing into and out of the shelter like it was mini tidal waves. I have never experienced anything like it in my life. But don't ever write us old folks off. We are hard headed and will use that determination to survive what was thought to be the unlikely. I believe I can speak for us all in saying we are glad to be here now."

Jack said, "Yes sir, and we are all very thankful for your survival."

Then Jack asked, "Harold what kind of damage did you see back at the camp?"

Harold said, "The best description I can come up with is it's all a big mess. Man there are trees down everywhere and I saw a lot of our roofs have been taken by the wind. It looked like the beach has totally been redesigned. There's a ridge of sand piled up next to the tree line keeping the flood waters trapped on the island. If the second leg of the storm doesn't kill us all, the sand dunes will have to be addressed first to recede the flood waters. Like I said, everything is just a big mess."

Sherod said, "Well if you really think about it, we were running out of projects already. In two and a half years we built an entire community pretty much from nothing. To everyone in this cave I say, we are all survivors. It will take a little while to rebuild, but don't we have plenty of time? It won't take us as long the second time because now we all have experience. What will take the longest is trying to find where the roofs got blown to. We all might wind up with grass roofs this time if we can't find the metal. Maybe God will replenish the debris field with new materials. He had that first batch just waiting for us to use. Anyway, don't start getting discouraged. We will all pull together and be okay, God willing that is."

The Islanders were fortunate they had chosen to take refuge in the cave. The storm would rage until some time during the night. Luckily due to Su Li's OCD condition, with the help of Jenny and Ophilia, they had spent three hours cutting up vegetables and fruit to serve the hungry group. There were many trays of cherry tomatoes, sweet banana peppers, carrots, celery, mango, pineapple, bananas and peaches. Chun Li who prided himself in always being prepared for the unexpected, produced crates of water bottles filled with water, tea, his milk mixture (Powdered milk mixed with non-dairy creamer), and fruit juices. The entire duration of their time on the island he had painstakingly cleaned and reused every water bottle available daily. At the end of any given day, there were 320 bottles of life sustaining fluids available and ready for consumption. This was the first time since their arrival that the Islanders learned of his extraordinary efforts. All were grateful.

It seemed surreal the next morning when Harold once again made his way to lookout cliff. Unexpectedly the flood waters had all gone. He had to work his way through debris and fallen trees, but the trip was much easier still than the day before. Once he ascended the cliff and pointed his binoculars toward the beach where the camp had been, he quickly moved the glasses away and rubbed his eyes. He looked again and got the surprise of his life. There, not far from the seashore, on the horizon, he saw a large cargo ship. It appeared to hold hundreds of large crates on deck. He soon rushed back to the cave to tell the others.

Harold ran as hard as he could back to the cave, many times jumping over tree limbs and trunks like an Olympic hurdle jumper. He entered the cave shouting, "Hurry everyone! There's a cargo ship on the horizon. It seemed to be moving away from our island. We may still have time to light the signal fires on the beach. Come on! Hurry!" Basically every able bodied man ran out of the cave immediately. None of them knew the rest of the story. No one knew that Harold had secretly watched as the ship turned away from the island. No one knew that he had already seen through the binoculars all the wood piles for the signal fires had been taken by the storm waves. No one knew there were now some twenty cargo crates scattered about on that very beach which held unknown treasures.

Along the way to the beach, there were many downed trees to find a way around. Jack and Harold eventually found themselves at the back of the line of men trying to see the ship. Jack whispered to Harold, "Do you really want to go home?"

Harold whispered back, "We are already home. The ship was leaving the area as I was leaving lookout cliff. There's pretty much no way we will be seen."

The closer they got to the beach, the more they were hearing the others speak of loving it here. Nigel French said, "I almost wish we would get to stay here. I fear the bureaucrats of society will remove Pierre from Elizabeth and my custody and give him to a blood relative. Do we really have to do this?"

Guillaume Rotge said, "We don't even know what we would be returning to. Violence in the south of France had reached a new high before the plane crash! What if there have been wars? Our home nations may no longer exist. I'm kind of like French! I don't know if this is a good idea or not."

Doctor Goodson chimed in next saying, "A lot of us could be in trouble for the actions we have had to take here. I have tried to save the lives of those who died in my care, but I have had to use some unethical means. You also have to consider the families of the deceased, they could have us prosecuted for illegal disposal of a corpse. We threw an awful lot of bodies into the quicksand pit preventing them from being able to exhume their loved ones for burial in their home countries."

Sanjay said, "Yeah, and what about Jack and Harold. We all know from their actions on this island that there is no way they could have been involved in the plane crash. But society warrants they find someone responsible and they are the only living people to blame. They could be convicted of a crime they obviously didn't commit and go to prison for life. How could any of us live with that?"

Doctor Goodson then added, "Besides that, I had just been served with divorce papers and assured by my wife there was no chance for reversal when I booked my trip to Europe. What if the proceedings were dropped when we disappeared? That would make me guilty of bigamy and you too Jack."

While some were shouting their protests, many were frantically trying to collect wood and brush to attempt to build a signal fire. Some of the men stood next to the ocean's edge waving their arms in the air to try to gain the ship's attention. Two of them had taken their white shirts off and were waving them like a flag of surrender. One man even had found the aluminum blanket which had served as the doorway to the restroom and was waving it as hard as he could. Jack, Harold, Nigel French, Guillaume Rotge, Doctor Goodson and Sanjay stood among the scattered cargo crates watching as the cargo ship lingered on the horizon. An erie chill swept over them as the ship's whistle sounded off: toot, toot, toot. The ship then disappeared in the distance. What did it all mean? Would the ship chart it's coordinates and return for it's lost bounty? Had the storm blown the ship so far off course it would be unable to find this island again? Or had Google Earth expanded during their absence to now include this region? Exactly what did their future hold?

THE END

BIO

Hello, my name is L. A. Smith. I grew up in a small town in Tennessee in the 1970's. Being reared mostly by my grandparents, I learned many things about being self sufficient and living off the land. I learned one basic rule of survival is to waste very little. Bits and pieces of their teachings are scattered throughout this book.

I graduated from high school in the early 80's in the top ten percent of my class. I went to work instead of college. I did factory work, bartending, and finally cleaning houses. I learned a great deal about human nature while bartending and housekeeping just by watching people.

For ten years now I have been married to a wonderful man who encourages me to dream big.

I was blessed with two children, a daughter and a son. My son spent six years in the military. He now works two jobs to support his family. In my opinion his wife works two jobs as well, one outside and one inside the home. This lovely lady keeps their home and their two children running like a well oiled machine.

On December 1, 2017, my 32 year old daughter died from an overdose. The grief from her loss was threatening to consume me. I chose to avoid anti-depressants and nerve pills. Someone suggested I allow my mind to wander and focus on unrelated subjects, possibly write a book. I decided to embrace this idea three weeks after my daughter's death. I dedicated one to two hours to the text before leaving for work daily. This awarded me peace of mind for those hours. Honestly I think it saved my sanity and possibly my life.

On the day I chose the subject of my book, the morning news did a story on Malaysia Flight 370. This modern day mystery sent my mind into a whirlwind. It is my belief the entire plot of ISLAND JET 370 was born that morning.

Writing ISLAND JET 370 gave me my own sort of virtual reality. The ever changing tones of the pages reflects the chaos followed by peace that define the " waves of grief" I experienced. Even though I hope ISLAND JET 370 will do good on the market, it has already been successful in it's original purpose - saving me. I hope you will enjoy your escape as well.

2-25-19

To Brenda
Thank you for
your support. Please
tell your friends.
God Bless You

Made in the USA
Lexington, KY
19 February 2019

31403393R00122